Sunday Dinner with Father Dwyer

Books by Jim Meirose:

Mount Everest
Eli the Rat
Inferno

Coming in 2019:

Understanding Franklin Thompson
The Box

For more information about Jim Meirose, including other novels and short work that has appeared in numerous venues, visit www.jimmeirose.com

Dedicated to my Mother
ANNA MEIROSE
(d. 1988)

Optional Books First Edition, 2019

Copyright © 2019 Optional Books

All Rights Reserved

www.optionalbooks.com

Jim Meirose

Sunday Dinner with Father Dwyer

OPTIONAL BOOKS

Chapter One
Packed, Sealed, Loaded, Gone

Chuggie the section boss pulled out the earplugs he wore all day working on the containership loading dock. It always was extraordinarily noisy there, beneath the great cranes thrusting out so far above the multiple ships roped up beside. He stood under the crane working to load the recently completed, fully-automated Dakota Maru, one of a line of three being loaded this evening. The paperwork told Chuggie that the giant ship would, by this time tomorrow, be far at sea on its way to China. China, imagine that. He'd never been to China, yeah, and he'd been thinking of China, the Great Wall and all—who the hell would build such a thing, you know—when he pulled out the earplugs as Booster's huge black Mackie's-crew pickup-truck was let through security, and he came out on the dock. This was against the rules. Private vehicles were not allowed here. Approval would require levels upon levels upon levels of paperwork to be signed. It didn't happen too often, and every time, when it did, it had been arranged by Mackie's outfit. Every single time. Chuggie walked in the direction of the approaching truck. This was special; he smiled; it was always special when Mackie's outfit sent something right down to the dock to ship. Something important and interesting needed to go, right now, today. Chuggie pocketed the earplugs as the big black pickup, brand-new and gleaming—as was everything associated with Mackie's outfit—pulled up beside him. The door flew open, and Booster came out, as usual nearly big-belly bursting his too-tight, filthy t-shirt, his hands black from hard work, his shaved stubbly head glistening. As he slithered from the truck onto the ground, a brown envelope dropped from the seat behind him to the concrete below. Chuggie eyed it, but Booster's big words boomed his eyes back up into his; he half-yelled at Chuggie, Okay, my man. Here's another special. Got to go, got to go on this ship right here. Got to go to China. Don't ask, the answer's, as always, yes, it has been pre-inspected. No need to look in. Come on, get some big guys here, this thing weighs a ton—and, at that very instant, Booster rushed around and unchained and slammed the tailgate down hard. In the bed of the truck sat a brand-new glossy blue fifty-five-gallon steel drum strapped tightly down precisely in the center of the truck bed. Corrosives: Do Not Open, stretched stenciled large across the barrel's side.

Chuggie nodded and raised a hand and waved out through the dark noise to someplace way farther than he could see. Two huge faceless men appeared out of the noise and came around nodding and examining the truck, and Chuggie stepped back, pointed up at the barrel, and flicked his hand down. The men flowed up and onto the bed surprisingly gracefully and effortlessly despite their great bulk, and knew what to do. The straps loosened, snaking in coils all around, and the sound of steel scraping steel merged out into the general mass of dockyard human and nonhuman and unknown noise, and in two or three minutes the drum came down on the concrete dock, the outsized longshoremen beside it. Stamped on the sealed top, a label stuck pasted, saying, Corrosives, dangerous! Do not open! And below that, it read smaller, To: Mr. K. Moon, Shanghai, China – call dockyard extension 3456 to arrange pickup. Chuggie pressed his finger to the barrel top, his eye flicked momentarily to the small brown envelope lying by the truck, then he turned back as Booster said, There you go, that's all we got, do the usual process. It's a special for Mackie. We okay?

Yeah, I'm okay. What's in this, anyway? You don't usually drop off a barrel like this.

Booster's eye veins needed to burst, so full, so red, but held, as he answered.

I don't fucking know, Chug. I never fucking know. I just know it needs to go.

I know, but I'm only asking because it's not usually a big barrel to China marked corrosive, and all—I don't think you ever brought anything before going to China. I bet…

Listen, Chuggers, you think too fucking much. Mackie does the thinking. We don't need to know everything. As a matter of fact, we practically don't need to know anything at all, except that payday's damned good when you been doing exactly as told. You know?

The eyes strained red, needing to hear the right thing. Or else…

Yeah, yeah, I know, said Chuggie, stepping back. As the strain in Booster's red eyes visibly dimmed, Chuggie turned to the large blank-faced longshoremen and said, Okay, guys—get this on board. Take it to that open container they're loading over there, we'll send it that way. One's as good as another. Tell those guys loading I said it was okay. If they give you lip, point them to me. Then I'll point them to Booster here.

Booster grinned a half grin from the right corner of his mouth. No more veins colored his eyes, as the massive faceless men nodded, gripped the barrel lip, steel scraped on steel, and the barrel and the wide-backed brute-men moved, disappearing into the noise and nothing on that side and were gone. Somewhere far off, some ship's bell rang, for some reason, as happened all day long. Bells and horns and whistles sounded from ships large and small for dozens of reasons, to kick this or that thing off, whatever, and always were shrill enough to pierce the overall noise. Booster turned back to the truck without a word of goodbye or thank you or anything else, and the truck immediately was gone back through the tall chain-link gate leading away toward the far-off city skyline. Chuggie looked to the envelope.

Damn, he said to a passing, filthy longshoreman, as he moved toward the envelope. Look at that. Shit all over. People just toss garbage down anyplace, don't give a shit—but the man didn't care, just nodded and grinned all stupid, and walked on, as Chuggie picked up the envelope, flipped it open, and took what was inside down into the side pocket of his mackinaw, slowly walked to a garbage pot by a fence, tossed in the empty envelope, and went back to work in the hard pounding noise. Everything gets lost, in the noise, eventually. The noise goes on all day, all night, forever, but no matter, everything lost gets found by somebody. And when it's found it's always a surprise, some unexpected good thing; a thing that would bring a smile to anybody with normal simple human feelings who's at the same time able to live a whole life of constant blasting noise.

Chapter Two
On the Free One-way Trip to China

Fertilization; the joining of the father's sperm and the mother's egg; this is when life begins, so, yes—eyes open, eyes open, do they? Eyes open, yes they do, but do they? Yes or no, regardless, pure blackness instantly smothered up into Foster's opening eyes, actually faster than instantly, enveloping him. His suddenly primitive face took form in the dark with large dark circles for eyes. Then he jerked up, they opened, expecting to see, but nothing; they gazed into deeper than pitch black. His lips moved but told him nothing; he just heard from someplace inside, Where is the spaghetti I just brought to my mouth? Where is the wide bright open space of the glittery bustling restaurant? Oh, sure, yes, I have wakened from a dream. A whole day of smoking and riding in Mackie's Escalade and coming in a joint and everything was smooth, the deal was done, and we were gone out to celebrate the deal that just went down; big for Mackie, big for me. Must be looking forward, really looking forward to getting with the guys and wrapping it up, yeah, yeah—shake it off, can't even see yet, woke up so fast, but shake it off and get out of bed, but…

His mouth, lower jaw, and throat were just now developing, so Foster's head moved barely at all and came against some hard thing over the bed; yes, of course he was in bed, where else would he be? The dream must have been so great it won't let me go, thought Foster—blood cells were taking shape, and circulation had begun; but shake it off, shake it off, God damn, never had a dream like this before, but his hands, both hands, went and met, not sheets and blankets, but something that shouldn't be; something cold, hard, curved, smooth, and invisible in the dark. Foster began breathing fast and felt all around to find the edge of the bed and the way to get up, but—absolutely no light broke through the black. No bedroom ever he'd been in all his life had ever been this dark. Up;

up is hard, flat, and cold. Down; down is hard, flat, and cold. Side is a flat circle all around, all around, all around binding tight the living, black, center, tar-like wrap of an imaginary business meal, that was Foster—no! No. No. Open up the damned eyes—see, feel, this is a restaurant table, something's gone wrong with it though that makes it impossible to touch. Hard, flat, cold is all. No light. No. no. Press, press, press...

Implantation!

Foster knew right where he was for the first time ever.

Nutrition, nutrition; do not think what you know this is; here comes nutrition, where better to get it from than in this restaurant, yes! Yes, here are Mackie and the boys, the guys, the men, and the light; Johnny chewed the spaghetti and meatballs, a sauce he had begun chewing before what had just happened; no, not what he knows it is, but; just some momentary brain wave zap. Thank God he had gone to the bathroom to piss, before. He had had to piss so bad that his vodka and tonic even tasted different when he half drained it when he came back. But thank God he knew where he was now, yes. And, they had all laughed when he did it; Mackie stood and lifted his glass in a toast when they laughed, that was how hard they'd done it, like they'd never seen anybody drain a drink before. They had saluted him just for drinking it all down. Johnny felt special, so special; he had made them happy, they were happy, yes he knew. The rest of the dinner and what lay beyond would be wonderful, profitable, wonderful, profitable, won—derful—won...

Johnny, you are the best! You are the best, you have done what we wanted and more! Right boys? And more!

Yes, Mackie—

God, yes!

Yeah—here's to you, Johnny.

Yeah. What they said. Right.

Boy, after tonight you're going to get what you got coming, Johnny! What you got coming, and maybe some more!

Johnny kept his eyes shut to stay in the restaurant, the restaurant was brightly lit; desperately he had to stay someplace, anyplace, all brightly lit; he pressed harder and harder the hard smooth curved cold steel before him; press harder. Sometimes pressing harder breaks through. Break through the dark, and the light it will come. The pressure brought up his vodka glass to get the last drops, and it drained down inside, where no matter how joyous the occasion for which the drink was taken, it is always hot, dark, silent, and immediately whatever ends up there begins to be drained away by the body; as a spider drains prey; as the tiny heart-tube beats sixty-five times a minute by the end of the fourth week; as in a wasp; but can't know this. Some things you just can't know. His hand came back from the dark smooth steel, and this movement somehow glittered his mind up to bright again. He sat cutting a large hot meatball, the sounds of laughter having been replaced by the sound of tableware and cutting and chewing and swallowing, all the sounds that flash by when the end of a great meal is being sped toward. Now, hold on, hold tight. Watch what you're speeding toward—is the urge to piss really spawning? Something had changed somehow after you pissed. Maybe you pissed and pissed to death. Maybe when you get just a bit too empty there's nothing else. Not even you anymore, somehow, huh?

Can a person piss too much and piss all the way to emptiness and death?

Why you staring at that meatball like that, Johnny? Never seen one before? Feeling a little funny, eh? What's the matter, Johnny? Come on, eat the damned thing.

Oh, sure—no, nothing's the matter. Just feel funny somehow. You know?

Shake it off, buddy. Eat up. Don't forget—after the meal, we get down to brass tacks. Right boys?

Yeah—

Brass tacks.

The meatball pushed all savory back in his smiling mouth. It brought him back, he chewed, and as he chewed he looked back into himself to check to be sure he was really feeling okay; before he was sure, Mackie said, Boy, Johnny, your eyes look funny. Your eyes look—hey, your eyes look like the eyes of some fake fortuneteller down the boardwalk. Just like that, Man! You brought me right back. You ever been to a fortuneteller, Johnny? I went to the fortuneteller that day, I was about fourteen, Dad let me. Mom would never have because she was a real serious Catholic, but she stayed home that day, and Dad said, Sure, Mack, go on. One time won't hurt. You know what I mean, Johnny? Mom gave a shit, but Dad didn't. Such different people they were. How they got together I'll never know. Maybe that explains me, Johnny—how I am. But, I digress. You ever been to a fortuneteller, huh? Ever wonder where you've been, or are, and how you will end up?

The question, I could not see. The question was simple, but everything seemed slower and farther away. Life moved from the sea to on land, they say. It took millions and millions of years, but we got here. It's much too far away, far away. Life has just barely touched the shore, it's alien, and it will be millions and millions of years more before it gets to the sand. Dry sand, the dry sand, the dry sand; let me drink. Yes, let me, yes, let me know.

I don't know, Mackie. Yeah, I been at a fortunetellers; but right now I need water, get water, I am choking—

Okay—Bill, there—get this guy some water.

As the water was served to Johnny, and he gulped it down, Mackie said, You know, Johnny, I was a pretty bright kid that day when we came to the fortunetellers on the boardwalk. Very glary and sunny it was that day, Johnny. The fortuneteller booth was open a little, and it looked so nice and dark and cool. I went in. The only thing I wanted to do at first was to get into the shade of the fortuneteller's awning. Hot day, you know. Blazing. You ever been out all day in the direct hot blazing sun, Johnny?

Yes.

It's bad—but, long story short, there was my Dad egging me on, and before I know it—I mean it's just a pretty dim long ago memory. You know how that is, Johnny—

Yes, said Johnny. But it was harder and harder to hear Mackie's story because, somehow, Johnny kept being reseated at tables further and further away. The bright-eyed staff just kept coming, touching him, saying, This table is reserved, sir. You must move—Will that table do? Would you mind?

Johnny nodded *no* each time, but it just made Mackie's story get harder and harder to hear, and Johnny strained, strained, and strained, nodding.

The fortuneteller had gold around her head and a big clear ball on the table, and her hands came around on both sides, and her fingers were so long they touched at the front. But no long nails; they were all clipped short. Short like when like they hurt they're cut so short. You know Johnny? You know, like when they hurt?

Yes—but please hurry up, they keep moving me, you are harder and harder to hear—speak louder, speak—

Look at his fucking eyes, said Big Sunny to the side—but Mackie said, Shut up, I'm talking to Johnny—Anyway, Johnny, she said, I bet you can't think of a thing to ask me—can you hear that?

Yes.

I bet you can't think of a thing to ask me, so tell you what, I'll ask me for you because I can see it hanging there in your head, you just don't understand it well enough, or maybe you don't have the words you need to say it right—Do you feel that way, Johnny, do you ever?

Yes.

Good—She said, I bet you would like to know what will happen to you at the end. Isn't that the most important thing to everyone? Isn't it true they just stifle the question? Isn't it true, that people are afraid of the end, to the point they can't even ask about it or think about it or even admit they know it's coming. The end is rushing up—feel it, Johnny? The end is speeding up for you. It's big and round and hard and colorless—I see you shaking, I see your eyes close. Yes, Johnny, sleep now, and for now, because when you weren't looking the end came like a brushing feather, so open your eyes and see where you are now, but—remember before you look at the end that it's coming because you screwed the wrong guy. You ripped off and lied to the wrong people. Open your eyes, see where screwing the wrong people and lying and trying to rip off the wrong people takes you, Johnny, look!

A glimmer came of something most closely resembling a worm, long and thin and with a segmented end, but it went down someplace underfoot, as the restaurant lights went out, yes out. There must have been a storm, yes, the light went out, and less than black slapped on Johnny's face suffocating, suffocating, need to get up and get out of here, where's the big red *EXIT* sign these joints tend to always have; can't get up, something's there all hard, cold, like things get in the silent dark, can't roll over, can't lean back, can't move legs, the dark is real. Pressure. Heart beating though. Had not heard that before. Arm, leg, buds form. But, that was long ago, so, how—face, twist the face, twist and turn and push and stretch the brand-new eyes, ears, nose, and mouth all around. But no, calm down, that's wrong. Pressure is all. Open eyes, just say pressure.

It's okay to laugh at the asshole now, Sunny, said Markie; yes, he said it, I heard it, he did—but they're all gone! All the voices are past and gone. Where! Where! Sunny is laughing and laughing, but—the lid's bolted. Everything moved and stopped and everything's happening wrong over and over, too fast to see, too fast to know, thank God it is that fast, because it's not something people generally want to know. Nothing outside; go inside. Go inside before the nothing outside gets you. Yes, you know. But get inside. Before the knowing gets you. All at once there it is, as an embryo with structures like the gills of a fish in the area that will later develop into a throat that, when developed, begins laughing, so what, laughing. Laugh on. Like you all laughed tying Ayotte up, and throwing him in the tool room, and by the end of the day they reported him AWOL, but he was in the locked tool room tied up all day. When they found him, he said, I don't know what happened. I don't know. Who did it? urged the fat Commander. Who? I don't know. I don't know. Did you ask him who did it? What, he doesn't know? What kind of people would do that to someone? Those kinds of people are bad people. Those kind of people, well—you ought to get rid of them when you find out who they are. What do you say? Do I hear you out there? Touch, push, feel; all black, all solid. At once Johnny knew where he was. He knew they did this once in a while, but he never thought they'd do it to him. There's words worse than worst, but they choked inside someplace because they haven't ever really had the time to be created. When such words are needed there's no time to make them. Get the fuck inside! Stop, stop, stop—it is safe inside. Get there now, stop seeing, be. Relax, breathe easy. Don't think or panic. Just be, back out, back out. There. Go in. That's better. Someone somewhere has stopped menstruating. A blessing in many more ways than the obvious. Contentment.

Chapter Three
Banter on the Ship to China I

Sunday Dinner with Father Dwyer, the only show available on the only cable channel available aboard the almost completely computerized, really big containership, played softly upon the flatscreen slapped up on the flying-bridge wall, as Skip and Noman, the two humans required by international regulations to be aboard, talked all hollow in the welded room.

Skip, you know, no matter how many years you are on these ships, there's one mystery you never ever solve, said Noman.

Oh? What mystery is that?

Noman slugged back his tall black beer. On the screen Father Dwyer was pounding meat.

Look! Look out there! All those damn containers, and the sea. The two are so different! So very, very different. The sea, now, you know, we've all seen what's under the sea. Depending on where you are, there's different things, like—trash. That's everywhere. That's the only thing that's really everywhere, but other stuff under the water, sometimes, wherever you might be, there's tuna. Or there might be shark. Or, there might be dolphin. Whale, even. And seaweed; tons and tons of a million different kinds of seaweed. All the way from New York to Shanghai, on a nonstop trip like this, all month, there's things under the sea that you have heard of and know about and have seen in books and all. You know? We know the sea. You know?

—Today, said Father Dwyer from the TV, his ruddy cheeks glowing, masterfully powdered up by Crisis Johnson the makeup technician, looking like a chipmunk, Today, we will learn how to create banana pancakes, yummy, yummy—and notice I said the word *create*. Not *make*. Humans from the dust of the earth do not create. God creates. Now, of course you know, I'm not God. And I say I create. How can that be? I just said only God creates. Well, here's why I can create. Because I am coming out of hundreds and thousands of TV screens on great ships all over the world. You know how they say God is everywhere? Coming out of the screens, I'm damned near everywhere. So, out there, to you, it's like—a creation. But, now, if you were here—here with me in the studio—what you would hear would not be a creation. I would just be making something from stuff that God created. Now, this leads to a line of discussion that I doubt we want to go through here. You know, said Father Dwyer, waving a super-long wooden spoon all around all directions, spattering and spattering even the edge of the camera lens with some ugly sauce, anything can be argued about. Everything can go a dozen ways. So, I choose rigidly to just go one way. I choose to believe I create these pancakes. Like God creates. Ok? Now that that is settled, I will peel these yellow lovelies and make you glad we're not making brass feet for some hippo. That would be too big and hard. This is why I took up cooking instead of rolling out ingots of iron, steel, aluminum, or gold. I can't do that, but I can do pancakes; pancake after pancake after pancake and all—I may not be a God, but no harm in feeling like one—

Yeah, it's something, said Skip idly, kicking a heel. It really is. Anybody isn't ready for when it happens, is in for a load of trouble.

Huh? What? Why? said Noman, looking down from the TV. What trouble? When what happens?

Here, this—everybody wants to ignore it, but, someday, and someday a lot sooner than people think, all the ice will be melted and all there will be, will be only the sea. Nobody's planning for it, you know—nobody out there who thinks the land is permanent—

Wait—what?

Global warming. Ever seen that lousy old movie, *Waterworld*?

No. But I heard of it. I think I seen bits of it here and there.

That's what it's going to be like. No more land. No more governments. No more laws. Just people all around on ships like this, all kinds of ships, big, and small, just floating around the world with no destinations but to stay alive, one day at a time.

Lord. You believe that? I don't know—

That's right that's why I never go on land. I'm either at sea, or at one port or another, where I stay on the ship. I can't step on dry land, just can't. Knowing what's going to happen—

—Now take this here sausage goulash, droned the ignored TV show. What about sausage goulash? I don't know, you tell me—what about sausage goulash? Well, here's what; you know damned well your brats love anything with shells and sausage. This goulash recipe I'm going to run by you will be one of the little rats' favorites. It's nice; very nice, nice as nice can be to make something like this at home for a change rather than buckling the squealing little banjos and banjettes into their stinking filthy car seats to drag them down to Friendly's one more time because you're a lazy fucker with a fat fistful of credit cards. Plus, made at home, there'll be leftovers! That will make tomorrow even a better day because you won't have to take them someplace or cook or nothin'! This is why God made microwaves and shredded cheddar that never expires—

—to me it's very, very bad, said Skip. And I am so sure it will happen any moment now that taking a step onto the land scares me as bad as if I was stepping off a mile-high cliff.

God, oozed Noman. Is that really true? God, that is awful. What do you do when the ship you came in on has to leave and you need to wait a day or two for the next ship you'll go on to come into port?

I don't know. I just chug vodka. I chug it and chug it and stay in whatever crap-hole flop joint they put me up in and just get all blacked out, and before you know it, I'm in the new ship and I barely remember being ashore.

If you're blacked out drunk, how do you know your new ship has arrived?

People know me. The guys in the company know how I am. The bosses value me. They send guys to get me and bring me on board. They put me in my cabin and lay me on the bed and pull off my shoes and let me sleep it off. By the time I wake up, we're at sea. Everybody knows me so well, they automatically set it up for every assignment I get. There's a cheap place booked for me in Shanghai right now, for this trip. When we get close to Shanghai, they send me a message with the detailed arrangements. They even—

Wait a minute, breathed Noman, cutting the edge of his hand down to pause Skip right there—I was told when I signed onto this ship, that all means of contacting land would be disabled at sea, because any such transmissions could be hijacked by terrorists or pirates or whatever, to track us. You mean to tell me that's not true? I can call people? Tell me how!

No, no, said Skip, waving Noman off. Every one of these ships has a secret super-encrypted link active at all times between the computers on board and the control headquarters on land. It's to detect and repair defects remotely in the ship's systems that might arise. I have the secret codes to tap into that link. It took a lot for this to be approved, and there's review after review after review, like that. When I enter the codes into the computer console on the bridge, a message will be sent back to me with the details of who I will be met by and where I will be staying. You could probably get the same thing, in time, but you got to prove you got a real need. It's a real nice setup. They book the place, they take me there, they even stock the room with vodka for me. They stock at least a dozen fifths for me, to start with. Hey, sure, oh, I'm out of it on land, yes, sure, but once back on the ship, I give one hundred percent. Sometimes one hundred fifty percent, or even more. I'm the best seaman they got. They tell me that on every review date I got. I'll do this until the great flood I told you about comes. Then there will be no land, and I will be at sea forever. That's my dream, to be at sea forever, forever, forever, forever—land is shitty, shitty, hard and ugly, and all infested and diseased. Fit only for vermin.

Hey, Skip. I like the land. What, am I vermin?

No, of course not. It's just that I—

Hey, I know that. Just funnin', ya know. I do like to fun people. You sure?

That's right.

That is great to hear. What I picture is different—

—Father Dwyer they called me! shouted the flatscreen. Me! Me, who never had a roll in the hay with anything more than my hand in my life! And Mom and Dad saw the sheet stains, I am sure. And bless them, bless them, they never said nothin'! My cache of stained, sticky Victoria's Secret catalogs I had in the basement rafters was gone one day. I went numb. They must have known! Must have! But, Mother just smiled and made me eggs to order every morning, just like these I'm showing you how to make now. Yes, or—

Skip!

—at sea, yes! Forever, forever, forever, and forever—

Skip! shouted Noman. Wake up! You're asleep again on your feet. You're standing there like you do—come on, snap out of it.

—forever, forever, for—

Come away, come back—here I'll spit in your face; I always snap you out of it by spitting you in your face—ready? Here—

Noman turned Skip's blank face toward his, and hocked up a big yellow plug of phlegm, positioned Skip just right, and let go—and a drip of snotty hocker hung yellow from Skip's face, and he came to, shouting, Now why the hell did you do that, for what the hell was it for, I ought to kick you to shit, wherever or whatever—

Noman stepped back and put up his hands.

You were gone again, Skip. Sorry, when you're again fully awake, your inner Skip will understand. You were stuck again. You know you get stuck. You were stuck. Skip!

The smaller blond tanned man shook his head, and said, Yeah, Noman. I get it.

Good.

They idly, silently glanced at the TV—suddenly smiling like brothers—up where Father Dwyer tugged at his too-tight ecclesiastical collar and barked, Toasted rye bread topped with chopped onion, ham, and fried eggs, makes up Strammer Max, which I am going to show you how to make after the next AARP Insurance-scam commercial. Strammer Max. How about that name? Nothing about that name tells you what's in it. How about that handshake, or that smile, or that hairstyle, dress size, or suit cut, or beard? Nothing about any of that tells you what's in it. Everything that's named is intended to hide the truth. The truth is intended to hide behind the exact opposite of what it is. How can anybody function in such a false world? So, Strammer Max will be next, after AARP gives you truth after truth after truth. Actually, because you know, at this time of day, only the elderly are likely to be nodding off before the television—

What was I talking about? What about? You were saying something about what? You said something. What? Before I went asleep—you were saying something. About the containers.

Uh, oh, yeah—the containers! All these damned containers on this ship. All going to China.

Containers? China? What about containers to China?

Noman waved a palm over Skip's words, and said, Here's what, Skip. The containers, like—like that red one over there at the top. The red one. The new one. The question's for that one and all the other ones. What the hell is in them? What the hell is there? There are so many—thousands even—aboard from stem to stern, from port to starboard, and they're all packed with stuff. What stuff? I always wonder. What the hell is in just that one red one out there? And multiply what's in that one by how many others there are—what's the number, hey, you're the one good with numbers? They taught you in school—Know Your Cargo! Know your Cargo! Know it so that if something bad happens, you can react according to the needs of the Cargo! They teach you that? If you're aiming for Captain some day? If that's your aim, they always teach you that—

Yeah, they did. But—

—Okay! shouted the TV priest. Here we are! Strammer Max coming right up! It's an honest meal, because its name leads you to expect God knows what kind of filth. But, first, a teaser; soup to start, followed by a main course, and then, yes, no, I thought you'd never guess, I knew you'd never imagine that Strammer Max would be the capper, the plus, the finish-offer, the end; dessert. How does the condemned criminal feel when they're finishing off the last few spoonsful of their last meal's dessert? I swear to God, I do—

Anyway Noman, said Skip, folding his arms and turning from the TV. How many of those big iron boxes do you think are on this teeny tiny son of a seaboil ship?

About sixty-nine thousand—but I know some of what's in these today. I was hanging around over the rail while they were loading. I saw a manifest. It said Container Williams number one—one hundred sixty fifty-five gallon drums with removable tops and locking rings and hardware—sixty-nine thousand pounds. There were two pages of entries like this. We got quite a few fifty-five gallon drums in this ship somehow, someway, somewhere. All empty. All quiet. All hollow and nothing. Nothing inside. Funny, you know. Pretty funny.

Yeah, funny. Sure. Funny as shit.

After they'd said this, silence walled between them, and each stood lost in thought. Thank God for ships, and for people of the sea—we're the only ones who will know how to survive, thought Skip. Land people were stupid. Land people like Noman.

He turned toward Noman, but Noman was looking down holding his chin in his hand, the way he had the day he got his orders for this trip in the mail at home. It opened to him and shouted up at him where he stood on his sun-drenched porch beneath a lovely blue sky. Lord, God! I'm assigned to a forty-eight-day round trip to China, at a minimum, he read—a mandatory, impossible to get out of, highly important trip to China! He stood in the sun beside his large dog and looked directly into the sun; this is not good, he thought. She needs me home. Can't leave when she's like this; can't leave her alone. Plus—

The TV on the wall insisted to be heard.

—Oy oy oy, you say, oy oy oy, what's this? gestured Father Dwyer. This is what? Salads and cheese instead of soup and dessert—oy oy oy oy, what's the catch? This is much too good to be true. What's the catch here? Strammer Max? I must know if this is Strammer Max. S'cuse me while I pull my fully loaded Mauser, that's never been fired in fear before today—

—how do I tell her, thought Noman gripping the bright white porch rail—What an awful blot of fear had flown up to bust him in the nose out of that letter. He stood looking out at the row of house boxes set down along the other side of the street, staring with the orders in his hand, feeling blood surge and flow behind his face. The beautiful day off had disappeared. He turned to go tell her—

But no, where is Skip? Back on the bridge, Noman's hand fell from his chin and he looked around and found that Skip had walked away. Oh, yes, he glanced at his watch. Damn. Late. Need to go below and do my duty, as Skip has done. Need to do what I need to do, to prepare to leave for the voyage. Don't think back to how she reacted when I showed her the orders and left the room. Have to shut out everything but what I need to be doing to prepare to leave.

Being on the ship was better now than constantly remembering her face. Being on the ship was better than the crying he'd done driving to the port, better than the crying she'd done when he'd told her, better than the bosses telling him when he called to explain why she needed him at home, Either work that trip, or there's no more job for you. Yes, shutting up, shutting down, and going to the ship was better than walking from the superintendent's office, his last check in his hand, with tears in his eyes, for her, for the both of them. Knowing that it was time to go to work, and realizing that Skip was not coming back, Noman felt free to wipe the moist flow of tears set to run from his eyes. Deeper even, he wished what Skip said would be true; that the water would rise and take the land and drown her fear away, but somehow spare her. Set her back like it was before. Before me; I ruined her; this would not all be, but for me. She would have her husband with her, when time has run out and she must face her fear—they had lost one, she was terrified they would lose another, he should be there if it happens, you should quit that job, quit that job, quit—

Noman set his lips tight, turned from her sobs, and went below to think no more. He left the blustering, banging Father Dwyer TV show alone on the wall, the fat defrocked priest straining to end his episode with a flourish, his sharp-edged words bouncing around the steel floor bulkheads, ceiling, and immaculately clean glass, wide windows, saying out beyond the glass to the forever sea, Sunday dinners are called *Alaska*! Yes they are, yes they are, and get this; they've nothing to do with what they're called. Alaska is not what a load of salads, cold cuts, cheese, breads, lox and smoked expired tuna should be called. That is a lie, a complete lie. And look, look—there's not even anyone listening any more now that I've got down to the bottom, flat, hard, black, complete truth that the word *Alaska*, used suchlike, is a lie! In the end, when everybody's gone, what is real becomes only lies!

Chapter Four
On the Free One-way trip to China

—A blessing in many more ways than the obvious. Contentment. Yes, Foster focused mindless for quite some time on the feeling he had of growing out to ten thousand times larger than he started as. Contenting, it was. Content, contenting; could both mean the same? At the same time, atop or underneath or in this feeling, he told himself he knew they did this to others, but he never thought they'd do it to him. There's words worse than worst, but they choked inside someplace because they haven't ever really had the time to be created. When such words are needed, there's no time to make them. But, calm, yes. There is life. And there is hope. Johnny Foster knew he was one tough-as-nails fucker. He stepped out and faced himself surrounded by the dark and said, Get the fuck inside yourself! Stop, stop, stop—it is safe inside. Get there now, stop seeing, just be. Relax, breathe easy. Don't think or panic. Just be in yourself. Nothing else—just yourself; life goes on inside yourself, as long as it needs to, it's not over now, so, push, there! See, when you're all calm, it all opens out, big, bright, and wide. It is always still yesterday in the Fortuna bar to meet Miss Sweetie to celebrate what I just got away with and to tell her what'd happen next. Look at her, look at her, her hair is so shiny golden so golden. There cannot be dark when it's golden so golden and flowing down such a beautiful woman as this. Breathe easy. Breathe easy.

So golden, so smooth, so flowing come the words from Johnny. At the same time, he suddenly felt small as a peanut. But the words came and went fleshing him back out.

Guess what, Miss Sweetie? Just guess what?

What honey? Has to be big, the way you sounded on the phone.

I made us a lot of money this morning, Miss Sweetie, a lot, a whole lot. We can get away.

Away? Away where?

After we eat and have a few, we'll stop at your place. Make sure you pack light.

Pack light? To go where, Johnny?

To go to Barcelona tonight.

For what?

To live. We got to go there. We got to lay low. I got us more money than you can imagine this morning, Miss Sweetie, so much it's kind of dangerous for us now for a while.

What? What'd you do Johnny? You fuck up somehow?

No, no, no. I just delivered a pretty big delivery for Mackie this morning, and it just hit me, why go back—why not keep what the creeps I gave the load to paid for myself—and for you. We want a life, honey. This is our way out. We can run away and be together. This money will last a long, long time, Miss Sweetie—we can go live high on the hog. I don't want no more boss. I'm sick of Mackie. I got to get out. You need to pack. Let's eat fast, pick up your menu. Go on.

You're ripping off Mackie? My God, no, nobody does that. Anybody who's ever even thought about it, just, well, they're just not around anymore. You'll get killed!

Maybe yes, maybe no, Miss Sweetie—but chances must be taken in desperate times.

Some suction came then trying to draw him gone from Miss Sweetie back all sealed in, probably summoned by the word she had said: *killed*! Killed! Just not around anymore! She is striving to sit there eating alone, seeming to be talking to some pretend person! And that was real. Everybody ends up killed someday and somehow, but no, not now—he fought to stay out of the trap, and she sat silently, and the small gaps around everything in the place at once were an instant away from oozing out sticky-gluey pus-like stinking panic—no no no no, don't let panic push up, don't know, don't see, easy, easy. Look Miss Sweetie in the eye, see—it's not dark all around, there's her eye. See? Just as it should be forming, it's formed mammalian, somewhat pig-like, but speaks and is good looking, so it all is Miss Sweetie, though everything really is so different now, it's like there's a new planet all around them, but, so, Johnny said into her eye, And all it means is we have to get out of here and lay low someplace far, and Mackie will look and look and look for his money, this is frightening, so grab the glob of frightening in the middle of the play, form it, make words, say them to Miss Sweetie, hard, and fast, and it's caulk, see; it caulks everything up and there she is again. Thank God, yes, he is still here with her. He is not yet make believe. Something is forming, and sliming, and flowing all around, he feels it there, why it is, who knows, but he is safe. It's coming to keep the peanut safe. Yes, the peanut, no!

Whew! Here she is, yes, here was Johnny too, yes, so he had to talk to keep it real.

We're in love, Miss Sweetie, he said quickly. And she registered surprise as he went on, saying, You know it and I know it. She stared, waiting to hear what was next. So, the pressure eased when the magic words came from him; yes, they do, and she's waiting, so I'm really here not there, so, I'm asking you to come live in Barcelona with me. I got tickets. Two seats on the redeye. Leaving in two hours. The place over there is the house I grew up in. It's a big house, just my Mom lives there, I can pay off her place now and pay for a nurse to clean up after her and feed her and all, and we can just go right over tonight. We got to get moving, get you packed, get to the airport, and all—so open that menu!

This is very sudden, said Miss Sweetie. Barcelona? Why Barcelona? And I didn't even know you felt—well, I'll just say this is rather sudden, and, I can't help it, this is the word keeps hitting me—rather surprising. And telling me right out you ripped off Mackie, I mean, that was not a wise thing to do Johnny, no not at all, if I say no to Barcelona, and you go and I stay back here, Mackie's guys are going to be around, saying, You were the last one of the bunch to see him, Mackie wants his money, my God, Mackie wants his money—and Mackie doesn't like to ever be answered with I don't know, if he asks a question. I might get a bullet in my head, Johnny. I don't want them put a bullet in my head, Lord God, why did you invite me here, why did you tell me this, why is it so crazy, and—I don't know the answer. Barcelona? Why Barcelona, Johnny? Why are you putting a bullet in my head, Johnny?—

Fade back dark veil between them; not as dark as the veil in a confessional but dark enough to blur Miss Sweetie, so, to fight back into the light away from the hopelessness encasing him, he said over her, You're going to get a bullet in your head sooner or later, Miss Sweetie. Keep hanging around Mackie's crew, with me or without me, you and everybody in that crew sooner or later will get, not just a bullet in the head, but many, many more bullets, all over you, you need to escape anyway sooner or later, so don't be foolish, don't pass me up, I've got money, a place, and with me you will never ever get a bullet in your head, no, no, no; and her voice was flattened to nothing; the veil remained the same; Johnny was tough and would not panic, ever, ever, and the veil lifted slightly, and the restaurant was easy to reconjure, but she was a mirror person, her face resembled that of a primate, not fully human in appearance. Johnny knew she was Miss Sweetie, so he said into the mirror, Miss Sweetie, please come with me to Barcelona.

And the glass did crack and fall down away, but there was another mirror, and her hands had webs between the fingers, and her arms were so tiny, but this could not be a mirror because then that would be how Johnny was, and he knew better; so, he said into the mirror again, Miss Sweetie, stop fooling like that. Please come with me to Barcelona.

Foster's pounding heart strained to rip from his body. Blood will squirt all inside, yes; and the second layer of glass cracked and fell down away revealing another mirror, smudged with the fingerprints of a fetus; yes they have fingerprints, yes at one month already, they do.

Multiple layers of mirror fell and fell and fell showing in turn a reptilian creature living somehow inside Miss Sweetie. A tail, might be pig, rabbit, elephant, chick, or human and the eyes opened on the sides and just a slit for the mouth and nose—and Johnny had had enough, so, tough as nails, he pushed through closer to her though her bones were barely formed and her head was much too large; something's wrong, so he started to say, loud, aloud, I am in the restaurant having dinner with Miss Sweetie, not sitting somewhere terrible watching myself be someone else—I am not Miss Sweetie! I am not Miss Sweetie! I—

Sir? Is there a problem sir? Do you need us to call an ambulance?

—am not Miss Sweetie—what? Ambulance? Why—honey—why are these men standing all around me? Why—

Please quiet down, sir. Or we will have to eject you from the restaurant.

Nonsentient fight/flight, fight/flight, fight—

Sir!

All the words Johnny had been saying condensed into a pinpoint of heart-pain fluttering in the dark in him. Mackie, he said, looking up. Mackie, good to see you. Funny to just run into you like this. Here—

Johnny was made lucid by the pound of the heart, and it still pounded, but he offered Mackie a hand to shake. Mackie just sat down. The jut of his chin was stony. His eyes, watery and cloudy, were nearly dead. He did not take Johnny's hand but sat at the table and clasped his hairy hands before him. Thick dark hair coated the backs of his hands, almost flowing hair like on a head, but up from his collar floated more hair, and this sight shut Johnny and Miss Sweetie up as Mackie said, I came here on business, Johnny—and thanks, Miss Sweetie, for telling us you'd be meeting little Johnny here tonight.

What? What—

Thank you, Mister Mackie, oozed miss Sweetie, who began rising and saying, Good bye, Johnny. I need to leave you and Mister

Mackie here. Mister Mackie's got business. It's not for me to hear. Maybe someone's watching, somebody else, maybe, whose business it is; but it's not mine, no—

Wait—Miss Sweetie, wait! Mackie, what is this—Miss Sweetie!

Everything all around shone hard-edged, crystal clear, and fully lit, and the young woman was gone almost as though there was really no door, no way out, like there was no way out for Johnny, Mister Mackie was here, no one walks out on Mister Mackie—Johnny was no longer hungry. Johnny's chest fluttered, and he loosened his collar, and—

Why do you look so uncomfortable Johnny? asked Mister Mackie. You're here for dinner. So, check the menu. Have dinner. I'll even buy you your dinner. How does that sound, Johnny? You'll get a little more of my money than you stole already. Enough for, oh, who knows? Go wild with the money, Johnny. What do I need it for?

Hands ice-cold, heart—Mister Mackie, I didn't steal anything, what do you mean?

Oh, Johnny, we been watching you all day. What do you think? A top man in my organization like you, I wouldn't want to keep tabs on you, make sure I know exactly what kind of fine job you're doing, so I can make sure you get everything you deserve? Did you think I wouldn't work that way with a valuable young man like you?

I suppose not, Mister Mackie.

Mackie smiled, and though the smile was silent, Salmon Fish and the rest of Mackie's crew came out from the back, and at last four men sat at the table and four men stood behind Mackie.

What is this all about? said Johnny. I—what has happened?

Wait, Johnny—hey, Fish, said Mackie—come here.

Yeah boss?

Go to the kitchen and order spaghetti and meat balls for Johnny. Nice big plate.

Okay, Boss.

Nice, nice—see Johnny, you're in the crew. You get the best.

But hey, I just thought of something I meant to ask you. Why did you book a night flight for two out of Newark to Barcelona today?

I—what—uh—no I didn't.

Oh, you did, and first class too. Not on the cheap like me and my men travel. Got to keep costs down when there's a big operation to run. Hard to turn profits these days. Hard. You know that, Johnny?

I—yes. Of course, I know that.

Since I know you want to travel, Johnny, I've got those tickets cancelled and have arranged a much better trip for you. Nicer place. Great trip. Won't take long to get there, either. But you got to trust me, Johnny. Barcelona? That's a slum next to this place. Ain't it so, boys?

Yeah, Mister Mackie!

Right boss!

Shure 'nuff!

All you got to do, Johnny, is eat all the spaghetti and meat balls, and we will then take over and make you very, very happy. Say Johnny, while we're waiting—want a few lines? Want some blow? It'll put you in the mood for the trip, Johnny. Very important, when taking a trip, to be in the appropriate mood. Do you know what I mean?

Ah, yes I do, Mister Mackie.

Heart pound came sharp—cold hands, hide them, yes—like fists on metal but no, just a heart pound. Meat balls. Fists on metal, no panic, no, see! This is a restaurant, a mother-fucking restaurant, but—pounding heart sounds sound out through surrounding hollow, empty, dark, round, sealed steel spaces, and all fades away, frightened.

But Miss Sweetie at least has a living new reptilian brain.

Yes, this could be worse.

But Miss Sweetie, at least, has a living brand-new reptilian brain, with a big future.

Say that in time with your heart.

This could be way worse.

Say that in time with your heart.

Makes sense somehow, panicky. Makes sense somehow, panicky.

All that has been learned by Foster is that he is one of two possible sexes.

Sex organs, yes, but could be either. Wait to know. Got to wait to know.

Makes sense somehow, panicky, but; teeth, fingernails, taste, the sex is, but which is it? Wait, wait, sleep, sleepy, sleepeth.

Chapter Five
Banter on the Ship to China II

Sunday Dinner with Father Dwyer, the latest hit show on their only cable channel, continued playing first thing in the morning, as it had day and night, episode after episode, for the last four days, soft upon the flatscreen screwed up to the wall, as they talked some more, clearly becoming bored by the routine. For Father Dwyer, there was no time. For Father Dwyer, every day was Sunday. For Skip and Noman, Father Dwyer did not exist. Just one more thing turned on and running all the way from New York to Shanghai, like all the other computerized, preprogrammed, automatic navigation devices on board and almost needing no one there, really, but Skip and Noman needed to ride along, for Insurance purposes; for the sake of some fine print, in the tiniest footnote of some properly-filed-by-low-paid-well-dressed-clerks, deliberately-notarized, sixteen-signatured, big shipping contract, on some very high corporate floor in Dubai, no doubt. Nothing like a ship there, no. Not like a ship, at the top. With plush carpet too. Yes. Very, very plush, vivid carpet. Not like the grey steel Skip and Noman trod on in their aching steel-toes every inch of the day. They were out on deck or amidst the containers, or someplace dark down below, but up in the empty, bright, midday-lit cabin, Father Dwyer's Sunday Kitchen played episode eight hundred seventy-six, of over two thousand, with probably more being filmed every day. Father Dwyer stood behind the slick kitchen counter, Havana cigar hung from his thick scarlet lips, shooting his blood-veined eyes straight into the camera, and stirring and stirring a long wooden spoon in a great dirty silver pot, possibly purchased many, many—too many, really—years ago, and smilingly speaking nonstop through the vapor-steam rising thinly from the pot. Father Dwyer's black shirt strained against his large fatty belly-ball, and his cigar bobbed in time with his words, flicking ash after ash down into the pot, as he spoke obliviously to no one at all but some red eye, probably on some automated hi-tech camera, with an invisible cameraman in the dark beyond.

This cooking, he said, is being done with some kind of obvious gift God gave you—we are all gifted by God in some way, you know. And I am master. It's like this; give me, you know, a pack of a hundred or more dogs—each one I pat gently as I say tenderly, You are the very best good dog in the world. The dog thinks that, to me, he or she is the sole and specially loved, good, possibly greatest dog, ever; the best of the best, you know. And he or she carries this through the rest of their life. They remember. They grow big heads. They always think they're better. They lead the pack day over day. They keep thinking, The great Father Dwyer long ago singled me out and said I was the very best dog. The dog thinks this over and over and always remembers to the day he or she dies, never knowing the real truth; I actually patted the same pat the same way and with the same words the same way to over one hundred or more, maybe thousands of other dogs, each of whom now thinks until death that he or she is the best, top, gifted dog. So, they are really all the same. And all the same actually equals very mediocre in most cases. Nobody's best when everything's best. Oops. Got to keep stirring. The great big pot.

Heh. Shit.

Pot. Great big pot.

Funny.

Silently, Father Dwyer stood pulling at his half-gone Havana, staring into the pot, slowly stirring the unseen mixture with his big wooden spoon, for five full minutes.

At last he looked up and said, contemplatively, You know, when I was still a priest, I was the Pastor of a big Parish. That Parish had a big grammar school. In the big grammar school were three hundred or more children—each one I hugged lightly, when the opportunity arose, and said, oh so tenderly, You are gifted, you are truly gifted. You are special, you're a great gifted child, and you will do great things; and I always said this making sure the child's Mother was near, listening, beaming, beaming and beaming brighter toward bursting, higher and higher with each hug I gave the child. Special, different, better, I'd say. And after I let go, the girl or boy went on, grew, and carried the belief I had planted for the rest of their life. They all thought at least once a day, Father Dwyer singled me out long ago and said I was the very most gifted one, the most special; I am better. They each went to their graves never knowing that, just like the dogs, the same hug and the same words were given and stated to over one hundred or more, maybe thousands of other students, each of whom lived a whole life wrongly thinking that he or she was gifted, bound for greatness, the best of all. The chosen. They are really all just the same. Dogs, students; students, dogs. All the same, all born, live, and die. Again and again and again. Like the planets orbiting, feeling safe, never knowing they're continuously falling toward the heart of the Sun.

But, that's astrophysics, and this is cooking; don't mean to bore you, you know, but now, look, look, look; here and now, I see the boil in the pot is way, way up, and the scald of the bubbles is bouncing, so back to now. Cut it off now! All done now! Look, yes! Off with the gas! Down with the heat! And though half a Havana's worth of grey ash has fallen into the mix while I just gave you your very most important lesson, I have given you the moral and point of why we cook, as it were, what is done is done. Scotty, my work here is done. It's all boiled. Yes, yes—cameraman! Here! The mitts!

Father Dwyer slipped on outsized oven mitts tossed to him from the darkness past the camera, the mitts all embroidered with cow faces, smiling and winking much cuter than any real cow ever could, and tilted the pot down and told the cameraman, Point it here; give them a good shot of this boiling, salty potato mash with corn beans and gore of dead vulture, by God! Look at it boil; watch it spatter higher and highest. This, my ship, lads, is the Eintopf, full of scalding hot swirl, spice, and color; beans or lentils, lentils or beans, vegetables and sausages and sausages and vegetables; see it, feel it, touch it, heal it—and in the next episode, I will boil innocent living crabs to death all screaming before you, yes! In the very next episode of Father Dwyer's Sunday Kitchen. Enjoy, fans! Lord God and Mary Blessed, thank you for this great cooking gift that makes me able to send waves through the screen, to come out of every television everywhere on every ship on the way to everywhere; land watchers don't matter. They will drown in the end. Life began in the sea, and in the sea it will end. Sea watchers matter! See ya', seamen! Carry on, go potty-pop fast during the next commercial, to be ready for the next installment! There are many commercials that need to run first, though. No, don't worry if nothing will come out your ass or wherever absolutely immediately, and be sure to take time to wipe up really good. We stay clean on our ships yes we do. So, then…

Amidships, Skip was in the middle of the massive job of creeping along on his hands and knees tightening and greasing each of the twelve-thousand-containers-on-board's worn and rusty mounting gear—old-school style hardware. By the end of the voyage, they all must be done. That means he must do four hundred and sixty-one containers each day of the twenty-six-day voyage. Of course, no normal human being can do that; of course, the regulation demanding this be done was written sixty years ago, when the largest ship carried no more than sixty or seventy small containers. That was now just ancient history, may well have been the Middle Ages. When they got to Shanghai, of course, the review and arrival status sheet would have the box labeled, *All mounting gear cleaned, freshened, painted as needed, lubricated and secured*, with an extra-large X, slashed across by Skip, who really only had been able to do a tiny fraction of the actual number of mounting-gear-sets on board. He could do about one hundred ten containers by the end of the voyage, about as many that ships carried in the nineteen sixties, because—primarily—of his imagination about what was behind the endless progression of steel-plate container sides, he spent his day creeping along, with his ancient universal wrench, and his half-full pot of axle grease, and his large, almost-completely-worn-down grease-wiping bristle-stick, which the common man watching would just think was an old, ready-to-be-thrown-out paintbrush, but no, they'd be wrong, because every tool that spent its entire existence aboard ship had a name of its own, and a special look all its own as it wore out through the years, just like a sailorman is almost the exact opposite of a landsman. Like a ship is the exact opposite of a warehouse on land; the ship moves, the warehouse sticks at the same spot for all time, as a tree is forced to do by circumstance, or like every blade of grass on the world is forced to remain where it sprouts until the day it dies, the smears of green seen on Irish calendar photographs are made up of billions and billions of individual organisms, creatures, men, and tree dwellers, spending all day atop gleaming corporate powerhouse symbols, set up to look real, but just facades.

Skip crept along in the narrow space between the containers, using a large orange flashlight to see his way because this place was like Manhattan: tall towers on either side of narrow streets spending most of every day in the shadows, and when the sun would move to flow its light exactly between the towers, it would just be there for ten minutes or less, probably just one time a day. The hour and length of the lit period might be somehow meaningful to some mystics behind the scenes, might even have been lined up to the stars and planets and the calendar according to some prophecy only known to the priests, like Stonehenge and other suchwise monuments. There in the land of the midnight sun crawled Skip shivering hard, and the cars and trucks and delivery vans and police cars of the city waited for him to slowly move on after cranking his wrench and painting on his grease and moving his flashlight around to see above and behind and around the big threaded rusty steel bars. They honked and honked behind him, but he had the weight and bulk of the undone work before him sitting as hard, large, and black as a row of great trucks inching along before him. Unfazed, he crawled down the very center of the road following the banging and the bristling and the slapping and clinking clanging of the work he was doing straining slowly forward on and on down the road between the solid steel buildings up and down, across and ahead, probably the strangest buildings anyone has ever seen in a city huge as this one, the kind of city where you'll find anything you want just so long as you never give up looking. Skip worked on, moving forward on hands and knees, exactly tuned to where he was, who he was, and what he had to do, but—something happened funny. At the bottom of this canyon of steel-fronted giant buildings all bolted and screwed tight to the road in a strange way, odd and strange even for the city, as though to prevent the buildings from falling straight up, a sound stabbed him, and *stab* is the word; because it wasn't supposed to be there; and if you're where you are every day and everything is exactly the same every moment that clicks on by, identical to all others, something different coming in a moment will sting you, hurt you, stab you, and finally, stop you.

He froze. He listened. What was that, was that something from behind the steel wall, what the hell could that have been, what the hell, what—some steel banging? And banging. And banging and banging and banging and bang—he froze, just as the condom commercial on the Father Dwyer TV in the wheelhouse was ending and the smiling woman faded and the banging was stopped before Skip ever heard it, it went on for a long time, but just a single moment.

Father Dwyer's opening music for this episode called number eight hundred seventy-seven was raucous and saxophonic and piano-heavy, and he stood in the music with a brand new unknown brand of cheroot stuck in a special hole in his face, someplace other than his mouth, so his mouth would be able to say the truth about the foods featured this time, which spread across the counter all cartoned neatly before the press of his tightly large black button-popping shirted belly pushing painfully hard to the edge. The cheroot smoke came bringing words from where the opening music used to be.

Okay, my pals, all my holy boys and girls—ah, I remember I used to go barge into the middle of fifth-grade classes at the Catholic Grammar School, interrupt the teacher, just because I was the big boss and could go anywhere and do anything I wanted, and say from behind my flaming Havana, Okay! How many of you fine boys will become priests when you grow up? And, of course every hand would shoot up, every clean, white palm would gleam happily waving—and then I would say, you pretty, pretty girls—so bright shiny and so super-pure, how many of you fine girls will become nuns when you grow up? And of course, every tiny fifth-grade, bright, unsullied hand would shoot up; and my God, the teeth, the smiles, the teeth. This, my friends, is where—I knew this class would enjoy ice cream, right then, right at that second, to wash over those wonderfully new tiny pearly teeth and begin the lifelong process of decay. Yes. That is a force of nature. Wanting things drives it forward. Desiring, obtaining, and consuming things that slowly will kill you is the strongest urge on earth; but I did not tell the class, no—I am telling you now. You! The strongest, yet, at the same time the weakest, desire on earth is to enjoy and let wash back over your beautiful teeth, only those things that drive the lifelong process of living long without disease and deterioration and pain, and being active and happy until the end comes up in the middle of the night, a gripping hand like an upside-down arcade game where you can put in money and move the claw and drop it onto the little stuffed bunny and pull it up—wow! We got it, we got, it, we—careful, careful—but the bunny falls away, because the whole thing naturally is rigged, like life is rigged to do the opposite—the claw shoots up guided by the Lord and grips your soul, and pulls it down from your sleeping body—and the cherubim all chant, Yes, Lord, we got it, we got it, we—careful careful—oh, yes, the Blessed Savior tries this every night of your life, but then, because you went to the doctor, or you went to the dermatologist, and had your prostate check and your colonoscopy and topped it off with only live food not dead food, and walked a few miles a day with a big dog that old ladies and children cross the street to avoid when they see the animal—because of all this, the soul slips loose and shoots back up into the body, and the Blessed Savior has no more money to try any more that night, so he goes back toward the throne leaving the cherubim disappointed, but the Father at the arcade says, we can keep trying, tomorrow's another day, and the Savior says, Yes, go on, see another dawn, and sleep comes up drowning.

This is the way I know people live on, are judged every day, let to live one more day over and over and over until the ooze of sleep takes them and they have, luckily, shot themselves another hole in one, all while jangling jewelry obtained by the woman in heaven that can't grip the pen to sign them off to die right now, right now... Anyway—I know, yes; what I was going to say was, here—and he swept his black-sleeved hand across, and said, Here is a carton of Ice Cream, here is some Sugar, and this is intended to show you how much sugar is contained in this container of chocolate ice cream, I, yes, I—yes right, this is not really good for you. And I know. I do. After I left the priesthood and took a few culinary classes online, and then got this gig, I also got a job at night as a dancing-master in a dancing studio, located in the basement of the town's funeral home. I learned to dance down there from God, direct, because of the constant praying and sorrow and crying and consoling that seeped down from the funeral parlor above, well, it touched me like I got slapped in the face with a red-hot frying pan by the Holy Ghost herself, and then got the son of God himself to drive the fabled golden spike right in my brain, and all at once everything clicked that not only could I pray, and cook, but also, I could dance too. And you know what they teach you when you're in Catholic School—if God gives you a gift, you damn well better open it and use it and share it or you will end up in a place everybody fears might exist, despite of what they've spent their lives believing—I—yes, what kind of a God do we have that will let you go on believing and then be punished for some awful thing we love or have, which, if only we knew it was really that bad, we would never ever dare to do! But—mm, let's dig in this ice cream. This stuff, that I don't yet know I'll eat enough of to give me a disease where I'll need to give up dancing; and oh, this stuff I don't yet know I'll eat enough of to force me to carry around this big soft globe of meat where my belly ought to be; and oh, this stuff, that stuff, everybody's stuffed up—walrus meat's tasty, but unfortunately banned. You know? I said, I shout—Do you know? Lord, you are so silent and dense—are you sure you're not in a German ship? Anyway, I'm wasting the episode—now, here, quiet, listen to me. About this ice cream—

Tokophobia.

Noman stood facing a great, tall, wide, ice-cold, rusted bulkhead in a dark space near the bow of the ship. See, on land it's called the nose, but at sea it's called the bow; cars might have bows and ships might have noses, someplace somewhere; believe what you want, but the true nature of everything will not change to suit your words. Noman held a brand-new scraper in one hand and an ancient, very heavy spray-bottle of rust-loosener in the other. The label was long gone, sloughed off by the constant ooze of the oily slippery liquid dripping from the leaky seal up top. Noman had always longed to know what the stuff actually was, and if there had been warnings on the bottle not to breathe, touch, taste, drink, spill, or do anything else with this white thin stuff but let it shower the bulkhead, he might be the cause of his spouse's inability to bear a child to full term and the root of all her fears. What is in this spray bottle that, if brought home on clothing or skin, or if having worked its way so deep into him that after some voyage the semen he shot into her was nearly perfectly pure wall-rust-cleaner made up of God knows what poisons—so, how lucky he was to work on a ship. What terribly, terribly, fantastic luck—to have this shitty job on a ship where you can't be home for months on end. He made good money on the ship, but maybe his working on this ship and doing all this scraping and spraying and breathing and coughing and getting covered with this very probably poisonous stuff, might have caused, and might still be causing, a problem worth no amount of money, no matter how huge or useful the amount might be that would be shit out into and over and slime up his bank account each month. They had lost one child to mid-term miscarriage, possibly because of this—and now Noman was here again, doing what just might make the one whose delivery was during his voyage fail to thrive. When he got to Shanghai—God, that word stuck in his craw—if there had never been a Shanghai and no need for a ship to go there, or, better yet, if the surface of the planet had been free of all water, all oceans, lakes, and streams dry from the very beginning, and to get water to survive you'd have to tap wells into the ground and suck it up like they do with oil—nothing on the surface to get on you, to seep in and contaminate and poison… And there would be no need for ships, and jobs like this, and he would be home every night with her as it ought to be, yes, the scraper clanged the metal, yes, the scraper clanged again and again, the clang and the scrape and the dip and brush and scrape at last turned him around, and there, there, look, look! My God, no, they are cheering and calling him out onto a stage, bright lit with an audience facing him from out in the dark, great hot footlights gleaming, the huge audience screaming and laughing, the way he often felt that he wanted to scream, laugh, run, strip, and throw himself headfirst into the steel bulkhead, which was really just balsa wood made up to look just like steel, shatter it to splinters and plunge through, down, and past an even louder cheering audience and slice into the water of some huge Olympic pool, with the merest tiny splash: a perfect dive! This made him a contender for the Gold, nearly the perfect winner, but—as a very evil wretch of a suicide had said so many, many, nautical miles and seconds, hours, days, weeks ago from his deep dark hiding hole, watch out for whatever comes too easy, watch out for whatever comes too soon—see your woman there? Your woman is there. Out of the pool, now. Up, onto the stage. There she stands beaming, having been brought secretly here on the ship, for a surprise reunion, like they used to do on TV for sailors and soldiers and long-lost brothers and missing children, people like that. And because, yes, because it came too soon, as the evil wretch of a suicide had predicted, Noman ran flat-faced full-tilt into the inch-thick steel bulkhead on the other side of the small dark space he'd really just been spraying and scraping all this time—going through the metal brought great pain, but he brushed and scraped and smelled the heavy fumes from the paint can, to the place he sought to be, impossible though it was, the fumes drove him there, and at last, there he was; and there she was! This cannot be happening, maybe they gave him something that just made him feel like he was working and working and somehow to be here and home too, and back and forth and scrape himself to the center of the big TV reunion show that he never knew a cheap outfit like this would do for such low employees. And the host with the hard-fast black hair and sweet suit said, Congratulations, Mr. and Mrs.—say what did you say your name was, man? Hey, why are you lying there? Say your name to me—open your eyes and say your name, it's really not a lot to ask a person who just ran superfast, clean, hammer-hard into an inch-thick solid steel wall, who the hell they are! Hey! Hey!

    Noman opened his eyes, quick—yes, there she was! Just for an instant, and then for some reason, a cast iron baseball bat smashed him in the face, and here he was saying, Where'd she go? to a host that had just congratulated him and his wife, and he tried to see her again, this time longer, but instead stood in the dark yet again, inside a container ship between two steel walls that had something to do with the pail and brush and scraper he was holding, maybe it was his job to do something messy and sweaty and hard, but: no! The fumes, dammit, the fumes of some kind of work someone had been doing deep in the great ship boiled all around much too heavily to be breathed. He shook his head, exited the compartment, and immediately felt better, and he went up on deck to get even cleaner air. My God! he cried to the blue sky! My God! And just as he turned, a town square bloomed all about him covering over the ship, and, there she was again! There she is! I am with her, must run—and again the bat swung from no place, and he was flat on his back this time, out cold between the bulkheads, this time having run head first into the opposite end of the compartment. Slowly, he rose. He was in the ship, for real, for sure. There was no reaching her before her time came. No way to know that their baby would live. It started coming then, all over again, so he stepped up to the wall and started wildly scraping and spraying and scraping and spraying her image that kept coming up at him and he'd clear it away and it'd come and he'd clear and—the bulkhead work got done that way. All the bulkhead work, not just some, but all, like this at least for a couple of days. Why do they build these great steel monsters full of crannies, cracks, and crevices and tiny spaces that need to be sprayed and scraped and painted continuously, like they say how it is on the long, long bridges; they start painting at one end, and the bridge is so damned long that by the time they get to the end of the painting, it's been years, yes, years, and they need to go back to the beginning like that, and there is no break ever at all. And again, and again, and again, they paint, suspended by thin lines over great heights. But at least they're in the light. At least they go home every night. At least when their wives at last give birth, they can most likely be there, no matter when, what time of year, or day, or year or day, or hour. None of this, Here she comes, scrape her back, she comes, scrape her back, away; no don't think of her; what's done is done, she has to not exist or else, or else, the fumes will boil up and drive Noman head-first into something too hard at last, and there will never be an end. Wild obsession's no good when you're confined; when it's life without parole, erase the rest of the world is what must be done. Then serving out your term is—nothing.

Thirteen decks up on the giant empty sun-drenched bridge, the TV continued to power out Father Dwyer's latest episode. Thirteen ice-cream-based dessert items, every one more of a belly buster than the last, spread before him. He threw back his seemingly painted but just highly flushed red face and put out his arms, saying, But never mind all that! Walrus are endangered, walrus are, you will sit in a horrible solitary cell with no toilet at all, if you choose to eat walrus, you better know; this is why that bowl there at the very end, the least fattening of all these desserts, is called the walrus bomb. Yeah. Why? No one knows. All that's known is that this particular dish was found on the table beneath the stretched-out, gunshot-dead, brain-splattered Raoul Blanco—remember the Raoul Blanco crisis? When the bats in the attic had found out by gliding all night that he wanted to base Russian intercontinental ballistic missiles just ninety-three million miles from the earth. Think of it! Think, think—this banana-republic guy wanted to do this on paper when only five years old. This, of course, inspired the next dessert in line, there, there—the banana split. Weaved together using only banana peels himself, in fact; he managed to walk without rotting from Portland all the way to Mt. Saint Helens, where they dump it in the hot, ever-hungry maw of the mountain. Oh yes, yeah, the legend states as clearly as day, from the wicked suicide that said to do it, the world never exploded, and we are here today because of Raoul Blanco. See? See how important this was that this dessert was invented? There's something to be said for a man who's on break in the back of the Dairy Queen and who's peeling his wilted lunch banana and then gets hit with a wonderful idea. You know, come here. Closer. Even closer. Here—on my lap. My baby-lap. Come. Now.

The empty, steel-walled, chrome and red and black ship's-bridge-room's walls and equipment all tried to obey, but they were built to stay where they were built, like trees are meant to stay forever where they are planted. He insisted harder and harder however, until the room and its walls and contents squeezed, huffed, and puffed, and managed to shrink-wrap themselves completely and tightly about the TV containing Father Dwyer. The room hung a silent void, no place really, with a TV-screen shrouded tightly within itself, just floating where the wall it'd been bolted to was not anymore, inside of itself somehow, and for some reason it just goes to show you that when there are no human consciousnesses around, things sink, sag, and stretch, and loosen, and drop, and fall away rusting to nothing in time, turn inside out and outside in, so that is why I am here! Remember! I am the bridge, this is the cabin, here is champagne, Merry Christmas! I am Father Dwyer, this is my kitchen, and you must listen to me or abruptly fail to exist! Cling harder, and listen! I have, as you have already seen, ice cream stuff here. Big strawberry caramel sundaes all quickly and sloppily made, but damned good, all the brown and white and red overflowing down and spreading across the table; the table, the floor of the man who shot himself because of you, yes—you have it all blocked out, but it was because of you! But—who is that coming? he said loud toward the approaching footsteps. One Father Dwyer priestly arm went out, and then the other, and he made the sign of the cross with his fingers, lest it be a demon that, though he was defrocked, he still was sworn to abhor. But, the young woman's voice floated on across the torn up disrupted crime scene that the sloppy ice cream maker had caused to appear right in front of the embarrassed priest, who all at once quieted and realized this was no cooking show, this was a crime scene, everything squashing together must have killed men and women a-plenty, and he thanked God he had arrived in time to where about half, though plenty gory, were still breathing, and if he hurried and hurried he could deliver the Last Rites; Crime Scene Cleanup, said the young woman in Hazmat who came up beside Father Dwyer—the crushing disaster! It's—it's just a cooking show! This is just a cooking show! Oh my God, the world has whirled, mixed up, and fully changed! He knelt in the blood. He prayed over the dying, several at a time because time was of the essence. Lives were slipping up and away heavenward, the same way that death had flowed down toward the abyss, over the rim of the top-heavy sundae, and the living began dying fast, and the young woman handled her obsolete Sears Roebuck Craftsman Wet-Dry Vac like an expert, splashed bleach all around, scrubbing with big brushes in and out the carnage, the priest and the woman slowly did their jobs, until she backed out the door leaving the room behind spotless, and Father Dwyer reformed into himself, standing behind the counter spread across the widescreen flat TV again, and everything seemed under control.

He stood, looked at the camera, inhaled the clean air, and exhaled, saying with a grin, Lord God, it's a good thing I am no longer of the cloth, because this right here before me is a fucking good sundae! And, I swear great Lord, he said, eyes closed, as he raised the sundae chalice as though it were the moment the wine became the blood all around the world every morning, I swear, I will not command again that the entire room compress around me crushing hundreds to death ever again. I did not, I swear Lord, know that I was going to end up a killer! I did not know! Please, God, forgive me! I of all people am no terrorist! I of all people! I, Father Dwyer! No, not—not a terrorist! No—and he held the sundae up toward heaven, and said nothing at all, for three full hours, and tears flowed down his cheeks the entire time. Father Dwyer bitterly wept. He tried not to think what he wanted to think: if this fucking ship was not fully automated, there would have been that Skip and that Noman up here watching my cooking show. Why would a person not go nuts and do rash things after preparing for hours and hours and hours and then, finding out they are not needed at all…?

Shit, true—but he blocked it. To not do so would be sin. Though no longer a priest, he also abhorred sin—so he strained to keep position, knowing that not to do so would pull him down to a very bad place that, mercifully, no human can even picture. But, that was TV; real, but not real.

Not unreal, but real, like the place Skip was dealing with, down the steel-walled canyons. Stuck in traffic, surrounded by people growing angrier and angrier like they do in the city, a place he'd been a thousand times in a thousand other voyages, but—that sound, what about that sound? Through the steel wall, there's never sound; the only other time he'd heard sounds in steel city halfway to Shanghai was the time the ship took that crashing and bashing during the storm-squall west of the canal, which turned out to be a whole container full of brand new Harley-Davidsons breaking loose and sliding off, gone into the sea. Big in China, those Harley-Davidsons are, he had been told, but how big? Skip did not know how big, until on the dock beside the ship he was approached by Rocky Rambo and Sylvester the Cat himself, last name Stallone. The big built Italian man came up to Skip, jabbing at him a large fat fountain pen all carved snakes and skulls, and shouted, Where is my container full of Cosmic Starships? My container shipment of ten Cosmic Starships appears to have disappeared, it appears to be. Are you of the crew of this ship? From New York? Huh? Skip swore, Yes; the bang went off again deep beyond the steel city wall, and it surged out the rest of what Stallone had to say, which was, That container was full of Cosmic Starships, each with a one-million-dollar price tag, each being gifted by me and Montegrappa and Harley and a lot of big-money fat men to the highest bigwigs in China to seal off a super deal of Chaos pens! Pens like this—see? This pen goes for seventy thousand dollars! They would sell like seals in Antarctica sell to Killer Whales—almost free for the taking, Lord God, the money is flowing in China, yes, in the upper crust, the big upper crust, they got all the factories here now, you know, they're richer than either my or Arnold's best fattest longest juiciest stools—

Wait, said Skip, raising his hand to The Stallion, There was a storm—a large one, with rogue wave after rogue wave, and we always lose a container or two, or five, or ten in such swells—it's in the contract, ask the captain, call the office, here's my card, look at the fine print, in a storm that could easily erase the whole ship, a few containers flying off into the drink is nothing, it's in the contract, read the contract—

Jack Armstrong styled those bikes, yelled Stallone crookedly between full twisted lips. Cosmic Existentialism is the style—that's the style—this pen is Chaos—but those bikes are Cosmic Existentialism, which goes perfect with Chaos; all of China would register like a perfectly plucked twelfth-fret harmonic in an empty dark place that's been dead quite for a million or more years if these had come together like it was planned—why didn't it, huh?—your fault may be your fault, everything's somebody's fault in the end you know, he said shaking a big fist, pen at the ready; but Skip backed not down.

See the captain! I can't help you!

But—

Another bang in the wall.

See the captain! I can't help you!

But—

Another bang in the wall.

Fuck off!

Skip looked up from the bright pothole in the road he'd been watching the past through and scanned the steel walls, on either side welded and riveted, and the bang sounded three more times, and he felt like he felt in bed at home at night when his large dog barked and barked and barked, and he had no idea after each bark if he should expect yet another bark, or was the dog now satisfied and the barking would fade away gone. He waited, the emptiness fluid of not knowing slowly solidified into knowing that if there was going to be another bark there would have been another bark by now, and if there was going to be another bang from deep within the spaces behind the steel walls there would have been another bang by now—so he crawled forward, and scraped and brushed and greased and all with his ancient universal wrench, and his half-full pot of axle grease, and his large, almost completely worn down, grease-wiping bristle-stick, which the common man watching would just think was an old, ready-to-be-thrown-out paintbrush. From the first container to the last, each day it was exactly the same; the honking honking traffic of the city and the impenetrable walls that stood silent all the way. But, there had been that bang. There had been. That bang. Yes, there had. But it's gone now.

Everything dies one day, even a single moment of a bang; a pinpoint, yes, just a pinpoint, yes, said Father Dwyer, you got to prick these sausages with a pinpoint so they don't blow up like pipe bombs on the grill. They're tight like steel walls. Nothing bangs inside. No nothing. They're dead meat, you burn to a crisp on a grill, you know, every food you cook dies tormented. Every food you cook once walked and looked around and smelled the air and tasted food. The taster becomes the tasted and all the—yes—the taster will become the tasted, oh, yes, in the end we're all sampled and judged and tasted by the creator himself, so!

And he thrust the great wooden spoon spattering scalding droplets, one of which went to the lens of the camera and caused the rest of this episode of *Sunday Dinner with Father Dwyer* to have Father Dwyer's face blurred out, by the sticking droplet, like on TV when it's that show *Cops* and they blank out in a grey blot the faces of the bystanders, the license plate numbers, the names of the stores, and the house numbers, sometimes even the graphics on the filthy, sweaty, three-a.m. T-shirts, because they have not given permission for their personal information to be broadcast loudly out into the world. You will all become the tasted one day, sinners, cried Father Dwyer from the flatscreen into the empty steel room with wide windows looking out into the endless sea, miles off to and over and behind the horizon, where the red dot was that told Father Dwyer there was an audience out there growing angry and angrier that there was no cooking being done, after all, they had got into their La-Z-Boys right on time and switched on their televisions and expected to see Father Dwyer, soft, fat, and jovial, cook up from practically nothing at all, a fine meal! One they themselves could make, if they paid attention and took detailed notes, which, of course, no one ever does.

And that, Mister Stallone, is why your container of ten Cosmic Starships is now a thousand miles away and several more down sitting peacefully on the sea bed, never to be ridden, ever. When the sun expands at the end and swallows the earth, those motorcycles will be swallowed also, never ever having felt the sweet caress of any Chinaman's narrow bony ass! So laugh that one away, Man of God! Laugh that one away! screamed Linda Blair. Back then, nobody knew what the devil she was trying to say, but here we are, in a whole new world; The Stallion knows what it means, but he missed the movie anyway, so everything all came to nothing! Isn't that a blast!? shouted Father Dwyer, flinging scalding droplet after scalding droplet, and this episode was actually stopped and redone so nobody ever saw him on the screen, his head blotted out as though crushed into the pavement by the front wheel of a fully loaded giant cement truck—anyway, enough of that.

Here, here, let me gather together the sweet things with great taste that we have killed to make today's episode of *Sunday Dinner with Father Dwyer* into a cohesive whole. And guess what, children, guess what, look—and he whirled around and at once was in a sunlit mild-smelling grove in a green rolling park before the world's most expensive stainless-steel barbeque grill, hooked up with a full shiny Rhino-brand great big grey gas tank, all set, cute big jungle animal frolicking on the side—Salads! yelled Dwyer, long tongue flinging spatter. He ran in to grip up the garlic he needed, the long sweet bread, the premade kebabs, and as he put the platter down atop the workspace, flies settled down almost immediately to eat from his dish as he raised a kabob and said, You know, I knew a great man, a great cook, who I learned from. When I was just a boy, touched by God of course but far from ordination, this great man taught me to barbecue. He taught me to make these kabobs. He taught me to make huge ones, and tiny ones, and ones in sizes in between, and when he was done with me, I, of course, grew into a schoolboy, and larger and larger I got, into the high school, and the college, and the first day in the seminary—for some reason I was waiting in the room of seven hundred folding chairs, outside the office of the Rector of the seminary, the biggest, holiest, oldest, skinniest, spookiest, most connected, big boss priestly Godly guy in the place, who made sure he spent two hours with each seminarian on his first day. I had a two o'clock appointment, continued Father Dwyer as he deftly switched on the grill, and he went on to say it was ten minutes before, and there was an old newspaper there. And as the blue flame licked up warming through the grill, he adjusted it deftly before slapping on a couple of steaks, continuing to not watch what he was doing but to stare at the camera, continuing on to say, And there in the paper was a picture of the very man who taught me to skewer kabobs, and below his picture it said *deceased*, and it said his name, and the top of the page said *obituaries*, and I tried to catch the date of the paper but it was ripped off, and all that I could get from the story in the few minutes I had before the Rector would have me called in, I read that the kabob teacher had died suddenly right in the middle of doing what he most loved, teaching mentally challenged institutionalized youths to correctly use skewers of every size, which was his specialty, and then—but the Rector of the seminary's door flew open and the gentle yet pompous man waved me in all smiling toothily into my face, and I left the paper, frustrated about not being able to find out more about my old teacher, but I had to go through the entry door to begin to become a priest, and you know, ever since then I have wondered if that bit of frustration at not being able to read the whole story is why I ended up—

Father Dwyer! yelled a voice behind the scenes—Father Dwyer, watch the flames! Keep quiet, concentrate!

What, what? What—

Never mind what! Keep on watching the flames!

But, but—

The Rector closed the door behind me before I could imagine the rest, and he sat down slowly and quietly behind his twenty-five foot wide and ten foot deep, high-gloss, absolutely bare, dark brown, nearly black, very expensive Italian-made desk, and he faced me surrounded and closed in all around by the floor-to-ceiling shelves of fat books, all brown with golden lettering on the spines, and I saw that the entire room was walled up this way, and I glanced around and could swear, even today, I could swear that the door we had come in through was walled over gone with books. The room should have been pitch black since there was no lamp or light fixtures anywhere in the room, just the books and the desk and the chairs and the Rector and me, bathed in some light that came from the Rector himself, somehow generated by the torrent of words that began flowing out over me, like great, slow, rolling, warm-lit ocean waves in the twilight. He said, said Father Dwyer's episode, going on and on from the lonely flatscreen no one was watching or hearing...

   And it went on while, thirty-three decks below, still in the dark, still afraid, sweet Noman continued to scrape, brush, and brood over the cold steel, battling back his worry for his wife all alone; battling back through the years, all the dark gone past, all the way back to when he'd been exactly as alone that Friday night, at the Strike 'N Spare alleys, and she came around the bar to take his order today, today, yes; today, right here, as the steel parted.

Can I serve you, sir? she said, all bright blonde. You look absolutely bushed. How about a Schlitz?

The rolling balls of the alleys behind boiled up around her; her eyes.

Into her eyes, he thought to say, as always when she came around the bar for the first time so innocent, Do you know, dear, that by approaching me you have decided to miscarry once, then twice, and develop a horrid fear of childbirth—that, of course, because I am a man and I am expected to forever and ever bare-back-fuck you as long as we are married without caring if you want it every day or not, I will dare give you, accidentally, a third fetus inside, and then take a ship voyage so long that when you face your terrific worst-in-the-world fear, that you will be medicated and numbed and talked to death by psycho-professionals that will call you tokophobic, obsessed with knowing you bear within you just another tiny, blood-tinged, white, stiff, cold corpse, with your legs spread wide, ready to give the thing birth, all surrounded by white-masked highly paid strangers set to help you safely deliver, I will not be there? I will not hold your hand? I will be on the other side of the world, I—and that this time you may even die? Do you know this? That there will not be love in that room, just death, icy cold, and love born only of the salaries requiring the white-clad mob to help you and then wash and go to the next on the assembly line—do your blue eyes know it yet, I've told you a thousand times—

Well, how about it sir, she said again, smile tilting. Schlitz? Bud? Coke? What? You need a drink. You need one bad.

I, uh, oh, yes.

Yeah, she said—I know the look, kiddo. You've had a hell of a day. Right, honey?

The balls rolled on and on, strike after strike, her punctuation.

We even have milk, she joked. If you can't decide, I mean. But, it might be—guess what?

Instant silence in her eye.

I don't know. What?

Expired, she laughed. It could be too old. It could be sour. It could be rotten. A Schlitz is what you really need. None of that goes rotten. How about it. Tell you what—first one's on me!

On you? Why?

I like you, I think.

But—I—

Okay, I'll be right back. Hold that thought!

A wink and a turn; and here drops the dark iron bulkhead, and the rolling of the smooth balls again becomes the scrape of the rust brush, and the stink of never-washed bowling shoes becomes poisonous fuming and foaming strange oil. And he rams his face into the dark steel, again too late to have left the bowling alley and have been done when she came back with the free Schlitz, standing there in her short uniform, looking around thinking, Where'd he go, where? and then, just forgetting as she turned tossing the little Schlitz onto the bar for someone else to clean up later, pour out, dump out, clear out, and render never was. And his face would not be pressed to rusted steel ever, ever in his life. He would arrive in China alone, as it should be, not followed by the terrifying fiery wall of guilt she has become and pursued him as gradually since that day. The heat was on him. The heat. This compartment's done, on to the next. What is the fucking time anyway? And as he turned, a thought flew through—he never had tasted a Schlitz. Why is that important? Where's that come from? Ah, let it go. Life's just thought after thought after thought. They come and pass and disappear and are less than smoke and vapor. But there are always more and more very real, hard steel bulkheads to scrape and be busy with in huge real-life ships like this—

And Father Dwyer spoke hard from the flatscreen, telling no one at all what the Rector of the seminary had said when they both sat.

So, the Rector had said—you want to be a priest, eh?

Yes, Father.

How valiant.

Valiant? In what way, Father?

Hey, listen. Don't call me Father. I am Jim. Just Jim.

The walls of books seemed to be inching tighter and tighter in, diminishing the room. So, I thought to talk faster.

Sure, Jim, I said—and I am—

Never mind who you are, what's important is that you were reading that paper out there! I saw you reading that paper out there! How far into the story in that paper out there did you get by the time my door opened to tell you, Come in?

I—

Never mind *I*! How far?

A small white fist slammed down and drew words out of me I was surprised to hear, but I was so afraid and sure I was going to be rejected by the seminary, so I said, My cooking teacher was teaching mentally challenged institutionalized youths to correctly use skewers of every size, which was his specialty, and then—and that's as far as I got, then, Father! That is all I can remember!

Are you sure?

Yes!

You did not read on further to learn how he went mad from the foibles and foolishness that made up his life, now that he was near eighty, near the end, still unable to retire because of no savings or pension or payments of any kind, and he began to slash and slash and slash, like this movie here I'm going to show, now open your eyes and watch, it's just a minute—

A screen scrolled down before the Rector, and from someplace behind glowed into the screen a human trunk, neither male nor female, being pierced severely from behind by a series of fast-piercing sharp steel needlelike knives, and the tip came out the skin and from each hole after hole that was made through from behind, a drop of blood dripped, and there ought to have been screaming when the tip pulled back out, but blood squirted then, and in a minute there were hundreds of bloody holes, so many that the screen turned to just a red glistening sheet, and it rolled back up into the ceiling revealing the Rector rolling a long thin red needle-sharp spike in his hands, and he said, Okay, then, Dwyer, now that you have seen what your soul will become, are you still ready to join us?

I sat. I did not know what I had just seen. It was gone and there was nothing, so I filled the numb nothing space with, Yes, I am still ready to join you, Father. The Rector only smiled, raised a hand, gestured, and I turned. And there, where there had only been books, was the door. I went out to the waiting room and looked around and saw that somebody had taken away the newspaper. Or maybe I had brought it in with me? But if I brought it in with me, I would never be able to look and see if the Rector had told me the truth of how the story ended. Due to that, I left the waiting room and went on and became a priest; but ever since then I have wondered if that bit of frustration at not being able to read the whole story is why I ended up quitting the priesthood thirty-five years down the line, to pick back up cooking; anyway, anyway, I digress too long. This is the day of the Strammer Max, as asked and answered. The bread, the cereal, the juice, the coffee the tea the milk the fruit that make up the whole motherfucking feast—

The crime-scene-cleanup white-clad woman had her busiest bloodiest day, I learned later. Years later, but; now, the Strammer! We take out ten big pots and yell, Courage! So, then...

And at that moment, out in the steel lined street, the last great dog bark banged deep beyond the steel storefronts, and while

Noman had been toiling and Dwyer had been reminiscing, Skip had been able to snug up, clean, and grease twenty-five container-hold-down turnbuckle rods, all the time surrounded by the chorus of barking dogs given rise to by that first dim but very, very fist-like tap-bang deep behind the wall someplace. Like a *let me in* kind of bang. Like a *let me in, let me out, let me in, hey, maybe I'm Jesus, and if Jesus came a'callin' today, would your house be clean enough, neat enough, nice enough and sweet enough to responsibly accept his holiness?* Or would it be always as the next container turnbuckle hold-down contraption, spider webbed, rusted, filthy, jammed, frozen, and wearing an inch of hardened salt-air rust? Thank God the rising sea will never take him; thank God that for him there's just street after street of container-hold-down hardware to deal with, but—Don't lose the Harley Davidsons this time, no, not the Harley Davidsons, this time, let it be a container or two of paper cups, paper clips, cheap made-in-China toys, or little blue bathtub boats—for tiny bathing naked boys who will never in their minds admit that each time they ease down in the tub they pee out in the warm goose-bump-raising relaxing-all-bodily-functions water—that got thrust and bumped out over and lost into the deep. Just crawl forward over the cold steel, at sea. Never on land again, never. On land you get hell, or you get drunk, or you die and go in some grave that gets drowned when the end comes. And it will, yes. Life began in the sea, and in the sea it will end; like lunch; lunch is here; yes, with Skip's, Noman's, and Father Dwyer's lunchtime coming, they began winding down, wound up, all three together at the bottom. As Skip began coming. Father Dwyer said alone from the bridge wall to no one, But that's a whole 'nother matter, you know, but—sometimes he asked himself, Are they really watching on all those distant ships or are they not? Am I a tree falling in the forest with no one to hear? Like a tree, I have no ears. Like this fish I fry, this golden boy, snatched up by youth, I have no ears. Is there really a whitecapped tossing sea out those windows? I have no eyes to see past the red glow of the camera. Maybe those windows are just phony photos painted up, like these fried potatoes you'd never think had ever been alive, they're just little dry parchment-like discs. I have no way to reach through, to touch them. Like these French beans and these greens with this pea soup? I have no way to grip one to me, crunch it in my teeth, or swish it in my mouth, let alone to do the terribly creepy gargling thing with the hot soup that no one ever does in public.

Noman pulled out his illuminated pocket-watch. Lunch was coming up, across all the steel boxes spread out and down and around, and through them. He sat his back against the cold steel, eyes not open to the dark, waiting, but feeling the need to wait for the Schlitz? Pay for the Schlitz? Or leave. It seemed like the thing to do. Leaving would have been the right thing to do. Just because you screwed up once, doesn't mean you ought to screw up, Daddy, shit, might as well get up. Go up. Gone.

To lunch.

And, with the men coming back to make him anew—to make him feel, fear, smell, and have purpose, their footsteps sounded from the stairwells on either side of the desk—oh Dwyer, Dwyer, Dwyer, Dwyer, give them dinner; sweet and sour pork, their steps, steamed rice, cucumber salad—Skip came out on deck from one side, called by the cold cuts—cheese, salad—and he ran right into Noman, called up escaping from having to again say, Yes, thank you to the Schlitz, and; here the three stood together in the middle noon of the day, and faced one another back up in real life, and there was Father Dwyer, here was his cigar smoke, there was his large belly, and yes indeed he was moving fast, hands unburned, fingers uncut, over the magical meal all complete on the screen, but nothing Skip and Noman can say will quiet him down, so, You know, said Skip, Why can't we turn that damned thing off? It's a nuisance, and we should be able to. It's just the same thing over and over. When we take our breaks, we should have quiet.

And now for a commercial break, a commercial, a commercial break, before—

Listen. You were the one who threw the remote overboard, remember that day? There's no shutting off, turning down, changing at all, in any way. Just because you got all angry. All angry like you do. You know you do. Do you remember what you were angry about?

Do not, I don't, no way, I can't—

Then it was real smart, wasn't it? Come on. Let's see what's in the fridge.

The usual black between show and commercial suddenly burst out, expanding, obliterating the room like some crazy unpredicted superheated pyroclastic flow—into absolutely nothing, because this piece of story's over.

Until next time,

next time.

Next time,

and maybe one last more.

Chapter Six
Further Along on the Free One-way Trip to China

—wait, wait, sleep, sleepy, sleepeth, yes; after some period of staying inside himself safe, yes safe, he tried to move. As he tried to move he smiled and made funny faces. Somehow he never could before, but now he can. Out in the darkness he wouldn't see, he seemed able to feel and move his arms. At the ends of his arms, he moved slightly, so slightly, so there would be nothing bad discovered or any pain, his arms, hands, fingers, feet and toes were all still there—they must be his because he is still himself, not no one else, which is what he really wants to scream, No, yes! Let me be somebody else who's not—not—you know what not, but don't dare think. Everything's there and intact, that has not changed, it all feels new though. New. Like something just budding up and popping out grown from some cell; yes, yes, yes, he was intact, and—now, he felt animated; talkative; self-confident. He could be anything, do anything, be anyway now—so, he dared. Yes. Dared open his eyes, and, yes! Mackie! Mackie and the boys, all sat jabbing forks. What's this, yes, there's a meatball to chew. The same one he took in before. The place is all right, all lit up and bustling and ready for him to talk, yes talk, yes; Mackie, talk.

Yes, for sure, Johnny, it's really in your eyes. It's all red in there—look boys, look. Johnny's got the sleepy red eye, maybe it's almost the time for sleepy little Johnny to go to beddy bye-bye. After tonight you're going to get what you got coming, Johnny! What you got coming, and maybe some more—ha ha—and for some reason the meatball spits out. Right on the plate. Eyeball red. Veins. Eyeball red veins like sleepy time night-night, but, Johnny says brightly, widening all the other's eyes, Gosh! Why did that happen? I am not fucking drunk. Just had a few of—of something. Here, give me wine. More wine, I want a wine!

You sound so happy, Johnny. Why is Johnny so fucking happy? Johnny can't be happy, because Johnny, you are gone—go away, go back away, don't you know you're gone? Gone on a long trip. Long and long—right boys?

Yes, boss.

Long fucking trip to China. You're tucked in nice, sleeping, Johnny, all sealed up safe, nobody can fuck with you where you are, where you're going. Turn around, back! How dare you come back to ghost us! How dare you come back to ghost us! Lemmie, let 'im have it! Lemmie—and everything expanded to a starflash like comes out the muzzles of big loud assault rifles in fully automatic mode, at night, in a cheap special-effects war movie. Got to avoid something very, very bad. Turn around come back, back yes, where the starflashes are not and it is black. Rub my face, God, it sweats, but, hands will not move. Pull, pull, push. Nothing above and below and around but cold hard. No. Piles and piles of people die and die and blanch all out, but; no, not Johnny. Remember: what lay beyond the dinner would be wonderful, profitable, wonderful, profitable, wonderful—won—here is now beyond the dinner. What will come? There. That's a normal question. You are yourself still. You are. Lights up! Surprise! There, she are, is, or whatever; open eyes, and—

Where she are? Here's the wide restaurant, she has to be here, and I got to have pulled it off, this is where I was going to meet her tonight after I got away with the Mackie-scam, and I was going to show her the tickets to Barcelona for this very night, after dinner. I told her to come packed and ready for a surprise getaway, but there's nobody in the restaurant, and for some reason there's pitch black and bright light at the same time, and—where—yes, here—I got the tickets, see? But—they're in the dark light and I can't read them. And I got the fat envelope that contains what we got now, fixed up for the rest of our lives—but, no, in the light dark I cannot find it. What can be done, but—ah—no, can't know, can't stretch, all jammed in pitch black where? Where? Panic fights to push up, no, no, no hallucination; open eyes shut, yes, okay, there she is, here she comes, looking around. Looking around for me. Hey! Hey honey! Hey, here!

Rap steel. She keeps looking around. Noise out through surrounding drums, absorbed, fades hollowly, and is gone, but she still looks 'round.

Panic and reason struggle—but, blink, blink, blink.

She's here. There she is. Honey, you came. I pulled it off. Look at these tickets. It's Barcelona tonight, after dinner. Real red eye, big old red eye. Big fucker penis-shaped plane; remember the time we smoked that great shit and laughed like hell at that? What for, honey? It wasn't even that funny, honey, but—that was good shit. What do you think of that honey?

She looks around. She looks at me but not like she's seeing, and then she keeps on looking around, for some reason she's playing a silly game, okay, darling, I can play silly games too.

Miss Sweetie, I am so glad to see you, I got here and the whole place was dead, I mean weird, you know. I almost started to laugh, it was so silly. So anyway—here I am. We are set. Here, give me your hand. I need to touch you—

No.

Faltering voice cannot bring her to life. Ever talk to a picture in a magazine but it moves and breathes and is really there but not there too, somehow, crazy? Can't stop talking, go on—all right, Sweetie Pie, I bet you're doing this on a dare. Or, maybe, if that show was still on, maybe this is some kind of candid camera. Here, look, I can be silly too. Here. I tug at my brand new ear. Doesn't that sound silly? Not laughing yet? Here. Under the table I am somehow nude and grip my brand-new dick. Hear me pretend to practice breathing for the first time that's not this, this fluid air in this damned thing? As I squeezed my dick, it's like I learned to breathe. Just for you, I breathe in and out and squeeze and squeeze the little member. It's really, really little for some reason, though, it's certainly not good enough to do a woman like you properly. What's wrong with you staring, you're making me all weird. Okay, okay, you win. Snap out of it. This is no grammar-school-child stare-off. No, it's not, you have won the bet. You have been able to completely ignore me for five full minutes. Hey, where the fuck is the wait staff? The place is dead, really dead—no! Don't rise! I have my eyes squeezed tight shut to keep seeing you. I don't want to see the black again. This is what we were supposed to do tonight! Please don't stand and put on your coat and look around like I do not exist. I exist, see me! I have ten fingers, ten toes! Proper! All proper! My God, no, don't leave! What are they paying you? Who did you bet with? Miss Sweetie! Please, please, no, I cannot get up, stand, or move, but you can! Don't be gone, please don't—I need to see you!

Eyes pop open, strain to see, the dining room goes, and the dark presses around like a tiny, tiny barrel, and the tickets have dropped someplace in the dark, but there's no room to move, can't reach down, can't get them, oh, I thought that only in space you are not able to scream; over, grains, center, nothing. For a while now, nothing. No thinking, nothing. God is merciful sometimes.

Thank God sleep kept Johnny from hearing his thought that God grieves every too-slow death.

Breathe soft. No, not death. Dreamy meadow. Death, no fuckin' way. See, here's why; feel the rocking and moving and shifting all day as everything outside unseen moves. Shifting, cuddling, comforting, still sometimes, and when still, drifting down soft lacy veil after soft lacy veil of gentle, light, sleep. Light late fall snow twilight.

Chapter Seven
Banter on the Ship to China III

Skip continued crawling slowly on through the gap between the stacked shipping containers, working hard. He worked as he thought, and thought as he worked, as, Jesus, Christ, almighty! Yes, that is all I was burdened with, sure. Nothing at all, really, no—just burdened with twelve brothers and sisters, four bedrooms, and only two bathrooms, and getting zero attention or care from the one we all called Mother. That was life, Doc—that's probably what soured me on land life. That's probably why I turned to the sea. That's probably why I prefer life at sea to on land. That's why, if I'm on the beach, kind of between sea and land, barefoot in the place where the surf just comes and it's fifty percent each sand and water, and I have water cupped in one hand and sand cupped in the other, I will always choose to shake the sand away from my hand, fast; and I will stoop to my cupped hand and suck up the water. It's salt, so what. It's water. It's always water—shit in it, or pure as fresh spring, naturally-baby-bottom-perfect heaven, it's all water, and it's all the same to me—suck it up. I will, every sweet drop—

Skip had been frozen in place on the deck of the Maru, at the sixty-ninth container hold-down he was faced with brushing to rustless, wiping to greaseless, slopping with fresh grease, and tightening snug, remembering what he told the psychiatrist the containership company sent him to, long ago, that one time they pushed him too hard, and he snapped. They had wanted to give him a land assignment; said it would be a step up in grade from being a crewmember; said it was something he'd earned for good work. Said it'd be his first step up the ladder. He tried, really tried to do the office job, he did, but—he walked off the job nutty, they put him on disability, he went back, ended up walking off the job again, this time even more nutty, so while he was on disability they sent him to a shrink, and he said over and over again, he said, but—

Suddenly the wire brush he'd been mindlessly scrubbing back and forth and back and forth over the turnbuckles during his deep wayback daydream slipped, flipped, and the sharp bristles scraped sharp across the palm of his hand, and he woke from the daydream abruptly, as a point-blank pistol shot had just hit him between the eyes; he slammed back down, rock hard, in the canyon of the steel city built of battered and rusty rough steel containers he'd been crawling between every day and would continue to crawl through and between and around until they dropped anchor in Shanghai and set him free; free, but, up on the empty bridge of the Dakota Maru, on the big wide black flatscreen TV on the back wall, there was someone not there but who always was there, and would never ever be free; the large-stout-cigar-smoking old retired pastor, Father Dwyer, whose image glowed out from his bright clean TV kitchen, playing continuously day and night, going over and over through all the sequential episodes of his great but failed cooking show, *Sunday Dinner with Father Dwyer*, which, as often happens with bad movies that close the same day they open and after that are only seen as choices for viewing aboard non-stop redeye flights from New York to Los Angeles, had been chosen by some bigshot boardroom fatsuits to be the primary video entertainment show on all the world's fleet of automated containerships at sea forever and on. When Skip scraped his hand bloody, far out on deck, Father Dwyer had just begun episode nine hundred, and sang the praises of the sweetmeats et cetera that lay spread before him on the massively expensive studio battleship-kitchen-sized stainless-steel worktable before him.

So, he crowed, See! Eighty, yes eighty, perfectly filleted dead ten-days-old perch. And not a smell to be found. No. And next, here! A stunning array of seven green moldy raw dried-up old pork tenderloins. After all, you know, it has been scientifically proven that moldy food is actually good for you. Like, take bread, he said, slamming the flat of his fat hand on the steel, The bread I buy, I actually will not use until it has begun sprouting those nice little dark green spots on its dampest parts; my mouth waters—see? And he pointed to his gaping mouth full of darkness supported by some blood red thing that might have been a tongue, and then he put both hands flat on the steel, and mouthed, And my perfect teeth? Did you see my perfect teeth? I never get any problems with my teeth, having lifelong eaten the food I do on this show live, before you, true and unhidden. Teeth, you see, and he looked around as though he did not want anyone out of sight in the studio to hear, before looking right through the screen in a very intimate and sincere way, so close you could imagine the pores of his fleshy face, saying, Teeth decay naturally over time. Everything on earth, as a matter of fact, decays naturally over time. Even the earth itself, the solar system, the universe, yes—even eternity decays naturally over time, except eternity, being eternity, will go on to decay more and more forever and ever, you know. This is actually the reason why division by zero is deemed impossible and why you can run Pi out an eternal number of digits, but—

And, with that *but*, he jabbed a large butcher knife into the air, and said slowly, We are not here though, to discuss eternity; that would need to go on eternally, to be done right and true, so, we're given this mere half hour to cook, and—cook we will, people—cook we will, and he swept the knife over the remaining foods, saying very, very quickly, as disclaimers and cover-your-ass words are said impossibly swiftly after radio commercials for anything that's about investing money, or about getting rich quick, or about making tens of thousands a month working from home, Everything here, of course, will be seasoned, with fresh thyme and garlic, but, the acorn squash candied with butter, pecans and brown sugar, unfortunately will not be available except upon special circumstances, and the baked potatoes rice and broccoli with cheese sauce shown on the show is not guaranteed to come onto all your plates either, and; and the homemade pineapple upside-down cake shown on the show may not be at all times available. But, never mind that. Let's go, let's start! Let's start with the dead fish, let's do! And he seized the first fillet, and spun around nearly losing his birretta and sending flying his ecclesiastical collar, and slammed the oily corpse into a frying pan, causing boiling clouds of steam to erupt and a dizzying sizzling sound to overwhelm the studio sound system. People behind the scenes jumped from their folding-chair slumber to readjust the controls. We must readjust the controls! Must readjust the controls, must—it got so intense backstage, off camera. Such a crisis, yes; such!

Countless levels of deep below Skip, Noman went on with his chore of spraying rustproofing solvent on the hard-as-rock walls, also deeply daydreaming to the rhythm of the scraping of the steel. Should I have left, he thought, before she came back with the Schlitz I said I wanted? Should I not have waited so long for her to bring the beer? Should I just have decided she was all talk and no substance? I believe that she is just all bogus. Why would somebody like her want someone like me? Way back when I was only eighteen? But, he thought much too long and much too deeply, as he sat pimply and red-faced, sitting on the bowling-alley snack-bar-counter stool way back inside.

Scraping and scraping and scraping and scraping and scrape, the rough drone made him think that, Now, here's where I should have got up and left. Here's where, if I had done nothing, everything would be completely different, no worries about any wife's health, maybe even having gone down another whole path and never stepped aboard any huge too-huge big-jelly of a containership, down buried in this silent steel box every day, with just me, myself, and all my regrets—will she come bring the Schlitz, should she come with the Schlitz, should I go—But all at once he was solidly struck from behind by a baseball bat and came to himself in the tiny steel compartment, deep down below. His hand moved scraping down just one of the thousands of identical walls of the boxes in the belly of The Dakota Maru. Bound for Shanghai, you bet, you do. You bet—his head turned, and back in the bowling alley again, he saw.

Here she comes around the corner, with two tall bottles of Schlitz—but why two, hey, why, he ordered just one, what gives, hey you—

Here you go, she said brightly red-lipped and toothy—and also, you know, guess what?

What?

She slid onto the big soft stool next to his and said, What's what is—like I said before—this is on the house. On me, actually. They don't give this good shit away.

Why are you buying me a beer? he said, palming one bottle that stood ice cold, wet, tall, and foaming. He poured it into the icy glass as she told him.

Because, I've been watching you, and, I think you're cuter than shit. And you're the new guy, so, anyway, it's my breaktime, too. Ain't that a rip? Think I'll spend breaktime with you every single day—here!

She held the bottle up toward him and he gently clashed his bottle into hers, and with her smile, she said, Here's to us, Pal. I can see it. I can *really* see it. So, aside, with that she paused to pour, and the black beer rose, and the big white head exploded, it seemed, with pure white beer flowing over in foam and more foam, and the very head itself joked to itself, I am very cute, smiling and proud to at last have been delivered to someone. It was dark and horrid in the case, just one of hundreds just like me, in the truck that I rode from the beer factory, in the case and cases piled with hundreds of identical bottles, so—why did this one, I, me, the true one, be in his hand all foaming with this guy watching the waitress busily and abruptly chugging down half the tall glass.

The tip of the bottle was foamed up white, and he came at her saying, So…

What is your name honey?

Noman.

Mine's Phyllis.

Ha ha, he said. Ha.

Why is my name funny? she said, as it began behind his forehead boneplate.

Silently behind his lips the answer formed, Phyllis, Phallus. Phyllis, Phallus—should she know what I'm thinking? Sure, what the hell! Everything in him paused and focused on Phyllis. He took her in from head to toe, did some mental calculations, and somehow got lost in all the flingflying numbers, so he lost control and his mouth opened and the answer to her question came right out on and over the marble bar, saying to her waiting eyes, I think your name's funny because Phyllis, Phallus, and Phyllis Phallus, like that you know, like that. Phyllis and Phallus are just two letters different. Two vowels, to be exact. Almost the same damned word. You know?

There, yes, I do! I totally get it! she said, pointing—I knew it, I knew. You're a thinking, walking, talking, dirty-minded but nearly a genius, fucking true man.

Haw! Phyllis and Phallus fit together so well, maybe they'd do a nice word-fuck, he thought bright-eyed, saying, No, I am no genius, no, I—

The bat slammed him wide awake in the steel ship's compartment. The cleaning solvent smell formed into a man built like a giant blue genie, up behind him, who slammed the bat down on Noman's brain again, and again, plugging him back to full attention to his life-socket spot that most people think is their job.

Where'd she go, where? And then he realized the genie had made him rise, and turn, and walk to get far from her. As for her, she just forgot and rose and tossed both Schlitzes onto the bar for someone else to clean up later, pour out, dump out, clear out, never was.

Now, Noman knew that for a while, the torment following him everywhere was erased for a while, at least. He would arrive in China alone, as it should be, not followed by the terrifying fiery wall of guilt she had become and pursued him, married him, and all the rest, gradually, since that day. Relieved, he kept scraping the gutwalls of the Dakota Maru, all in the here and now; up, down, up down, spray, look, okay, then up, down, spray look, okay—but she came out of the steel and asked him, You there. I never got your name. What have you ended up doing for a living?

Noman explained in great detail all he had done and was since that day at the bowling alley when he'd turned from her, and as he scraped, up and down, up and down, he told her; it was safe to tell all of anything to someone who wasn't there.

Out at sea all the time? Doing that shit work? That's a hell of a job to have, said Phyllis. But hey, listen—look what I got today on the way in, look, do you think this would be a good birthday present for my Grandfather? Here, wait—and she rummaged around someplace in her clothes that all of a sudden became unnecessarily voluminous, flowing, and gownlike, and held out to him a wooden set of Soviet-Union-Leader nested dolls. The largest was a man with a gigantic birthmark at his bald hairline, whose name Noman couldn't remember. Oh, he said, as she deftly took apart the nested dolls and the Soviet leaders stood on the counter, largest to smallest, bathing in the gently hard but soft roll after roll of the distant bowling balls, each roll ending with a sharp sloppy crash of large hard bowling pins all scattered, making her pick up her Schlitz and say, Well, what do you think? Pretty cool eh? Russians, you see. Cool.

Russians.

Sure, he said, his word flipping a switch restoring her clothing back to the simple plain uniform of your typical bowling-alley snack-bar attendant. She had no bag, no usable pockets. There was no place for this bulky thing in her clothing, anyplace—but there it was. Miraculous, miraculous, a sign from whatever's above, brightening the bowling alley lights even higher, and he knew that, yes, that was where his life forked forever. The name of the largest Soviet leader came from the steel wall; Gorbachev, it was; and Gorbachev said clearly and plainly, Noman, this is the one. This is the woman for you. You are now in love. I am a dictator and am never wrong. You are now in love—never matter what love is. You'll find out as the years pass, as in: Here, says the stranger you encountered that day in the park. Here, take this pill. Never mind what it is. You'll see when it comes all over you—

But—

Slam! The genie bat!

After the bat hit him, he was gone from the tiny fume-filled steel dark box way down in the great ship. A pure white space all around him shone that he held something new in his hand.

What is this in my hand in some pure white space? he thought; God!

A set of nested container ships, each full of smaller container ships, each containing another ship, and another and another on to his last day—caught him like a fish, had this Phyllis—life without parole, baby, yes, she had put him there and put him good.

And right then Father Dwyer held out his skillet of badly burnt dead fish, and said, There! See! Mold is nothing to fear, fish do not rot, and look, look. Everything burns. Isn't this a stunning sight to make you lick your chops until they're bloody! But never mind this, next is breakfast! and he tossed the fish, skillet and all, into a huge off-camera garbage bin, sounding like a professional-level bowling top-gun's extremely hard, violent strike, no way that was a spare, based on the noise. Had to have been a strike. Like a great Olympic high dive is marked by scarcely a splash. Father Dwyer was a man of God, who was never wrong, and he knew it. Pulling his black, silly, old-fashioned priest's hat down tight, he faced the camera, and said bulge-eyed and veiny-faced, Breakfast now, yes, breakfast. It is the day for breakfast. That's what's cool now. That what's going to be happening, in just a little bit, after you're shown this Boeing commercial. Why on earth they have Boeing commercials on TV to be viewed by the poverty-level simpleminded is beyond me, but—here goes!

The commercial played everywhere at once, but narrowed down to a place and far away where Pa turned to face Ma, in an old rotting house where they were stealing cable, on no ship, no ship at all, and he said through his beard, Look at that! Just look at that plane! and he threw aside his squeezebox and leapt from his duct-taped recliner, almost tearing his waist-length beard off, crying, Look at that commercial! Look at that! That commercial makes me want to buy a Boeing product! Let's buy a great big plane! Sure, let's buy a great big plane—from Boeing! Yes, Boeing! Yes, let's—grab up that phone! Ma, Ma—let's do it! Pa stood with his back to Ma not caring that the commercial was over and Father Dwyer was back, hands out, saying, Sorry, I know the commercials waste your time, but they're a necessary evil. Pay the bills you know. Pay. *Pay* might be one of the most important words ever, but—this is a cooking show after all, and we are to talk about breakfast today. Forget Boeing, it's gone, dead. Think. Think of a big, big breakfast. I am sure you wake each day, leap from bed wide-awake, breeze through your shower and shit and wipe very well and all like that, then you immediately run downstairs ravenously, clutching the railing of course, to stay safe, because of your history of bad falls. I know, you have learned the hard way that you could be a little too hungry and step off the step a little too fast, and the last little cute cloud that might not yet have dissipated in your brain, might cover and blank out your sensibility center, you'll instantly turn stupid, and you'll shoot full blast down the stairs, tripping, falling, rolling, banging, cracking and straining as you fall and fall and fall—and your spouse, who rose early out of love, to have a big fat omelet all steaming and plated and set out for you, will hear bumping and crashing and cracking and straining noise pouring in the kitchen door from out by the stairs, somehow—and there you are sprawled out spread-eagled, on your fashionably expensive hardwood floor. There might be blood too—but no matter. Your spouse will now realize that they have to go in the kitchen and put the omelet in the oven and leave the oven door open, because you don't want to harm the great, great, omelet, it must not be allowed to get either stone cold or dried up and overheated, to scald your mouth, while you recover your wits and stand and finally come for breakfast. Yes, you will. You will, because every time you have fallen down the stairs in the past, you have shaken it off and come to yourself, and you rose and came in to whichever meal awaited you, but—but what has just happened is much more serious. Maybe this time much more is bruised and ruptured and broken. Flags should be waving and crowds should be roaring and you should be stranded, unable to cross the wide, wide road, to be able to blink and move and rise once more, because the parade in honor of your premature death is so noisy and busy and thick and endless, and—but oh, I'm afraid, I think, I digress again. Here is how that omelet you never got to eat, was made. Whether you lived or died of the fall is much less important than me telling my audience of containership seamen how this fat yellow spicy cheesy stunning omelet was made. But, I guess we must have showed you how it was made, because there it is, right there before us, all made and hot and steaming and delicious.

So, let's turn to the bacon. Little piggies grow to big hogs, and bacon comes some way nobody is ever shown. That whole time between the living hog and the bacon all wrapped tight in the supermarket display, is unknown. Blank. Undisplayed. Nonexistent. Not to be spoken of. It's just, some kind of magic happens, and—there's the bacon. Get it out of the fridge. Cut the plastic and unwrap it. Slam down the skillet onto the stovetop, just like this, watch me! Put in a dab of oil, wait, wait. Go piss. Good time to take a quick piss. Come back and the oil is steaming and sizzling, kind of more than we like to see, but after all, this is just reality TV, so just pretend the skillet is perfect, and peel off and drop in strip after strip of bacon, and slow sizzling starts to rise. The sizzling rises and solidifies and falls, and in no time, you're ankle deep in it, then knee deep, then waist deep and suchlike, and then—your arms are pinned. Submerged to the neckline in hot solidifying sizzle of a silvery hue. And since you're pinned, you've no choice but to watch the bacon darken and darken and stink up, smoke up, burnt, and destroy itself, because it lets itself stay in the skillet and burn itself to cinders, and beyond. And as you are forced to watch this horrible sight, Pa in the other room is on the line to Boeing, Ma is clapping her hands with excitement, and Pa is explaining, saying, But why do you have commercials on all the little people's TV shows, if what you're telling me is I can't buy a 777 over the phone? I can kind of see why shipping such a big awkward item might be a problem, I mean I can, and I can definitely see why we have to move our rusted out 1953 Skyliner Trailer to a much bigger lot that can accommodate the plane, but—what the hell is that burning, Ma? Smell it?

I do, but—

Something's in the kitchen on the skillet burning!

No, it's—

Yeah, you got stupid again, and started frying something on the skillet and came back out to watch old Father Dwyer rattle on and on about food, and forgot, you old goat, that you were cooking!

I am not the hell an old goat, you, I—

But, said Father Dwyer, taking back control of his show—just like we don't really need to go into what happens in that blank space between the big live hog, and the bacon in the pan, we really don't have to go into what happened in the blank space between Pa delivering one too many insults to Ma, to when he lies quiet on the floor by the kitchen door, ripped in half all bloody and gory and red hot stone dead, from a hot lightspeed shot from the smoking double barrel ten gauge he so prized since a boy. It lies, muzzle smoking, right in the blood. And Ma is gone, where'd she go, Ma! She somehow knew, she had to get out, before she got buried up to her neck again in police car sirens like happened before with the rising bits of sizzle off the skillet going volcanic on everything and sealing everyone in like it's some kind of Pompeii. I mean, an omelet and bacon, for breakfast, we have talked about, and we have gone through the pertinent processes, so, here—here! Look! And Father Dwyer flings the second burnt skillet into the big dumpster off camera, and lets the crash that surrounds him all misty fade away, and then puts his fists down on the edge of the immaculate countertop, and looks into the camera, with his look of priestly God-given power, and says, Now, then, so; breakfast's gone, never was, but here comes lunch! In the next fucking episode, I will say, Did you like this breakfast? Wait till you meet the lunch! More later in episode nine hundred one, after these words from our sponsors. Get ready for Boeing again! As a matter of fact, this brings to mind a big deal I lived through. I was with Harry Truman at his lodge on Spirit Lake when the great big supersonic eruption happened—I—

But he was interrupted when the Boeing Commercial cut him off, even as Skip out on the steel street in steel-container city on the deck began to realize he had scraped his hand much more seriously when he got careless with the razor-sharp wire brush, across his palm. The canyon he worked in was very dark and the bloody pool gathering gradually around wherever he pressed his hand to the steel deck to steady himself as he worked could not be seen because of the deep shadow, and the pain had not yet hit. The blood was invisible, just like the blood inside him was invisible, so he must not really have sliced deep into his palm because the blood on the deck and the blood inside him were exactly the same, and, since he was alive and moving and scraping and dreaming in the dark slip of shadow between the container stacks, it must be that he was not cut or bleeding at all; so he worked himself into his normal calm trance he always wore as a shell around himself as he, all day every day, cleaned, greased, and tightened the container hold-down hardware, and it felt cozy, very cozy, that the earlier scrape could not have really happened, and here he was, squat, safe inside the great containership surrounded by all the sweet water he knew that one day would cover the world, and he would then transition into the sea creature never to touch land again because the land will be no more—before the end of his life, let the flood come, he prayed to the swarm of gods surrounding him unseen, which he picked from to pray to depending on the nature of what he was praying for. Some gods can deliver on some goods, and some on others. Some gods cannot deliver on anything because they are false renamed mirrors of the others. But, right now, kneeling in deepening blood that was really not there, that was inside and outside himself all at once, he had no recourse but to pray. He prayed that he would live to see the day the land was no more. It was so bad in him and so strong in him that just thinking the word *land* almost caused him to vomit up great blasts of bitter bile. They would end up docking again at Shanghai, and once more he would be tortured, forced and driven to go onto the land. Skip thought, Well, I can just jump off this ship and start behaving like there's no land right now, I can throw down this brush and this grease pot and heavy wrench one last time for good and go up, and out, and run in the sun to the stern, and leap after kicking off these heavy painful high-top steel-toes the company issued me ten years ago, that are fully worn out anyway.

    Skip never asked the ship company for a new pair because that would mean they'd send him to a shoe store everybody called Cheap John's, which carried all kinds of work boots and suchlike, and that would mean going out of the dockyard and inland much, much too far from the sea. The sea was like oxygen to him, not having the sea that he lived and he breathed for near to him for even the time necessary to go inland to Cheap John's, be fitted, get the shoes, and come back—he would asphyxiate away to nothing in the store, though, he knew, not for lack of oxygen, but for lack of the nearness of the sea. It would take too long. Not to have its rotten polluted heavenly heavily scented presence nearby wrapping him around making him forget the land that was just under the floor of wherever he was; the thickness of the floor keeping him from actually standing on land, combined with the knowledge and smell and sounds of the sea he held onto so tightly inside, kept him going until he could get away, board his next assignment, and get out of sight of the evil poisonous land again. Being aboard ship he was fine and happy because he did not stand on horrid dirt, but on pure, strong, innocent, manmade steel decking, below which he knew the warm soft sea the ship was sliding along was near, still so near, and he dreamed again deeply and calmly of the day when the land would be gone. He could feel the sea seeping up and on and around him, and it soothed, so soothed, what a drug mixed with his rhythmic brushing, greasing, and tightening, the moves each exactly the same as the water rising, but he reached a certain instant which had been speeding toward him from the future since the moment he badly scraped over his palm, and blood began to flow. Emptiness and weakness began rising in him once the sea was up and over him and gone above—and he lit the small flashlight the company issued to all the seamen, and the light poured down and out and over, and he saw that he was kneeling in a pond of hot blood. He whipped the light onto his scraped palm and the blood unseen all this time came into view dripping, dripping and squirting from his palm-wound, and he realized—yes, realized— this was worse than he thought.

 He, he thought, Goddamn it, I am bleeding out. My word, my God, bleeding out, bleeding out, and he shot to risen slipping and sliding and thought, weak and slightly hallucinating in circles spinning around the edges of his eyes, that he needed to be in the super-modern ship's automated medical department right now, right now, so *right now* that he ran slipping and sliding in the blood fearing oh so fearing, and he pulled the medical department toward him from the future by running at it with his fat legs, and he got to the elevator that would bring him to the level where the department was installed, but the elevator was as dead as he soon would be, so, like a lizard scurrying into the hedge by passing tourists as though this was some kind of crazy vacation resort, he climbed the stairs, blood spattering and squirting from the holy palm, and got up to the top level, and went to the door of the automated medical department, leaving a steady trail of exactly evenly spaced red dots on the floor behind him, and pushed the bar that opened the door that let him in, and thank God he made it, he made it, and ran up to the machine panel set in the wall studded with buttons, screens, and big, big, leather-trimmed holes, bigger holes, and doors also great and small, and the sign above all this technology said, SYMPTOM: BLEEDING OUT.

It was a big room with lots of automatic robotic doctor machines each with the sign of its particular specialty blazoned across above, but thank God, the first machine specialized in saving people who are bleeding out, and it was even free. No insurance hassles, no waiting, all free—and his eyes scanned down the small print panel of how to use this automatic Dick-Tracy-style doctor he had never needed to use before, and he read, the print was small, and, fuck it to hell, he'd left his reading glasses at the scene of the accident so he needed to think fast, read slow, squint hard, and hope he had enough blood left to understand what sequence of which of the hundreds of multicolored buttons on the control panel to press, to activate the robotic doctor who would then take charge and tell him in a slow, lo-fi manner of speaking, what to do next, to save himself.

As he studied and poised his good hand to be ready to push the proper buttons once he had deciphered the tiny series of ten hundred hieroglyphics, far above, past deck over deck of solid steel, on the bridge, Father Dwyer had taken the place of the gone to the past Boeing commercial, and began episode nine hundred and one of *Sunday Dinner with Father Dwyer*, saying to the empty steel bridge room, Hello! Here I am, with the next episode of my show, the name of which is such a household word on every far-out ship at sea, to tell you all about how, pardon my French, you can make a neat lunch of a turkey wrap, but first I need to continue the story I started last episode about how I rode out a massive volcanic eruption, in the Pacific Northwest, whose brand name I am not permitted to mention, because the people that run the volcano never sent in their check to buy air time here, so; here it is. I sat with Harry Truman, yes, *that* Harry Truman, in the Spirit Lake Lodge drinking cold black coffee and exchanging anecdotes with the wizened old man across the rough-hewn table he had made himself forty-four years earlier. Badly done taxidermy of various species looked on from the walls.

Quite a table, Harry. Quite a table. You made this yourself, did you?

Yes, I did—and you see this tabletop? This great big wide knotty pine thing? It's a single slab of wood from the widest, largest tree ever carved apart by hand by one man. I called Guinness about it, you know, to get this into the Guinness World Record book, but they said they had no such category as largest tree ever felled, cut up, and made into great slabs of tabletops et al, by one man with just a Swiss Army Knife his father passed down, that *he* got from *his* father, and as a matter of fact, the history of that knife goes so far back that somehow, magically, it appears that one of my ancestors hundreds of years back must have succeeded in creating a kind of time travel machine that they used to zip forward future fast, grab the knife, and get pulled back as by spandex or a big rubber-band backward-slingshot contraption, back to their given socket in the great wall of the distant past and slammed the knife into the family vault, to be passed down the generations until it came to me, and; I swear to God, it flew right at me from out of nowhere when I was out walking the dog, and I caught it with one swipe of the hand, even before my brain knew I'd seen it! All of a sudden, I had it!

Had it? I said—great! Good catcher, huh?

Yes, very good. I just grabbed it down in a swoop, and I had it. Lucky I was on my toes, and it didn't slice into me or the damned big dog.

Oh, yeah? You're a dog lover, then, Harry? Where's your dog now? Is the dog still alive? I like dogs. Where's your dog?

Gone, said Harry. Gone of old age. Suddenly, very, very, suddenly.

Oh, that's awful. But at least you got the cats now.

Oh, yeah, the cats are okay. Good dog is hard to find, you know. It's usually all fatty. Not good for my Cholesterol. I settle now for cats.

Yeah, I love cats and dogs too—

Hey, don't fib me—but dogs taste much better. I long for the taste of dog. Don't you?

Huh? I started, jerked up, adrenaline wave tsunami; all my relaxation rushed away past the walls; out, all gone out the crumbling chinks in the rudely hewn log walls. I leaned at him, saying, What? Did you say taste? What taste? Taste of dog? How do you know the taste of dog?

Amazingly bug-eyed and red-faced, he became.

Huh? What, don't you know? People out in the woods like me, raise all the cats and dogs to get fat, slaughter, cook, and eat. Don't you, man? You look like a city Parish Priest, where nobody knows how to *really* eat, but there's something lit in your eyes when I said how I raise the dogs and cats for food. You know—

I leaned at him, hand up, saying, No, no, I don't know. Wait—something in me says—don't believe the cats are all for—

Listen, don't cut me off like that. Let me say the whole thing. I was going to say that I've already planned the little calico on top the radiator over there for tonight. As a matter of fact, let's cut this short. Pretty soon, I got to butcher her. Plus a couple others. She looks real good. Kitten is a delicacy. I got quite a few of 'em in a scrap container out back. You think she looks good, Father? You can come with me get a couple more, Father. My trucker buddy Lucas Barnes brought up a whole shipping container of pups and kittens that washed up on the beach down his summer place in the sound. I mean, don't be shocked, Father, after all, there's no grocery stores or any place to buy food within fifty miles of this place. And even if there was, Father, my old DeSoto out back hasn't been started in around fifteen years. And I'm afraid, actually, man to man, to try and start the damned thing. Then I'll know for sure it'll never run again. I don't want to know that, Father. That would weigh too heavy. It's better to eat the fixin's I raise myself. After all—they don't know what's going to happen. They don't know fear.

The small calico cutie sat snug, eyes half closed, the very picture of innocence and contentment, listening to the two strange big others across the table debate, and dead air surrounded us long enough that there was time for me, the all-seeing holy man, to look into my blurry globe God gave me, after all, what he was hinting at was so bad that the floor actually started to vibrate in time with a rapid series of sounds like thunderbolts, from outside the cabin, and I hoped to hell my crystal ball would still work in a thunderstorm because I knew the factory never tests them for that, but something made me check my watch—something made me check, and it read, May eighteenth, nineteen eighty. See, I got that fancy watch as a Christmas gift from my parishioners; that watch could tell you anything; your height, weight, depth, speed, mood, or altitude, and lots of other stuff. So just as I saw the date and time, the big bang came, the mountain blew, and the shock waves came, and the world rattled hard; like the world was attached to the tip of the tail of a universe-sized, taken-by-surprise timber rattler.

Harry rose from the beautiful table, and I started to rise, but he waved me down and said, No, no, the mountain's blown, but it won't hurt us. You've a safe haven with Harry. A very strong haven with ten-mile-thick solid steel walls, floor, and roof all around. I see it's coming, a big dark cloud is coming toward us, it's about a half mile away, but it's just clouds and a little wind is all, so sit right there, Reverend. Sit right there—and when it passes and I've proven no mountain can match me, we can pop a cork or two in celebration. You yes with that? What're a few little passing gusts, anyway?

Oh yeah, yes, with that, sure, of course—but it's getting pretty loud out there.

Loud can't kill ya', Reverend. Loud can only annoy, pass by, and be gone and never was—and with that word, the cloud and the roar and the heat and the ash hit the wall, and it pushed in and broke to splinters and flowed over Harry. The cats were all tossing around awakened and screaming by the whirling swirl of loud, fast, scalding heat that woke them so rudely. They had no idea that they were being saved and transformed into something unfit to eat, and the eater was dissolving too. They actually were much more angry than frightened. They were little glowing fireproof missiles bouncing around the crumbling, windy, black, flaming room without even time enough left for them to feel pain. And somehow, miraculously, I had been put by fate behind some glass wall, and I was in the front row of the theatre, in the dark but lit up too, very, very happy to be able to stay alive, watching the space where I'd just been, where Harry was disappeared under the now-flaming rubble of the blown-in wall, and I think he was really right, you know? He said, Loud can't kill ya', and no mountain could match him, because it hit me like a couple or three or four mortared-together bricks stuck together in one block right in the face; I am here and now talking to you, in my kitchen; Harry is long gone dead, and cannot be killed by what just blew up in the mountain while I was with him; I felt, viewers, and I feel now, that I ultimately will be canonized for what happened that day, when a man was made indestructible just long enough to survive one mighty blast that was probably just as powerful or maybe even more powerful than a big fat sneeze from God himself. So, all you viewers crushed together in the little red-eyed camera I talk to during each episode of this show, about food, all food, food like this here waving cold pizza slice all spattering around, tell me what you think of all this so far. What? I cannot hear you, no, I cannot, no—there's too much spatter around all over, and underfoot too—and the winds are like winds of some other planet. Lord Jesus my Christ, too wild and windy and loud there on the other side! But wait, I am so sorry, what about the food, after all it's a food show you know; I think I was nodding, please forgive me. Sorry. Really sorry. This should be about the fresh soup the mystic soup girl makes each day—for example, today is Tuesday, and she'll bring chili, the mystic's favorite. And instead of all this palaver about volcanoes and Harry Truman and all, there were supposed to be *oceans* of special Russian soup discussed today, as well as a few taped remarks from Mister Vladimir Putin himself, when he was young, skinny, shiny faced, just a boy, with spindly, wrinkly girly legs, and the exact opposite of any kind of leader—but you needed to know what Harry and I went through in that cabin, yes, you did, you did, yes you did, but anyway—

  Father Dwyer shut up, lolled away, and called out immediately for his low-paid and badly treated, baggy-pants clowning-around pretending-to-be-happy lightning-fast heavily-tattooed ex-con cleanup crew, to come and zap the place up nice and neat so Father Dwyer could go on and talk about the next food on the agenda. He stepped back away to make room for them, but his moving away simply revealed Skip, in the infirmary, bleeding out, but still struggling, madly punching at the rows and ranks of buttons on the computerized doctor-machine in the Automated Medical Department, with nothing happening at all, by God, he pushed his arm deep into the leather-rimmed hole in the panel he assumed you would thrust whatever was slashed or cut or ripped across into or against, as he moved from pushing individual buttons to slapping the button panel again and again, panic-stricken, randomly.

The room swam swirling around the weakening Skip, its revolving faster becoming a blur, like the porch used to do years ago, when Skip had one too many Ripple Wines. How much time do I have? he thought as the room sped up, whirling—Dear God, when will my blood all be gone and the shutters of life be closed over toward me and my window of life be closed and unreachable and unknowable, way before I have a clue I'll die soon and have some chance to say a prayer and make ready; and angels will quietly come up behind and take me gently by the arms and soothingly, kindly whisper close to my ear, Your time is over, young man. You did not rip down and open your palm because you slipped or didn't pay attention or anything like that. The Lord on High slid his finger down the who's-next-to-come-up-here-now book open before him, and your name was there. He stated your name, and when he states your name in heaven, it is a signal for us, the angels of death, to come and pull the appropriate strings, pay off the appropriate people, and make the secret cash-only deals behind the scenes to close you off from the world. Death is not dying or destruction or disappearing or being gone to nothing forever, no; it's simply the door to your current world being closed down tight, and you're locked out, and it's time to turn and enter the next. There's nowhere else to go. And, everything alive must move on, go someplace that's next, that is, unless they're vegetation or any form of life that lives its whole life rooted right there. So, Mister Skip, let go, turn, look at our faces. The deal will then go down, and we will have done our job as always. We have done this job for every human being since Adam and Eve themselves. Turn and see us, yes, turn, and see us. Do it now, please, do it now! Come be born into your new level—the words went in Skip's earholes, and stopped as he again slapped his palm against the panel of buttons. No, I cannot die, shake it off man, shake it off—this was the kind of death-dream

Mother had told him about when he was just a dirty-diapered infant on her knee. I know you're just a baby, Son, I know you don't hear me and probably don't even know who I am, but take it from me. Life will pass in a flash, and then the death-dreams will start. All the dreams you have in your life that you think are meaningless are just pushing you in tiny increments toward the last big one you never ever wake from—the big one, bigger than the kind of big one they're waiting to hit California—

Ma, hollered Pa from across the room, lowering the Daily News he used each evening to block out his miserable failure of a minimum-wage life, the daily news that pulled him in and he walked through the stories about the rich people and the successful and glamorous people on his favorite, mind-blasting, society rich people's gossip page. He was right in the middle of ogling the nearly nude, big round arousing breasts of the pinup girl of the day, but Ma's words to the boy destroyed the experience of this ogling, so he lowered the paper, hollered, Ma! And this was the switch that always shut her up and locked her eyes to his. He said into the eyes, to the great relief of the infant that, unknown to them, could understand Mother's every word, he said, Why are you telling our son those lies? None of that is true! Why are you trying to poison my son before he's even over his first week on this planet? Here, here, Ma, give little Skip to me. Here, boy, to me. Look I'll even switch off the Hitler Occult UFO conspiracy TV documentary show I'm watching, for you, my son. My little son who will be great someday.

Ma did as told, and brought the boy to him, as the TV went to dark with a tiny faraway click of the remote, and he gently took the boy onto his lap, and bounced and bounced his leg, cooing and *ah* and all like that, he played with the boy, and from the hole in his sour-smelling raggedy-rag of a beard came the message, You, my boy, will go on to great things. There is nothing as horrible in the world as death! You will beat death, my boy, you will beat it! You will be the first person ever since the creation to never ever die—do you hear me, good boy? Your Mother is wrong. She likes to make up stories. You know what stories are, boy? Stories are where you spend your life inside; make believe stories, all make believe stories, that's what we all live inside till we die.

The smell and sight of the unwashed beard and the raw, repeating, annoying breath of his Father who would be deep in the ground about a month later, made baby Skip look away—and he bugged his eyes, and shook his head, and spit quick to the side, when he found that the Computerized Doctor machine had all lit up with red and white lights, strung on rows around a screen he had finally slammed into life, where a fake digital person smiled at him and said, I will help you. You are here for help. Nobody cares about me or thinks about me unless they need help. This is the burden of every doctor, human or otherwise. Do you know how many Doctors commit suicide in this country every year? Well, I'll tell you. Male doctors do it at a rate seventy percent higher than any other professionals. Female doctors, though, get this; two hundred fifty to four hundred percent higher. And, since nature takes what remains of the dead and forms something new out of them, these doctors end up put someplace. Get ready for this, son. I was once a human doctor. What kind doesn't matter. They built this new experimental shipboard automated doctor, and then they needed a brain for it, and since it would be murder to rip a brain from a live doctor, they looked to the freshly dead, like me, and snatched up my brain and fed it into some computer through a funny, impossible-to-understand rat's nest of wires, cables, and dust, and dropped pen and pencil and whatever, and here I am! I am all digital. My body's gone to ashes or less someplace, and here I am screwed into place and put to work now! This is the next life for me, ah, well—but what about you? So, sonny, what is your complaint? And before you speak, know it better be about stopping you from bleeding out dead; this is what scares you, and you came to the right place, but if and only if that is true. Is it true?

This question, of course, went to exactly the wrong place, because some Russian hacker years ago, who was secretly employed to wreak havoc by what was left of the crumbling communist party, came surreptitiously into the gizmo-guts of inner-digitized-space and made sure if that question was ever sent over some wire into the big super-complicated make-believe cloud someplace no one sees or really understands completely, it would land in some random place, and it rolled and stopped miles and miles away and finally sideswiped Father Dwyer's cable show.

When it hit, Father Dwyer spun, seeking who, what, had shouted that at him, and he cried out, What? Yes! Of course, it's true! I never fib! from the flatscreen screwed to the wall of the bridge, having heard his honesty questioned by some far out coward, from someplace in the miles and miles of network connecting him to more and more miles of all different networks, one of which happened to graze across and resonate with the signals from some kind of computerized doctor he'd never heard of, which for some complex reason was somehow watching his show with a mechanical frown frozen on its face, but Father Dwyer, completely enraged and scarlet-faced, shouted back, What do you mean? again and again, cupping his hand over the earpiece containing whoever or whatever had questioned his honesty. But, he turned and realized the hordes of unseen seamen viewers had not tuned him in to hear him rant to some crossed wires down-network that none of them could relate to or care about in any way. This is the problem when no one scarcely speaks to each other face to face any more, really! Everything's connected by this or that network's cables or antennas or satellites or this or that screen in cars or at home or in bars or sitting in some coffee shop full of people but totally alone, all phones all around all lit-up phones, blocking—and my God, yes, for sure, he thought but dared not say for fear of losing the very last viewer remaining—there certainly never has been and never will be some computerized doctor shitfaced phony gizmo like that.

Impossible! But, anyway, said Father Dwyer, turning his fat gaze into the red light floating in the dark before him, We're not here to waste time. Lots on the agenda today. First look at this—and he stepped to the side and pulled from a shelf a gigantic blue plate or platter of some kind, piled super-high with every kind of baked goods; donuts and cookies and little cakes and oddly shaped and sprinkled unknown treats of some kind, and brought it to and onto his worktable with great effort, because the platter was over four feet long and was piled high with so much pastry and baked goods that it had to weigh over three hundred pounds. Father Dwyer, being relatively elderly, overweight, out of shape, and never seen without a cigarette or a cigar, said to the red light, Excuse me, I am a little out of shape, and really need to catch my breath. With that he leaned on the worktable with his elbows, and suddenly snapped harshly, No! It is not wrong if I am out of shape. It is not wrong if I waste airtime silently catching my breath—what'd you say? Jesus, really? And he put his hand against his ear and his face took on a listening-hard squint and crunch, and it became very apparent that he was being spoken to by someone of authority through the tiny earphone bud plugged into his ear. As he listened, first his chin reddened, then his cheeks, and up over the forehead—just as though some invisible, fully loaded paintbrush had been brushed up tight to his face and spread red paint from bottom to top. He began to nod, and his mouth became an open hole that somehow did not move at all but just let the words ooze from the hole and somehow spatter down into the microphone clipped to his chef's jacket. He said, Listen, no, I do not agree. Don't you realize that it is very probable that just one or two seamen are actually watching and listening to this show, and that's being optimistic? They might all be busy with whatever they got paid for doing every day, and maybe nobody at all watches this show, on any ship, because they just broadcast the same episodes over and over for year after year—it's a wonder the tapes haven't all worn to nothing, but—no, listen, let me finish—but I truly believe that no one watches this show at all on any of the ships at sea, most of the time or even all of the time. What? Sure, go on, lecture me now. I'll listen. Go on, talk and talk. I'm here. I've said all I have to say.

And Father Dwyer deftly lifted his hand to his ear, pulled free the ear bud, and tossed it out toward the red light in the dark before him. Ain't that just the fuck, he said toward the light. Somebody thinks they are my boss. Somebody fat and homely in a five-thousand-dollar Italian handmade business suit, sitting in a huge corner office high up some skyscraper someplace a world and a half from here. What do you guys think? Go on, tell me, I know you're there, it's just that you're in the dark all the time. Actually, that's funny, because most people are in the dark all the time, no matter if there's light pouring on them, or dark snug hugging them all around. Talk!

We're with you, Father, came from the dark, expressed in tones and cracks that meant whoever said it hadn't spoken a word at all for the last five to fifteen years—and more followed, one after the other, and they all kept on going, wreathing Father Dwyer all around, causing his face to brighten as though the Lord himself had appeared before him, or some kind of mystical vision. Only once or twice a year did anyone speak at him out of the dark surrounding the bright piercing dot of hard red light. He listened hard.

We are with you father, you're right, no one is watching—

If no one is watching, you can do anything you like—

You are the greatest, Father—

Yes, the greatest—

And the words and phrases grew so dense that after about three days they had blended together into a howling wind that never stopped. If they had been humans shouting from the dark, the effort and their sheer number and nonstop praise merged into a single musical note, fat as the fattest saxophone or tuba honk that was really not a honk, which typically lasts a second or two, but was an endless roar which smothered over the platter of food, and smothered over Father Dwyer, and took over and filled to packed tight the whole of this episode so full as to bursting and the whole platter of food went to stale and was ultimately left alone on the floor of one of the hallways in the broadcasting building, where year over years critter after critter and every species of vermin and rodent and pest had at it until everything was gone, and after more time, the platter was even pinched by one of the after-midnight janitorial contractor crew. This guy, whose name was just one note named Ned, knew the platter had value. Ned put it up for sale several years beyond the voyage to Shanghai on which he'd pilfered it, and it never sold, but some young blonde perky long-limbed lanky feminine entrepreneur saw it and reproduced it and, long story short, ended up rich after millions were sold by way of infomercials on land TV, and, just by Godly lucky chance, one was used to serve up hors d'oeuvres at the formal get together after Father Dwyer's massive flower-stenched unbearably long and boring closed-casket funeral. He died by being run over by a massive cement truck while rushing to the studio and stepping into the street as he was distracted by finding a human hair embedded in the Dunkin' Donut he was wolfing down, in his haste to be on time. Hairs kill. Hairs kill. Yes, hairs kill! And the episode ended up being completely wasted because Father Dwyer had put in extra effort preparing, by personally making a stunning upside-down cake and baking two loaves of wheat bread for the show, working late into the night despite his advanced age.

Thirteen or more levels below, Noman was slowly scraping the same tiny spot on the same steel bulkhead and still hearing in his head the words, *How to be a Nut!* A great book! A book titled *How to be a Nut* would go down in history as the best book name ever.

Phyllis stood before him as he scraped his wire brush up and down her fat steel belly, knowing somehow subconsciously that this was fine because where she stood was really just a steel bulkhead of the great Dakota Maru. And, because she was only a steel bulkhead, she didn't say any more to him, and sound was still valid inside Noman's vision because the constant over-and-over rolling of the bowling balls and the crashing din of the pins being blasted backdropped her perfectly. And from that point he did everything she told him to, and ultimately they married, and all the rest up to the horror of his not being present to calm her through the terrifying childbirth to come—

No! No! This must be stopped now, his nails ripping down his face at last demanded he say—into the steel he flung it—

Phyllis!

Phyllis!

I cannot ever have married you!

The steel stood between them. Only now, with this steel between them, could he hold her to what she had finally told him; if you don't decide what's what here and now, I will move on and you'll never see me again!

No; hold ground.

Enough suffering.

A fork in the road formed unseen on the other side of the bulkhead and sped forward.

No; hold ground.

Enough suffering.

—if you don't decide—

The fork touched the steel, flinging balls down all the lanes, combining in a single multiball skysplitting crack.

Speak!

No.

The searing-hot crack faded to a pit of quiet. No bowlers were rolling. No pins were crashing. There had never been a Phyllis. Phyllis was gone, never was, just nothing, all zero, zero. Just zero. Noman looked up from the stool in the bright-lit, empty, silent bowling alley.

What the hell am I doing here? thought Noman.

Why a bowling alley? How did I get here? Nobody is here, this is the snack bar, everything's locked shut and turned off, and it is cold in here—oh, yes, there's a clock. It's exactly twelve. Twelve but which twelve, light or dark? I don't bowl. I never have bowled. This place is bizarre—and as that thought faded, Noman popped off the stool and ran to the main entry door, and the door was black as he approached, and night shone dark through the door as he tried it. The door was locked. It was twelve midnight, why was he here? What the hell, I work on a fucking ugly-assed ship going to China. And not even halfway there yet, but—I had had something on my mind.

Yes, I had been very upset about something.

What, what? It's on the tip of my tongue.

Must be nothing, must not. It is far more important to get out of this mess of being locked in a closed bowling alley at midnight. Midnight. Yes, I know. Here goes.

Noman ran and snatched up a large bowling ball and hurled it through the entry door glass, shattering it, and an alarm rang up. Got to go, now! Got to go—and he sliced his way through the oval hole in the door and went forward to the steel bulkhead of the compartment deep down in the belly of the Dakota Maru, and stepped back. In the pitch black he looked around and sensed the job was done in this compartment. Funny, funny—he didn't even remember doing it. Funny how you can do something in your sleep somehow, and bang, you are done. Like driving someplace back home and arriving and not remembering anything of the drive, because your mind had been elsewhere—shit. Shit, good, thought Noman, and he grabbed up his wire brush and his rag and pot of stinking solvent, stooped through the low opening to the next compartment, and started all over again. The brush sang and sang shrilly against the steel in the pitch black. The song wrapped around Noman's head and formed like clay being molded into words, whispering, in the sound and tone of his thoughts.

What had I been worried about?

What had I been having heartburn about?

I'm young, single, and see the world.

That sounds wrong somehow, but—it must be the solvent fumes gone in my lungs and up to my mind. Up to my mind. Calm down, Noman. But something felt missing and gone in his brain. Something had been in it making some kind of pressure build and build, and it hurt all the time, but now it is gone and there's an empty space—but no, no, get a hold of yourself, man—shit, you're young, single, free, and see the whole world. Think of that. Things are good. The brushing went on, and the solvent ran down the steel wall, but Noman didn't see it, how odd he had learned to so easily do this job by feel, in the pitch dark. Scrape and scrape and scrape, pour solvent across, repeat; what a job. What a wonderful job. Wonderful yes, and almost lunchtime. What more could a simple young man want than a good lunch?

The brush went up, and came down peeling the steel, and there in the hole in the steel was the bridge and the light and the TV on the wall, and Father Dwyer was in the middle of his show that no one anywhere was watching anymore because everything got repeated over and over—for the millionth time Father Dwyer said from the screen, Okay! That takes care of breakfast. Funny how you get full of breakfast between six thirty and eight, and three hours later, here comes lunchtime. How odd is that? Your life with flesh and skin peeled away is just hunger followed by fullness back to hunger and fullness and hunger again—this is like your heartbeat, men! That is funny, but the world is funny, too—if not funny, how can I still talk to you after I die. Oh, yes—I will still go on talking to you after I die, forever. They say that in a few billion years, the sun will swallow the earth, but they never tell how civilization will adapt to survive as the sun grows to fill the sky and ultimately swallows the earth down whole. What will that be like, my God, what will that fucking be like? How bad will it hurt to be dissolved that way? Every single thing on earth, and even the planet itself, will die into just a little tiny bit of star-stuff dispersing out inside the sun, and will never be, just like when people die today. And tomorrow and the next day and the—Shit—but sorry now, but we got to get back to business. Sorry if I bored you, but remember I used to be a preacher. I fall back into the used-to-be a lot, then come back. For lunch, you'll watch me deftly set up a restaurant-quality salad-bar you can have at home for parties and holidays. Then we'll cover a burger made with quinoa, black beans, water chestnuts, red peppers, and garlic. Isn't that just so sexy, tasty, and magical? And I get to do it over and over and over and forever, until that final end we'll all face like I told you before, I—but no. No more on that today. Let me get busy pounding out this lunch. You'll want to eat immediately after you see me do this. And you will need to eat immediately over and over and over through your life like cars need to gas up over and over and over until they're dead, and scrapped, so—

And it so happens, at that very moment, Skip was in the Medical room, deep elsewhere in the ship, being scared hairless by the escalating shouting from the digital doctor inside the screen before him, which continued to hammer home its question of, was Skip scared to die, and the question came over Skip, and suddenly stopped after saying, I have shaken you enough, you're awake now, so puke, shit, piss, or barf out the answer! I am getting very irritated by all this resistance from you! We cannot heal you until you answer!

Okay, okay, said Skip, defeated. Yes, said Skip. Of course, I am scared to die. You happy now? Can we get to my wound now? Before I pass away?

Of course. That's why I am here, after all. But I have to tell you, I happen to know all about you. It's really a million in one shot that we should meet up like this. You know why?

No. Why?

Here it is; listen. I was, as I said, once a live human. Just like you. But in the future, when some person we both know got old and passed, the Master took away their head and came to me and squeezed the head dry into my skullcap and I was reborn and tuned in and turned on, and here I am; or, should I say, here you are. Like, I mean—my God it's too much, too much—I need to tell you, but you'll never believe—

What? Spit it out! Get to the end before I collapse from blood loss!

You aren't going to die, I will fix you, but, hey, you know, you live humans are very funny, you live people don't have a clue how time works, no. Nothing alive does, no. No one. Get this, man, and trust me, it's true—after you died, the corporation came to your deathbed and cut your head off and took it away and processed it, creating me.

What? What does that mean?

I am you, Skip, said the digital doctor. Your brain was melded into me when this machine was manufactured, back here, about ten years ago, because they needed to get a new bunch of Automatic Digital Doctors out the door.

What? How—

I am you after you died. You are asking yourself to heal yourself.

Huh? I—what do you mean, you are me? That can't be. You are nuts!

No. Not nuts. You just healed your own wound yourself from this machine while we were talking. Look. No more bleeding. All healed up too. And also; because I have been through this process out in the future when you gave up the ghost. And beyond you, past and present, I have healed about five hundred patients.

Skip looked at the wound. There was nothing there. Not even a mark.

How the hell did you fix this? You must have me hypnotized or something!

No, it was simple. I just reached back into the past and eliminated the wire brush you carelessly cut yourself with, before it happened. Simple. When you know how, of course. Out in the future, when you finally died, time travel had been perfected. It turned out to be relatively simple, actually. You know?

Skip stood with his face frozen and numb, as the screen went on to say, In a way, right now, you are looking at yourself after you die; don't you think that's neat?

I don't know. I'm confused. Explain some more.

No, that's it, you're healed, we're all done, I will now shut down and you can go back to work. Oh, and by the way; we checked, and this procedure is one hundred percent covered by your shitty insurance policy, the one you bought on the cheap. On land, you would need to have referrals and get stuff notarized and have a prescription first, but you're lucky, you're on a ship, and they don't require anything special in that case. So, let's go. You have a lot of work to do on your ship and in this machine right now too, since we are both the same person—the only difference is, you are alive and I am dead. So, so long, keep safe, press the red button under the screen, and we are all over in more ways than one. Go. Push. Now. Bye.

Skip pushed, and the screen turned dark, quiet, and cold, and his dead self was gone from the screen. All of a sudden, for some reason, the Medical department went ice cold. Dead are cold, yes; cold as the dead. This is some kind of nightmare that I will wake from, he thought. Think, think, back to when you cut your hand—think! Keep thinking as the brush slides across and back on the container hold down, but what's this, what's this? The wire was all at once gone from his hand. He looked back and forth and around, and it was gone. Skip could have sworn it felt as though he had never held it, but: things do not just puff out of existence, so—he rose, steadying himself on the battered red Hanjin container, and began to search around. After searching for an hour, he gave up. He stood in the steel street between the steel city walls; without the wire brush, he was useless. Useless!

All the blood that had shot from his hand was gone also, but—since it never had really happened, there was no thought of it in his head.

I got to go see if there's another one in the tool locker. I mean it's in the ship owner's manual that there's a tool locker, but... he had not the slightest idea where it was.

I got to go ask Noman, he thought, and the thought grabbed him by the feet and moved the feet back and forth, making Skip walk. The thought was like a machine some poor paralyzed wretch would have strapped on and could only use it until the wide black Velcro straps pulled tight around him began to become excruciating. It walked him, saying over and over in his mind, Must get another brush, must get another brush, must get another brush, and at the same exact time the TV show *Sunday Dinner with Father Dwyer* was between episodes playing commercials sounding unintelligibly like pleas for help, over and over, as pleas for money in exchange for things, like—must get another brush, yes—buy a fucking Lexus, yeah—must get another brush—Toshiba, this fucking Toshiba, cut to the chase just, please, Saab, for money, Saab, peel away the glitz and glamour, stop trying to give people erections for Range Rovers the way you go over the top to sell—must get another brush—GE, Honda, grip the shaft, rub, stroke, yes—OHSU, Red Bull, Southern Comfort, Tap King—Is it me you're looking for, is it me, is it—

Is it me you're looking for? at last came from the sudden presence of Noman before Skip. What, Skip, you look all flushed, what's the matter?

—Honda Hands, VW Golf, Kellogg's Fruit Loops, must get another brush—

What brush, Skip? A wire brush, like this?

There it is, there it is, there it is—Yes, Noman. Where is the tool room?

I'm not sure, we need to look around, it's up here someplace—

—must get another brush—

Well, hello, again, viewers. Welcome to episode nine hundred and three. Just think. Before we wade through the slough of food we have to show you today, let's meditate, meditate—

This might go on forever. Ain't that something?

If you've watched every episode, raise your hand! In the red dot through the hole to the real world, hear me, raise your hand! I cannot see you!

We cannot find it!

How can I see you?

We cannot find it!

I can see you though, even—

Where might it be?

—even though I know you're there. You'll be always there.

Let's start lookin'.

Never quit. No—

Oh, what the fuck, Skip. It's lunch. We'll look after that.

Okay. Sounds good—

The quest was buried in the backwash of the hunger that sat hidden until Noman waved out his arm in a most tidal manner. They went to lunch.

Chapter Eight
On the Free One-way Trip to China

—light late fall snow twilight, yes—but on waking, panic set in, but; don't yell. Oxygen, don't use up oxygen; please don't yell. Please, my face, pray for me in the Church lobby before mass. After six o'clock Mass, wander out. Been in there too long and prayed perfectly knifelike to everything; each sit, stand, and kneel also, done perfectly, precisely. When kneeling, the good book says, do not lean your butt back on the pew to rest, so never do it. Like in Catholic School, the large mysterious frightening black-draped being of a nun that wanders and watches, and would poke any boy on the side that it caught dozing or leaning their butt on the pew, kept the class honest. Have to shit, bell is rung, need to piss, bell is rung, but; need to go, as taught, can get out to a rest room to go; how about I ask this other guy waiting on the corner across from the Dunkin' Donuts I'm suddenly back at, whose name is Lucas. He stands talking to one of the other regular gang of guys waiting for day work, who is a large man named Walter, but I feel I have peed myself in my pants, cripes almighty. Need to leave, get new pants, silently hollers the steel all around, but—Lucas turns to me and says, Do you know it is a fact that every fetus begins urinating into the womb very early, and, once started, pees every forty or forty-five minutes? So, don't worry about it. We understand. We can see your—well, your problem. No need to hide it. If I were you, I would do the same thing, what the hell. But I'm not you. So, I wouldn't. Get it?

Yeah, said Walter in a deeper slower voice. I Get it. Do you?

They spoke nonsense in my view. I turned away and pushed my hand down my pants, and felt around. Dry—everything felt very warm and soft and absolutely dry. The penis in there was shrunk all flaccid, but there was a penis there, yes, a pretty well-defined penis there. So, I am developing okay. Why had I felt myself urinate?

So, I opened my eyes and Lucas and Walter and everything else went absolutely pitch dark, and absolutely silent, and again, when I felt out at everything all around, there was just hard cold steel, and the bottom of my space was puddled, urine smell from the puddle got very strong, and I struggled to feel in the dark, where I'd felt before, and everything, yes, everything was drenched; bad, bad, bad; bad was all around. Very hard to breathe, too. Very hard.

Eyes shut, and again I see the street and the Dunkin' Donuts, and Walter and Lucas are in the middle of yelling something to me.

—Wake up! Lord God, man, how do you sleep standing up like that? You, I swear to God, I never seen the like of it before—

Where? Where is Miss Sweetie?

Me either, said Walter. I—but yeah, yeah. Hey Lucas, he's back now.

Yes, he is—hey guy! You always do things to scare the shit out of us—hey, I bet you guys didn't know, that toward the end of its term a fetus will shit in the womb too?

What are you trying to say? I'm not—

Eyes sprang open, and big fire hoses worth of darkness gushed in my eyes, and I felt it going down through flushing me raw, and coming out, and before I could help it, it was coming into my pants, and it was hot; and there came Mackie again, across from me at dinner, up on his heels, doing the toast! I Mean, I thought he made this toast already, but no, there he is. Doing it, saying, Johnny, you are the best! The best!

Maybe I'm back there and I am safe?

You have done what we wanted and more! Right boys? And more!

Dear God, yes God, I can stretch, stand, walk. No more steel, side, top, bottom sealed, I guess holding my breath and closing my eyes made it, now, never had happened!

Yes, Mackie!

God, yes!

Yeah—here's to you, Johnny—hey, everybody, wait a minute. Johnny, why'd you stand up in the middle of my toast? It's not polite to stand and wave your arms, and all, when I am giving a speech to my men—what you got to do, shit? You got to go take a piss and a shit? It's something like that's why you can't wait till I'm done, because you'll slime your pants in back and front inside, and end up wearing trousers that got a professionally hand-embroidered multicolored technicolored surrealistic kind of butt? Huh? Huh? Huh, boys, what you think—should we let him go, or what should we, what—over the *what* overcame the laughter, and over them all and everything laughter, so I disappear in the great thickly wave of laughter that pounded across the room drowning Mackie and all his boys onto the shore, up past Dad struggling to spear the earth to death many years ago, with the tip of our not-rented-but-owned, ancient-looking, great, big, tall, beachy-as-shit umbrella, all flecked with mold, waving up to the sky. What? Where? I thought you were dead, Dad—I thought you were dead—I—fingernails? Already, there's fingernails. Look at my hands.

I have fingernails!

All's well in your growth's what that means, stated Father, the cadaver. Yes, it is that, even though I am. Go away. Back to the side of life you belong in. You have years yet to come over here. Look in the mirror, you've got a human face. That's a good sign you are developing nicely.

I stood. Developing? Developing. The laughter was tarry and gooey and threatening to drown—I watched it, watched it take him down, but, what am I talking about, thinking about, laughing? I made this whole world of endless greasy goo engulfed up everything, by my own laughter? I sense I am laughing, but I am not. Why do I sense I am doing a million things that I'm not? Nothing is to see. Nothing is to hear. But there is everything around everywhere. Sleepy. Need to sleep, want to sleep—gone over, going over, gone—going, what's that? That's Mackie. Where is this? There is, what's he say, huh, what say it, huh—

Boy, after tonight you're going to get what you got coming, Johnny!

But where is this? Oh. The table. The dinner, but—

You're going to get what you got coming, he repeated, and maybe some more!

Yes, stand, Mackie's done, turn to go shit-pee, but; fall over, just fall over, but no, something blocks me; a fire hose of black India ink fills in the steel. Up, down, all around steel, all filling with black India ink, otherwise known as the absence of light.

My God! My God! This can't be, where are you Mackie, I know you are here, Mackie, please don't do this, Mackie, I don't want your money, Mackie; I swear to God I don't want it at all, please? Please, because this joke is starting to hurt a little bit. The air is bad, Miss Sweetie. I tell you girl, let me out, get me out. Curl in a ball. Where did Miss Sweetie go? Curl in a ball like it hurts. My thumb is here, wet and warm in the cold ice steel puddle of filth thick in the bottom. Thumb in my mouth to suck. Nothing else will soothe. Where is Miss Sweetie? No, no, she didn't do me like it looked like, Mackie. Not Miss Sweetie, No, no; she is only yours.

Chapter Nine
Banter on the Ship to China IV

So, after a long tiring walk across the gigantic, state-of-the-art, fully automated container ship called the Dakota Maru, the only two men on board, Skip and Noman, sat eating in the bright cheery lunch room behind the bridge. The watery, tossing, lightly splashing whitecaps filled the big windows to the side, all the way out to the bottom of the blue sky.

International law demanded that even fully automated ships must have at least two crewmen on board, to handle the infrequent big dangerous crises when the computers lose control; as such, Skip and Noman had nothing but busy-work to do, for about two long months. This was another of several exactly-the-same days, with several dozen more ahead out to Shanghai from New York and back, very, very slowly; yes, yes. That slow.

I'll tell you, man, said Skip, cutting the food loaf before him. I still don't really believe you aren't married. What happened to all your worries? Was it really just—all in your mind? Why would that be? How?

Noman chewed, chewed, winked, nodded, swallowed, and said, Yes, yes, I was very deluded, but it's all clear now. I guess I just didn't want to take this assignment. I made up the best excuse I could think of. I guess I wanted to be excused from this voyage so bad that I didn't let anyone, not even you, know the real truth. God, am I relieved. How the mind can get twisted. You know? You actually can force yourself to believe your own lie!

Hey! Tell me about it! Hah.

Plus, this job doesn't help any! This has got to be the world's shittiest job!

Agreed, said Skip, as they hunched down digging at the cold bowls of shit, leftover shit to begin with, expired prison shit they had been given to eat during the months-long voyage. The spoons and bowls clattered and scraped in time with the voice of the ever-present, not really there, Father Dwyer, up in the wide flatscreen television bolted to the wall out beyond the stench.

Today, intoned the priest, across, through, and below and around the two seated, silently eating men, You know, see, as long as you've not got some harrowing physical nervous or mental condition that prevents you from quality sleep, sleep on land is a great comfort, escape, and odd dreamy time. And if you don't get enough, you can over-the-counter buy numerous sleep aids—this-PM, and that-PM, and even just plain old PM-PM. So, sleep is inevitable on land. But, as you men well know, at sea's a different cookie altogether—

They bit down on their stale lunch loaf, listening.

—sure, the ship rocks and rolls and tosses and turns, and even with that you can probably get some kind of almost decent sleep, but how about those North Atlantic blows, eh, men? Yeah. Lack of decent sleep can even give you a kind of voyage-long narcolepsy. That's when you fall asleep without warning, instantly as death comes if you get a shot to the back of the head.

Boy he's got a way with words, eh man? came through Skip's long difficult chew.

Yah, 'e does, burbled up, out from Noman's last swallow.

I even knew a fellow cook, continued Father Dwyer, on a past voyage so damned long, who was slicing up a big, fat, long, hard vegetable of some kind, and had an attack of narcolepsy so bad, he stood there asleep slicing and slicing, numbly not seeing, over and over until the other cooks in the kitchen heard the crunching and ran over to find he had, in his sleep, cut two and a half full fingers too far into his hand, without even waking. This narcolepsy thing is just too weird, and just too dangerous, for anyone using sharp tools in a hurry in a fast repetitive manner. They couldn't save the fingers; no doctors on board, not even monocled Germans. His religion said, Only German doctors. That was a shame; he bled out and died for lack of this.

But now, back to now, speaking of knives, and speaking of apples, and happily not plagued with narcolepsy, we will—we will make a roast roadkill, with apple—here's the rule all seamen should live by; always keep your belly full, to absorb the queasiness that creeps inside, in time growing to a great ball of squirming worms, and drags you by the face to the side of the ship, to puke, puke, puke some more—

The priest went on and the crewmen quietly relaxed, nearing the end of lunch, hearing in the gaps between the jaw-crushes and the swallowing down, Skip in particular recalling his quirk—yes, thank God, in the name of Father Dwyer—that he always needed to be on the sea. He reminded himself how lucky he was. As he reduced the brown matter on his plate down smaller with each and every bite, he felt whatever fit he'd had was passed, except, deep down—an undertow in the deep reptilian brain that never can be heard, it is so down deep—he could hear it saying, I am in you, and you no longer know who or what you are, and I am deeply disturbed. I don't like to be deeply disturbed, something is different now, there's something you know in the upper levels I can't see into that has changed everything; something large is different. Somehow you are confused, and no one has told me what is different—somehow, I sense you don't know if you are about to be born or if you are about to die, or somehow magically have split into being in both states at once. It's something like that, like—like remember that computer monitor they had in the office down Florida, years ago when you had not yet decided to give up life on land, you had that new job in that computer consulting office, and you were using that fat, wide, eighties-vintage IBM monitor, and it suddenly looked as though you or it or both had suddenly snapped into double vision; you were confused, as I am confused, and all at once, a hand came and slammed into the side of the monitor, and everything slapped clear again, and you looked to the left, and up, behind, and there stood one of the masters of the place, whose job it was to train you, Kent Dazey. He smiled, and he spoke quickly, saying, Hey, Skip, my man, this monitor's on the blink. We called IBM and they came and looked and couldn't find why it goes all nutty looking like that, but they said just give it a good hard slap when that happens, and that would always make it right. We said, how about we replace it with a new one, and the IBM suit said through suddenly sparkling eyes how much that would cost, so we decided—to the deflation of the IBM guy who smelled a sale coming—to keep this one, thinking that a slap in the side was free, and no problem, as outside of that, the thing worked perfectly well. The sale smell left, and so did the suit, taking his mysterious pitch-black fat briefcase with him and fading away to dim forever yesterday. So, you see, we're cheap, said Kent Dazey smugly. And cheaper is always better, he threw last from his smiley lips.

Yes, that was something you, Skip, learned years ago, from a master of the craft, years back, when you could still bear to live ashore. And it's been smooth sailing since, but now, here today, I have to speak and say there is something different in you, way above me, that is quite unsettling; so, since you are no more than a smelly soft machine of flesh, bone, blood, and general muck, atop which I just sit and man the controls, how 'bout we do what Kent Dazey recommended and slap ourselves silly on the side of our unnaturally large rocky head—go on!

And Noman jumped his chair halfway back to the bulkhead, as Skip's hand came up like a gunshot, slapping himself hard as he could upside his head. Noman feared an eardrum'd burst; Skip looked dazed, so dazed—Noman began to rise, speechless, and stepped around toward shipmate Skip to see what was wrong; what had happened; what was he thinking to cause this. But Skip's eyes cleared, his stricken pallor faded back, and he said, You know, Noman, I read a paper on the internet last night, that confirmed once more my core belief that we have a global crisis that calls for international cooperation to reduce emissions as rapidly as practical. Otherwise, the warming will continue, and it will be just *Waterworld*, just like that shitty movie, *Waterworld*, and you know what, fucker? I can't shitcan wait. Now—

Noman was so relieved, so relieved, a tiny spot of urine seeped into his underpants without his knowledge, as he said, Skip! You sound like the old Skip! Skip, why the hell have you been acting so weird?

Huh? What?

Weird!

Weird? How? What the hell are you talking about, Noman? You always ask such odd questions; you should talk about weird, you actually spent a long time thinking you were married and you had a pregnant wife, you even had me feeling sorry for you, but today, God, today you tell me that's not at all true and was just in your head, and you are calling me weird? You're the weird one! Listen, hey—and what's more, I been—

Skip it, man! waved out Noman. Enough! Enough! Let's just be.

Skip? You said Skip? Hey—that's my name, laughed Skip; thou shalt not take my name in vain! How dare you, landsman, insult this future merman of the deep!

They exchanged shocked glances, at once melting away, revealing smiles, and they sat and laughed for a while, deep from their smelly slimy bellies right out their mouths, about what an odd day it had been so far. It had to have been caused by being at sea so long. It had to be because every minute of every day was exactly the same aboard the Dakota Maru; and Father Dwyer was still just starting to preach, about, of all things, how to make a meal of roadkill.

He said, Now, the roadkill you use, got to be heavy on meat. You know, not just any roadkill will do. First thing you need to do to never, ever have to buy the main component of your meal, is to always watch the sides of the road. Any lump coming up in the distance might be a candidate for a meal. Look at it this way; you go down the supermarket aisles and look at stuff on shelves and in displays and in frozen items' shiny refrigeration units, and they all flow by, and you stop and pick this now, that now, yes; and that and which whatever. Switch your thinking to the following; every mile you drive is a mile down a market aisle. Now, the food items might not be as close together as in the store, but they'll be there. You need to watch them coming up. As they come up, you slow. Do they look freshly dead? Were you past that spot earlier? Was the roadkill there that long ago? And, as a matter of fact, how long ago was that? You need to keep track of every dead thing lying in the trashy gutter. You need a little pad and pencil, but of course you know you cannot make notes in a pad with a pencil and drive too, so…listen at the end of this episode, and we will have for sale to you a little recording device you can hold in your hand, designed, made, and sold in all the United States' fifty segments, for only nineteen dollars and ninety nine cents, by The Only Way to Eat is Free Corporation, located in Georgia and soon to outbranch, just as seen on post-midnight bleakly bleak television sets all across, yup, just the same as three a.m. on those same tubes worldwide, yup, it will just be a little box; but that smart little box will file, time stamp, which week, which month, yup, for the item you describe in your own words, when at the same time you press hard as possible, yup yup, the little magical blue button right here in my scrubbed up clean palm, and it will keep everything cross-referenced, ordered, sequenced, and prioritized, and it can tell you when you ask it to, that the roadkill you found on the road cannot still be fit two days from now, yup yup yup, and it will generate a set of GPS directions which will tell you where to go to stop and pick up this night's dinner, on your way home from the office, it will generate cooking instructions which will be based on Ace of Spade's rule, which is: Thou shalt not consume today's roadkill before yesterday's is all gone, and all from prior forevers as well, and the little box will also inform all the little boxes of others who dine on this fine food, that if the item you are going to take from the road is on their waiting list, it will be removed. The Only Way to Eat is Free, Inc., will also send you a second unit, absolutely free, if you act today and call instantly and directly after this very canned episode of my show, *Sunday Dinner with Father Dwyer*. That's right, free! To give as a gift or keep as a spare, though because these things are sure to last forever, and take about a penny a unit to make over in some sweatshop in China where people work with no piss breaks until the day they either crack up or die, there's really no point in having two. It's a marketing gimmick, natch? A marketing gimmick, yah! Okay, now, so. Using this, you got your hands on some dead little filthy hairy rag of pale, completely-drained-of-blood, smelly hot flesh. But finding it is just the start of the fun! Now, you got to know what to look for, as in signs of palatability, so that you don't go and gurgle-gush out the whole meal you choose to make and eat today, if you don't start with something edible, rather than sickening, as in slimy, rotted, all nauseous, loose.

Now, when you get an animal icy dead from the road, there are things to check. As in anything you do in life, you need to check things before you do them. You need to check there's a gangplank present when you step off of the dock. You need to check no cars are coming before you cross the street, and you know, by the way, I learned that the hard way when I was about eleven years old. I was walking the sidewalk up the hill in Milltown, up Washington Avenue, and I was bouncing a little ball quite idly, thinking to the blue sky of everything in the world besides the ball; the ball abruptly bounced weirdly off a crack in the sidewalk, and shot out into the road. I went after it into the road without looking both ways, and as I grabbed at it, I stumbled and fell on my big ass in the road, both knees skinned raw, and I looked up, and here came a big black Dodge to nail me, but it stopped at my face right here; this very face. Just in the nick of time, the brakes worked and the chrome plated word *Dodge* on the deadly thing's nose, was stamped into my mind forever, as being something you should do to get out of the way of any evil event that is rushing up to kill you. And yeah, I was just eleven! I bet none of you viewers remember something you did when you were eleven, that you are sure that you were eleven when you did it; and that you remember it because something about kind of tattooed it someplace inside your pitch-black skullcap to ensure that you will never forget. I got Dodge in my mind forever! Dodge! Dodge! Dodge! And a Dodge that would be a valuable collectible classic today! But more likely rotting into the ground behind some barn. Or, crushed even. Totally never was, just a false figment surging up about every decade from my aging grey matter. Who knows, who cares, you know, but; back to you; each of you listeners, tell me in turn, tell me crisply, neatly; because you are seamen who should keep your minds shipshape and everything squared away all just like the rule books say; your minds should be tougher than Krupp steel; talk now, and I will hear you. Think, what is your personal Dodge? What is your personal Dodge, what color shape or size or level of deadliness, or level of pure pleasure? What is tattooed inside your skull? Look inside! Learn to look inside! Learn to look both inside and outside! Be like the television you are watching me on! It's a fact that the televisions you are watching that are installed in your obscenely massive container ships are the only televisions in the world that can watch you while you're watching, completely and clearly. Now, I wasn't supposed to tell you that, but; yes, we are watching every movement you make to ensure the voyage is going as planned, that the computers are all running perfectly, correctly, and all the GPS systems and related spatial networks, lasers, and cosmic-ray counters and Geiger machines, and what boy Lego figurines constructed special for your very voyages you are enduring, are totally valid and precisely in effect. Know that the television you are watching is not just a means of entertainment for you seamen, but a means by which the unknown masters of the ship in huge spotless conference rooms in tall black glass towers on land are making sure you are doing your duty, day by day, crisply and smartly, like you ought to be going, and doing, now.

And right at Noman came, guess what: his own personal Dodge—the thing, whatever it was, he'd got rid of, great and powerful, the wave you see a few times in a lifetime that is lit just right while rearing and breaking and there is something solid, dark, and quite large inside. Maybe some old log. Maybe some old board. Maybe some dead fish. Or maybe some live wildly snapping great white, come to get you, get you, get you, get; Noman rose quickly to get away, and guessed Skip had also; like clockwork they knew it, it was bound to come, the back-to-work bell rang faster and higher, and Noman did not simply walk, he flew, to escape the wave-Dodge full of God knew what bleak unknowns, coming at him. Noman did not want to see or know his personal Dodge, somehow it had him locked up for the remainder of his days, but he always made sure, he didn't want to know or care, he just knew he had to escape; feared so horribly, run from so quickly, the wave did its job of putting him down in the steel square dark room thirty stories below, with his brush in his hand, which he plunged into the stenchy solvent, and ripped down fast, unzipping the wall, and the expected great gash opened, and he stepped through, escaping just a second, one tiny split second, the fumes, the fumes, the fumes, the fumes, and there he stood way back, aged nineteen, on the parade ground spread sunny before now, yes; Noman stood dressed smartly in the pouring sun, with his cap pertly tipped and his trousers creased, one of a mass of clean-washed dressed-up military men on parade way back then, in his military costume with his military weapon empty of its military bullets and thus, harmless, held straight in a vast expanse of straighter weapons held higher still, and the sun was up in its proper compartment, and the great single-star general in baggy pants came toward him, one man at a time down the formed up line in open order, to inspect each soldier.

Noman was once more not a man, but a soldier. Five or more

years it would take to become a man again, from where he had been frightened back to by the surging Dodge that had bashed itself to death in vain on the beach he had run from, back up to some sort of today where he'd feel safe again. The general came before him, and took his weapon, and it nearly spun as a propeller in the old general's liver-spotted hands and then got thrust back into his, and he was fully there as he had been once before, actually many times before, but who's counting? Now's what matters. It's always now, here on the parade ground, not years out in the bowling alley, where she waits frozen ready for the moment to come and to pounce and take Noman for her mate, and—but, no no no—no, the wave. Know not the wave, the Dodge hidden there—yes, now, the thing is the nearly senile, sloppy, suddenly-barking-out-loud general.

Soldier, your uniform's a little ragged. When was this jacket issued to you, soldier?

Sir! A while back, sir! I don't know how to measure when exactly, sir! Maybe not yet, maybe years from now, or maybe way back in the past, sir! You know, like yesterday, last week, or years ago, from now—maybe even not yet really at all! Sir!

From really at all, what?! barked the general.

From really at all, sir! spat Noman.

You mean, from the now, when the bowling alley is just a plan on the drawing board?

What bowling alley are you referring to, sir!

The one you're headed toward. Where your personal Dodge awaits.

Personal Dodge, sir?

Yes. Personal Dodge. As in with tits and ass. Are you afraid of tits and ass, soldier?

No sir!

You have tits and ass, soldier! What are the possible other parts you may fear? Any that you or I might have, soldier? Any that you or I might have?

No, sir! Nothing you and I might have!

All right soldier! But remember; the bowling alley is just part of some spark in some architect's head, and part in some architect's pen, and part on some architect's paper. And that is just, first draft! Many years will come and go until, once more, the moment of truth slams down! So, you see, son. You've years yet to worry, son. So, come on, get loose. Loosen up. Slack off a little, you know? Have a mushroom or two. After all, it's nearly the sixties.

Yes, sir!

Now, you know, soldier—your uniform must be perfect! So, let's see—

Several days passed, until at last the general stuck his face in Noman's again.

What are you afraid of soldier?

Noman woke, blinked his eyes, and said, Nothing, sir!

No tits and ass?

No, sir!

Good! Next, your boots must be properly polished—here, let me see—

The general stooped. Days passed. Day/Night/Day/Night cycles passed about him. The rest of the men undressed, got into sleeping bags, slept, got out of the sleeping bags, dressed, and like that around and around and over and under and here and then and day after day after—all for one pair of boots, one pair—of fucking boots! You know, I; never mind. Continue.

The general's face came up, forward, out of the boiling blue of Noman's dark uniform.

I heard that, soldier! I heard that! What are you afraid of?

Noman woke, blinked his eyes, and said, Nothing, sir!

No tits and ass?

No, sir!

Good! Now, all your creases have to be perfectly sharp! Here let me look—

Again, Noman stood still, did not age, did not dare speak, for nearly ten days. The general's head bobbed up. Again, he asked the question, and Noman said, Nothing sir!

Good—next there have to be no loose threads, dirt, marks, ruffles or abnormalities on any of your kit, or on your body that's all hidden because it's improper to be nude! There has to be a straight vertical line from the middle of your toes, up to your trouser zip and button, through your shirt buttons and aligned with your face. And no male anatomy bulging inappropriately against the cloth, to spoil the effect, if you know what I mean! Let me look!

The general's blind hand looked, as Noman thought; days, yes, I know there will be days—days like this, yes, days—

It is not flawless, soldier! It is not! Why is it not?

I—I don't know, sir!

Buck up, soldier! Sociological research has shown that standing tall and looking confident, even if you are not confident, is a good way to become confident. Did you know that truth, son?

No sir! I did not know that!

Oh no? Really. Then I guess you were not listening in class! So, how many other great truths you should know by now have you let fall in the passing dirt beneath but a second, then gone? So, I suppose you don't know either, that by behaving like a soldier, you affirm to your self-identity that you are a soldier, and will therefore act like one. Do you not remember that?

Noman tried to speak, but it came back off his tight lips and made a silent burp, mixed with the taste of bile—sick feeling, yes, sick, must chew ten Rolaids then chug a large water kind of sick, yes, that kind that will just sicken and sicken and sicken, but into his face was barked and re-barked and barked again, more and more sickening every single time—

Do you not remember that either, soldier? Do you not? Do you, do you not soldier—Do you not remember? Where are your eyes? Dare not close your eyes to me when I am speaking!

The word *speaking* came in Noman's ears and said, Speak, yes, go—try and see what happens. And he did—but just bile surged in a wave followed by a hotter thicker multicolored substance mixed in a morass of large and small fragments, no spoken words, none at all, not a one, and it came up in Noman.

And do you know, soldier, do you know, sailor, do you know, marine, do you not either, what the fuck, what the fuck—as a full hose of filth came flooding straight at the chest of the general, driving him back like fire hoses do demonstrators hurling rocks after dark with fires burning in steel drums that bums stand all around as the cold settles and the snow falls, and flying gas missiles shot from the police, deep inside Noman, fighting off scores of enemies; these enemies stood in the guise of this old general, stricken back multicolored with vomit of every possible kind and size and stench of chunk mixed in colors, all mixed up in dense liquid, and he fell back, his silly little one-star helmet blown off and back, he fell back full length, the back of his skull shattering on impact with the concrete of the parade-ground, on which no expense was spared to construct it to remain hard as granite for all eternity.

Arms gripped Noman, as his knees buckled—the stress and strain of the months of training and struggling and straining and striving to be the perfect soldier had slowly been building a large hairy blister of gross resentment in him as the fetus of a devil grows, is stressed and stressed some more, until this at last happens, meaning many things; that Noman should never have been a soldier; that the aged general should have retired when he got his first sad consolation star, too late to ever get enough done before being senile to ever possibly get another; and this was the start of Noman's last story.

The Army spat him out dishonorably the very next day. As he was driven to the gates of the garrison at twilight, under heavy guard, wearing only the ill-fitting clothing he had worn down to the recruitment station seven years ago, and only having the three crumpled dollar bills that had been in the pocket of the baggy black pants from the day he entered the Army base to the day they forced him drugged and screaming back into the pants to kick him the fuck out for killing the general with the world's largest gushing puke one man had ever shot-gunned out any kind of maw, the memory neatly stepped him out back into the steel compartment containing his present-day job in the Dakota Maru, his steel brush came down, zipping shut the zipped open maw he'd gone through before and came out of now, and there he was again, slowly steel-brushing with hot solvent the thirty-third of the five hundred ten such compartments he'd scrape down for no reason by the time they arrived in the Port of Shanghai! Ah Shanghai, Shanghai, there was something very significant about the approximate date they'd get to Shanghai, but—

Father Dwyer, who was just then saying, no one hearing, except, well—maybe some other ship someplace at sea had somebody watching, or maybe several people watching, or maybe actually dozens of hundreds of people watching, as Father Dwyer often reminded the red eye floating in the dark before him in the studio. But here in this room on this trip to China, Dwyer went on to say, You know, some of you may be getting a special treat, to be seeing this show. That's because this show is automatically beamed to all the myriads of cargo ships flying under every flag and traveling endlessly from continent to continent. Cargo ships, cargo ships mostly, container ships most frequently, even big oilers, tankers, and LNG carriers so dangerous, yes; but; here and there a forward-looking passenger vacation cruise line has decided to make my show available to their landlubber passengers as well—and he went on to say, These lines are forward-looking because they will go to any lengths to give their passengers the complete out-at-sea-with-no-land-in-sight experience. And my show is part of that. Who the hell is Father Dwyer, they might ask you in a cab in New

York City, or, Who the hell is Father Dwyer, they might ask you on a bus, or on a plane, or even on the cheapest most out-of-date cruise that a big, tubby, out-for-your-money-pockets vacation-agent may have got you booked on, for mere peanuts—anybody who would say that had got a peanut's worth of what the real at-sea experience is from the hucksters who ticketed them with cheap for-shit tickets—Who the hell is this Dwyer guy? What's so great about the guy? He's a guy, just a guy. Is all. Yes, is all. But if you're in some pagan-based there's-no-Jesus-Mary-or-Joseph religion, or any club like that, you might say, Who the Hell is Jesus? He's Jesus, just that Jesus. Is all. This is similar, really quite similar, because in many ways, Jesus and I are very alike; except, of course I do not claim God's nature. This cannot be done. This must not be done. I certainly do not. But, think a bit. Read that last sentence again; you there!

What does he mean read that last sentence again? Huh? What? Huh? Why?

Say it again!

Why?

Say it again!

Why?

Say it, and say it, and say it again!

No!

Yes?

Not *yes*! No!

Father Dwyer stated quite frankly, Well, you know, if it were not for the word *not*, I would be a blasphemer. How powerful is one, tiny, three-letter word: *not*. But, maybe we better change the subject. If I'm a three-letter word's worth away from plunging into the deepest fiery flames of the waiting, longing, licking hunger which is Hell, one tiny step from stating that I am equal to Jesus, which, if it's not blaspheming I don't know what is, I better step back! Yeah—back to the subject at hand. The fucking cooking.

This is, after all, a fucking cooking show. *Sunday Dinner with Father Dwyer*. Not the fucking and the cooking with Father Dwyer, but the fucking cooking with Father Dwyer. You guys hear me?

The blankets writhed on.

I guess not. Well, as in cooking. See what I mean about the three-letter words? They're dangerous. They trip you up. They can bring you down. All but one; one little bitty word for something so known that it's almost unknown. Yes, that's it—you in the back, who just blurted it out! *Egg* is the word. Egg! Egg! Okay, egg—and as sure as security is ushering the wiseguy in the cheap seats out who guessed the word, we will go on and on and on and—on!

Yes, went the laser-like drone of Father Dwyer, going on way above, saying, Yes! This! The deceptively simple, yet holding universe upon universe upon universe within itself, egg. That egg. This one, yes! This one I hold aloft now—I—tell you what, I will do a trick, I will drop it and before it hits the floor, I will open the cabinet and slip out the skillet and get it under, and the egg will splat all shattered and sticky and yucky inside; and we will make scrambled. Yes, scrambled. Yes—hereletgotheegghereitisfallingopenthecabinet-stoop fortheskilletpullitoutgetitupandunderandsmileand—splat!

There it is, splattered! As we say in the business; car-crash splattered!

Oh!

God!

Oh, Lord, God, yes, I hear you, I'm here, I heard. What a thrill this all is! But, with this egg, well, that was a true magic trick. Nature is one thing. Magic's another. Behold, your humble defrocked priest turned magician. See me flick out the shellbit from the pan. And, since the sea you men see out your porthole when not so busy in bed, looks exactly the same as the sea looked back before mankind harnessed fire, we might have a few million years to wait before we can light this burner I'm gripping here, as a matter of fact, this burner and stove and all might be—might be the mystical sacred object that holds all of matter across the universe together. Just like that word *not*, which is the grand key to the cosmos, this knob on this stove being turned to off right now, yup; if turned, and no flame came right behind, it would mean we are in the time before mankind had harnessed gas; imagine that? So long ago!

What the hell is that?

When the hell did mankind harness gas anyway?

You know damned well what that is!

Jesus, God—and if it does not light, and if the maintenance crew of blue-clad on-call short men they will send to solve the issue cannot get it lit, it might be that it is really just illusory and gas has not yet been invented and that the whole ship, the whole long wide so-real vessel, may be a magically created boat of a kind that we are not really on vacation in, or on the way to some business meeting in China for, after which we will return to our original homes, but of a kind that will sail us to a barren land of stunted colorless stark-naked super-ancient cannibals, who are waiting on their ragged lava rocky shore with long spears in hand for the liner you think is a liner but it's not, which will run onto the shore and then be blinked out of existence by the spell cast by the bony-nosed witch doctor flailing long-feathered chanty bell-ringing jangling things, and when the ship becomes what it really is, which is nothing at all, all passengers will be in the water flailing and flailing desperate to stay alive, breathe hard, and make land quickly, but a hail of spears will quickly make short work of them, and there'll be good eatin' in hut-town tonight!

Mah! Maaaahhhhh—ooooo!

Yeah, I'd go *ooooo* myself, too; some really good eatin' and a' head rollin' and all such games played before what you thought was time, but really wasn't, had an instant to begin. So, I ask—you there, out there where you are, or you, or you—or maybe you; do you want to take a try at lighting this burner that always worked before and you are sure will always work forever, now having heard this tale of mine, want to turn it? Want to? No? You? No? You not either? You mean you don't want to dwell in Hell with the big Nazi and all the little and littler Nazis nested inside him like a Russian wooden set of nested dolls, who were only following the orders of make-believe mystic magicians that just had mail-order PhD's anyway? They chose to turn some magical knob; or maybe they chose not to. But, gee, my God, Lord God, the egg! The magic egg I so deftly dropped, has burnt to a crisp black knob in the skillet while I was doin' all the palaver and what-how, not! I guess I made the choice very, very simple for you. I turned the damned knob, oh, myself, and mystic pale pygmies are not waiting at your destinations to spear, butcher, eat, laugh, and play around with your entrails after all! Oh, silly me. Silly, silly, me, but anyway; that egg was just the first of twelve. What of this next one? How wise might this one be, eh, eh—and after that, the eleventh. And the twelfth. And so forth. So, let's shut the gas and prepare for the next. But look out the porthole this time, when I turn on the gas. Dare you look out? Dare you? I dare you—dare to look and find out if you will see sea, or shore, or what! So, bye, that's it for now!

Nothing is real might be true, children—not just three words nipped off some song.

Screen snapped dark; blanket pushed away; naked and spent they lay, smothered in stationbreak and suddenly speaking much too fast.

What the hell did he say? What the hell?

I think, he said, breakfast is usually eggs-to-order accompanied by either sausage, or bacon. Or some such dither-bobbly!

Hah!

But! On the very Dakota Maru, out on the cold steel between giant ten-high stacks of Hapag-Lloyd, Maersk, OOCL, and tens of others of packed-full, dented, rusted and worn steel containers, Skip went on with his assigned job of working hard, while clutched in his gut by his never-ending hatred for the land. Black, slimy hands, cut and not cut, dead and notdead, he thought not about these things for fear of what they'd lead his mind to; there were three forks for the mind-genie to take, and it pondered all turbaned and smelly but luckily locked hidden airtight in his head. It decided to simply just put the thought of the evils of the land over to the side someplace in some random swirly cerebral folds, and brush by brush focused Skip to pondering in a simple circle, why Noman had risen and stormed off back to work, without waiting to help him find the fucking tool room. In the tool room, he had said, he knew, that he badly needed a new wire brush to grasp and shove back and forth over ice-cold steel turnbuckles, the rest of this single one of what might as well be a thousand shitty days, because weird things had happened, and his brush had simply snapped gone just like that, never even existed. But luckily, on the way back to steel city, he had by some dumb luck found the tool room easily. The bright purple steel door swung open smoothly, a rack of new tools stood up on the far wall; and there, front and center, were the brushes. All new clear wood handles. All bright brush-bristles glistening. Skip hesitated; tools he'd used all his years at sea were always old, filthy, greasy and worn out. Skip had never seen a clean new tool. This cache of new tools smelled too wrong, too clean, too much like some kind of little Mom and Pop hardware store on the land he dimly remembered being dragged to by his father, so he got out fast, after gripping a new brush, then, as the purple door sealed back away the evilly clean smell, he stopped. Right next to the tool room door, an identical door stood set in the wall, hinges and hasps and all of it, all, but solidly welded shut with a perfect smooth heavily-rusted steel bead all around. The door woke Skip's Genie, who sent the slow sway of the ship up Skip's legs, as the Genie always did when he was completely confused and two plus two somehow equaled five and the first two was out of phase with the second two, and it was saying very clearly, I am the Genie. You are facing something I cannot understand, but yet, at the same time, strangely do; look what is sloppily stenciled across the wall all faded: Dead In Here. You, Skip, do you understand that, why it says that, or are you out of phase too, with your life-self stood on this side of the door thinking some few instants that you remembered your dead-self on the other side of the door had spoken to you out of some make-believe machine? Yes, it's what I said; your very dead self on the other side of the door. I am you, no, I am you, no you're not, yes I am, no I'm not, you are dead, no I'm alive, but no, no, I beg your pardon, and at once, stars exploded in Skip's face and he opened his eyes and there was just a tall wide welded-shut door like a blank headstone standing there saying Dead In Here—and his rational thought generator pumped words up to his mouth just short of speaking, Wow, what a door! What does Dead In Here mean? Good god—and a voice too tiny and sweet to be heard over the noise that underlies everything in existence came up from the brand-new brush he hotly held in his hand.

It said, I am the same brush you lost, but I am when it was new. Yes! I am the same brush you lost but I am when it was new. Everything that's old again comes new. Everything worn out goes back to when it was new to start over. As a matter of fact—

But just at that instant a large hand from long ago came again and slammed into the side of the IBM monitor that had evolved into the head of Skip gradually and gradually until came today; Skip woke, turned, and no, no one was there—yes, he must have hit up against the sides of his head again, as always when his thinking blew him out of line, and as once before, everything was right, nothing surprising or out of the ordinary, and for sure, for sure, he had never been on the other side of the welded-shut door. He had never seen the welded-shut door. He had no idea nor was it any of his business why it said Dead In Here on the door.

Yes, and look how it's welded. All tightly welded. Being welded shut is kind of, in the world of steel stuff, kind of a forever moment. Sealed welded boxes are sealed forever. Sealed fifty-five-gallon steel drums are pretty much sealed forever. No escaping out or in of. Just forever inside. Black and dark and quietly forever. That thought gave him pause, fear of a sort, but mellow and distant enough pause from the flat awful day all left behind gone, to right here, right now, just about feeling fully alive again, scraping the new brush one thrust at a time back to old. So, now, he lay on his side on the busy steel street, Soviet army trucks, tanks, buses, and United States railroad cars crunching and crashing past. There was even a rickshaw or two on the street, chasing a lashed-up, skinny, pale, running-fast guy; a miss is as great as a mile, you know—he lay brushing the hold-downs of a big Maersk, and drifted back to wondering why Noman had been acting and talking so weird. That seemed something safe and calm and harmless to wonder about. They, after all, were about halfway to China. Weird acting and talking as Noman had done only usually begins after around the second month and when almost home, thank God. When almost back to land, Skip was. *Waterworld*, Skip. Think *Waterworld*. Or Chip, or Skip, or whatever fucking name she goes by today—Chip tapped his forehead lightly with the wooden tip of his wire brush, and everything made sense again. Like whapping the side of the computer terminal. Like robbing the plump black-clad IBM salesmonkey man. Like—being shocked as hell when applying the wrench to tighten a long rusty turnbuckle; but ouch! Ouch! Being surprised actually hurts one tiny second that's gone before it happens, and Lord, God, this is a problem at least once every voyage. It's all rusted up tight, too old, old and dead, and—the right thing to do is to cut it out with a torch and put in a new one. The reality hit; yes, yes, I am sorry, but; it has to come out. We got to cut it out. It's that tight, that bad—yes, we got to cut it out. The dentist told Skip this the first day he went there back in his babyhood, after they'd papoosed him all yelling in the chair. His first memory was of a person who he'd gone to for help had told them they could not help, unless they hurt him first. Where was Mother, Mother, please save me; but the length of the frozen-solid rust-locked turnbuckle came up over and around, and back to him thinking that the right thing to do is to cut it out with a torch. Burn into it, purify it, kill it, and give birth to the next one. May the next to endure torment please slip easily in out of the slimy birth-canal hole. Go from here. Go suffer and maybe you'll end up here. As a matter of fact, you will. Yes, yes—got to cut it out with a torch. Skip rose, again a man. Back to the tool room he must go. Torches must be in the tool room. Yes, in the tool room. Skip trudged between the steel walls expecting to go past the tightly welded Dead In Here door, and to enter the tool room, but; Noman came from no place, his blood all running down, his fat hand slapping against the welded-shut door, his mouth stating, half-yelling breathily, My God, open! My God, my God, whoever's inside, open!

Noman, said Skip; what's wrong, what has happened?

I need medical help, I need fucking medical help, I need help! I am dying! I am too young!

Why? What—young? Who, what?

Noman showed Skip his hands, the blood flowing.

My God! blurted Skip, in perfect but completely unknown unison with, My God, yes, My God! shouted by Father Dwyer, way up front far from Skip on the big flatscreen, deep into episode nine hundred nine of his unending cooking show, which at that particular moment had no viewers.

Yes, he said, Yes, God, just look at this, and he flopped over and over on the worktable before him a gigantic, roughly rectangular, hundred-pound slab of well marbled meat; it made one think of a blood-red summer sunset, with bright white spiky jagged lightning bolts flashing across. It was a sky of meat; not a slab, not even a sky, but a world of meat, freshly killed, harvested from a large, hairy, killed-by-motorcar creature, unrecognizable; but unrecognizable could mean I can't see it's good, but could just as well mean I can't see it's bad. So, the men in the road scouting for Dwyer roadkill meat who worked for The Only Way to Eat is Free, Inc., stabbed the meat as though murdering; and the meat was not bloody, but glistening and tasty looking, so the two carved out several dozen slabs and threw them in the back of their pickup truck, and thus through the proper channels the meat found its way to Father Dwyer's cooler, and he grabbed it up not knowing or caring what it was because it looked good, it smelled fresh, it was not bloody, and he winked at the driver of the pickup truck who delivered it three hours earlier, who sat on a milk carton, smoking, skinny, obviously summer-sweating heavily in a long-sleeved threadbare sport shirt, with a large, filthy, stained, decades-old cervical collar strapped around his neck. The driver's eyes were intact and clear; hence he was a fresh kill also, had he not been still alive. Watching the smoke go in and out his mouth, Dwyer paused and asked the man, You there. Yes, you. You work for the show, right? You an employee of The Only Way to Eat is Free, Inc.?

Yup, said the smoking man. Meat we got; you look good today? Do we please you today? Do we please?

Oh yeah, yeah, but I was thinking of explaining to the viewers today how to tell good edible roadkill from bad, spoiled-rotten-as-poison roadkill. Since you're here, and you probably know a lot more about this episode's topic than I, would you be up to coming on camera and telling our viewers how to tell good dead from bad dead meat from the roadside?

Yeah? Yeah. Oh, sure. Will I get scale?

What?

Union scale. For being on camera.

Yes, yes, yes, of course, laughed Father Dwyer from deep in his fatty bellyglobe, almost dropping the worldslab and almost spitting the cigar into—who? Who is this? This strange man out of nowhere, who? What is your name, my man?

Lil' Albert.

Yeah—okay, said Dwyer, nearly spitting his blunt stogie into

Lil' Albert's eye. Get up, come over, come up on camera with me, and after the show you'll have several reams of paperwork full of questions handed to you, and you'll be pointed to a small plastic chair by a young lady who you will remember nothing about but that she was blonde, and she'll give you a pen that barely writes and will tell you to take your time, I mean there's no rush, no rush at all, but hurry up and fill out these forms, most of whose contents you will not have the answers to, so that you can get paid, but that no one in the back office will read because they just piss money away everywhere anyway so they'll cut you a check, and the paperwork you spent three days filling out will already have gone through the incineration process, but you will have your money. So, get up, stomp out that butt, and come up on camera with me! Come on!

Father Dwyer came back around behind his stainless-steel worktable and slammed down the meat, splat, onto the cold steel, dead, but edible, healthy, good looking, and tasty. Lil' Albert came up beside Father Dwyer and popped his knuckly, skinny, bony fists down on the shiny steel, slightly splashing out splatter from the meat blood thinly seeping out across the table. His shirt was spattered across in a line. He ran his hand across the spatter as Father Dwyer bellowed at the camera obliviously, saying, Here, friends out there at sea. Let me introduce Lil' Albert, one of the best men in The Only Way to Eat is Free, Inc., group, every one of whom know good meat from bad, firsthand living and the dead, amen.

The dead center of the mass came and sat the parishioners soft on their pews.

So, Albert, what do you—

Albert raised his hand and said, Father, just a minute. The lights up here are damned hot. Can you turn the lights down? I get too hot, I can't think, it is not good to think Father; can we?

Dwyer patted Lil' Albert soundly on his shoulder and said, No, no, I'm afraid we can't put the lights down. We're on TV, you know. We need the lights on, OK? Anyway, he went on, facing the audience once more, shouting out, So, Lil' Albert, what can you tell our viewers about how you separate good dead meat found on the roadside from bad?

Lil' Albert stated confidently into the red light of the camera, Well, first, we look at how the dead creature was hit. It's the point of impact determines how much meat is salvageable. My experience with broadside impacts is not good. Internal organs usually rupture and taint the meat. Not to mention all the bloodshot meat. As in hunting, a head shot saves meat. Yeah—hey, one minute; Father, are you sure we can't turn the lights down just a bit? There is sweat running all down under this shirt, and this neck brace is choking hot, too.

No, no, said Father patiently. Just keep on telling them about the meat. You'll just be here a minute a minute or two, is all, maybe three maybe, is all, whatever; go on, he said, slamming Lil' Albert's blazing shirt shoulder soundly down, in, and through the skin.

Well, okay, here, said Lil' Albert, red-cheeked, hot; tire treads over the body usually means a bloody mess. Squashed meat requiring a spatula to remove from the asphalt also should be avoided. Also—if the eyes are intact and clear, the animal is likely a fresh kill. Cloudy eyes hint that the animal has been dead for some time. Over four-five hours—hey, Father. Listen, listen. It's too damned hot up here, I got to stop.

No, no, no—keep on, you're doing fine, yes go at it, man, Skip shouted again and again and again, looking down from Noman's shattered hands, to the great red pool spreading on the floor around his stricken shipmate; yes, you need medical, God damn, I know, but—

Okay I'm in! Get out of my way, I got to go in through the door!

Slipping and sliding on the slimy grisly deck, Noman rushed in the opened door. Skip looked the door up and down; it stood no longer welded; the sign said Medical—and the door beside the tool room somehow had changed, also, to a tall side steel plate welded permanently shut. The Medical door almost had closed behind Noman but Skip's boot tip shoved it over open and levered Skip in through the door following exactly the trail of blood droplets following behind Noman. Up on the far wall, yes, read it; Symptom: Bleeding out, it yelled quietly, calmly, just like before, and Noman stomped his ass down like a big wide boot on the little black leather circular seat and looked into the dusty screen and pushed and slapped and punched painfully at the knobs, levers, and buttons all around the screen, spattering red droplets all around, and at once the screen glowed, and Skip hardly knew what was happening before he found himself in a small room, as dark, moldy, and damp as a Catholic confessional, looking out a round hole filled with glass, right into Noman's wide round frightening face, which he'd pressed into the Bleeding Out machine's screen. Skip knew not where or what he was, but all of a sudden he opened the eyes he didn't know were closed and found himself saying at Noman's anguished face all flooding over him, I will help you. You are here for help. Nobody cares about me or thinks about me unless they need help. This is the burden of every doctor, human or otherwise. Do you know how many doctors commit suicide in this country every year? Well, I'll tell you. It's a large number, yes.

Jesus Christ, Jesus Christ, Jesus!

Yes. Very large.

Noman on the other side said, Thank you, oh thank you, to the digitized pixilated doctor, and thrust his hands to the elbow into the leather-ringed arm-cureholes. He did not know the anguished fear exploding back behind the Doctorscreen, he just felt his hands back there somehow being soothed, caressed, soothed, caressed—and he opened his eyes, and there he was looking out from the snack bar chair out onto the vast brightly lit never-ending array of bowling lanes, the balls randomly flowing down across the lanes, like droplets of blood seeping from some kind of crazy horizontal wound. Years he had sat there. Years after doing the gush-puke on the general, but years before slowly steel-brushing in the hot solvent the next and the next and the next next next of the five hundred ten dark steel compartments he'd scrape down for no reason all the way from New York to Shanghai, and back. Ah, yes, Shanghai, Shanghai, there was something very significant about the approximate date they'd get to Shanghai, but the balls rolled teardropping horizontal tears from his eyes; it's something about the bowling alley, the Dakota Maru, and her very lengthy trip to Shanghai; something very sorrowful in between; something very angering and saddening all at once; someone saying, Do it, or lose everything. Do it, or lose anything that may have been gained between the snack bar stand and Shanghai; between releasing the ball, hearing the roll, and then the blast of the strike, sorrowful, happy and sorrowful all at the same time, once, years; yes—the years compressed in one instant of pain; the balls roll, the brush scrapes, the solvent boils, the strikes and spares blast, and Skip's there when the blast clears; why, who, what, when—Noman dropped his eyes down from the rolling balleyes, and came up beside a small suffering woman, and a girl never-married, bundled all up in words, breathing, Can I serve you, sir? You look absolutely bushed. How about a Schlitz?

Huh?

Noman looked into this woman's eyes, embedded magically in a copy of Skip's, and she's there with them rolling bowling balls into the distance crashing the strikeblast out, unveiling Shanghai! And, he jumped from his bunk in the dark, someplace still dark and stinking so the only thing to do became to climb the ladder up, higher, up, up away high, and out. The tap of the drop of the brush rang in the steel, as he looked up at her, stating loud and clear, No, sorry I don't drink! How dare you think you can make me drink! Go away, leave me alone, I have much to see, much to do, and to see too, so; I got to leave the alley, yes; got to leave the alley! Yes; remember, remember; you are zero. Nothing but zero, and remember there are two kinds of zero; zero that started as zero and has been zero ever since, and zero that had been something higher more and better but that something had tapped in deflating it back down, to zero. Like a female that is not pregnant can be so the same two ways. A man who is not lying with a woman can be so the same two ways, also. Like this—this bowling ball I am lifting, as I turn my back on you, strange woman; this bowling ball I step with toward the glass front door of this bowling alley, that you have forced me to become locked inside of after closing, to trap me into knowing again why the date of our arrival in Shanghai is important, because you never existed yet; you are afraid, so afraid, so alone, yes—no, no, I will not think it; there goes the big black ball flung out quick; shattering, blasting, through the tempered glass door, making a hole I may leap to the dark through, and remain unmarried, which, of course, can be two different ways; unmarried because never ever got married, or unmarried because once married and now—no don't think more, face facts, you are ignorant and selfish; no, leap, leap, leap; leap!

You I said; yes! you! You are ignorant and selfish! Leap disappearing to the dark.

Noman leapt through the front door of the bowling alley, but at the moment the door never was again, he snagged his out-flung hand over a last remaining shard. He nearly slipped down away, nearly adding insult to injury, straddling the sudden spreading pool of blood.

You are ignorant and selfish! Leap disappearing to the dark.

Tendons and flesh ripping brought pain; but he did not recall the moment he was snagged, or what he was doing, coming from, or going to when he was snagged, he just knew: must heal this wound; this is not the same as the blood of the savior; this is where Noman climbed up and out and came out a door, slipping and sliding toward the medical department, and ran smack rip tear right through the sudden Skip that shot up before him, causing

Skip to bristle, goose-bump, jump, and yell, Noman! What's wrong, what has happened?

You are ignorant and selfish. Leap away; disappear into the dark.

No! No, I am not! No!

Where are you hiding the door, Skip; where? Oh, there it is—let me by! My God, let me go in there! My God, my God, whoever's inside, open! My God, I need medical! I need immediate—if not sooner—medical help, I need help, I'm dying!

Why? What? Huh? Spit it out, man! What, do not ram me, don't ram, hey!

Noman ran right through Skip, reaching—Yes, the door, give it! Yes, the door, open it!

What?

This! yelled Noman, lifting his hands, splattering a red mist over Skip.

This!

My God! blurted Skip, as Noman turned away, not wanting to die of a bleed-out, knowing that there are two ways to have lost all blood; to never have been born and be nothing that ever needed blood at all, or to have been alive and cut open and drained to empty. At once, the bleeding-out machine's screen reappeared holding a face he knew. The smile of the face was soft and airy and told him to yank on his arms, and he was aware again that the doctor machine had been needed, sure that's why he was here, but why was he, really? Oh, yes, silly me. Yes, his palms, oh yes. They lifted to his face. Yes. Just palmlines. Clear, clean, intact, healed, soft, and purely just palmlines, on Noman, God's creation.

Oh, my God, thank God!

You are ignorant and selfish, leaping away disappearing into the dark, but, such may even so still be God's creation; these words faded back with Skip's God face receding back in the mist of the big round screen, before Noman could know it was Skip and not God in the machine. God in the machine, God. God the great doctor in the big machine; the big flat black machine on the wall up on the bridge where Lil' Albert continued crying, It's too damned hot in here, Father! Let me strip to the waist because it's so hot in here! Okay?

No, wait. Albert, no. Don't do that.

Albert, regardless, ripped at his filthy sweat-stained cervical collar to remove it, as he would in moments rip off his shirt, his belt, and further, until enough had been removed to provide relief from the heat of the studio stage lights; beefy plump-cheeked Father Dwyer gripped his forearm. The priest's cigar crumbled ashes all down the stifling, never washed, jet black priest-shirt he'd worn forever, as he cried, No, no, Albert; no no! We must remain clothed here, it's just hot during this one episode—go on talking Albert, go on, you've done fine so far, so what else about this roadkill eh?

The burly Father Dwyer twisted Lil' Albert's arm behind him, making the filthy, skinny man grimace, and as he shook his head no, no, no, Father Dwyer threw his whole black-clad burly self into the tightening arm-twist, and shouted in the ear of the agonized man, who listened gasping, eyes strained shut, chin dripping with flying sweat drops and tears.

What else, demanded the burly priest—what else about the roadkill? Huh? Huh?

Down squeezed his fat hands, causing Albert to ooze, Okay, okay, yes I can tell you that creamy discharges around the eyes or other orifices indicate a sick animal. If the eyes are gone, leave it alone, let it rot, go—please, let me go please, it is so damned hot!

No! shouted Dwyer, droplets forming on his forehead. The priest twisted Albert's arms back tighter, squeezing words from the thin man's face like toothpaste from a tube; Albert said, when the pain meter touched extreme, Okay, this I'll tell you; I can tell you that rigor mortis sets in within a few hours of death. This is not a deal breaker depending on other indicators. The steak in the butcher's glass counter has undergone the same process of decay or tenderizing. Father, fat guy you are, but; please let me go now, you are killing me, let go of me now, let go you slimy wormy flunkie! Here!

With a strong sudden writhe, Lil' Albert twisted free of the weakening fat priest's slimy sweaty hands, and spun to the end of the worktable; then, quicker than a tug on a magic zipper, stripped himself down from the neck, to the beltline, flung the shirt and collar and all at the camera, where it caught, stuck, and caused screens to go dark worldwide, just as Father Dwyer shouted, No, God damn! Albert, no! The audience can't know, no they can't they can't, no! No! Here! My God, they can't see the tattoos!

My God!

The tattoos!

Through the scuffle behind the black, Albert's words wove in and out from the general loud rattles, bangs, and grunts, somewhat like that in a *Cops* rerun on TV, when for the hundredth time fifty fat blue men strapped with clattering gear, guns, and radios attempt to subdue a small drunk man at three in the morning, in the poison ivy bushes at the roadside, on a hot summer night when the humidity's skyrocketed, saying, Fleas feed on the blood of warm-blooded animals. Brush the hair on the carcass and inspect for fleas like you would on a family pet. If fleas are present, that's a good thing. Fleas won't stick around on a cold body—my God, Father, no my God, please stop, just stop—

God damn it, stop resisting, or: more charges will be applied! Your sentence will be long, cold, and weary. Here, tighter! Feel my strength, bastard?

This is art! yelled Albert; we agreed, these are not mere tattoos! I am a work of art!

Stop resisting, or we will crush you. Here, feel that? Yes. Feel it. Now.

All right, okay, let go, damned Jesus—so you also need to consider that there's usually blood involved when animals come in contact with three thousand pound machines speeding along over the highest speed limits in the world—all right, all right; give me my fucking shirt! Rip it away!

No! cried Dwyer. No one can see you like this, no one, thank God when you stripped down the shirt flung up on the camera! And you're also damned lucky that this studio is fully automated too, and no fussy, skinny, pissed-at-never-having-been-recognized-as-an-up-and-coming-star in this business, will get all fussy, all self-involved, and rip the rag from the camera, because no one can know where I got you. I will seem crazy to take you marked as you are!

Father, look; these are marks of God, we agreed! said Lil' Albert behind the blank screen. These are signs that mean no one can touch me! These drawings were all earned, I told you—and you just smiled. You were so different then. I was your boy, you said it was all right, you said I could have the job, you brought me up on stage with you. Why?

Because I thought you would behave! I did not think you would strip down!

Clanks, rattles in the poison ivy brush, the sweaty blue men struggling, crying, Give me my shirt, I can put it on, I need this job, don't rob me of this job, please officer sir!

Shut up and talk; stop resisting, let us cuff you. It's all poison ivy here! We got to get you and get away from the ivy! You not listen we will pound you! You will have blisters and burns! Talk! Talk on!

All right, damn you, yes; the next thing to know is that blood all a-spatter over the road would mean there's too much damaged meat to salvage—hey, look, Father. I told you. I was initiated; here, on my chest, see this woman? This rose-woman? I am of the elect, you believed, the day I signed on, after my prison sentence was up. You said, You are welcome, Albert, to The Only Way to Eat is Free Corporation! You said that; we shook hands; my dreams were fulfilled; this rose, I had earned, you believed! I thought you believed, we were a train on a track all flying-like, yes, so you hired me—here, my shirt! Get it, give it—

No! Go on, go on, the show must go on to the end, the end! The end! Quiet down, do the show. People are watching. The—end! Just *stop resisting*!

Okay, okay, no reason to choke me, daddy, not choke me, please—uh, I think the next thing we go by is that the color of any blood present at the kill scene should be dark red, like, fresh blood; listen, Father, my neck is aching so—lay off, please—

Shut up, no! Talk—talk. Go on, go on. You with no fucking shirt! You crossed the line, so this is your first and last broadcast, because you ignored my rules! Look! See! You!

What—gaaaagh, don't squeeze so hard! For the love of God!

That heart inside a triangle there—you told me what that meant, and that that was your passport for thirty years of a very busy life in prison!

Dark puddles of blood have been there, been there a while; it means the meat's no good.

What meat? My meat, your meat?

This meat—this meat, here! I grind you like this!

The sound of a two by four against a hung-up ice-cold side of beef rattled the screen nearly loose from the steel wall.

Damn you, skinny bastard! How dare you strike me!

It seems as if it is strike or die at this point! See the naked woman all raw spread on my chest? The one with the nipples that are my nipples too? See her sweet well-oiled breasts, priest? I bet you want her, and behind her, me! You're beating me for deeper reasons! As in secrets told in the quiet confessional! The secrets, the secrets, the secrets you know, they are luscious! The breasts have deeper meaning, yah, I never told you, but no, no—noo!

Shut up now! Go on!

I refuse to submit! You are the devil; I will not say yes to the devil; I won't!

You! Here! Tighter now. Like that? Huh? Like that, you bastard?

At that a wobbly and confused Skip, unsure if he was among the living or the dead, stumbled onto the bridge and stopped, facing the blank flat black TV screen all shouting out from the wall; shouted out shouting, out shouting, out: Flies are a bad sign, Father, don't kill me please. A fucking bad sign, very, very, Lord God, stop choking me, Satan!

I read in a book that involuntary tattoos are made pornographic if the victim has unpaid gambling debts—I knew that, I did! And I hired you anyway, despite the sloppy tits and the sloppy ass, because you have a way about you. That's why I hired you!

Flies lay larvae in wounds and other openings of the body.

Yes! Yes! Yes, I hired you because I thought you were going to do as you promised, to turn over a new leaf, and you were doing so well, until now, up here, I said no one can see you nude, no one can see the scrawling all over you—those—but you are so stupid you almost showed yourself through the network to every ship at sea! Sailor? Is that how you think? Here, I choke you harder! What? You think this job is on board some damned prison ship, is that what you think man? Sorry, but this is a family show! Hah!

Hard upthrust gag, shooting with spittle.

Ugghh—God, no, let me go! Let go, ease up! Look at my nautical stars, damn you, Father! They are on my knees, see them? They are scarred and painful, to make me remember that I kneel before no one. There are also two on my shoulders. Every move of my arms sets them stabbing! They make me remember to not fear authority. Only God can give authority. God gave you none, Father, sweet lying humper of a reverend. Listen, look, what, hey! If you let me go at this point I will just turn and confront and attack and gouge your eyes instantly. I do not need your phony job. Nothing's been the same since I got out of prison. Nothing's changed since you found me bleeding in the street. I was like roadkill to you. Something to eat to you, I was. I want prison again! I want prison, I want home! Let me go so I can turn and grip you and end your useless life—

Dwyer gagged Albert quiet by the throat, yelling, Speak! Finish! Get back on topic! Get on back, this is a show, do the show! Go on! Now!

Ugghhh! God, no, okay. Here; a few flies around the corpse isn't a bad sign. Unless the animal had a wound prior to being struck, and already was full of maggots—Jesus, God, Lord God almighty, you're a damned strong priest, Father. Rather a devil of a priest, you are; horny damned dark, howling, horny devil of a priest; that's what landed you on here with me, I bet.

How many bodies have you trailing behind you? How many dead? Huh? Speak man!

Ahhhhhh! All right, yes all right, I'm near the end, sure—

Flickering flashes crossed the screen, making Skip think the picture would appear and explain in some way all these crazy yells and screams; but the flashes faded as the rough choking voice finished talking about the skulls on its knuckles. It cried fast, quick, See the skulls on my knuckles! That's my number of murders. Murders, yes murders! And you will fill one more if I ever can get free and turn this scene into something else. Maybe something about a live deer found in a backyard long ago, it's hindquarters splintered from a days-old vehicle collision, the legs and hips slimy and red and totally half-covered in a quarter's worth of maggots, but—the eyes, yes, something about the eyes, and the crucifixes there, right there, see? Under the fur there? That means whoever was talking was not of the authority to approach and attempt to humanely dispatch the poor live dying-slow deer. So, she went back in the woods forgotten, to someone else's regret; Skip swayed back and forth on the steel deck of the bridge, completely shut down, frozen and confused, as the screen finally said, Heavy on meat, heavy on gravy; light on the vegetables. What's that, now? A swastika? Yes? Is that what you're wearing on your chest these days? Well that is more than enough, you're fired, and no loss; because we successfully got to the end anyhow! Here, here, here! And, all at once, a bolt struck and woke up Skip, as the black ripped off from the screen, on which simply stood the familiar Father Dwyer in the surging bright light, who'd just flung something large, ugly all sweaty and a-flail, thrashing off-camera, having just commanded the skeleton crew in the last of the blackout to eject the horrid thing that no one at sea could ever see, all the way out the building, and he tucked his shirt, wiped down his face, and smiled at the camera all calm, surrounded on all sides by his chrome and stainless-steel bright-lit gleaming kitchen, saying, Okay, then, folks, that wraps this episode! I can't explain, I can never explain, send us a card or a letter and maybe upper management will explain, but I'm sworn not to. I cannot, cannot, cannot. Any questions? And, yes, yes; Skip took a step toward the screen, raised his hand, and started to ask, but before a word could come out, Dwyer's raised hand slashed down, saying Good! It's good there's no questions! And, across pulled another Aspercreme ad, which Skip turned from, having used that ointment years ago and discovered he was allergic and ended up covered in baseball-sized hives, plus nothing tasted like anything anymore.

 He turned and walked back in his head to the moment he'd stood off the great ship's bridge, in the dark silent room back behind Father Dwyer, staring into the round glass hole into the dark, again and again, yes, but it came at him this time, not from him: Nobody cares about me, or thinks about me, unless they need help. This is the burden of every doctor, human or otherwise. The eternal burden of the Gods. Do you know how many Doctors commit suicide in this country every year?

 Skip raised his hand, and, not being able in the dark to see it, he felt he had none, yes, plus, somehow he had no lips either. Muted this way, he struggled to answer some question he'd somehow forgotten in the middle of his being asked it, so, soundlessly, he rose;

and, thinking that this meant he at least still had legs, he rushed out the door he found luckily in the dark and turned around to the blinding light all around, and the sign on the door took him back.

Tool Room

God, Jesus, what, no! And, what's more, the door beside was again the steel plating welded shut under the ghost of what had said Medical—and he quickly turned around and around, in his head quietly shouting up another headache, saying, Where is Noman? Hadn't Noman been all bleeding? No, no, guess not, he breathed, before plunging through the tool room door to get that which he'd come for. A torch, yes. A torch to cut away some rusted solid turnbuckle in the steel wall by the steel street full of army tanks of all nations and eras all rushing that he'd come from, and in a mere snap, it seemed like he had the torch and was back on the steel street with the army tanks rumbling, idling, still there, thank God, still there, Jesus, so; it was safe; so, he started torching through the frozen steel as though he'd been there all along, yes! But why did the flame make him see miles and miles of baseball-sized blistered, allergic, innocent suffering flesh? Wow—and the steel gave way, sucking up the flame, and the torch both. Why? Where? Where'd it go? Yes, don't say that, think that, because there must have been a torch, you fool, 'cause the steel's sliced through, but God, why, yes, it seemed the company let the Dakota Maru take to sea without adequate inspection, which might lead to unthinkable disaster far out of sight of any land, if not on this trip, then on another, that must inevitably arrive, as it is written that—Ouch! he cried out, snapping his face quiet, his finger pulling back from the scalding, still, steel. My God, why is it still hot? We are days out, and it's still hot, yes—there must be a fire in this container, whose container is this? My God! He rose feeling the cold steel up and down, and knew, No, there is no fire, so why are the mysteriously severed turnbuckle's stumps all flaming hot? The burning bush, yes; must be the burning bush; yes! The burning bush! God! Only God!

God's watching me, no my God, God's watching!

He stepped back, all fearfully aghast. In the eye of God, Skip was brimming with sin. If nothing else, just the porn-flesh upon porn-flesh upon porn-bones, -flesh, and -blood, all dog-eared, stained way back under the mattress of his bunk. Somehow, no, oh my God, no, Jesus made flesh had discovered his porn, and the turnbuckling quickburning bush spoke booming all out loud, crackling like Hell might crackle.

Though he was no Moses, God spoke to him. Maybe God was practicing to speak to Moses later. Skip's just a test for God. Or perhaps an exercise to improve all the flubs in dialogue God had committed the first time he tried out his play for Moses. The bush a stage! A stage for God! Skip backed off, fear level rising. If you were in a room for one hour with God, his Grandmother had said on her deathbed, if you were in a room for one hour with God and could get any question you want answered, what would that question be? Having asked that, the bush fell back into a turnbuckle again, that had never been rusted solid tighter than welded in the first place. No, it had not. It was fine, yes, all smooth, shiny, and loose. Why? Skip stood staring. What, what. Something about blisters, yes. Blisters, baseballs, and Aspercreme. He turned and ran padding the barefoot floor to get fast as possible to medical, because never in his life had he been able to properly scrutinize the state of his back. Hives, itch, bees, and wild blackberries. Need to run for home, yes, need to.

Yes! Skip turned, running, slipping and sliding over the ice-cold steel, not watching, just thinking, There's baseball-sized blisters all over my back, baseball-sized blisters all over my back, baseball-sized blisters, baseball-sized blisters, baseball-sized, baseball-sized, baseball-sized, yes—no, foot, don't stop, I'm still moving but, no, black slam of head on something hard flashing, down on the steel all prone I am. Prone and sliding and what was I running for? What was I running for in the dark, eh, what oh what oh what oh, eh—

Father Dwyer boomed Skip down, swarming words out in every direction, saying, shouting, So! So here you are, seamen! Episode one thousand of *Sunday Dinner with Father Dwyer*—an achievement we will celebrate by allowing the Lord my God to speak his wisdom from this teeny tiny burning bush; and on the table the camera panned over a little Christmas-tree-style bush, live, or fake, didn't really matter, because here comes, comes, comes the Lord Thy God. Yes, the Lord boomed from the small pretty fire, Supper is smaller, but is otherwise similar to lunch! What else do you need to know, hey there, Father? What else? I am God, you know.

Uh, said Father Dwyer, through his short fat flushed fingers pressed to his lip, I thought you were going to run the show today, My Lord. We talked last night, I knelt before the main altar in the inadequate heating of the great chilly church at nine in the evening in this here January, all dark around, heat turned down, silent, silent; as befits great holiness—I prayed, Lord, come do show one thousand tomorrow, I will prepare the bush! God, please!

What bush? you said from the sanctuary—blowing out great cold winds saying it again and again demanding an answer, What bush, what bush, what bush, what—and in the gale, I screamed at the top of my squeezed-out lungs, The burning bush! From the bible, my God! And the wind stopped instantly. It was like, like—

Like what? said God impatiently from the bush—What? Hurry, man, hurry, stop blubbering, my time is precious, you know, I am important, I am the boss, I run all 'round heaven, all meetings day and night! Come on spit it at me, man, don't waste my preciously holy time!

Okay, okay, it was like one day, Lord, when I lay in the back seat of a moldy, damp nineteen-fifty Ford, laying, watching pounding rain which someone I never will see again was driving through toward home from the weekly trip to visit Grandma, so mundane, you know, so mundane it sounds, yes, I know it does, I know, but—

What! cried God shrilly.

—but the rain, I was only just used to rain, and he who runs the clouds shut them off. And in less than a snap, we were sailing along through a bright sunshiny day! Cutting along fast, smooth as a cruiser! My Lord, God, my Lord, I had never ever been wakened so fast, so hard, and so completely! All the raindrops instantly came together into wires running, dipping, and rising from pole to pole as the car pushed faster now toward home, now that the weather was clear! Do you get it?

Yes I do!

Are you sure? It was magic!

Yes, I am!

Say it again!

I am.

Then, thunder!

And Father Dwyer awoke embarrassed more than even all the husbands fallen asleep to embarrass the wives next to them, in bright-lit churches 'round the world just before it's time to rise at the start of the seven thirty a.m. Sunday mass—Dwyer jumped, writhed, and pounded the tabletop, which also had been snoozing, and which when wakened absorbed the burning bush, God and all, down through the stainless steel, all gone.

But, there's no hole, how did it go, there needs to be a hole, yes—

Take! cried a voice from the forward dark, snatching away the end of the sentence. Take one of episode one thousand! Of your show! Remember your show, sleepyhead? Remember you are here, and only are kept alive by the state to do episode after episode of your very fake all plumped up and overrated stupidly foolish stumbling along for far too many years, containership cooking show?

Table talk! My God, it is true, table talk is all too real—Dwyer strained to think out words to keep the ropy episode going to the end: Supper is smaller, but is otherwise similar to lunch! he cried—Jesus Christ, people, when I say the word *supper*, what pops in your mind? Why do I have to tell you what to see? It is there, within you! Supper, I say! Yes, supper! Think the word, think it, look inside at what's there to see!

Father Dwyer's eyes now fully opened, and he sat at Mother Babushka's dinner table. She was a grey crone, all hairy, and she was interviewing him for the job, back when he was a deceased boy, brought to life by electronic signals from someplace, holographically probably, from some vast dim unknown left behind—Why do you think you are suited to the job, Mister Dwyer? Why? Mister Dwyer!

It is Father Dwyer, ma'am, he slid out politely. Not mister. Father.

Father? What? Why father?

I am a man of the cloth. I want this job! I can cook, chef! I know I can!

Okay. We can talk about whether you're really a man of the cloth or not, later—but now, describe me a supper. Big, fattening, spicy, summer-evening supper with friends, all casual but not really.

Huh? What do you mean all casual but not really? I don't know.

Why don't you know? You should know!

Please tell me!

On the wide flatscreen, far out on the Dakota Maru, no one stood idly to see the end of the pitiful episode one thousand that had just been taped, and thank God, the company snoozed too, and let it go. It should have been purged, yes! Purged! Yes, purged from God in the burning bush, way below now all trapped, in the big dark slimy steel box containing Noman, which, frightened by the holy bush, spat Noman out into open water. Ice cold like a Navy seal in the winter surf at three a.m., after a snowstorm, being barked barked barked at by fresh-as-a-daisy gigantic winged drill-sergeants, so unlike the recruiting commercials that Noman will never see.

Yes, Noman?

You out there Noman?

Out there all cold and wet and needing to piss?

Not to piss in the water!

Not!
No!
Not!
Noman?
Noman, get the hell back to the beach, now!

Noman got footing, stood in the water, the ice-cold wave-splash crashing behind, yes him, helping him toward the beach, a few more feet with each surge, propelled like whale-farts all surging, and there appeared a spot of light from someone on the beach, beckoning. Thank God, I am destined to be saved, he said to himself, and he strained ashore from the ice-cold dark wet, came toward the light, and stopped up against a voice saying, Noman, Noman, you are once more a failure. Why the hell did a wimp like you apply for this unit? You are the worst loser! The worst I've seen in my seventy-five dim years!

I—I—

Noman found he was much too cold, wet, and shivering to answer.

Why do you not answer, trainee? Why do you not answer? Obey, and answer. Obey!

The light spun around and folded into a tiny fir tree, bushed out all spiky, matching the bone-dry words coming out winding as a huge warm towel, all around Noman, saying to him, Noman. Look around. Life is a steel box; your life will be thrown away into floating steel boxes all welded 'round, yes welded all 'round! The name of the ship will be, Dakota Maru!

What? Well—oh my gosh, my gosh, I—I know that name sometime, but not just yet.

The towel absorbed the drenched chilled words Noman tried to force out, and the tiny tree in the air with dark all around continued to talk from its glowing gut, You will end up in my belly, Noman. You will work in my belly for twenty or twenty-five years, as corrosion, metal fatigue, and the stress and strain on the containership

Dakota Maru, which is your home, will take its toll, and we will be at the Sri Lanka shipbreaker's yard, the light grasping down at you and the steel all torched through, all fallen away! See the light coming down, see it! See it. Life as you know it will change and you will be back where you were when you were living month over month, living evil, escaped into the scraping down of the steel, to be vomited out into your real life as God, that's me, intended it, but no damn you, no, I—

The glow pulsated, pausing, pulling at Noman; the pause grew and drew words from his mouth that he did not know until they came up, around, and plugged tight, sliced stabbing pain into his ears, as, Tell me, why do you stop? Talk to me talk! I don't know where I am, what I am, who you are, no, you're not God, see? You're not God, you big faker. You ran out of steam just like the fleshly mortal blood-pumping thing you are, not human obviously, but certainly no God. God is—

The tree flamed up, cutting him off, the burning bush went all gone to the fire that went up the flue heating the bottom of the stainless-steel table before Father Dwyer, glowing it up so hot that the priest could use it as a cooktop. Good, good, no dishes to do Father, no, no, no dishes to do, no loss, not at all, no, not now and not ever!

And, with that, all around Noman appeared a gagging mouth letting him go, cursed to slide into right where he started, the face of Phyllis receded away forward, back into visibility; it came over swallowing him where he sat way back in the bowling alley, with her question grasping him back onto the very stool he thought was already sat on once and vanished into just a smoky memory, and she came moving, speaking all around him in the bright light of the bowling alley again, with the ball-rolls pressing behind her in a most sensuous manner.

Can I serve you, sir? she said, all bright blonde. You look absolutely bushed. How about a Schlitz?

My Lord Jesus, cried Noman.

She laughed at him, eyes bright sparkling, before he could answer, and Father Dwyer far above flipped his fresh pancakes, and Skip, wherever he was, said, Noman! What's wrong, what has happened? What's wrong, what's happened?

My God, where am I?

What?

What, Skip?!

What happened, to your—

What? What!

—to your hands?

The question brought Noman's palms to his face, all very crooked long lines.

Wounds! Dear God, my God!

What Noman?

The stigmata of the Christ! Please God, please God, no!

Huh?

These wounds! This pain! This blood! My God!

Damn you man, get a grip!

A clamp tightened down on Noman's shoulder, telling him no, his eyes don't see hands, they are closed somehow; bloody hands glowed into his veiny eyeballs from implanted seeds placed by the Automated Doctor into the back of his lids. Open! The hands went, gone! Light shone all around a big fat black head talking; shining spiky and hard like the light around the shadow of the moon on the sun in an eclipse. Out of the head fell words. Yes, yes—no stigmata but just out of the head, words, to the floor, all bouncy.

So, I have to say, Noman, the fact you never actually got married is a revelation to me.

After the words plunged down Noman's gut, they pulled along like a bright yellow caboose sliding behind Skip's face all charging forward, and click, yes, great, it's again the lunchroom.

Wow, yeah, oozed Noman into Skip, wreathed all around by the foursquare eat-space—and I got this shitty job because I thought

I was married; have a Schlitz, sailor-boy; she said that, just that, and I had to run. I knew, I knew. You know what I mean?

Yeah, but hey, Noman. Your hands are shaking, look!

Noman's coffee cup vibrated all a-splatter alongside his tremor, which stopped as soon as he looked it in the face; and it thought to itself evasively, out past visual range, hiding, I cannot let him know I am here; he cannot know the real world hiding all around and behind that he must never see. Everybody has a reality lurking just out of range that they must never see. Everybody—yes, you too, Noman. So, talk! Distract yourself now, yes now, baby you—

Oh, Skip, that shake is nothing. It's nothing really, just nothing, you know.

As Noman brought the cup to his lips, the fact of his coffee having gone cold because of all his unconscious time-consuming shenanigans caused a rift once more between himself and the lunchroom's reality, as: It's really nothing, yes, nothing at all. What's more important for me to now know more than how deeply Phyllis is plunging down her tokophobia steep-ramp, which is targeting her for termination into the Shanghai bullseye date which is rushing up, all baby, you know, hung up to be sexed like a baby chick, flying at the dead center? The bullseye, yah, uh, no, yes—Oh, Skip! How the arrow fears the sudden-stop slice into the bullseye, ah, yes, no—you wish—yes no, but a lash filled his head with lightning strokes, sweeping Skip away again, as the painfully ugly big boss behind shouted down all close, hot, Get up, Noman. Get up, I caught you again. Get up, you coward! Here, let me grip you! On your very first day, you cannot be so lazy! On your very first day, you cannot be so afraid! But look out there!

Turning, Noman saw a hulk in the distance, being stripped, and—he cried against the vista of darkness towering one at a time off out to the horizon, at the iron giants, the hulks near and far, melting up-close to a line of creatures utterly dark. Are those tiny ones creeping, there, those, are they ants? No, they are not ants; they are Noman's fellow workers in the knee-deep mud swarming with hair, guts, rot meat, dead leathery sinew strands. No, he thought, no, not in that filthy… but at his back pressed the ugly big boss's hand, from his great booming voice, repeating, Join the line of ants, Noman; join the line, yes, go! On your very first day, you cannot be so lazy! On your very first day, you cannot be so afraid! Noman; join the line, yes, go! On your very first day, you cannot be so frightened. Grit your teeth. Grit them bloody and go on!

Noman's bare foot touched the ice-cold black mud, for the first time, and, No, he thought, no! It would have been better with Phyllis, yes, with Phyllis yes it—

A spark struck miraculously from the touch of flesh on mud, abruptly changed the channel, as; Father Dwyer burst through the weak tissue-paper football-game-style banner made just to last five minutes, saying, Sure! Yes!

No no no no!

The Dakota Maru!

No, Lord, not that!

Not the Dakota Maru!

You, it's not even close to the time you have to break the Dakota Maru!

Break? How?

Dwyer gripped up a fish from the nearly liquid stinging mud.

Stop, yelled the splashing, crashing down, sucking toxic mud. Stop!

Clouded over fast, then reappearing in the bright light of the film studio, the large silver fish slimed against the scaling Father Dwyer immediately began administering. The fish yelled as Dwyer scaled hard, not realizing in his passion that life still pumped through the silvery suffocating creature. The fish yelled, Stop! Yes! Stop! Oh! No! Oh—as Dwyer once more stated off the teleprompter the praises of the sweet, sweet, sweetmeats et cetera that lay spread before him on the massively expensive studio Iron-Chef-quality super-sized spotless brand-new worktable before him, as: The twilight is down, the scales are up the front of my habit, thank God we have a large rusty remanufactured very cheap washing machine rattling around someplace in the rectory, that would get this clean, after the show, when we have scaled, fried, and consumed the chewy, finely fashioned demi-glace right here; and it will be time, though I never sleep, after God blesses my left leg and knee-hip with essence of lidocaine and Romero bros. scorching yellow salve. I will bed myself neatly and comfortably, and that will be it. Yes, and as I sink into the dark mist of night, I will be relieved that it is finished.

No! cried the skinny wild producer-tress named Mary, newly appointed after Lil' Albert raged through the offices cutting hearts, hands, and heads neatly and messily away. And, after accumulating a bouquet of these, the misfired badly hired ex-con Lil' Albert shot down the building, plunged down the elevator, smelling freedom, but when he shot through the silvery sliding doors onto the expensively tiled and grouted ground floor, he slammed right into a blazingly loud grand-finale firestorm of a supercop-volley. From the center of the bouquet bloomed the prior-producer-tress, Diana; Hearts and hands! Hearts and hands! Here are their hearts and hands, Lil' Albert had cried, even though gut shot, turning from the pistols back into the elevator, which pistoned him down to the devils of Hell, quite quickly, loudly, all scarlet and bloody; clean tiles no more; clean tiles all spattered. This was the instant they promoted Mary, the next-in-command at the studio, namesake of the great blue-robed virgin above, to be the Father Dwyer assistant. She leapt from the dark right into the action, screaming all witchlike for a do-over of the current episode; sweetmeats are not fish, she shouted broadly, stopping the action with a tiny wave. Fish are not sweetmeats and sweetmeats are not fish! Who loaded the teleprompter with yesterday's lines! Huh? Dwyer, man, stop now. Now! We got to do the intro over again, and again and again. Come on, guys!

Dwyer glowered from under his great brow, saying, Why? Why? Why is that, Mary? I was on a roll, this is my fiftieth year, you are new and green, so I will be always right, that's a fact you need to learn to live with, yes; I—

But a horde of helpers came out from hiding behind Mary, and flowed all over Dwyer, as Mary flung off fiery gales of laughter, and enveloped him higher and higher in a mass of small slimy slippery living very plump squirming eels, like the ones as a boy Skip and Noman and he had set on the concrete platform above the Main street dam in Milltown. The eels trapped in their dirty rusty Dinty Moore can were all a-squirm to escape wildly. Amazing how they just flow up and out of the can, said Skip. How do they do that? Dwyer squinted hard, pulled his stogie from his plumped-up lip-socket below his fiery young mustache, and told the small boy, They are special. That's how they do it. And, you are special too, yes, you're a great gifted child, and you will do great things; and as usual, he said this after making sure the child's Mother was near, all listening, beaming, beaming and beaming brighter toward bursting, higher and higher with each hug he gave the child, and more, yes, yes, yes. Here—

No! cried Mary, waving. No, no, no! Those are the day before yesterday's lines! Who's in charge of loading the teleprompter today?

As Dwyer turned to face her, the dam slid aside and she transformed into a simple photo of a vista of giant-hull hulks, off on the mud-flats all in the haze, that he once saw in a National Geographic the boy sat leafing through in the dim room, long ago. The haze of time pulsated all around him, and here she came, in her presence, behind, saying, Don't turn around, son, no. Not around. She sent the tentacles of her smell out all around him, and though her son did not hear what she said from her lips, the words lingered in the smell, and he heard it. In the magazine page, up through the barren vista, came her face. He did not need to turn. She was both before and behind him. Something about hearing—but not seeing—her coming, made him think of the Medusa. Do not look on the Medusa, an old book had stated, maybe an encyclopedia. The book smelled old, moldy, obsolete, and damp. It had been carried to him through the shadows of the huge dead hulks dotting the mud plain. It sent him faster past the insects lined up, all the dead slaves. The slaves never have names, he mused, walking.

No show that day, said Mary the new producer, as though she were his mother. He disobeyed, she commanded him again, palm stretched out; no show today, said Mother Mary. He begged her in the dark under the covers, to bring him what he wanted. Please, Mother Mary, in the name of your beloved son, he prayed as he'd been taught, in this way that would never be ignored, so taught the nuns. Her smell pulled back away; he breathed clearly. There was no magazine. The room fell away.

The fish! What? cried Father Dwyer impotently into the empty studio. Where the Hell did my big silver fish slither to? Who snatched away my stunningly half-scaled still gleaming fish? No, it can't be returned to the wild like that, all ripped open like it was, like that; we tore out the scales, it cannot live! No, no, no. It cannot live, it cannot, no—not without scales!

Stop! No! No this can't be, no—cats entered the light licking up the scales across the grass, silently. Noman lowered his hands and they were not his, they were Father Dwyer's, streaming with blood, from the dying small animal he'd worked on all day, yes it was a female in heat. But now it is five days dead on the blacktop, dead, dead, roadkill, slimy and stinking and covered with large loud black buzzing flies. So, down he went, on his knees in the blood, and began to weep. And Skip could not take it. Far too much weeping today he had undergone; the Dakota Maru's walls that had recorded it all, being cold steel with the usual steel trap memory, told Skip in his skullcap that he heard so loudly, after the Dakota pushed its own PLAY button, mostly being an antiquated almost worn-out cassette job from the seventies; yes, while eating lunch with Noman, Skip said, Why'd you have to lie, Noman? Eating shit, not eating shit. Which is it? A way with words, yes, no? Ran from the hammer-blows raining down, remember? Dead, or alive? Ball peens or flat? Which is it, alive or dead or dead or alive? Thank God for the sea, and for old Kent Dazey, monitor-slamming into the broadly pinstriped IBM fat-suit, that forgotten one with the big airy gut, Yes, *Waterworld!* Yes, yes, yes—don't dare insult this future merman, laugh laugh laugh, dead or alive or alive or dead, Skip! What matters is, you got away! Chunks of hot bile all flying from the dark at your face, brush by brush you live your stinking life, but it's time for new tools, tools, new tools, new, now—Oh, no God, don't let my huge swollen blue hulk of a genie die here, when the large hand from long ago is still a'slammin', hit in the head one time too many, me, yes me, I'm talking about me, Mother, Mother, please do save me, I'm rusted tight at both ends, yes, enduring all this shit a moment at a time at a time, Mother, save me! Lord God, look at Noman, he needs my fucking help! What's that got to do with my bloodflow; bloodflow running, Doctor, no, please don't kill yourself, please do not let me see you fall on that lancet, no, ignorant selfish, ignorant selfish, selfish, ignorant, did you not know I was a teenage Godface one hour ago in the prickly God-bush, loudly brawling with close friends in the poison ivy, until one hour after daybreak from the shrinking God-bush, you insisted, What the Hell happened to your hands? What? What the hell, I; now why'd I say that? Did I say that? Who said that? Noman, your hands are shaking! To be distracted from your symptoms, which are only there when you are brooding over them, come on down here, up above the plunging dam; in the scorch of summer, wipe the sweat from your brow with your stiff sandpaper towel, your nose, your chin, and—sit and dry as you watch the amazing eels, all a'slither; all a'slither, those silly eels! Silly, silly, no, far too much weepin', yes, yes, watch the eels; they rise flowing all around you; eels over your mouth, your nose, panic pushes it all up, yes, and there go your eyes. All gone are your eyes, yes, yes, oh, what? Is that you, that is you, yes, stop shaking man, stop! See, you know wieners show up in unexpected places: sometimes fried in onions and served alongside an omelet, sometimes chopped up in soup, and once served alone, boiled, as a sort of appetizer, mainly all in Germany; yes Germany, sure 'nuff Germany, mainly in Germany, hey! Yup! Sure, no, here you go Noman—tossing off to you—grab and run with it, Noman! Go Noman, go! Tell your full, ugly, story—make it more interesting than looking down through your voluminous files of botched post-op extreme Botox injection photographs! Go Noman, go—

And, after screaming all that, Father Dwyer flew his robes back with a twist, and out from the hot dark of the Priest's nether regions, swarmed into existence from Nothing, some damned Noman: yes, the ship is long, deep, and skinny! So, where am I, what am I, sure, I had lunch with Skip! I told him I was never married! He told me that in his opinion, we have the world's shittiest jobs! I yelled, Skip! Why'd you go batty? Here, here—eat my food! Why did you slap yourself upside the head like that? You nearly made me pee my pants! Oh, yes! Laughing, joking, Skip! Uh-oh! There's the back to work bell, a'slicin'! And with that, remember you rose to get away! You dodged the waves that managed to drown me, and you ran! Gone back, you went, to your small steel square stinkingly unhealthy poisonous room. You then zipped the wall open, stepped out in the parade ground—and my word, oh my God, Sergeant! I did not mean to leave the base AWOL! I cannot be punished by not going to the parade ground for graduation! Dear God man, my dad and my dog are driving four hours to see me! So, you say you're a baggy, sloppy, retiring-tomorrow, sad-lifer of a single-star general? He glowers and you nod into it, slinging back at him his very own question, so he fell on his longsword, then he came out of the glowering face before you, with mushrooms in his hand saying something about the sixties. Shocked, you strain to see his grin, but no, it was her! Phyllis, Jesus, why did you not ooze to me, I am into mushrooms, Noman, plus what is your name, boy? I think I might want you, she said, and in your horror you turned, following some large black hard ball full of fingerholes, through the jagged glass shards and splinters, and ouch, oh, God no, your thumb was off! Off, dear God, you knew—and in your shocked quick haze, the Lord touched your head, and put on you the marks of the stigmata! Remember, Skip! It was God-damned funny! For no reason at all but with a good reason I shouted, Medical! Need Medical! Yes—then you gripped my arm, I reached you just as I started up the chilly steel ladder, that was so fast as that, it was—you yelled back with phlegm and spittle, into my face you showered me, crying, We need medical! There it is, there it is, there it is, yes! The machine came at you, scooped your ass up on its seat, and I don't know what was wrong, it just spouted all over you in a strong, deep voice, Nobody cares about me until they need help! Why? Suicide? What is that about suicide, no, with one last shout of, Jesus Christ, you thrust your hands home with much red spatter, and sucked yourself automatically back to Phyllis, and you did the whole damn thing over again and over and over and over again, until you, at last, every one of you chorused to me, all together, You, Noman—yes, you are zero, and zero, she said, you picked up and you said, Skip, your face had been in mine all along, I felt as joyful as we feel in the instant when God crowns us down with knowing that the dream was not real! Face fading back, I lose you, Skip, where is your face going, huh, sinking to the depths perhaps dead of the below zero water, huh? All stiff you sink so quick, my word—you fade away back through yourself, killing the winged giant drill sergeants, pissing in the water of every pool that comes your way, for over sixty years I pull you ashore, pull you, yes, thank God, I have saved more lives than a cat now; so, is this the last life? Yes, no, maybe, sure, somebody taught us from in front of her blackboard, That is something only God knows, he has known that since the very big bang and the dark winged ones came out of the mist to the breaking surf all screaming through my face, Thank God, for no, you are not a failure. Maybe a wimp but no failure, sho''nuff'! Go run and embrace the sudden burning bush, but yes, no, maybe it is a bush of foot-long needle-thorns! So, life is a steel box. It just materializes, just like that, around us! We work in the belly of this ship twenty or thirty years, but then what? Then, where are we, no! No! Noman reached out superfast then, zipping open his wife Phyllis' belly; yes, open, my wife, Phyllis! The truth does hurt, when it's born via caesarian! Noman knew at last now in the light, he was in her all along, she was just his chrysalis, he grew, and shed her, and she crumbled dry to the deck, fit only for bunny-food!

What happened, what happened?

What happened to your hand?

No, God—I tossed that t-shirt, I just didn't have the guts to—

I say, son, listen! You told me, Skip; what happened to your hands, what happened, to your hands, sure, yes, look at your hands man! You are on my snow-white shag with those dripping red dots spattering off your hands, you had to know you came on my gleaming carpet with every intention of marring forever its loudly quiet but strong whiteness!

No! cried Father Dwyer—look up, up, man! See where in hell you are!

Wait, wait, what do you mean *no*? You dare say *no*! As though I wouldn't know you must be either Skip, or you might have been Father Dwyer all along, saying, A small buffet of sliced breads, deli meats, and cheeses at every meal, so if the main course is not already smothered in cheese, you can add your own, sure, you maybe can, you know? And, also, consider you are offered additionally a wide long thick rare china plate of chunky super-green iceberg lettuce, sometimes with cut green peppers and mealy tomato, which gets recycled into the following day's huge salad bowl, then burdened with ever-heavier dressings, until it can no longer support the weight and must be immediately trashed; you, Skip! You, Noman! Yes, there you are! Are you ready for inspection, eh? Birth, growth, maturity, decline, disposal. Is it time for that for you two, eh? Huh?

Dwyer writhed loose through the screen, wrapping Noman and Skip solidly tight as you'd roughly pull the drawstrings of some industrial strength super-invulnerable garbage bag not available to the general public, Go, out, down!

Into the lifeless surging water, they plunged!

As the Dakota Maru reached the end of her service life!

The last voyage begins now. The long, long last voyage, to Bangladesh!

Yes, you, we all know what happens when we arrive at Bangladesh!

Diminishing into the distance, she beckons for Noman and Skip to finally man her; they breast stroke quickly, catch up, board! Yes, to arrival! End! Last, star implosion; going, going, gone, dead, calmly, all of us end up in the quiet twilit mud.

Chapter Ten
On the Free One-way Trip to China

—not Miss Sweetie, No, no; she is only yours. Yes only yes only yes only yes. Worry, worry, worry and worry, why worry when what's worried about will wear to less than a nub, then gone. Sure; pause a moment. This can't be; yes, yes, that is it. Close your eyes and shut me out, says the wide round dark cylinder overflowing with worries that are not really there. Ah, good. Yes, that's right. Teeth painful and throbbing from gnashing hard through the thick brush of wood-ticks, mosquitoes, and drenching hot sweats all night, at last can rest. See, it's true, it couldn't be that bad. There's no need for that last push to rake up and bag what the teeth sliced through and away and let fall to the grass all behind. Garbage. Garbage. Nothing could cause so much garbage. Thank God there will be no more. The place to put it was almost full. There was never any garbage at all, actually; it was just a cheap, overly long play, perfectly performed as though almost real, but now past the bushes any size or strength of grey-brain can see that it was all just make believe on a false stage set under the kliegs. So, this is when the stage crew pulls the rope that glides the curtains together, and this is when the actors' eyes are all supposed to pop open and pull back away, and there goes the stage, sliding, pulling over the dark of the bedroom before the cast, who breathe deep sighs of relief. Wow, hey, shit. It wasn't real. But the last tiny words from the last tiny bushes lying on the grass, cut and dying, need to be all heard before the last word opens the last set of eyes. These are yours. It will take the words forever to open the eyes, yes it will, there's ages to go, this is a nice peaceful breather of a spot, nice warm words goose-bumping cold that will pry loose for many years, surely, Listen, the words say, life's just one big moment. Eternity holds its breath; life starts and stops; then eternity exhales and strolls on. That's what the Doctor said. That's a healthy way of seeing all around as life rolls by, one sidewalk concrete square after another. Life is one big dog-walk. It's a quest to find the perfect dog, and the perfect way to walk. That's all your desires boil down to, in the end. The end is meaningless when one has got everything that one ever desired. The fun ride is over. The play park gates will be shut up locked. You got to just pull your head out of the mud right now, wipe the stench from in your hair with the towel handed you by the surprise of an attendant, and as you search for coins to pay the attendant this unexpected tip, this last fact razes everything that's gone before. Up until just before eternity exhales as a factory bell-buzzer signals the blue-men, it must be time to go. The everyday mortal invisible tripwires have all been avoided. There were close calls, but just brushes they were. The tip? Huh? Something about a tip, what, where, oh well; there's no need to tip the sudden frozen dripping-with-thaw-water chocolate bird, whose left wing brushed down over a sun-sized solid brass ball all hung there. In one hundred years the wing will brush again. And over and over until the ball is worn to a point so small it just quivers and evaporates. The bird brushes once more and thinks the ball is still there. The one-eyed bird blinking, brushing down once every hundred years forever, until the bird is so far ahead no one could possibly see it again. Has it been taken and will not need to brush down again? Or is it just too far away to see? That's a good question. Yes, class. That's a good question. Anybody know the answer, class? If you think you know the answer raise your hand. Come on, come on. A guess at least?

What? Hey! No questions? What kind of class is this? Holes for eyes are in all sixty-five young students. All the holes expand, growing together, pulling up inky liquid from way deep inside. The best potters let the clays form themselves. Deep under water, it's dark and confusing on which way is up. Follow the feeling of that air bubble to the surface above which again panic settles in; what panic, why panic? These shut eyes can't see anything to fear. Just still, solid absence of noise. Too hollow to stab, cut, hit, kick, or curse. Curse is a word. Sure it is. Curse. Curse. Curse, but a breath must be taken, eyes must pop open, taken breath, opened eyes, taken breath, and open eyes, sure; the truth's icy bare curved steel which, after all that, is still around.

The watched water never boils. Never. And at the never point here, panic sets in, but—don't yell. Oxygen, don't use up oxygen; please don't yell. Please, my face, pray for me in the Church lobby before mass. After six o'clock Mass, wander out. Been in there too long and prayed perfectly knifelike to everything; each sit, stand, and Kneel also, done perfectly, precisely. Life is over, you say, Peter? Life is really over, but how can it be still marching? How can the ball have been thrown when here it is palmed tight and hot? If the boots were thrown in the fire, why do I hear them marching? No, no, no, not! Life over; step by step, extreme panic builds, breaks through, explodes, but words come, a will to keep it back. Quiet, relax. What's living? What's dying? What's this horrible in-between place? Why be given life if it's going to end like this? Honest, out of school childhood, sweetheart can't get work, no no no no, no interviews please, no, none, no, not; we just got time to get down and go in the daily laborer pool.

Run down the steps with shoes just half on; when kneeling, the good book says, do not lean your butt back on the pew to rest. No, never do it. Like in Catholic School, the large, mysterious, frightening, black-draped being of a nun that wanders and watches, and would poke any boy on the side that it caught dozing or leaning their butt on the pew, kept the class honest, and will single you out. The have-to-shit bell is rung, and the need-to-piss bell is rung, but; need to go, as taught; get there, as taught; can get out to a rest room to go, but how? Oh, sure, how about I ask this other guy waiting on the corner across from the Dunkin' Donuts I'm suddenly at for the thousandth time, whose name is Lucas.

On the hit list to the rubout is where he is, sure, says Lucas, talking to one of the other regular gang of guys waiting for day work on the street. The other guy is a large man named Walter, uh, oh, but can't go into that now because I feel I have peed myself in my pants, cripes almighty. Need to leave, get new pants, sound stiff as if rolling around the steel drum—what steel drum? No, God, no—stay where you're at, smile at Lucas.

Lucas! Hey Lucas. Big wind today, eh?

Oh sure, sure, says Lucas, turning from Walter—and he goes on to rattle off, Hey man, do you know it is a fact that every fetus begins urinating into the womb very early, and, once started, pees every forty or forty-five minutes? So, don't worry about it. We understand. We can see your—well, your problem. No need to hide it. If I were you, I would do the same thing, what the hell. Go on to the bathroom in Dunkin'. They won't make you buy anything.

But, Lucas, it's not just the periodic wish to pee. It seems like mere pee, but it's actually a wish to not ever have been born. If I could go back and catch mother and father copulating, I would stop them like dogs and yell, No, don't do that, don't, you are condemning me to this! It would be far better for me to have never lived. Please, please, Mother, do not give me birth! Be like me, I cannot do it. Half the world can do it, and half cannot. I know, I know. So, in this handwritten letter I can truly say, I am developing okay. Why had I felt myself urinate, she replied? So in honor of my long gone Mother, I opened my eyes, and Lucas and Walter and Mother and all went totally flat black mixed with absolute silence, and my hands moved feeling everything all around; just in the dark we felt hard cold curved steel, and the flat under me was a puddle of something, I didn't know what until the urine smell from the flat bottom strengthened, and I struggled to feel down in the dark, and everything, yes, everything below me was drenched; bad, bad, bad; bad was all around; see what I mean, Mother? Oh, please, please, Mother, do not condemn me!

Men, a BAC level of point thirteen to point thirty percent leads to this stage, which borders on alcohol poisoning after consuming an unreasonable number of drinks in just one hour. And, the resultant confusion gives way to emotional upheaval and extremes. Coordination is markedly impaired, to the extent that the person may not be able to stand up, may stagger if walking, and may be completely confused about what's going on. So, watch your drivin', goin' in!

Yes! He has. Yes!

My dear God, yes God, I can stretch, stand, sure; it's a miracle to be able to walk, God I am stiff as shit, where was I, where was I, think where I left off, before the—don't say it. Keep it like it is that there's no barrel all dark and cold and around anymore. No need to say it anymore because it's gone and over. Good God—no more a horrid dying body. God was wise to make us so there's no feeling after death because being dead must be unbelievably painful. The boss' speech told multiple times that those in this stage of intoxication are highly likely to forget things that happen to or around them. Blacking out without actually passing out can happen at this stage.

That's all it was, was blackout. No death right behind. No more steel, side, top, bottom sealed I guess, no more holding my breath and closing my eyes to make it now never had happened!

Yes, Mackie!

God, yes, go on!

Yes, you may begin to feel your baby move, since he or she is developing muscles and exercising them. This first movement is called quickening—say Johnny, is that it? You feeling your insides quickening? What, you trying to give birth to yourself? Huh? That does not work, Johnny—hey, boys, what you think—should we let him go or what? Should we, what, hey!? As is, he's a fourteen-point-eight percent chance of survival. And about half of these survivors are brain-damaged, either by lack of oxygen in the airless moist womb, or too much oxygen from the ventilator. Funny they save them, then just let them die again; but, no time to talk more. Everything's around, everywhere cold and solid. Still living, yes living, but the solid steel walls are—no, can't know. Don't know. It's not, there's still a way out. Listen, no more heavy thought. Sleepy. Go on, sleep, you want to sleep—gone over gone over gone—going too sleepy to care. But, what's that? That's Mackie. Where is this? Still the toast? My God, any time closed eyes come, up shoots the crazy toast again.

Chapter Eleven
Banter on Ship to China V

Skip knelt in a sudden, squally, driving, ice-cold rain, near the thirtieth set of container hold-downs, scraping out deep brown scaly rust from one of the tightening turnbuckles. The Dakota Maru was now fifty-five days out, in the heavy Southern Ocean zone of freak lashing storms that came and went quickly, sometimes violently raging and pounding several times a day. Which ocean doesn't matter; any ocean is just an ocean. What area doesn't matter; any area is just an area. All that mattered was that wherever the ship had come to today, this moment the sky could be blue, the sun hot and bright, the ocean smooth as glass, and then, that moment, wham: darkness fell from some backstage area beyond the sun—multiple times each and every day—that somehow the sunlight yanked up short at the end of some rope formed of lightning and thunder. Its abrupt stop caused the sheets of ice-cold rain riding atop it to break violently free and plummet down on the ship, smashing hammer-like down on the decks. Skip, whose job was always outside, on deck, had to work exposed through any weather that might assault him, and must continue through all daylight hours, with no running inside for shelter from heavy crashing foaming seas, blinding rains, whipping winds, or near-zero icy conditions. This day, the rain fell hissing hard against the back of his heavy yellow rubberized waterproof raincoat. Sometimes, when the rain got so heavy he could not see a foot in front of him, he thought of fictional seaman number two, Noman, many levels below, probably not even knowing there's a storm; Noman's job was a safe, dry, inside job; a true breeze. Noman may not even have been forced when first hired to get the special heavy-duty stiff-armed rubbery raincoat, which was not provided by the shipping corporation, but that every crew member had to buy with their own money. Five hundred dollars on the dot, not including tax. Cash only. Now Skip's hand pushed out through the nearly solid rain, feeling the rough outline of the drowned ice-cold hold-down turnbuckles and nuts and bolts and extremely fine threads cut into the shaft making earsplitting noise in the smelly old brick factory out in the farmlands that had been flattened by a few dozen jet black wrecking balls some years back, where the hold-down hardware for all ships was manufactured, to be replaced by a bland retail mall within which beige was the primary color; like the office, neat and dry and bright he sat in the day he'd been called back to the land by the management. Blindly he fingered the thread of the shaft as the office light pouring silently all around parted, to reveal the wonderful manager who had just come in and sat down facing Skip, settling down in his big-shot high-backed leathery gold-studded rich-man's chair, such as all the upper-levels were required to have but that they needed to buy with their own money, just like the raincoats on the line seamen had been. The large forbidding chairs cost three thousand dollars each; and from the pile of wasted money his own chair represented, the wonderful manager said, So, I see you were able to make it, Skip. I have been looking forward to this. I've been told of your enthusiasm for your assignment.

Skip returned the volley, simply, brightly, and shortly, snapping, Thanks. I'm glad to be here. The directions on the memo were perfect. I got here early as a matter of fact.

This word-status went out at the wonderful manager, but got pulled down neatly between the wonderful manager's legs by the strong suction of the great pile of money supporting him. The pumping words hit and penetrated the throbbing moneypile, which signaled his lower gears to rotate and push the rote interview script he had memorized far longer ago than his memory could ever cogently reach, way up his gullet, and up up up further to his face, where he could easily read it aloud from where it scrolled across on the back of his specially treated eyelids as he blinked his sightline on, off, on, off, thus saying to Skip in a sincere, off-the-cuff manner,

You know Skip, you were called here today because I wanted to talk to you about your future. There's an immediate opening of opportunity for you; a promotion to management as a matter of fact, which will enable you to increase your pay by more than three thousand dollars virtually overnight, you little tiger, you. Yes, you heard me right; you are a tiger. Yes you are. But, anyway, what that means is that we in management are all tigers, and there's room for one more to claw their way aboard. That's right, Skip. The whole executive team knows you are a tiger. From our separate but similar money-perches, yes, we each have watched you and considered and discussed and all that baloney, and have deemed you worthy of nothing more than having your very own manager's money-perch, too. We're very sure taking this promotion will pull in place beneath you a much more solid seat for your financial future in the company, you know? Would you agree, Skip?

I suppose, yes. But—why me? I don't see what's so special about simply doing a good days' work. That's all I do, you know. What I am told, and that's it, no more. You know?

Yes, I know. But, great men are always humble. Listen; you have been chosen for promotion. This will move you up a notch to a junior navigation officer's level. No more freezing cold outdoor work in the pouring rain and ice and snow all day. No more tossing and rolling in heavy seas, to upset your stomach, which was never meant for such punishment. So. What have you got to say about that? Seems like a no-brainer, to me. Don't you think?

The wonderful manager sat back quite pleased, with fingers intertwined atop his genital area, but luckily the coarse cheap fabric of his trousers intervened. Skip's mouth gaped, but no words came, as he spoke his secret back and forth thoughts behind the newfound manager's mask that the wonderful manager himself had just slapped onto his face, sparking up also flickering shards of spark-flaming tinder deep in the dark inside Skip generating feelings wrapping words alive and throbbing, these being, OK, very good—my groin is warm now, must not let on now, where will my office be now, aboard ship or where now, start to talk now, ask real fast if it's really three thousand dollars the company will lay on me, making Skip say to the wonderful manager—Lord God, that sounds great, Mr. Wasdyke, where will my office be, it will be amazing to travel the seas with a nice office computer and sunny sea views for three thousand dollars becoming in time five thousand, yes, my groin burns, where will my office be, Wasdyke, I asked you, where will my slot be where I'll be churned to bloody every day for the next thousand years, Huh?

My groin is afire.

Sure, Skip. Those are good questions. I can tell you that what we have planned is to groom you for a step or two forward, and down the years maybe more, into a large fat-cat-manager's padded grey soft-walled cubby spot where you will be assigned to cook up big solutions to imaginary problems. Good, huh?

No! Not good! Why on land? I like it aboard ship! I can work remote from some ship, with my computer. People do that all the time, in a few decades there won't be offices at all.

No, no, no, shook from the wonderful manager's long full greasy beribboned oily mop. You have to be near us, Skip, so we can watch you and judge you; you are not mature enough, not yet close enough to being a fully alive house plant; not yet mature enough to survive outside, not yet ready to be dug into the garden in the back yard, all wild on wild, as you are. Yes, it is so, and the hard work you've been doggedly doing for years, that you never thought we were watching at all, is now all growing, maturing, and blooming toward the day of your final soar. What do you think, Skip? Huh? Lord God, how lucky you are. If I had got such an offer when I was your age, well—I can't imagine where I'd be today.

Gosh, said Skip. But I can log in from a ship, why is that unacceptable?

No, said the wonderful manager's french-cuffed arm thrust out, down, and across, which by the way, is the self-slashing pattern most often used when committing traditional Seppuku, pulled across the wonderful manager's instant-by-instant of now-flowing time all across everything in every direction, all solid, not protesting, or, at least, not very much. Isn't this what you want? Isn't this what everybody wants? Three thousand, four thousand, five thousand dollars, drifted quick across, backed by the flaming walls the conversation had ignited and now flailed up flaming, shouting, yelling, This is what I wanted when I was your age; sure, I was fresh faced and wet behind the ears, a very green sleeping boy, just like you, I was! Welcome to the Pet Salon, small Skip! Hey, let me scratch you. You seem quite a fine dog! We do a fine little grooming here, know you, small breed Skip! Here we do to death all the puppies which are tossed unwanted against our front door between three and six a.m., but not on weekends; no, but we guarantee that from days one through five hundred, and all around all hours of the clock, we will grip, love, and find homes for these newborn baby beasts, and this at all hours, boy, yes! This at all hours if necessary, but; here we are now face to face. So, here! Boy! Here, up boy, up! Get a treat boy, yes, get a treat! Come on! Yes, come on now!

So, yes, time notched back an instant, to when atop a steel grooming salon table long, long, ago, set Skip's sudden four canine paws; held by a tether, struck down in the classic pose. The clipper ran back and forth over Skip, all buzzing; but no, wait, the clippers buzzcut down under to his belly, and his thigh muscles, and slipped back under his pulled away tail buzzing into his spotless pink rectum, as the fur fell. In my breed, honey, does the wind blow? Staffordshire, what; Chow Chow, what; Sharpei, what; and Golden Retriever, last but not least, what; sure, grooming's impossible to do if it's not administered by a professionally hard-talking lawyer like me! See, said Father Dwyer, into the maw of the red dot in the dark facing him, this is the two thousandth episode of my wonderful cooking show, tailored of course to the needs of the average low-level automated modern containership seaman, and to best continue serving the gustatory needs of these sailormen, I have just come from uploading an attachment to the management that says there should end up being no less than two thousand more episodes of this cooking show filmed! So, let's pray, my little reverends, pray; pray enough, and if you live long enough to pray a total of five million prayers, you'll be plucked away to be offered a lifetime sunny Californian Rosicrucian membership, with the multimillion dollar application fee waived, to boot! Sure yeah, it's not for nothing they decided eons back to start putting dead people into personal and private rectangular holes in the ground, because down is where all flesh and blood ends up—and the sinners who pursue fleshly desires follow after. See, you do not even know that back down behind this giant iron and steel chopping and working and slicing and mashing-up cooking show island, I am nude from the waist down, and, hey, no, not! Got to think of the company's image, after all. They were kind enough to catch me and drag me and force me to be addicted to food talk all my life. So any way, no way, here I am, yes sir, and we need to get on to the next dish on the agenda for time is a'wastin' and a'wastin' is time—hey hey, they used to jokey jokey-joke with me saying, If there's no one on the bridge to hear Father Dwyer, does he make a sound? I took that joke, went with them, and laughed and laughed and laughed at it as well, because I sensed it wouldn't deny me my future, fame, fortune, or hatred or rudeness, because I already had all of that long ago, when I was a young, typically obnoxious man all caught up in God—but yes, he said, shoving aside the show for a minute, no loss actually because no one is watching, which must be a lie because you are reading, if you see a tape or transcription or text record of my show, does your seeing it and hearing it go back through the tube or paper or whatever, and cause the show to make a sound, when back then no one was watching and thusly, it didn't. If no one sees the fresh head cheese on display in the deli cooler because the store has closed, is it still there? Or the car speeding by on the huge interstate, or the dog barking chained in the back yard, at three a.m., or whatever more items or issues the big boss flipped the alone switch on for causing them to A: disappear, or B: do what they can only do when no one is home and the dog and cat are locked on the back porch and the opportunity and motive are there to call it crime for me, Father Dwyer in the flesh after all, to spend a moment or two reminiscing about my rough-hewn boyhood? No answers? Good! Because regardless, here we go going ahead with it. Hey!

He stepped back, thick robes a-flow, and coughed up something from way down deep, which he spat unseen onto the floor behind the work table, licked his lips, raised his face, and proceeded to take advantage of this opportunity to indulge in a moment of verbal masturbation, as, Let us start at the beginning. Was I a boy once? Yes, I was. I became ordained after a rough, stony, stinky childhood, more like a raw red hot dog than a boy. I threw myself prone at the feet of the Bishop, along with around fifty thousand of my fellow graduates. Out boomed the Bishop from up and above, blasting his thin feminine voice out burrowing through the thick air seeking some in-range ears. Boys! he said, just lie prone for the next several weeks, while I read to the thin number of actual parishioners seated way behind you, in the dried up cracking and crackling ancient back pews, right behind your very own very proud friends and even prouder families, that we will be collecting money from after the service in the gloomy ice-cold drafty back vestibule, for our purchase of a full set of vestments for Bishop Crane, not yet deceased, and his immediate team of direct reports, the total number not to exceed ten thousand, and also not to fall lower than five thousand fine young skinny deathly pale pasty-faced men. These vestments, he continued, will be fully reflective of the sinless state of the hearts and minds of these devoted Catholic men. One or two of these men are certified spotless by the Church, birth babies also, and ultra-clean, etc., meaning that these have never committed a single sin since they were in the womb, and that is made even more impressive by the fact that they have maintained their spotlessness for seventy-nine and eighty-two years, respectively. So, in conclusion, in reverence for these sacred men, we will gather up wheat, separate it from the chaff, and then make some calls up and down the forever expanding exponentially miles-long dataflow, and sing up some prices from underneath all the hype-ads, so we can deliver the best possible deal, God willing! So here; you might think from the way I'm singing that all that is yet to be done, but no! Nos! Nona comprenday! We are buying, we have bought, we have seventeen complete five-piece Roman Vestment sets, crafted from pure, one hundred percent silk. The colors range from purple, for Advent, Lent, and times of penance, as well as white, cream, red, rose, green, black, gold, eh, eh eh, take your pick, said the glittery garbed nearly space-suited pinch-faced silver-helmeted saleslady that abruptly burped up and blasted in from out of nowhere. Go try them on, she said to me curtly. The lowered flutter of her super-long lashes, said she thought I was up to no good. Come, she said, they're over here; she turned her back and walked me away. I enjoyed following her luscious silky mane; silky, yes, silky, yes, and the sway of her flat-chested silky swathed back—and then she stopped, half turned around, in a swish of long supple skirting and pointed to a shapeless mass of cloth bunched in a tall pile on a long silver table. Here, she said—seventeen sets as you told me on the phone. Take them to the fitting room across the store and try each on. Take your time.

I looked at the massive pile almost burying the table, and said, I don't know if I should try them on. They're a gift I will spread across seven holy males' malenesses, and they are all either much, much smaller or much larger, in width, height, girth, and all like that. Dimensions, you know. Everything is in more or less of some dimension. So, I don't think I'll try them on. What's the cost come to? Let's make this quick. I got holy mass still to do today. Tell me how much. I have cash.

No, Father. You cannot buy an item of clothing without trying it on.

What? Wait—why is it that no store I've ever shopped in before has had such a rule? Who is in charge?

No point in talking to the masters in charge. It is store policy that must be fed, and cannot ever be bent.

Wait, no. Get me a manager. No masters, just managers! Now! Okay?

You mean a master, not a manager. We only have masters. But sir, we cannot—

Don't tell me again! A manager, now!

Sir listen, please listen. Keep in mind that each set you are buying has two-percent gold bullion fringing on the stole and maniple. This makes them something we will not let leave the store unless we are sure. You must be sure you'll keep them, not ball them up wrinkled and soiled from an unsuccessful try-on, which would set people shouting, making you angry, and possibly in your anger treating them roughly as if they were just so many rags for a workshop. We would then never be able to resell them. There are only so many of these in the universe, Father. Carelessness over time could lead to there being none of these left anywhere far or near, anyplace that God takes the credit for having long ago created! Plus, be aware that—

Aware of what? You mean, you've got more shit to sling? I seethed. I was close, I swear to God, very, very close to slugging her. My hands formed fists and swung at my sides. My face was a tormented scowl. I swear to God, I nearly slugged her. But she just went on rattling over me, as I stood in the unstoppable gusty gales of flowing stone-hard words, trying hard not commit multiple felonies.

This is what I was starting to say, Father. You probably do not know it takes the death of between seventeen hundred and twenty thousand silkworm Pupas, to generate enough silk to make just one chasuble. The work, imagine doing the work. It's like, you know, it's like—mass assassination done in some mass assassination clinic.

What? Assassination? Deaths? What deaths? Thousands of what must die? Back up to that part please, yes; to the place in your recording where you switched from don't give a shit to actually caring, even though you won't be moved! What has to die? Spit it out!

Silkworms need to die. In the pupa stage. It's like twenty-five thousand abortions. Just for the chasuble of one set of seven full, of which, in each, the chasuble is merely the smallest of about a dozen items that make up each set. That's what dies.

She stood nodding and winding her reddening hands together.

You know, I think, no, Lord God almighty, I don't know what to think—

She leapt in the gap and added, Plus, about three thousand cocoons are used to make just one yard of silk material.

My, God. Maybe no. Maybe we don't want silk then, I told her. A smile grew on her serene set face crying, See, I was right, mutely into my face. See, I was right, wrapped my head tightly like a cocoon all suffering just one of thousands of others all also suffering knowing that when the wrapping's done, the only thing left is to be murdered—how 'bout that Skip, how 'bout that; that's worse than being doused with some hot land-juice, don't you know! Land-juice! Define it Skip. Don't run away like a big hairy hunchbacked mess of a coward—stand your ground, man—define it right this minute please, huahhhh? Land-juice, yes. Got that land-juice all inside all hot, don't you Skip, don't you, yes, so rip, tear, and claw loose from the groomer's table, snap the painful neck-tether away off yourself, and scamp scamper out now a dog, why am I a dog, no don't think that, no don't, God said to me, Tell Skip, and I had to, or the cobwebs over the slot waiting for me in Hell will be swept away in preparation for my delivery. Like Pop Oscar said so long back in some loud-lunged shout of a dancehall, God prepares two places for us to end up in. Which we end up in depends on us. A mansion is prepared in Heaven, and a superheated coffin is prepared down in Hell. It will be as bad as the thundering sheets of heavy solid rain pounding down today are, or it will be as wonderful as a thousand years of heavier rain pounding wearing the earth down from planetsized to moonsized to beachball sized to basketball, softball, baseball, tennis, pingpong, all bouncypopping, and rice grain, ballpoint-pen ball, grain of sand, to spores, to end of sentence period, and then half, then half of that, to half of that, to—Jesus Christ, Skip! Weigh the costs and the benefits; a mansion needs maintenance, but a superheated coffin does not. Get it, Skip, get it, yes do, you get it, no, don't you, do you, can you, will you, no? What the hell do you mean, No!

Skip's eyes popped open, and his face came up and down, and in front hung a grade-school-style front-of-the-classroom roll-up-and-down home-movie screen. On the screen played the wonderful manager halfway through the latest sentence of the Skip interview, as, Isn't this what everybody wants? To have an opportunity to obtain a free map clearly portraying the inside track to making the title of wonderful manager is a rare treat! Skip, I'll forgive you your somnambulism, which I find very rude, but it could just mean you're a super-hard worker. I rather like you, how 'bout you come here, yes, onto my lap here. Oh, please drop your pants first, Mr. Skip. Drop your pants, Skip, drop, drop your pants, here; Drop 'em and the briefs too and let me get a grip of your dickie the privateman—huh—

God! exclaimed Skip—I need to go sir, I don't really need a job, this was just a lark. I mean, you know. It was a bad decision for me to come here.

Nude from the waist down, the wonderful manager rose and stroked and stepped and stroked harder, and reached, but not with a hand, but with a—

Skip shouted the wonderful manager back with a wave.

Listen, bologna—just like that, yeah, stock still and listen.

Skip reached in down his gullet, though choking and gagging, he managed to flip the very-last-resort electrical continuity switch, which everyone has but no one knows about, that only becomes available and apparent in times of crisis, as in moments from death. The flipped switch caused the acoustic shouts of the wonderful manager into impossible-to-hear digital subsonic intermeasured and intermingled pulses that delivered young Skip-boy from a forever flawed life, made so by early exposure to and use by some pedophiliac pervert. The pulse took him back, sat him back at the desk on the ship he served on all those years ago, and he went ahead and made the opposite decision from his first response, and he respectfully turned down the offer to go on land to be interviewed for a big opportunity. Skip often, out in years beyond, thought back to that moment and asked himself, Why did I decide as I did? It would have doubled my salary, and I would have been able to settle down and marry the dream family and have the big new house in the tract-wonderland and also would have been able to obtain a large brown American Staffordshire that, strong as he is, a bluenose pit can muscle-tackle down in any kind of prolonged scrap in any season, weather, or midnight low temperature or frozen rock-hard snowbank.

Detecting a problem crew member in his studio staff, Dwyer pointed at the red dot hung in nothing before him, like a brick wall looks the instant before the two-hundred-mile-an-hour super-funny-car—which halfway to the traps blew its very expensive, chrome-plated, pretty, shiny, giant, noisy motor—impacts the wall and explodes to nothing-shards all fly-flashing up and out and down and flaming all red-hot into the distance the driver will never get to experience, his having involuntarily given up the ghost on impact, on that sunny happy Sunday afternoon at the racetrack. Turning from that ghastly sight, more than one shocked former-race-fan viewer will not even hear the question, as, Who the hell was Emile Lagouis? And the fake studio audience member who's really an actor will not know the answer, Lord God, the answer is worth half a million, but I don't have it. So, after the time-buzz, the suity shiny Host turns around with his microphone all relaxed, and broadly tells the crushed contestant that Emile Legouis was the son of a textile salesman and, one year later, taught at the Collège d'Avranches as an agrégé for English and later as a professor at the University of Lyon. Well, I have to tell you Mister Hostman, by the skin of your chinny-chin-chin master craftsmen's wide-windowed quite forward house, the child who has fallen will never ever rise again, not horizontally, no, and also not vertically, no, nor neither any slant in between, no, stated after issuing exactly three mocking guffaws, no, by the fake studio audience member who's really an actor, no, over again and again to the ragged end of the gameshow's airy television transmission. But, on Dwyer TV there are no gameshows, so the reminiscence that's just been shared with you never ever happened, not by Caesarian, nor by vaginal methods of delivery. Any questions?

Father Dwyer stood waiting, but he had chosen the wrong medium for his first press conference and only found out the hard way that cable TV is strictly one-way, yes, at least as of this writing, that's all it is, unless the new ones are spying on us, as some theorize. He froze, waiting forever, looping and looping and looping back to finish the story about his ordination by the unnamable Bishop who needed donations to a war-chest to gift extravagant vestments to a small town of aging priests who probably only have a small number of holy masses to do before they drop dead anyway. The Bishop went on to say, to continue that, When the wrapping's done, the only thing left is to be murdered—what I concluded, you big gang of what, wait, what are you guys all called, yes, I know, candidates, yes, that's it! You are candidates, that's why I was led all senile to this podium and propped up to give yet another meaningless sermon, over you, you, and you, lying prostrate for some reason I cannot fathom the logic of, and the rest of the ten thousand of you lying there in a row all stretched out to the horizon. How about counting off? Like the army. After all, you are soon going to be foot soldiers in Jesus' army! Go!

Why have you lain silent for a full ten minutes and not begun counting?

God! Still nothing? I swear, someone must have slammed down the priest-popping machine so hard you've all had your talking tongues and related voice boxes shaken too hard, and they have died of some kind of bleed-out! I know, yes I know, the works got to be broke, because so many got turned out in this seminary graduating class that you collapsed everything by sheer force of weight. You probably collapsed things like stadium stands, and many of you died in that tragedy, I bet—though for some wild reason, it didn't even make the local rag's police log. The campus as a whole, hey; does it still exist? Or did you cause that also, by sheer force of weight, to rock and roll the earth so hard a ten-mile-wide sinkhole instantly swallowed down the entire college? Did the multi-level modern earthquake-proof dormitories pancake all down flat, and, thus, like the stands and the campus and the dormitories, kill off almost half of your number, despite which hundreds of you survived to lie in a line prostrate as you are? But no, no, my God no, we are all about to die because the pressure of you not having enough room in the supersized big box Cathedral, the weight of you weighing as ten thousand redwood logs piling up looking for room up against the creaky walls, will explode, actually explode, this cavern, yes. Come, men, which I am sure you are because this is a seminary, run with me out the door single file, Indian style, while there is still life in us to run fast like we were thieves, God yes, thieves with approximately ten thousand slathering howling large aggressive dog breeds thundering after us pounding their hundreds and hundreds of gigantic rock-hard paws, all pounding and pounding; I'm not ready to die, so come, oh, let's go—

Hey! Your excellency! Stop right there!

I stopped and turned, and six thousand prone men still lay face down on the marble. I saw no one looking like they had just cried out. Imagination, it must be, I reasoned. I turned only to get once more roughly grasped and spun back again by a torrent of shouts.

Your excellency! We want to know the end of the story about the vestments!

What? What? No, I—

The end of the story of the silk vestments you were gifting to Bishop Crane and his devoted crew! The woman in the store told you silk equals mass assassination! What did you end up doing? Vestments, or no vestments, and if none, then what?

Huh?

Yes, the Vestments! What about the vestments?

The truth then fell on me; the prone men had chanted those words down into the marble so hard the entire cathedral had resonated blasting the words super-amplified into my nearly burst drums! So, my dear candidates, I will go back, remount the pulpit, and wrap up my great big homily now; I think the cathedral will collapse extremely slowly—slowly enough for me to speak at least eighteen hours or more. Good, men of God?

Good. Yes good!

All right, let me first dispose of the silkworms. I left the store shaken and went slowly down the street, tore out and flung away my ecclesiastical collar, took a woman for a ten-night-long fuck, yes, over and over, morning, afternoon, night, morning, afternoon, night, with Lebanese red, while blindfolded, and finally escaped, and tore off the blindfold so I could see my way to the toilet room, stumbled inside and passed the longest water of my already too lengthy bishop's-career which I was astounded to realize I had been holding for ten days. Turning back to the bed, it crawled with silkworms, each the spirit of one dear creature, and so many so many, six inches thick, drifted over the bed, snowlike if I were twice my size, but that is another matter entirely, but there came up from the crawling mound the woman I had been ten days with, and she was the sales-person in the Vestments department of the big-box store down the block. I moved to grip her, to kill her became quite important; but when I gripped her throat, it puffed away in a thick burst of vapor, and the words came up at me; I thrashed! I tore! I kicked, and she said words, yes words, clear pure words again and again, as, Many die so you can look good, die so you can look good, yeah, as that dog that burly charging snapping dog coming out stage left—no! Nooooo!

Now looking at the playback I can see a great bull terrier big as a towering houseplant all withered and greatly concerned, spring, leap, come and go, taking my whole upper torso away clean, separated like stamps separate at their perforations, as just-washed, with not a drip of blood dripping. Pouring, raining, hissing red cats and snarling, slavering masses of giant blue dogs, totally not power-trained, came down, ran off, and were gone; I could not count them.

Okay, all right already, I'll get to the point; more silkworms are killed in a single year to feed the industrial machine than there have been humans living and dying since the first-burst-start off the starting line of earthly humankind creaturehood-being.

Wow! roared the wide row of prone candidates. More!

Okay! Yes, now—about the saleslady. I'll cut to the chase since the stone walls have been closing on around this coordinate for several decades! Here it is!

I killed the bitch!

A low rumble of a reaction rippled across the line bordering the candidates lying in shadow rumbling out toward a nameless daughter from someplace outside in the sun that I set up to trap them. Time to drive the largest of the sharp stakes home now; repeat the hammerswing, yes; I killed the bitch!

Roar-surge domes the crowd before me, but I reattack.

And! Yes, and—I got life in prison without parole for her death, and said all masses and taped all shows, here in my permanent home, the State Prison, where I have just been rerated to a trusty.

Whaaaat?

No, shush. Let me finishee upsy; there never was a Bishop Crane. The story was all to get in and infiltrate the layers of pretend holy pap you've been swathing yourselves with every day since you first snuck in to start up this abandoned seminary. To make you interested enough to follow my tortured logic to its end, as in, I now must hand the torch off to Father Dwyer. I must leave now, go, let everybody out, class be dismissed, or not.

No, what about our ordinations? What about the tens of thousands of us, lying here for your touch to run down, who need to be ordained today?

Yes! came a spear of a lancing voice just missing the Bishop's oversized head, whipping by past, embedding itself into the cameraman, who was cast down lower than a hundred times more repetitions of the story would be deep, probably sunning on hot bedrock, tanning, yes tanning herself all dry, cracked up, to bounce to yourself again, this time, the third time, you will know the end of the story, don't worry. But now here is Father Dwyer, older than the oldest known actual cement sidewalk, grey. Father, yes Father, they lie there waiting; spray them with the rest of the show, thanks for the airtime, now take us to the story of the unpopular, very, very, unpopular indeed, all the dead Boars' trail of bloody fleshlumps born to vomit; an impossible to eat Boars' head headcheese. Father! Yes, Father! Let us clap for Father Dwyer, come back on the slumbering deeply-foaming storm-waves of this here remote beach, and dry as a bone nevertheless. Father Dwyer!

Applause; standing ovation; stone-thick black noise, through which Father Dwyer came into being, at last speaking with a smile.

Okay, that's that, now is now, and the topic right now is head cheese! So. What on earth are the prime qualities of head cheese? Here they are: first, microscopically small it is. It is always laid out on every mealtable, it's just hard to see, when it's microscopically small, like it is. Second, everybody secretly likes it, though it takes a gun to the head and multiple cries of Mau! shouted in a smelly swamp-hut in the burning desperate jungle to force people to take the first bite, like in some war movie, like it is. Third, once ingested it will cause immediate understanding of who exactly Louis Camazian was, like it is. Fourth, so, here it is, Dwyer Musketeers! Here it is, like it is, like it is, it is; the fourth final truth on which all reality lies! Shout it out!

Yes, Father Dwyer! chorused the prone priesthood candidates. What is the final truth on which all reality lies?

On this, men! The last question is, How many characters should a story have? Ask it!

Yes! Tell us, Father—How many characters should a story have?

None!

True!

Into just a wisp of dissipating smoke, everything compresses. Up where it used to be swims a giant blue manta ray, bearing a plate loaded with multiple yellow slices of Noman's current brain-state cross-section backup synch-point. Eden La Falda, he thinks it is, as he answers the hollow question that occurred to him from someplace in the boundless liquid void sliding slowly by under the Dakota Maru, on each side of the Dakota Maru up to the waterline, and back past the Dakota Maru left behind between two portly, long, foaming masses of air and water mixed, called *wakes*, or, if taken together, simply *the wake*. The wake of the Dakota Maru slowly faded to nothing into the question repeated again by the sea-humanoid swimming along under the ship or attached like a remora onto the slick slimy layer of barnacles studding the underside of the ship; the question came much too long because the answer popped after the first two words of the question slid from the mouth of whoever it is that goes there; yes the one, the only one, who repeated, Where, Noman, was somebody's hiding place when the strife ended, and the bloated memory popped, and it was time for all evil to get away with murder? Where, Noman, was somebody's hiding place when the strife ended, and the bloated memory popped, and it was time for all evil to get away with murder? Where, Noman, was—

Eden La Falda is where they got away with murder! This is the answer, why do you keep repeating the question, are you not hearing the answer, I just gave the answer the fifteenth time, so make me the fucking puzzle piece I need wrapped all around with stylized fleur-de-lis; this one I hold here; here is the sixteenth repetition; Eden La Falda! Again!

A quick spark of silence then struck, saying, lighting, Where, Noman, was somebody's hiding place when the strife ended?

Christ almighty, I got to go up on deck, puke, cough, puke, and raise my nostrils to scoop down salt air! cried Noman, clanking down the hard wire brush and making loud pounding with his feet one by one toward the slippery climbing ladder welded to the side compartment ahead outside and to the left outside attached like the remoras, but so much more tightly. Noman gripped the eyelevel rungs one by one as they sank by at the same pace as his climbing which, from the ladders point of view, is simply just another of ten thousand smelly climbs it has endured since the launching of the Dakota Maru, when the champagne bottle smashed into the jut of her launch-time bow, but no matter, it didn't do enough damage to keep the keel from pounding up questions to the quickly ascending Noman. The answer to your question when it finally comes might be EMP attack, or it might be Eat, shit, piss, and play, which is, finally and all, the answer to what question? Yes, I am the host, you are a contestant, here's your money, yes; Merry Christmas, go on and take it!

Thus was the chain of adjectives that climbed with Noman up the ladder until the top came down, and he pushed it back up, and the hatch clanked loudly over, letting him come after thrusting and pushing so long and so unfruitfully that he leapt out of the hole into the sun and also into a wall of cheers, and he stood there asking himself, Where am I? Why a ship? Oh, yes. Tokophobia, the sallow lime-head heard again and again, leaning back on the soft, near-new kitchen of the psychologist's couch, listening to her decision as to which syndrome name should be applied to Mrs. Noman's unique and anguished disability.

He had come on his horse and run smack into Phyllis, in the flesh. No, please, no, not Phyllis. Phyllis should not be real, and I cannot be back again in the family room in my recliner and Phyllis in hers, staring at a rerun of the very big hit, My Six Hundred Pound Life. No, no, Noman, Phyllis was replying—it is not exploitation at all, this show. Damn you, you piss me off, you think you know everything, got all the fucking answers, gosh, and tell me again, because I don't really believe you, why again do you think it's not so bad that on my estimated delivery date, when my fear will be rocketing, you will be in Shanghai never the less? Why is it not worth the effort to push harder on the company to let you off the hook and stay back with me, when you and I both know my tokophobia will drive me over the edge because you have left to go play grabass with the boys way out to sea? Huh?

Phyllis' face then formed to a cold steel spike shooting over, spearing Noman tight to the recliner like a mounted bug for study, and, like a bug fearing for its life, Noman waved his arms and kicked his legs to ward off the impending fatal word-injection to be administered via needle next-formed from her heart, flying from her, and plunging deep into his arm. The plunger was pressed, his muscle filled; they missed the vein, like all poor nurses do, curse them; but the muscle was fine and would do in a pinch, so they injected into Noman's body, somehow, by some kind of black magic or blue or red or white or—magic all magic it matters not the color of the murderer, it matters only that the correct end result is attained, as the serum flowed to fill him with death, saying—I know you are somehow behind the death of my previous babies, I know that when you at last die you will be cast into a brand-new wing of hell, where in every room the guests are met by a mob of slavering razor-toothed slime-bound raging fifty-foot full-term fetuses, just like this one here, yes this—die! Now! Die, die, die— pretty babies, cute babies, pretty unborn children, come; his name is Noman, come to him kill him slowly, very very, yes, oh so slowly! Feast on him, bite, rip, chew, feed on the God-damned feast that he was always meant to be! Feast! Yes, viewers, on all the ships at sea, are you, ahem, I said, are you? Yes, are you—uh, yeah, that's right, you, you, and you—are you all up for a mutha'-fuckin' feast? Huh, I bet you are stumbling and strolling by on life's extremely long, very old, and quite worn out boardwalk, and know you, know you all, that regardless of the outcome for poor Noman, you can still look forward, all you innocents, to the additional items up for grabs on only the most special occasions, as presented via mostly unwatched flatscreened TV tubes at sea, by me, Father Dwyer; tubs of yogurt, for instance, or sliced melon—what, no. That's right, I said no, not *slice*, the golf term, as you suggest, but the cutting method *slice*, which is just the first of many such methods, such as chip, chop, dice, hash, julienne, mince, saw, scissor, cleave, rive, split, gash, incise, rip, slash, and slit. What? What's that you ask—I cannot hear you, you cannot be important though, since you were seated way in the back row by the security staff, who should have and I am sure did really check your press credentials, and you were found to be the perfect opposite from being qualified for a front row center sweet seat. So, I slice at your dome with this handy utensil! That's right, I slice you! And here comes a tiny drop or two of blood, and to avoid prosecution I will throw the slicer off the Bay Bridge at midnight, where it is and always will be the greatest show on earth. The creatures of the night dark deep will get a show; come swim down and see the deadly bloody evidence that was never discovered. Hip, hip, take your seats at my three-ring circus of a half-hour cooking show, and look; see me? I don't think you see me, I don't think you can, oh, yes, Who is this, you say? Hey, this is my carefully licensed dingbat skinny-slipped pale little waif of a used-up stage manager, who does its job exactly the same as the one Steve Allen had on his early to mid-sixties landmark of the very prototype of the now classic late-night variety talk show, televised even, handed to me a note a few minutes ago that reads, Do not address anyone seated in the back half of the audience rows, for two reasons: 1. It's damned pitch black up there, you can't see that you don't accidentally address one of the few people back there who may not be there at all, unless we can call them Mr. and Mrs. Seat, or like that, the Mr. and Misses' holy big emptinesses, cursed to only ever be seated on ice-cold seats which have never seen the warmth of even a single human ass tightly and super-sealed nastily and dangerously seated, sometimes with pinned and needled hands thrust sharply in the underbutt crack where the pot meets their fat pale flesh, their fat sweet cheeks all perfumed to cover their always stinking sweat-caked and super-gross skinny little thin-cracked butt-like anuses. There you go, there—but where was I, where, huh, was I anyway, sister, please sister; do not let your butts press together or something like that, is where it was—you're your carvings both old and new, if they've ever been carved, they're you, and: 2. It is too far to be heard, it is way out in the deepening dark, which bogs down the sound of any human voice, even the ones of the finalists in the every-summer hollerin' contest, held every year in Spivey's Corner since nineteen sixty-nine, but that lies full length in the cemetery now along with ham radio and the classic-car hobby; but you know, not to offend anybody, but, the remaining practitioners of these hobbies are typically one rack short of a full meal, thoroughly washed and precisely surgically boned by master butchers who took the best parts, only leaving the aging, the stupid, and the slow, and spanked them smartly on their heinies to send them quietly in the only direction still available, which, toward the silent shady wood whose leaves are slowly turning to the color of, is toward the autumn of their lives. Yes, then the next cruel cut, Noman—Noman and Skip, how 'bout the next word: *chip*. As in, chip it away, chip it away, chip it away now! Yes, that chip! Now, how am I going to get through the next dozen or so words of kinds of cuts, when I just took me about four hundred days to get all the way through *slice*, to say enough all the while twisting and turning to get to the good dirt and get rid of it, so there is no way any one of you seamen and seawomen, you dwarves and all you short and all you tall, all taken together regardless of size, could ever mistake the quick sharp word *slice* for anything other than itself. So we can feel good about that one but are instantly dismayed when we rise from the corpse of the first cutting word, and see that there are sixteen more cutting words to smother in logic and knowledge all of their fearsome miserable qualities and reduce them to harmless, virtuous, inert, formerly deadly, mere objects as natural features like canyons, cliffs, hills, mountains, and dry riverbeds are merely objects we never see at all after a while because they always have been and will be forever. Like when on the first dog walk with each new pup, the creature will spook when a car comes by, spook when a person with another dog walks by, even spook as each house is approached but when it passes, and after several hundred are passed again, the dog learns these things are just inert objects with no will of their own to cause them to eat their favorite prey, which had been all they wanted but after they got it, just became worthless again. Trees are pretty, but to a dog, mainly worthless. Houses are pretty, but to a dog, mainly worthless; so, he pranced his dog along daintily, Skip had a dog as a boy and pranced along daintily, and, this boils everything all down to the etymology of the word *skip*, as used for Frances Servon, the silly boy, skips along in the sun all the day, Skip; the boy, the silly boy, pranced along so far and so wide, that the backward, toothless, smelly, middle-ages peasants said to each other after he had gone through several hundred dogs, and after he had pranced by them for a thousand years, mummies though they were by that time, they reasoned that, There needs to be a special word for that. Eh, Clara? What would you say?

I think, said Clara, who happened to be the only degreed teacher in the village, I think that that particular step should be called by the name of the young man now old and probably by now dead who we first saw doing it. What do you think, Tim?

I think that makes sense. We got to grab him when he comes around and pulls into the pits, but the officials have said that the name of the moon is what we should call the step.

Why?

Because when the moon is full is when the skippers start to skip and skip. The moon is behind it all, you know. The moon. What I said.

Ah! cried Clara, thrusting her dagger-sharp index-finger at Tim—and did you just hear, it is not possible you did not hear—okay, Tim—yes. You may disappear now. You said the name it will be called—yes, the name it will be called and the name of my just-conceived son. Skip, it will be. Yes, yes, Skip! I swear I knew it all along, I—

You! stammered Father Dwyer, popping back to crystal clear consciousness, and gripping Clara by her firmest body part—you! You have hijacked my show! You are just about as much below qualified for anything a person can be, as anybody else ever has been who inside was thoroughly not! Begone, back to buggy-lugging beef sides from frozen freezer-meat railroad cars for less than minimum wage, in the rearward reaches of the TV station. These two creatures actually lower than the word *creature* was meant to describe—othermen, come, securitymen, come, take them out for legal lynching, beating, and shooting, yes!

There is no money in doing a cooking show that practically no one ever sees!

We will then, no, my brothers, sisters, and related nonessential children—we will become a gore video show, yes! If you are shocked at this out in viewer land limbo, cut us off now, yes! What is about to happen, you may find disturbing—a quick demonstration of all possible-cuts! Bring the first one out, now, yes, that one—the girl one! Here, here, yes—right there. I will now begin the work, and look, my hands are magic! I've not been Father Dwyer all my life without having developed some physical, mental, and cross-universal muscles, like: here I move my hands fast to a blur, and—chip! Look—in the blur something sharp came in my hand, chipped off her nose, and there—my hands all stopped, I hold nothing. I swear, swear, by God; the perfect crime commitment accessory that ensures the murder weapon has never been purchased to be traced to me that way, and that will never be discarded so crudely that it may be found, allowing tracking back to me by trace DNA, bullet-bore analysis, if a gun, or whatever. I simply will the weapon I want the blur to produce into its general direction, causing the mystical slicing away of the equally proper body appendage from the condemned, and forth again and again through the rest of the cut types, as chop, dice, hash, julienne, mince, saw, scissor, cleave, rive, split, gash, incise, rip, slash, slit, and all like that, as detailed in the thin, yellow, cheaply printed, very chemically smelly—snifit—mimeographed pile of rulebooks of which, we need to make sure there are enough for each contestant to have one, which, if not true, would cause the entire tournament to be cancelled, but that there are not so many left over that we've wasted as much as a dollar or two for each sliver-slip fragment of the shredded unnecessary outdated rulebooks, packed down in the bank of tall garbage-trash cans strapped to the sides of yonder log cabin, log cabin as in Honest Abe, the movie that went directly to DVD—and, so, there are—yes, a bloody mess surely, but a good clean kill!

Wait!

What?

Come with us Father, your mind needs rewinding, said the black-clad ninjas all in unison, that had instantaneously rushed in at Dwyer from all points of the compass sparked by his loud, exact, simple blurt, *what?* from some hiding place out in the unknown space beyond the flimsy walls. Mostly their kind are installed, but never needed; but if they are needed only once, multiple deadly tragedies are averted. So, they chanted at him in unison still, saying, We need you to take a sabbatical, like you and Skip both have done to be cleaned, you, Father, mentally so, need it; the boardroom gods in Abu Dhabi have determined it necessary. Did you forget, Father, that your show is monitored twenty-four-seven even though the listeners at sea may not always do so; or their loved ones to whom they have provided access as an exercise in maintaining togetherness during the long separations caused by the ever-longer sea voyages lined up today?

The boss of the ninjas reflexively nodded, the body language of the absolute truth, as often displayed by Big Pope Preston I, whose stand-in was in the process of rising to the very top of the cruise line corporate hierarchy. Yes, sighed Skip, sliming his already slimed bed slimier still, and the smell told him; the land, yes, no. Smells like land. The land yes, no. The: land, yes-no! Smells like land. That last was the best of all, so Skip rose. Lord God in heaven, I have done it! It stole from my body and covered some small regions of the soft plateau called by short-sighted humans a bed, which has many and varied purposes, ranging from the new, pure, absolute virgin's favorite solo activity, of the male and the female's absolute variety, to the used-up, pushed-out, pumped-out, saggy, experienced males or females of each and every species, pets and owners, owners and pets, to sleep or wake, to dream of it all your life but not working just that tiny bit more, toward the finish line. But Skip swept all this detritus off and away, making room for the surprising but true fact: he was at sea.

I am at sea. The blue sky.

I am at sea where there is no time, because the blue sky above will last as it has from planet-birth to dissolution within the expanding dying sun, long after I am dust.

Lord God, thank you, muttered Skip. But got to shake these cobwebs spidered all around, all waving, all alive; very creepy, very, and, said Skip—hard to be around, so must get away now. Yes, right now. Because the creature slavering to bite into me is a creature of the bone-dry dead land. Get away, damn!

Cried the grammar school teacher, Sit down, Skippy, you must learn this lesson; it is not my lesson or your lesson, but this! Yes, this! This is today's Goddamn lesson! Listen! To the lesson! Have I made myself clear, students? What can you expect if you buy in, or, said differently, what will your brother demand of his little chicken-shit sibling when he is on his deathbed and it is too late to do any more than just one single thing, what? Do you hear it? The thing, yes, I hear it. Do you? Skip, answer me!

Wait! cried Skip, sharply raising his hand; he had been administered a mild shock in his large, nearly impacted bowel, that told him to come up from the dream-world of his calm brain-space and look out at the world. He pulled away from the shock, opened his eyes, and saw layers of hot glue forming on his hands, and then realized that all this time he'd been nowhere else but this very spot, bent down to his work deep in the valley between the towers of sealed containers, with the rain still pounding loudly on the back of his heavy yellow rubberized waterproof five-hundred-dollar raincoat. Yes, all right, I have been here all along, so! It is time for a well-earned break—and he rose and straightened, the water pouring off his impervious slicker, and turned to find his face pressed up against the sudden soundless arrival of a field-detective-leader of the fabled corporate personnel inquiry team, who had been sent via supersonic super-helicopter from far off Abu Dhabi, where the clean bright gods of the great shipping company who man the internal personnel scanners had paused it at the next anonymous crew member, Skip.

Oh, God, look at this one. This one will probably not make it, said one internal organ of the shipping corporation to another, as they both gazed into the giant boardroom screen containing Skip's large milky-white sunken-eyed face.

Yes, said the female internal organ—this one will probably not make it because it's so far into its mental escape from the bleak grey boredom and depression and other similar symptoms of being at sea one time too many that it needs to be shaken, stirred, and awakened.

True, nodded the male internal organ—and the best painless way to accomplish that would be to send a detective and cause this one to have to answer for its mental whereabouts for approximately a week or a week and a half prior to when the last screen-shot was taken.

I agree. Let's send out the inquiry team—and this is especially critical in this case, because this is the one who passed up the offer to become land-based and to get a great raise.

Yes. This is extraordinarily urgent. The team must be there now.

Snap!

So, instantly then, smack on the now, the lead member of the inquiry team materialized and shot a thin stream of jet-black words into Skip's eye, straight up inside further into his lumpy, warty, thickening brain—the first step was to perform a mild lobotomy to loosen up Skip's mental impaction, the second was to quick-scan the internal memories behind his face that every one of his species has but that God has designed in such a way that no one, with no exception, is ever allowed to consciously remember, and, third, to develop the newly formed line of interrogatories pried from underneath Skip's cauliflowery, deeply fissured brain, which then in the next moment the pinprick of the detective's droll voice drove home as a simple verbal question, the tone of which demanded crisp, sharp, one-word answers directly point-to-point from Skip's eyes back to his, given immediately if not sooner.

Mr. Skip! Did you walk off the job today and revisit Mr. Wasdyke's office? And, if so, did you this time accept, or turn down, the job offer to step into a Manager's grey padded cell back in the offices on land?

I did not walk off the job today.

Why then is it in your mind a memory stating that you have?

I don't know. Listen, let me by, I need to go get some air!

No, there is more. Stand there unmoving, I need to get to all the questions today.

I am all wet and ice-cold, and I need to get some air!

Stand there!

I will brain you! Let me by!

No, no, NO—

Pow! Slapped Skip's burly seaman's knuckles against the yielding lower jawbone of the usually feared but always found to be weak and afraid when attacked back, great big bully of an inquiry team field detective. The jaw bent, splintered, and snapped, and Skip pushed by and mounted the ladder, but the wounded, shock-driven, tough-as-nails detective followed as if its mouth pain was nonexistent, feet pounding, hands slapping its way up the ladder, shouting, yelling, Hey, hey! Come back, I want you! Its grounds to fire you to harm me! I say, listen and stop and listen, its grounds to fire you to harm me, listen and stop and stop and listen and its grounds to fire you and blacklist you also, industry wide; yes, it is, it is, stop stop—

Skip paled all cold: I cannot lose my job, cannot, no, cannot, here goes, yes, no no!

His steel toe work-boot shot down and smashed the detective soundly and solidly in the center of his wide tall face. At that moment, he also willed the scent of his anal sphincter, unwashed since the Dakota left home port, to enter the nostrils of the detective and blast him away, then to go on blasting detritus from the yard toward and into the road, with this increasing lawn-service gang with the usual several hundred ear-splitting, two-cycle, gas-powered, revved-to-the-max, industrial-strength leaf blowers, as may be found swarming all over on any given sunny day on the green grass of any given well-kept split level in any given quiet neighborhood under any given big blue sky. They threw noise up for any given number of miles and out sideways all around for any given number of blocks. No baby could sleep, and neither could any night-shift workers lying in a hot, artificially dark, closed-in, stuffy room, sleep aids churning in their pitch black bellies, lying—eyes pressed shut—trying to believe it is really midnight, as it is actually three quarters of the way 'round the world, on the twenty-third floor of the gleaming chrome and tinted plate-glass, great oblong boardroom, where the black-suited upper-bosses have moved on to looking at the plans for the Dakota Maru, while viewing clips which indicate the great ship's trending timeline zooming toward total obsolescence, then on to driving up on the low-tide beach of the breakers' yard in Bangladesh, where tiny antlike turbaned bearded men will swarm up and engulf her into a pile of scrap within which will be buried at least one obsolete wall-mounted television, not worth picking out and cleaning up for resale, which once presented the constantly flowing surging and moving image of the *Sunday Dinner with Father Dwyer* cooking show.

Come with us Father, your mind needs rewinding.

What?

Come with us Father, your mind needs rewinding. As all rented videos were required to be returned rewound, by all video rental stores in the early to mid-nineties.

What?

What, is that we, in a sense, have rented you, and, now that you have a couple thousand episodes under your belt, you need to be upgraded to a more modern version, but still keep the primitive charm of your dated but effective-for-your-target-audience delivery. Come with us! Come now!

But I got a show to do!

Your fans will have to make do with reruns tonight, I fear. Come quietly, Father, come now. Here, come on, don't make this any more difficult than it has to be, eh—

Do not touch me! You treat me as an ingredient! I know you!

Father, come. Come now.

I am not merely an ingredient for your moneymaking, swampland country boil-pot! Shrimp and crawdads, surely, yes—but not that! I know what you do!

Come father. Calmly please. Your very words are hot with instability.

My show! I need to do it!

The Detective's hand sliced down and slapped against its thigh.

Father! If you do not come, we will take you to land and set you free with no job! And, if you do not come, after you are set free we will refuse to tell anyone thinking of hiring you, out in some badlands, barren and dust choked, under the slice of the noontime sun, no I am sorry, yes, the Father worked here, but we don't like to talk about why he was let go.

Really? Lord! He seems like such a mild and serious and very intelligent priest!

Well, I'll lay it right out; he is not very intelligent, plus not a very good cellist or double-bass player at all! Much too many false notes, you know. Full of clinkery, tinkling, off-key drab-drops down to the concrete floor!

Are you sure?

Absolutely.

No!

Yes!

I—Dwyer started to continue resisting, but his old heavy frame was heaving from all the yelling, and with each exchange it came up, a wave, come at him like a freak beach-breaker all full of driftwood jagged and deadly; no job; deadly; no job, no; at his age, Lord no, and it went back and forth and again and again, until, he tired, first.

All right, you win, he sighed, and instantly out of the studio formed a room with concrete chairs set in the ground on either side of a concrete table. The room was a perfect square of freshly hardened yet not cured concrete, full of heavy hot air settling in layers, radiating wet concrete stench, starting his head spinning until it became a blurry, whirly, black platter, spinning like a record baby, round round, round round! The spinning sped up and up, and Dwyer flattened and pulled out into a steel rod turned by a motor underneath the platter, and the quick sharp needle settled into Dwyer's grooves, cut into vinyl sounding all pure, and it sang out the musical conversation, as: Father, did you leave your post and go to a hut where a small man screamed *Mau!* at you to push you and force you to eat a head cheese sandwich on rye? With, as you do well know, accompanied by orange juice from China, yogurt from Canada, milk from the USA, a red sauce of unfathomable spiciness from Korea, and curried ketchup from Germany—which, by some coincidence that could never really happen, is exactly the tape of the rerun of your show that I told you we would put in to cover while you were brought here for your very critical, possibly life-changing interrogation? Huh, were you, were you, were you, huh? Tell us, tell us now you are spun up to the proper speed, now I will jog the needle and you will use the black magic you are suspected of performing to smoothly answer right up and out making vibrations from the spin of the gleaming black vinyl platter of truth! I will let you stew here and run out the answer, and as it will take a week or two, I will have more than enough time to drink my fill of my favorite brew in my favorite bar with my buddies. See, I was going to tell you I was going out to take a week-long piss, but as we are demanding that you tell the absolute truth, the least we must do is to return the truth in kind, even though you will no doubt prove a slacker and be relieved of duty. So, bye for a while, relax, me and my men will be back. Come on, men, let's go, we got to get the third guy on this ship, let's see. His name—the name on this printout is, huh, this can't be right—Noman? Can that be a person's name? Must be a misspelling—probably supposed to be Norman, get it? Noman, Norman, Noman, Norman—see, after a while they merge and blend and fuse into Norman, and—our GPS system will guide us to the nearest Norman. There, drive faster! We got several bundles of ten thousand horsepower each, bolted down in this rig—faster faster—all worldwide crazy we can snoop as needed, but no, there, that house. That large split-level. With the old Chrysler rotting five inches a year into the old lawn by the house; pitted, rusted, and lost, and used to be bright blue and brand new. Let's go on in and get the bastard!

The nasty, brutish, and short fireplug door-basher came up around the head detective and swung his two-ton solid-steel ram into the already fairly well rotted door, and through the frame, just now all hung with shards, swarmed the inquisitors; a woman stood pregnant before them holding a silvery television remote. She began to say, What the hell is this? but, right when her mouth opened, the chief detective responded in advance, words that would be a fitting response to any question that might come from her, namely just a fast, wordless ram of a black, cylindrical, bitter, rock-hard plug of silence several miles down her throat, choking her silent and injecting the words the detective sharply shouted, as, Where is he? Where is Norman, we need to interrogate Norman. Where is he? The GPS says a Norman lives here, so where is the Norman, the Norman, where is he, let us look—

No, no, no, no! she said. There is no Norman. There is only a Noman, and he is far off on the tossing seas striving his ass out toward Shanghai!

Why did he go there, what has he to hide? Why did he not stay to consent to see us?

He tried to stay! He tried so hard, and he swore to God he

had no choice but to go, or he would be fired with one very strong forever blast, and we would go over the brink to homelessness; he fought the Shanghai assignment like hell, he even gave in a confidential doctor's note about my horrid condition—oh no, no, it's not contagious of course, it's not that kind of disorder you know, a thing of the mind not the body, yes, I'm sure, I do not speak unless I'm sure, so: don't worry your pretty little sweet-cakes about it, please. But, I hope you are not here from the big outfit he works for, whose top talent are probably out of this world angry for his having aired his beefs in public like he did, in that radio broadcast—

Wait! Hold it! What radio broadcast?

What? You aren't aware of the worldwide radio broadcast he used to shout the word? My God, how can you do your job when you're so out of touch—well, actually, April fool's, there's no radio broadcast. I just threw that on you for effect, to shake your voice-rattle. So, what? Are you pissed I messed with you? I hope so, I do! Your kind's such fun to piss off!

No, we are not pissed, not at all, we are not as emotional a breed as yours. But we need to speak to this Norman about why he left his post in the not-so-distant past. Get him please, he no doubt is hiding upstairs, leaving you to get rid of us, so he can come down and you two can take off your masks, and resume your full-scale marital screaming match. We are no welcome wagon, old-grey-lady-style volunteers with no lives and with time to kill because our husbands have been stricken with strokes or any other thing you can name that blasts a body into being bedridden. We are not here because we have great rags to chew slowly and then more slowly and down and down incrementally like that, spending enough hours to kill our prey's afternoon; we are not the kind you have to actually cross the line into rudeness territory to get them to leave before your rage dims, and when he comes down it will just be like shooting each other with highly-phallic-by-design, meant-to-train-young-children-to-kill, Nerf-N-Strike Modulus ECS-10

Blasters which go for less than a dime a dozen in every dollar store in this state according to the most holy Google, and once that's done, the second step out of the minimum seven thousand steps to the end that might end up consuming your entire lifetime when only in the last moment before death you pay attention to your having been immobile for hours, days, weeks, maybe even years or multiple reincarnated lifetimes—

All right, already! I will tell you what I have been straining to know about my sweet spouse. Yes, I won't deny him; the one you are seeking information on is my spouse. Here is what I know—I met him in a bowling alley. I was shucking vittles at the snackie in a cute blue uniform. Very, very pert I was. He sat there not bowling. He looked somehow lost, so I went up and held him out a beer and said, Can I serve you, sir? You look absolutely bushed. How about a Schlitz?

He said nothing—but I knew the gears were grinding; they circled and circled silently behind his eyes. They stopped. The gate to him reopened. I tossed in more words.

Well, how about it sir? Schlitz? Bud? Coke? What? You need a drink. You need one bad—I threw those words in the crusher and again, the gears began to grind, saying, I, uh, oh, yes—finally, he petered out, so I shoveled more in.

Yeah, I know the look, kiddo. You've had a hell of a day. Right honey?

The balls rolled on and on, strike after strike behind him, and his gate at last hung open, silent, and vulnerable, so I pulled a grenade's pin, tossed the grenade in, and got back.

We even have milk. If you can't decide, I mean. But, it might be—guess what?

I threw some more shovelfuls of silence through his gate and at last, the blast resounded. He clogged, gasped, and spurted out like a food fragment flung from a successful extra-violently-applied Heimlich—I don't know. What?

Expired. It could be too old. It could be sour. It could be rotten. A Schlitz is what you really need. None of that goes rotten. How about it. Tell you what—first one's on me!

On you? Why?

I like you, I think.

But—I—

Okay, I'll be right back. Hold that thought!

He disappeared like a light switched off in him. A sudden sense of being startled surged to take me over, but I threw up a verbal wall to stop it, saying, Where'd he go, where?

And when no one answered, mister smartass failed-pet-detective turned human-version, I turned, tossed the beer back in the cooler, and was sure I'd never see him again, but what I didn't know and still don't know—but God is giving me the words to tell you—he is out at sea on the way to Shanghai desperately trying in his deep, stinking, cold steel box, number seven hundred of the thousands of such boxes that are joined together forming a large great chunk of the Dakota Maru, or whatever he told me the name of the ship was, he rips the door zipper down and steps through into the past to block and sabotage and derail our marriage so that it never was. That something, huh? That's what he told me, and that's what he yelled at the men holding the straps of his filthy super-tight straitjacket when they took him from me for what turned out to be forever, saying over and over, Hey you, Loonie, hey, you will never make it in pro bowling, nay, at least up to now, at least, yes; bowl after bowl rolling, tossed by him—missing way wide of a strike but who really gives a damn? I am way too old to shoot for pro bowler now, anyway! Why do I say that? Well, here's why—and Noman doesn't even know about this. He found me in a bowling alley for a reason; I was born knowing how to bowl; in seventeen prior lives I have been striving for the brass ring of being named professional bowler; and maybe in prior lives I had been, but you know, there's something untrustworthy about the process of lives cascading down; the life starts out being a lot like a perfect new simple rubber stamp, with everything that makes you you imprinted, which makes the first life it forges on the anvil of the universe sharp as a razor, perfectly defined, already professionally puffed up and pulled as a perfectly detailed life description from the planet-sized shapes, forms, and everything else that encases the brand new life, defined to perfection by some unsung hero of a craftsman. But, each time the born-live-die is complete, the soul's image is a bit more blurred; but, it becomes the next stamp to spark the third life, and the same, and the fourth and the fifth as well. Until it does not strike anything that can be alive anymore. Until it stamps out a useless person without the ability to remain alive and viable. It stamps out a person that just gets flushed away with some random human's menstruation fluids. That is the catch-all, a little unseen, hidden auto-abortion that is when us humans actually die for good. Didn't know that, did you, Mr. smart detective? All prior deaths are illusory, illusory, yes yes—yes—

Get to the point, woman! You ramble on too hither and yon! Make sense, please!

Okay, anyway, I ended up flopping, washing out most colorfully from my striving to qualify for professional, I felt fuzzy and nearly pins and needles all over, I felt achy-jointed and flatfooted and very, very, dumb; inside me was an arson scene, and what's worse, the arson was already too long in the tooth, quite the cold case—so they sat me down aside and told me, I better give up right now. That shook me, and I said, What will I do with my life? All the years that common, uninteresting, everyday people spend schooling and learning and rising toward some fruitful career, I had spent bowling twenty-four seven, I had not eaten or slept all that time, I had not showered or combed my hair or brushed my teeth for all those years, just my right-hand fingertips were craggy and cracked into a bowler's callus—the coach stopped me right there. He said, Phyllis, listen; and so, I listened.

The bowling alley owners want to take you on as a snack bar manager.

Huh?

Snack bar manager. Yes—they told me to ask you if you'd like the job.

Job? Bowling really over, is it over? The coach dissolved under the flood of gushing thinking bursting out like I had ruptured inside like some badly engineered and treacherous to live downstream from, great big cement dam. The flood came; Lord God, I need clothes, I've not worn clothes yet in my life; Lord God, I need food and water, I've not tasted anything since my last sip of momma's magic womb-juice; I need to brush after I eat; before death you get a last meal, after birth you get a first meal, Lord God, it's mad, all mad, crazy and mad, it's enough to make you leap, shout, I—

Hands came on me pushing me off the coach's lap, he laughed, and I stood back up and he sprayed me with, Well, I guess that means you'll take the job! Is that what you meant to say, Lash Flickery-Lips? That's your growth name, you know. Like it's—it's kind of an alias. Phyllis translates to *Lash* in this universe, your last name that I dare not say translates to *Flickery-Lips*, you know? You know?

So, yes, I see—so when do I start peddling vittles? Grey hamburgers like they sell at aquariums and museums and zoos? I can stand to go to those kinds of places, you know, at least I could prior to the tokophobia gripping hold of the thighs of my brain. It's in a dark space you know. Hey, listen, Coach, I bet—you know, someday I will read a book where a guy zips open a steel wall in the smelly close belly of an aging containership and springs out through to prevent a marriage, more yet, to even prevent there having been a meeting at all—say, maybe if you are that guy, Coach, you can use your powers to send me all the way back, after clearing it with the fiery grand creator that I be blessed with an ear for music; that is not me by the way, but just an example, of what one who spent twenty solid years learning an instrument, only to come to the conclusion, given by the sign on the bricked-solid dead end, at the end of the twenty years, that said, STOP, YOU WILL NEVER MAKE IT, because you are TONE DEAF! So, you see detective, my striving was to bowl but the sign at the end of my dead end, which by the way was also bricked solid but not with bricks but by used-up, burned out coach after coach after coach, that my mindless elemental liar of a bowling-ghost laid on me saying, STOP, YOU WILL NEVER MAKE IT, because you are WEAK AND PUNY AND HAVE NO INHERENT SENSE OF DIRECTION AND WORST OF ALL YOUR MAGNIFICENT BUTT HAS YOU WAY OFF BALANCE ALL THE TIME! So, you see I almost changed direction to take up an instrument like the other loser I didn't know was in parallel with me at the time, but: after I dragged my poor farmer of a Father to ten Four at the Top concerts, all held at Tepid Corner Ballroom up off Times Square only on weeknights and after midnight, the coach pulled my leash as I have stated and offered me the job. He said, Phyllis, listen; and so, I listened.

The bowling alley owners want to take you on as a snack bar manager.

Huh? Me? Uh.

And the rest, as they say, is history, and I have nothing else to tell you. Unless of course you just want to suffer through the hundredth telling, with minor variations, of the same damned revolving door to another and another nothing state that has been my life!

I, said the detective, am not sure, as I say every time. Let me think about it a few centuries, maybe we'll want to hear it, and maybe we won't.

No, no—I am done now and am sure that you won't.

What makes you so sure? Can you read minds?

No. I can shoot a gun.

No, wait, here—no don't—

Finger twitched making tiny explosion creating intense pressure driving hard metal slightly pointed object, simple object like one pebble of millions laid out across a back yard, causing another rubber stamp to be renewed and flipped and stamp out a new life for the detective; and hopefully that mother, whoever, wherever she is, will not be prone to develop another case of tokophobia. After the new detective was born and was grown and once more was whole and healthy and again a full-fledged detective, he went with his men to see the subject, object, and probable cause of the mystery, Father Dwyer, in the very flesh. The reverend Father Dwyer was poised behind his iconic bright shiny cooking-show-of-the-absolute-heavens-style Jesus' spirit church-certified food preparation surface, otherwise known as his counter. The priest gazed out at the large, loud director's clapboard about to be slammed down sending everyone within line of sight the usual begin-the-shoot magic symbol and Dwyer's mouth opened ready to say what he always said and was sick of saying and oh my god, oh my God, let me get past this gig, let me retire, yes retire, let's start now, yes let's, and from his mouth he pushed air, but, instead of what he'd planned to say about the pros and cons of a lifestyle that mandates endless flows and gushes of spewing words about some food, or this, or that, but instead a hard, razor-sharp voice came out, stopped in the air before his face, turned, and jammed itself into his mouth and past to his hindbrain, as if a red-hot rod jabbed words down in his gullet sequentially pouring, saying, Hey, you! You, Father Dwyer! Hold it there, yes, right there. I have come from the corporate office to investigate your supposed absence from the show either mentally or physically, just to know how you filled those several hours, more and more again and again—are you disillusioned with the work, is that it? Is it time to pass the big fat baton to a new gal or guy and slowly recede into the world of dim, and from there to the world of dark, and from there I can't tell you, when you enter there you must be totally engulfed in surprise that will jolt you and tell you to tell me the God's honest truth about, did you abandon your post or not? And, if not, where is the proof? And, if so, was there a true emergency life and death need to do so? And, if so, please provide notarized signed and stamped certification from a mental or physical health care professional, who must be no lower than the rank of MD, and this proof to be provided immediately when asked to do so, unless you have not prepared for our visit and completed the necessary documentation exactly as specified in preparation for our appointment, in which case your ass is up shit's creek. Listen. I say—

No, wait, said Dwyer back out directly into the tiny hole in the tiny tip of the red hot rod of a word-driver, thus ensuring the words would reach the detective after no more than two dozen long-path DX laps around the big jelly-fat super-blue globule we live on, Wait, I was never told that I would have to have any documentation prepared, much less that this witch hunt was even afoot at all, or that you or anyone at all from corporate was going to be here to meet with me to question me, interrogate me, all hell-bent to not believe me like your kind always does! After all, I am the major star burdening the wirelines on your puny network, and, so, as such, leave my God-damned soundstage absolutely immediately and right now. Leave this instant, and as for your mouth, zip it, yes! Leave without another word, or I will call tangential security!

What, those feeble old blue-hat seniors?—that are too old and feeble to be allowed to carry guns? Those guys you mean? Ha, a funny joke—

SECURITY! While I await their arrival, you do not exist—here, let's start the show now, men; on this vessel, reconstituted iced tea is served with every meal. Nobody on board drinks water at all, and here is why. It's the myth about the albatross, it is, so shut up—

No, I will not shut my hole, Father! Why did you revisit, on company time, the Mau hut? Ring a bell, Father? Mau! They yelled *mau* at you again and again. Though it is abandoned now, you had to call, just had to, eh?

SECURITY! No, I deny you. There is no you. And even if I am wrong, there's big loopholes I can exploit—but I got to go on with this show, right boys? Here goes, where was I, oh who cares, let me skim off the film from about my cerebellum, which says, When I asked for some, Michael, confused at first, kindly brought a case of spring water to my room, even though actually, I have no idea what that means—uh, wait—guys, you are here, thank God! Cut the camera!

Father, how are you? Did you call security? said the tall wide blue spectral big goon and his gang of buddies that had just slimed in through the door, reared up, and come down, becoming a slimy cylinder encasing the detective in their large, long, capturization pod.

Yes, but—oh I see, yes, you got him, you encase him now, that's great—

Huh? What the hell do you mean? I got no one—and neither do my men. He has become us. Because, you see, because of corporate headquarters budget cuts, we must all wear many hats. I and my men are indeed security, who, because of our mission, must double up as the detectation staff.

What the hell is detectation?

Do not try to distract us! We therefore relay from our deep blue bellies the earlier detective's fervent query, which was: why the fuck did you leave your post in the middle of a show, bitch, or bastard, or whatever else you may pretend to be? Which is it anyway, fat smelly priest who we are told mixes up meatloaf with the two bare hands you just used to wipe your canyony ass-crack after your daily bout with the runnies?

Huh, I—canyony? What the hell is canyony? Dear Lord—canyony, and that other word, what was it, what? The word from before?

Huh? Why—how is that pertinent?

Never mind why, maybe I'll tell you why when I think of it. What the hell was it? God, if only I could remember. It's slicing the tip of my tongue, no, not the death by a thousand cuts—please not—

Priest! You are trying again to distract us. This is very very,

very; unfair.

What?

Unfair! Why? Your ears dysfunctional?

Dysfunctional? Did you just say-dysfunctional?

Yes, we did. Why?

Their just stated words sank out of sight like a wedding party whose dance floor had just disappeared and shot all attending boy-girl pairs into the proper number of frilly-covered king-size beds way down in the darkness, so there would be no delay in starting their over-wedding-night athletic assignments within which they must strive to successfully create their own personal fetuses; and in their place flowed a super-grand announcement from all the thousands of PA speakers arrayed all around spiraling in welding the last words of the announcement down, as, *Winner! Winner! You have said the secret word! And the prize value accumulated since the last secret word was said, over thirty years ago, is forty-three billion dollars, cash!*

What? said the stretch-mouthed blue man, throwing the words of the detective deep down way below its gullet, saying, What the fuck is this? This is some kind of hoax, this company has not got a pot to piss in, the books are cooked thirty times over. The company doesn't even have that kind of money, this is a jailbreak, this amounts to a serious crime, come on Dwyer, turn around, back up, put your hands behind your back, you are under arrest—

No no no, but the walls opened, plucking Dwyer away to a safe distance, and tsunami after tsunami of flowing green plunged at the blue man and began to flow in around him, and the amount specified flowed toward, over, and around him to bury him under forty-three billion green paper slips called dollar bills to crush him, knowing his death would be easy, up and up and up came the waterline, all braided and fresh and airless and smothering, and the last thing the blue man with the parasitic detective swallowed deep down its unpleasantly hot humid belly heard before smothering under the weight of the currency was, *Okay, get ready, get ready you lucky son of a bitch or whatever she calls herself, here comes your prize flowed all out over you!* and out it came, out it came, it came and bulged and mounded up and became all molded hot and steaming, the very spitting image of Skip being called up toward the steel grooming table in Dog and Cat Salon grooming position number three, which looks like but is not the ballet dance from hell!

Up, boy! Come, here, up!

Hands intertwined under his belly, and the hands pulled him up as great industrial slings pull great boats from the water and swing them around to the cradle meant for their maintenance to be done on for next season, growing season of the dog hair and anal gland stink and scratch and hull barnacle scraped with a blue barrel to the side for to shovel the sea filth scraped away so carefully, rule one is do not mar the hull's finish, do not scrape bloody the flanks of the dog, do not let the barnacles and the rest of the unidentifiable sea-wrack on the ground floor, beneath the boat dog, the hairy mass needs to be swept, raked, and shoveled thoroughly and often so the boatyard salon the boat dog is groomed in will be neat and inviting for any future guests; Skip stood on the table, all fours, noosed up again to the frame of torment as it is called in dog world, the frame of torment, the half-hanging cruel braided noose nearly strangling, yes, but maybe not, because the slide of the brush comb and clipper-whiz down over the lean sides rippled with ribs, and if a dog could have goosebumps—do dogs get goosebumps, huh?—maybe it is not true to life, but it is a hell of a ride to take, so Skip stood there and up came the third coming of the sloth-detecting fuckoff-detector of a detective, saying, So, Skip, it is true! I see you're getting, let's see, sure—you're getting a nail trim, anal gland squeeze, and hot spot salve applied to any necessary rashes, scrapes, bumps, or raw-licked itchy areas, so Skip—Skip! You there in that dog, Skip? You there?

Yes I am, barked the hypnogogic man in the dog all hidden.

The groomer worked on the dog as the detective slammed out with great heat and smoke, So, I have caught you red-handed! Here you are getting a grooming on your dog-side on company time. This is serious, yes, very serious, I see also you tried your best to change your body and mind, mind and body, to purebred dog, with a concrete pour hardening in your brother's transverse colon. Sure, they got you standing like a dog of granite carved for a palace all noosed up to be kept still just like every other pet in the place, is what we see. That is really where we should all end up, being pampered like pet dogs of the one percent. What, the Dakota Maru container turnbuckle-tie-down every-day-all-day-in-every-weather rust-removal job too much for you son, hmmmm? Dying to get back to the land to dump this sea job? It hasn't turned out be the cup of tea you thought it would be? As a boy, we know as a fact, you looked at Jane's Fighting Ships under your blanket bed tent and with your Ray-O-Vac flash light blowing the dark away from the pages like the same kind of machine blows leaves off patios—you know now several hundred Mars years into consciousness, that it had been a big flub to get addicted to the big, steel, indestructible, bouncy, floaty hulls all gouged out and scarred up from a lifetime of hitting large four-by-four driftwood lying just under the whitecaps, each leaving its signature though all are namelessly dumb with age now. Everything you've touched or noticed in your life is encrusted within you or without you, whichever being decided by the basic nature of the thing itself. So, Skip, there are the charges. What do you plead? Guilty, or not guilty?

Well?

What?

Guilty or not guilty!

Suction suddenly locked onto Skip's bent back, and, sealed in place by the yellow, drenched, five-hundred-dollars'-worth of stretched tight rubber raincoat, pulled up, getting Skip up though he did not know he would be getting up until he had already been up between five and six days, which exceeds the duty duration requirements of a containership seaman of his relatively high attained grade. Once up, he turned around, and though no one was there beside him in the plunging, freezing rain, he had to answer because someone had asked a question about if he was guilty or not guilty.

Of course, I am not guilty! What the hell would I be guilty of? And, he went on saying, shaking his worn steel knuckle-buster, I love the sea. Why would I leave my post as you say, and jeopardize this set-for-life gift of a sea-job that I have aboard this here fat, dumb, and happy, leaky tub of a Dakota Maru? All on the land are doomed to die! Only at sea is there absolute safety! This is why I want the job, sir! I want the job, is the bottom line, so? What do you think of me?

Well, you're not the kind of candidate I usually hire. But, you are the kind of candidate I absolutely need. So, Skippy my boy, we will groom you to absolutely peerless beauty. You will make a fine permanent member of the Maru at-sea Crew! Welcome aboard boy—

Woof!

Awwww—isn't he cute!

Yes, he is!

He is a very, very, cuddly-cute boy.

Breeder?

No, shelter.

Shelter? God, you made a miracle.

All right, said the interviewer, rising—here, let's shake hands. You have a fine job now—wait and see. Life on the sea is all different even for a normal person, let alone even more so for a stumbling bum of a jackdaw-voice big jelly with a miserable flat-Annie killed and hidden up your throat—so, then—here, shaky-shaky! Here, congratulations, the Dakota Maru, you will find, equates to a mansion for a Rockefeller! Slung slings, hidden canes, hidden walkers, and press outlets hushed up by tons of money. Okay? Come on, come, come with us.

Sorry, I'm not interested, said the very sober young Father Dwyer. I want my impact to be felt across all ships; across the whole planet; I want to create and command a race of atomic supermen who will dominate the earth!

What? Huh? That is some large ambition, said the interviewer as it formed quite fluidly into the detective from the top boardroom; I am sorry you don't want to start by getting your foot in the door by joining the crew of the all-hallowed Dakota Maru—but wait, wait. I have something here, yes—yes, yes. Father, do you know how to cook? Here's the perfect job that will slam you home aboard every ship in the fleet, and, even in the bedrooms of selected landlubbers done doing the nasty, too! But, I need to know, from you and you alone—did you once more hear for the first time the Bishop pleading for donation to the Bishop Crane vestment fund? Did you hear the Bishop's story about the store and the silkworm genocide? Did you, like all the other Germans did, turn your back on the truth?

No, no, no, said Father Dwyer. Quite the contrary—you know, it's also true that everything I have told you up until now has been total fabrication. As a matter of fact, God came in me on wings of gold the day I was born, while I was not quite done being forcibly forced to squeeze out through Mother's vagina, just because some foolish mortals had conspired against me and made the species-wide phony rule that when nine months of any fetus's gestation has come to fruition, every womb-dwelling parasitic fetus-child needs to be forced out through its mother's vagina, whether it wants to come out or not, and though most do not want to ever leave the wonderful womb, just want to spend as much time as possible manning the uterus they have been issued, and steering their unknown dim Mothers through their lives, not wanting to and only letting the crowd of white-coated mindless medicine men tear them free while they cry their scummy asses out, and for the next seven or eight decades, it will be proven to them time after time that life past the womb is just broken up increments of striving, failing, adjusting, and striving and failing and adjusting, right up to the day when reentry into the next womb in line occurs; and then it is time to start all over—so, see, Master Dwyer, that everything you will experience from this instant out to your old age, and just before your death, will be totally meaningless lies and fabrications. So, I know that because of that, you, Mister detective, are also a total fabrication. You don't really feel real, do you? Admit it. Come on. Admit!

No! shouted the detective—I admit nothing. You are so, so deluded; made pompous and much larger in your head than in real life, by your spoiled rotten lucked-out life of being star of a cable TV show about cooking this and that, that's really—

At last Father Dwyer's arm cut down the words, which at that point had been quite too much, as he cried, No! Since I know you are not real, and that it's no longer food for debate, don't bother me, fake shadow that you are. Let me do my show of explaining to my camera how Monday's lunch of fried chicken leg will be accompanied by a picture of an adjustable wrench.

Why that?

Never mind why that et cetera, it's been proven you're not real, never were and never will be, so go and pick up the adjustable wrench and take it, take it and use your considerable anger and muscular anatomy and swing it around and through spattering my brain bits into those men off-stage over there who are going to rush you and straightjacket you after you become a murderer who has walled off the past and for the first time in your life have come lucid to yourself and felt alive with the guilt of having killed me, and by this act we together have created a situation, unique to the prison you will be sealed away into for year after year of appeals, to await execution, where Jesus will be handing you the keys to your new-built mansion, on the beach with great views with its very with-it open floor plan and its very with-it stainless steel appliances in heaven that, since being installed, have been waiting for you, over on the side of time walled off from mine entirely, and then he will hand you his realtor's business card, and you will go into the house into a wide vacuum-tube room wall-lined with ninety naked well-built ten foot tall virgins. So, now that you've been figuratively put to bed for the last time by my rhetoric, Good-bye, sir!

Why, you bastard you bastard you bastard you; here you go, sir. The company has had it with you! I am not gone, no, it's you that must be eliminated, here, here, with this; and the wrench flashed into sight from where it had been hidden in the wide Indian-grass field the cooking show had become, after being thrown there by an angry Navy veteran motorcycle-juicer, enraged at the size of the busted knuckle the slipped wrench gave him, under his sunny day Saturday sixty-five Bel-Aire's hood, spun round and threw, changing magically the steel wrench to blur through the air, perfectly arcing up and down into the middle of this here field, where it will remain for approximately forever, and at most, infinity.

So, Noman—I was lying, I am not Dwyer, I am the detective. How did you not know that, Noman? How did you miss that fact, eh? Were you distracted by a pour of liquid voices, flowing by under the keel unseen just a half inch under your feet? Do you know of the patented super-greedy mecho-remoras specially bred to clean your very own long steel keel? Do sharks know of their remoras? That would give you a clue! And, since whales also sometimes might have remoras, you are really rather like Jonah, you know. You know?

No, more like Ossian actually. Ossian, yes. See this, Phyllis? See? Right there in that town.

Noman dissolved back away from the detective barrage back to when Phyllis had dragged him out to the Stumble and Strain concert, because he cried the blues that they would only be in town one time, and after that never again, because she had had a vision of their charter jet blowing up and plunging down into some sea someplace which ends up being much too deep for either diving or dragging or frogman-driven demolition or scrapping of any kind. On the way to the concert, Noman got them lost. They ended up hundreds of miles north of the place Stumble & Co. was going to perform. What had been done was simple to do. As Noman's fat forefinger punched the starting and ending points into the GPS-Traveler-brand, absolutely cheapest Chinese export device, improperly; and instead of being on the way to Ossian, NY, the machine threw back at Noman, all warm, sweaty, and gassy and Chinese as it was, the town of Ossian, IA. And now the car, which may as well have been an old baby Yugo or an AMC Matador, sat in the after-hours parking lot of a Roman Catholic Church in the seventies twilight, battering away the point they each had to make, but it was more like she was meant to win, because he based his knowledge of which Ossian was pertinent on his prior night's meditation kneeling on his special very colorful completely new prayer cloth that he'd found in some abandoned murderer's house down the block, which was only intended to be used by the stone cold sober, and attempting to cerebrally bore into all the supporting documentation that had been delivered twenty years out, under the prized S&S concert poster he had bought to give to Phyllis as a token of their close friendship.

Why the hell didn't you use the computer to get directions? she sniped.

Probably because computers are not invented yet, Noman stated in fact-tone.

The falling twilight pressed on, around, and up and below, and the smell of the dark suspended them far off the ground, up in the thinly and more thinly shrouded soft press of the mattress beneath them upon which they performed their first experimental coital coupling. Wetly, she ran to the bathroom afterwards to wash, and he gripped his pocket pad memo-book to record his first impressions of Phyllis' private parts: let's see, long, deep, tight, and slippery, is Phyllis. Willing to do the mouth thing, but cannot put her sharp teeth aside to gum me rather than draw fang tooth needle tipped pin style cuts down on my long but soft, droopy, drippy, smegma-caked, smelly you-know-what stashed safely and darkly behind my pants zipper, etcetera.

Clean as a virgin again, she came back to the bed. It's really something that you should be telling me this, said Phyllis.

Telling you what? he asked, his eyes rising from the memo book to hers.

I—I seem to remember you telling me something, but—

But what? Are you going cracked, Phyllis?

She looked up from the naked, hairy, male crotch her eyes had settled on, which she had been stroking as though the stroking would lead to a seminal ejaculation full of the memory she sought. She strained, knew she was straining, yes, they had missed out on attending the Stumble and Strain tribute concert but there was something far larger, fatter, plumper, and better—yes, he had, someplace in the last twenty-four hours of superheated dripping with various bodily fluids and worse, told her anyway that he loved her. It had swarmed out yellow tentacles all wrapping, winding, unwinding, and braiding. It had shunted her to the taken-track. To go from unwanted and tired of trying, to taken! Just in less than an instant, a life is changed, and she came to and again locked heavy, intense, and tight over his bulging and frustrated eyeballs. They felt pained like muscles never used, because of all yesterday afternoon's grabs, grasps, and passions; but, like any gang of juveniles suddenly cooped up in their victim's actual house, they interpreted the heat come up in them as a nonverbal command to trash the stupid place.

Condemn the place, damn the place, plant the seed of tokophobia in me, you bastard, thought Phyllis, thousands of miles away, soon to either go through with giving birth again or to commit suicide or worse, to come back after the death she was sure she would find during labor and foolishly marry the same uncaring worthless type of man again. A man like the man maneuvering the same type of interrogation simultaneously as the one she had just endured, also tuned one step downward as are many guitars serving big names from the past who are dead now, with the reason for the lower step given as this takes the pressure for a reason dropped on the floor never told, and lost. The detective sat in a plush, soft easy chair upholstered with copies of old Southern Hemisphere navigation maps portrayed in muted, hushed colors. Thusly, the chair asked up through the lower tracts of the detective, up into and up his esophagus, and out his mouth converted into speech, asking, Father Dwyer, did you turn your back on the Dead and Dying in the Collapsing Cathedral you fled for your life from long ago on the day of your ordination?

Father Dwyer had had enough foolishness. As though the off-camera Detective had never spoken, he rebelled against the Dubai Corporation by turning to the red light in the dark before the stage set and talking sincerely, in deep, moving, ecclesiastical tones to the audience which may be no one or millions, no ships but millions; speaking, saying, Viewers! We have been distracted by this endless onslaught of psychedelia enough! We return down to the purpose for which we were born: for me to conduct this cooking show as a loop running forever, and for you to sit and watch and listen until the end comes for you one by one, and again and again I will continue until time has withered and stripped your ever-seated and ever-engrossed skeletons of their last scraps of dead salmon-flaky tissue. So, back to cooking we go. Here; we need to demonstrate the making of a breakfast called Melba on Toast which may be formulated and cooked only every other Friday, and put on the sill of the open springtime kitchen window to cool like the hundreds of pies were when they were made by the same heavyweight, vintage, sturdy, old-world babushka cook-people that now out of that rather pained past reappear, each being startled into screaming by the sight of her own personal Melba and all being snatched away by the savage needle-sharp, slavering, gaping maw of a super-quick sudden wild tiger, that came at us after just one instant of materializing, of sideswiping the house and snatching the melba, then in the next instant plunging out into its own reality, through the image of ours that we don't expect to be anything at all like the one the tiger went behind. So, continued Father Dwyer, you have just been given a demonstration of one way that adherence to old customs in the kitchen leads to waste.

So. Now what? he said, planting his outsized fists on his hips. I think we don't have anything else on the agenda for this morning, viewers, so, enjoy the following fifteen minutes of Landowska playing the Goldberg Variations over and over again for however many repetitions it takes, while the engineers behind the scenes that I'm told are real and do exist, take the opportunity of this break to perform some system tests and tuning that will ensure that this program will be as legible to you for the next two thousand years or so as it has been for the past two thousand years or so. You know that Jesus ran the first cooking show for worldwide containerships, played professional concert piano, guitar, and trumpet, and accomplished many other things during his first thirty hidden years? Why, sure, it's true, and furthermore, he—

Father Dwyer, cried the detective on the other side of now, who had long ago tired of Dwyer's ever-rising-in-volume-and-intensity tirade, Father, quiet down, please do, as I have given totally up on you, and will report to the executives that you are out of your mind, a lost case, so I have moved on to interviewing Skip over here beyond, so I can't see you, but you squeal somewhat like a big porker of a farm sow, a sow who is not really an animal but who is almost but not quite human as you or me—

Skip?

Yeah, Skip. A viewer.

I don't know no Skip. What ship is he from?

Dakota Maru.

Never heard of it. Maybe then you can dissolve to nothing now, since I am tired of your bleating rudeness. Must you stoop so low as to remind me that I will never meet a single one of my viewers, and I will never feel the happiness applause brings or the happiness praise brings, or even the sadness of bad reviews; I don't even know if what I am doing is good or bad—oh, of course I believe it is good, but—I would not be the first or the last deluded person who chases fame down the wrong path that leads nowhere, not knowing they're bound for nowhere until the priest makes the sign of the last rites over them and a hush falls on the room all around, telling them this is it, as my brother said on his deathbed, or that hey, looks like the time has come to die! And that's the last signal that we should get the fuck back to Dubai, damned Frenchman!

What? I am not a Frenchman!

What the Hell are you then?

I—I never knew for sure, you see, I was adopted from a migrant shelter in the middle east, way back when—

Never mind when, what, or how! To me, you are just another fucking Frenchman!

Ok! Ok, sure, well, that's quite enough! Jesus Christ, I will dissolve now! Jesus Christ, you are so damned carried away with yourself that I must just—melt. I cannot take you, Dwyer! Never in all my years of detectation have I seen a creature like you!

Listen, pal, calm down. And, this is the last time I will tell you, *detectation* is not a word! Dissolve, melt, or however you need to break yourself down to reenter your endless series of laboratory beakers in the secret English meth lab you were an unwanted byproduct of!

My Lord and my God!

The detective flickered sinking to the deck of Father Dwyer's kitchen, and now was just a liquid that began absorbing itself down through scads and scads of fissures in the grey steel, each too tiny to see, but large enough for a spill to seep through. Detective, snowmelt, human splash-puddle step, or urine, or whatever: when melted to liquid these are all the same; all the same, as a Greek god's tall, wide, and deep golden museum-quality sculpture-bust. The dribble sucked through to the space below, which held only one extremely filthy mattress, atop a rust-rodded, cheapy, tricky, cunty, dickwad mess of a bedframe. The detective juice collected to the back of the mattress already so sodden with various fluids and crusted over with wetting and drying and wetting and drying that the detective puddle up atop the crust only created a small sizzle as it bored partway down into the crust and then settled, stopped dripping, and spoke to the one sitting there, saying, Skip! Skip, our meeting did not go well, either.

Skip looked up and saw the detective sizzling, boiling, and waiting. He wished he had not turned into a dog so he could speak like a human. He'd been three hours barking and crying as a dog, and what's worse he was never even told by the prankster that did this what sex of a dog was he. But, though he stayed silent but for a brief whine, the simmering puddle cooled and reconstituted and reformed itself into a living breathing near-human biped, which yanked a clipboard out of the air and looked at Skip and said, So, let's continue, here; your name is Skip. Let's do this quick, and then you can help me back to the kitchen where I need to prepare a feast for five hundred.

Skip tilted his head, trying to tell him, No, I can't talk. Can't you see I'm a dog?

Do you care at all about bringing to justice everybody in the chain of silkworm murder, sale, distribution, and purchase of silk by the hypnotized public?

Skip tilted the other way, saying, Listen, pal—can't you see I'm a dog?

I will take that thought as a yes.

How can that be, I—

Would you feel intensely gratified in knowing, for sure and for certain, that you will have taken part in saving millions over millions of tiny soulless lives?

Skip pawed the ground and yelled, once.

God damn, Skip, what did I do to deserve that yelling?

Yell.

What does it mean when you yell, You! What does it mean when I command, Fetch?

Yell—

Father Dwyer just above, called a halt to his show, blew his ears open, and said, what the hell is that? There are no dogs allowed on the Dakota Maru! Men, out back there! I know it's early but hey, help out, track down the f---ing dog! Scour the ship from stem to stern and get his ass off overboard, and move fast men, because you are men! Get him!

Father Dwyer. Father Dwyer, I must know the answers to a few last things.

What? Who? Where are you!

Never mind, here goes, just answer me now, just listen. The question is, did you confront the Bishop who lorded it over your ordination, about his love for the fuck, for brutally bringing his men to tears, about his long-ago sentence of life in prison without parole that he escaped because of a clerical error that no one ever noticed, and murder, if it is applicable and proven he did the slaughter? Answer. Yes, answer. Think hard about the answer or you may find yourself reduced to far less than you already are not.

Look, listen. You came in here again only to screw up my segment again, this time about the totally unknown and esoteric Kalte Platte dinner which I am trying to show my worshippers how to make, even if these worshippers exist only behind and up someplace deeper in my face that a small one like you could never see no matter how wide and high I gaped up my face to let you see, and the dinner was going to be topped over by the rare and hard to make artwork known as happy little Porky-Pig-faced deviled eggs. Hey! What do you have that's so damned urgent that this very key episode of *Sunday Dinner with Father Dwyer* should be fouled up and pre-empted entirely, maybe, if you get too involved?

Well, what I have, Father, is—

Wait—Men! Get that dog! There's the dog! Get it! Now! Now!

Yes, chief, yes, cried Lil' Albert, the last man Dwyer could always count on—okay; here, doggie, here boy! *Swipe!* Dammit, missed him, damn, he is a fast little bastard! Here, baby, here, yes, I know how to do this, I had dogs in the jungle much faster and tougher than this—*Swipe!* Oh, oh, no—

Lil' Albert mowed down the spot containing what was left of the Detective, and the shade it had become through all the beating and battering and yelling and screaming activated the inner switch labeled, IN CASE OF IMPENDING DEATH, FLIP THIS, and that pouffed and puffed the Detective into being sent instantly back to Dubai, lain prone and naked on the long CEO's-meeting-room conference table, naked because the emergency teleport was not yet developed to the point you could bring anything along that is other than you. The detective opened his eyes and found himself surrounded by hollow-faced empty suits of the highest-level-attainable rank in the corporation, next to the Grand CEO itself, out in New York City.

How did the mission go, they breathed over his nakedness, raising goosebumps, which were the last pleasant thing he would endure prior to telling them, The Mission? What Mission?

Lil' Albert chased the little Skip-dog, shouting, Here! Here! several hundred times until he collapsed, out of steam, only to find little Skip, all concerned for his play pal, licking out the filthy oozing inside of Lil' Albert's waxy right ear.

Dwyer stooped to pet the irresistibly cute dog, and when he touched it, it became a large plastic unpainted scale model of first seaman Skip, himself! The show was still taping; Lil' Albert lay unmoving and possibly now a vegetable due to the crack of his head on the steel deck and the lickslime in his ear which, left uncleaned, could lead to a fatal infection; Noman came through the steel wall also then; he'd been climbing the endless steel ladder toward the

Sun, remember, remember, remember, remember, but ended up stuck at the studio wall, which he then zipped down expecting to go back to Phyllis who needed to give him Hell more and then a whole lot more, but beyond the zipped down wall was not the Four Nuts in a Nuthouse concert he expected to meet Phyllis at, only he slammed into a head-on collision with huge explosions hammering his spirit away back home—and he melted down into a second plastic model flanking Dwyer, who, standing in the center, was ready to continue his show unaware that he had just lost his only two viewers and had nothing much to do now forever but stand on his green hilltop, pissing eternally into the gale-force forever wind—and the screen faded black; the show was over.

Hey, Noman, did he drop his pants? Did you turn down the land-job offer? No one does that! Why are you so damned confused and mixed up? Huh?

Hah! Skip, if you had to spend four hours watching TV in the family room with Phyllis, you would be happy to go to sea permanently, too.

They walked away, and went their ways separately, moving fast, stone-faced and grim, facing the great shipping corporation's endlessly shifting and morphing superpilingup of sloppywise totallystumped gameshow days.

Chapter Twelve
Checking in With the Winner of Today's Free China Cruise

—days ago, plus hours gone, plus all the minutes then, yes, right, yes only now, in this instant here, here yes, here; where I finally sleep, but fitfully. But still the place. Laughter is all laughter, not knowing that the vertical gaps in the laughter would solidify into up and down pumpkin-shaped Halloween up and downs, Halloween curving back and forth all gap-gashes separating the Halloween ten peeled orange segments, only good to eat when freshly laughed at and again and again but not for too long because the ones ripped away first will already start decomposing way before the whole thing's done. Knowing this, and fully awake and beginning to be conscious, the being-between-states-of-existence individual is aware somewhat of its surroundings; the steel curve ran around the invisible, dry, spread, nailless new hand. Foster thought, Yes, sure, all right, the whole world's a dream that will come around and save me and smother me with the resumption of waking life, what a mother-fucking life, but hip hip hooray, it wasn't what I thought, I was only in some closet in the back of my attic-of-a-mind temporarily, something stored from some juvenile nightmare; they say after all everything a body's ever been conscious of is kept someplace in storage, seems like a waste though, really. Seems like a waste of available space, but then again, the big brains say that only a tiny piece of brain gets used across an entire life-line timeline, or whatever she called it, calling out loud to be heard clearly by hard-of-hearing adult commuting students up dozing in the back uppermost row of the amphitheater semi-dust bowl of a gigantic old-fashioned yet modern-in-a-way-also classroom, yes, classroom is indeed the widely used term—but now I am awake from the ancient, ought-to-be-purged-out dream-memory, yes—*Ouch!* My head went against something real above. God, God, what—oh, I remember now. Steel. It is real steel is real, oh no—just as the skin of these hands, though I can't see them, have, in fact—in the pitch-dark solid pen of cold steel—turned reddish and wrinkled, and, from the hands up the arms to the body but unseen, the veins are all visible through the dying, suffocating, panicking translucent skin. Now, a sentient life form I was; the words that said that echoed from the left-behind, stretched-out, holy, quiet origin-pocket in that great body made all of the past that now falls behind and away gone, leaving me alone. But, no; what, Miss Sweetie? What, how did you get here, what do you say, hey, what do you… hey, what is funny and not funny at the same time in the same person stuck like a stick in the mushy ground of the blistering big here and now! Do not shit me, yes this is steel! Yes, do not shit me, it's steel all around; and it suddenly dawns; this is a steel barrel. The barrel is sealed and the air's limited; as is the sense of place, okay let's play a game; this is a cylinder going far into space and I am a hero, and I am unlike Laika, I am really alive, CCCP, I am really really, well. That yes. Yes, that's right. What a way to fade away gently, in company with hordes of worshipping, ticket-holding, paying and hollering and shouting, generic, same-faced customers. Yes, customers. Some say they are always right. Customers; white packets and money and… Okay, Jose. The customer is always right—what? What, you think this is funny? And who the hell are you?

Who?

You! You are a doll-like man. You make me remember. I—I seem to remember you are the Father of one of these fresh-faced little kids. You and I, or maybe just I, have become a sentient human life for the first time. Or, possibly lives. Mackie; Lord yes, I just told myself your name that I had forgotten. Oceans away now; see, if I try and see you, I'm always trying to see two, like me and you. This is possibly also when each twin realizes it, him, her is a twin. Hey, Mackie, where the hell we driving to?

To celebrate you, Foster—what else is more important than that? Don't answer—I'll tell you, nothing is more important than taking you out to where me and the boys will see to it you get exactly what is coming to you, from the start right to now the finish.

So, things quieted. Trees pastured lonely horses and no cows slid by our cruise. It occurs to Foster then that someplace, somewhere, sometime, someone said there's two ways there would be no cows in the field; first, if cows that once were there have been taken away, or, second, if there had never been any cows in the field at all. You know that, Mackie?

Mackie said, I can tell by that comment, that you have reached the point which some pro-choicers define as the point where human personhood is attained.

What?

Personhood. Simple as that. You're just another person spat from the deep bloody dark place your mother bloody mother shot you out all fresh and wide awake with years and years of life most probably stretching before you, you know; and I know you're not comfortable being given a break like this, an opportunity to carve and hammer and twist time back onto its anus just south of its rattle, and restart your ruined life. Lesser men are given no such chance, and great men do not get such a chance either. You are in the middle, and your outcome is on the tippy toes, on the fence, somewhat of a dead heat between Heaven and Hell. Thus, it logically follows, of course, that we have to try you over one time, maybe more, the way the time flies do, but at the same instant you look back and a moment ago feels like years. Time—and how it is perceived—is wonderfully chaotic. Don't you think, huh? I think it, I do—

Mackie, slow down! You're going to hit the stopped car coming after us! Oh gosh—

Mackie looked up from the region of his belly button at the large car face coming, and, as tears flew misty all around, he hit the brake, the bell, and the whistle and the buzzard, and did all the other things that would cause the general public to wince when they read in the pages of the thermometer-wordpaper the age of the driver of the causal car: eighty-nine years; and I swear to God the car just ran away! I pushed and pushed the brake and just went faster and faster, and that was that, the second burst to shards, and now that is how I ended up way up here standing in front of the judgement seat with white pillowy clouds writhing over and around my poor red-hot circus seat. The matineed show was done before, so we small boys and I—just me—went up in the holy place, and I tried the rightmost, carved, tall, wide brass door that weighs a ton, I think. But I did it, I got out—

They smashed silently into the WRX's rear and landed in the dead room; where is this place? It is round with flat ends and, no, there is a barrel in the corner. A barrel in the corner of the banquet hall, and there I am again with Miss Sweetie and the boys and Mackie toasting again, getting quite very sloshed, and I am suddenly back eating dangerously writhing and coiling spaghetti pasta thicker than telephone poles and bowling-ball-sized meatballs, breathing quite heavily, all panting to roll, and, get this; baby's finger and toe prints cover the ball; Lord God, baby's finger and toe prints cover the ball; Lord God, the room grew brighter with each bite off the giant, raw, red, blazing, hemorrhoidally-skinned balls, and here again rolls over Mackie's old speech which he just dusts off and reloads for every single bowling ball baptism he encounters. But, no matter, Foster by now has gained another pound, his eyelids have begun to part and his eyes have come slightly open; his hand coordination has increased, and he can now move the thumb in opposition to his fingers, thus he can now grasp the eating fork at the banquet table, but then again he could do this before and so, he didn't know if he was coming or going until a shudder and shiver tore through him waking him somehow out of some stupor, but it turned out to be Mackie toasting, saying, Johnny, you are the best! You are the best, you have done what we wanted and more! Right boys? And more!

Yay! chorused his hoodlums; I bet, I bet this is a brand-new drum, cried one hoodlum thinly from the back, because his eyes were open though he was still pressed in the darkness of the womb; his eyes were open, and he saw nothing, but not yet the lack of nothing, because that doesn't appear to anyone except in the last lit moment before death pulls up over; and, even then, it is only anticipation. Johnny, you are the best, repeated Mackie. You are the best, you have done what we wanted and more! Right boys? And more!

Yay! chorused all others that would find themselves on future trips to China—extraordinarily boring long slow trips to China, ending up nutty as all people spending their days knee-deep in eyeballs each of which was independently hand-plucked from random mobs of gesticulating people with red eyes full of veins like sleepy-time, night night, knee-deep, deep; deeply stripped varicose veins dance around the dining room all night on fragile-looking, spindly, brittle, veryfast veryquick legs a'shuffle. Yes, baby responds to sounds by moving or increasing the pulse. Plus, little deposits of fat, which retain heat, have begun to form. It's good these lifers on the *Sunday Dinner with Father Dwyer* cooking show's crew have just all sat down in one place for a staff meeting. The trunks of the pachyderms are all swimming and twirling, and the rattle-and-pop vibrations up there where you're sitting on the porch say to the trained, educated, very pale-faced shadow of a person that struggles in, that struggles out, in and out, and in and out, and all like that, just so the uterus can begin to allow some light to be seen so the seedling tinyplant begins to distinguish between his and her lightness and her and his darkness. There may be jerking as hiccups erupt during this process. But—the steel is still the steel. the pitch-black, cold, curved way hits are done these days, one barrel in a million buried, but—no don't think that way, eyes, keep squeezed-shut on the lids, play's what's real now—breathing heavy, where's my truck and tools and soap? When you grab yourself digging, you should see a doctor, said Miss Sweetie. She motioned for the waitress to refill her hard liquor; and it comes, this must be a hypnogogic event this here this here thing; Beautiful Woman, Miss Sweetie, and our meeting in the Fortuna bar where celebration will take place; if the relationship is born prematurely, you may survive after the twenty-third week with intensive care, so, since it is Christmas, you may drink yourself, Hiram Holladay, being barefoot in his snow-white stash, into a state in which you have effectively rendered the body incapable of clearing the toxins generated by alcohol metabolism; and, get this; your baby is about twelve inches long and weighs about two pounds at this point. And you, said black-robed judge Newman from behind the high-gloss newly refurbished bench, you are probably also guilty of drinking yourself into being no longer able to respond to stimuli. It is not good when the air is half the thickness it was when you arrived here in this darkness. But, as long as you avert or shut the eyes off from the situation, it will remain a dream only viewable in dream-state, in the thickening, close, closed air, all terrible lying atop you, keeping you down, yes, no, the steel, the closed air becomes merely darkened not dark quiet not-stuff, not looking like Paris any more but more like this; the fetus is much longer, a large, segmented, thousand-legged dancer gone away down the drybed. Sitting in a stupor or passing out. The lungs' bronchioles develop, even though regression such as inability to control body functions, incontinence, and vomiting as Preston noses up and facilitates the interlinking of the brain's neurons with Foster's actual fall, his actual inability to stand or walk, the higher functions of the fetal brain turn on for the first time, yes, if a person has reached this stage, medical assistance is necessary, yes; If we have reached this stage, some rudimentary brain-waves indicating consciousness can be detected, yes; if we have reached this stage, like you, you could potentially choke on vomit or have breathing problems at this stage, because the gag reflex and respiration are impaired as well. The procedure is going well. We are where we should be, and your pal pinned up there with the cherry tat spreading out from the pee—peehole, there;

yes from the pee—peehole, the conviction will be discovered, the sealed files telling us that that guy over there is able to feel pain for the first time. Sleep rose in the darkness and enveloped and took away Foster. Yes Foster, the specially cut-up, stabbed, and sawed at and severed, tiny little new-victim lurching and lurching, yes like that, you sweet thing, I love to watch you eat, you know that?

Chapter Thirteen
Banter on the Ship to China VI

Noman and Skip sat at break as Shanghai edged nautical mile by nautical mile nearly near enough to allow the wind out of the correct quarter of the compass, to bring them over faint odors of something on some grill on Earth, cooking and sizzling it seemed, maybe forgotten because the cook had had one too many beers and fallen asleep someplace in the house, creating the situation that said the meats on the grill would juice up, brown, crisp up, burn to lumps of charcoal, and then finally flame up in a way that would send up a boiling, acrid, grainy, choking plume of hot, hot, touching superhot, yes, yell from the pan flame up, and no more, and carried the feeling of sea, say sea, say sea, and one last time sea, and then abandoned the stovetops, and simmer down smell several thousand times fading to unsmellable, but able to tell those out at sea, land is near, and shall come nearer. Careless barbecue cooks are every seaman's friend. Noman and Skip sat on opposite sides of a welded-down solid-steel picnic table, located in alternate seamen's break room five, on the other end of the ship from the automated unmanned bridge, away from the ever-blasting booming Father-Dwyer-Only-and-Forever flat wall-big screen HD tele-screen-console on the other side of the entrance to the bridge from the usual breakroom that they had used, where every break, lunch, and visit of any kind meant sitting in the midst of the swirling eddies of the words, music, laughter, tapping, slicing, and joking from Father Dwyer who's aboard and not aboard at the very same time, but; as both seamen were working more toward the ship's butt end than the other, and because the Dakota Maru seems about several dozen football fields long from her backbutt to her knifeblade of a sharpedge of a bowbaby, but; if they had gone to their usual break room swimming in Dwyer's singsongy foodpatter, by the time they got there it would already be too late to make it back to the ship's colon-space; so they made the decision that they made, and Dwyer, without knowing, would be missing his entire audience of two and would be speaking into a vacuous superelectronical mellowly lonely alone space out of which, down, along underneath, through the walls and everything else, the Dwyer-voice beating the drum signaled land, probably hold, hole, like the empty hole in your back, almost Hell, but not as ice-cold. Haw. Because it was quiet and there was no chatternoise to stifle their thoughts, their minds flowed in different directions, but both beginning to take aim at the problem of making ready for landfall in Shanghai, bright lights big city in the big bellybutton of the so-called bulls-eye in the butt-land, center of the trip and turnaround spot, wild China.

Skip choked up and spit for the thirtieth time at the cruddy steel wall, and said, Noman, I need to go to the bridge.

As Skip rose, Noman said, Why? We were told there was nothing we needed to do there, unless, oh sure; you want to fuck off up there for a while, sit down all comfy and full of prison food and stretched out and laid back to watch the Father Dwyer show, huh? Addicted to the show now, eh? Addicted?

No, no, no, please no, not that never ever, laughed Skip. Here's what it is; we're getting close enough to the terminal in China that I should check to see if they've sent me the information about where I'll be staying in the Port of Shanghai, you know, like I told you. And to make sure they get me my vodka and all, and of course to find out what and where's the place I'll get and stay wiped out for the couple of days we'll be laid over.

But, ah—why can't you just stay aboard the ship? We're taking this same ship back to New York. Why get off at all? There's no need to get on land.

Noman, my boy. You don't know the ins and outs of this terraphobia syndrome. We might as well be on land when the ship is docked. I get just as crazy on the ship or off, you know.

This close to land equals land, to me. Land has a big harsh aura around it, it is so evil. I actually am starting to feel the tingling of my brand of fear in my extremities, you know, because we are drawing nearer to port. Thus it follows that I need to get blasted on the ship, or off. And the bottom line of this logical thread is that, since being in possession of any type of intoxicants aboard the ship is grounds for termination, either in port, at sea, or in or at any possible in-betweens, it is clear the only logical thing to plan in this circumstance, is to hole up in some cable-ready hut on land, get unconscious, and stay that way for as long as is needed. I need to go to the bridge, to make sure that all is in place. I'll probably be a little bit late getting back to my post after I go up there, but as they say in any work-at-home arrangement, when the boss is far away the telecommuters will play! But—Noman, you look puzzled. You puzzled? Do I need to go over any of my brilliant thoughts, sayings, attitudes, or mannerisms with you a second time? Or do you just want to go back to the beginning and start this break all over again? Hm?

Oh—no, no, we don't have to do that. The only thing is, what you said, what was it? Oh, yes—telecommuter. What is that? I don't think I ever heard that word before!

Oh, sure. Before I came to sea I was in the systems design field. We used to telecommute all the time.

Hey that's all okay, but you're not really answering. Just tell me what that means.

What? Telecommuting?

Yes. That word.

Uh huh, that's when you pick up your work and take it home on your back and drink lots of coffee and are only connected to boss-land by a couple of twirls of insulated copper, each ten to five hundred—maybe even thousands in extreme cases—miles long. Theoretically, you could start to work remotely from any of the outer planets or galaxies, or further yet, yes, even further than we know exists. It's all no more boss. Not even hardly a shard or a splinter in your life left, of he, or she. No more bossie, moocow. Quite the happiness warmly radiates up from your fully loaded, leaky, splitting, used-up, blood-red, vein-covered, painful-looking, hundred-fifty-pound-at-least-when-gone-unmilked-for-weeks, quite plumpity udder; but, you know Noman, I really got to run. I need to check out the state of my on-shore arrangements while I'm thinking about it. I don't know about you, but I am very overwhelmed by the beauty of being at sea for so long; I have a constant buzz on, as a matter of fact. The best drug is being at sea, as I have said to you in the past. Plus, I bet you didn't know that—

Wait, wait wait, Skip. Hold that thought. You go too fast for me. You've never said anything about a long voyage being a drug to me. I know you haven't.

Oh, yes I did, flowed out Skip's sudden smile which was meant as a signal to tell Noman's hibernating smile that there is mutual humor connecting us right now, in this now, which as we all know is extending, all the time extending, creating now after now after now, after and after forever. The smile connects us. Arguing is set to null in our heads when we are locking smiles you know, I bet you didn't know, did you? I bet.

I am lost, Skip. I think that perhaps, mayhaps, happyhaps, super-for-surehaps, you have been at sea for too long. Either at sea or passed out drunk while still alert and aware; that too is possible in this universe, but, that aside, quite frankly I wonder how you can go so long without while you're getting the willies of withdrawal from Honey's out-back hut stuck in the last slot to the outside world, or whenever, whatever inside that burns you.

You have a right to your opinion Noman; remember, it is fine to disagree as long as you wear a smile that the other may see whenever, what?

Yeah, I suppose that's so. You ought to be going though. The bridge is far off. Say hello to Father Dwyer's hung up deaf and dumb TV set program for me. I'm going to go back to my job. See you on afternoon break—or at lunch. Careful of all the jagged and stumbly iron and steel trip hazards deliberately built into the ship on the way from the farthest end to the nearest end, to deter us from going too far too fast.

What? What trip hazards built in?

Hah! Got you. It's about as true as—no, but never mind.

You are such a card.

You too. I'm going back to work. See you.

Yeah.

At that very instant all alone and screwed to the rear wall of the flying bridge, the TV set flowed out the silky satiny rolling words of Father Dwyer. He had just got done making a torrid yellowing point on the politics of that day. That was always a dangerous thing for someone in the holy food preparation class category of the assorted TV media to stray to because he knew food and only food, but what the hell, ninety percent of the human race has enough to eat, the rest are in the horrible downward traps like scuttling spiders down the netting slung over the side of the long tall stinking warship leading to the boxy hulls of old-school LSTs packed with nearly dead men that will receive their coup de grâce from faceless mobs of blazing fascists hiding in enormous hollowed out concrete blocks on shore. Unaware that Skip was starting toward him that very instant, he finished his point by stating that from several thousand joints for us to get into, saying rather loudly, or at least he thought it super-positively true that, given the state of uncertainty and the high risk thereof, humanity better get its collective foot off the accelerator!

That is absolutely true, so, seamen at all and only points of the compasses, the topic today, is the pancake breakfast. And, as if that weren't special enough, it's about Sunday's pancake breakfast. You see, Sunday is a very special day in so many ways, you have to use the descriptor *Sunday's* before anything done that day. For example, when was the last time you saw something made more special by use of the descriptor *Friday's*, or *Monday's*, or whatever. See, *Sunday's* is a quite special moniker to hang in front of something. It's almost like how I came up with the name for this show, *Sunday Dinner with Father Dwyer,* you know. The first agent that I hired to try and get this kind of show going, wanted to call it a whole array of quite stupid things, as follows:

Priest's Pantry with Father Dwyer.
Devil's Poison with Father Dwyer.
Rut of the Slutty Dog with Father Dwyer.
At Jesus' Joint, with Head Chef Father Dwyer.

And another five hundred more examples of ratings and popularity blocking names were barfed up from the agent to the table before me, with no character or sense to them—utter nonsense and garbage and everything ugly all rolled up in big fat tangles of gasoline-soaked sheets. We put the names all wrapped in the sheets in the road next to the white line that was laid down fifty years prior that you could see very well on the first day of its life but that now, fifty years later, was very invisible, but I know where it used to be, so; that's right next to where we put all the silly names; off to the side, in the fast lane. That agent thought we were putting them there for safekeeping, until we could get together and sift through them some more, drop some, make more, oh, yes, like every asshole who doesn't know they're an asshole, he thought my IQ was quite a bit below his, but his was not high enough to know that after we went home for the night after a very pleasant good-bye that he did not have the brains to detect the tone in my voice equaling *good-bye, and screw off, because I am done with you, there's not going to be a next time, baby fat cakes,* oh man, no; and he didn't even know that the middle of the road where we put the crate of names was right in the bulls-eye path of probably several hundred tons of giant eighteen wheelers all night long, leapin' and a' froggin', their nearly dead drivers caterwauling into CB sets all day, smushing up the names and merging them totally with the pavement with not even a stain left on the blacktop by the time the mornin' come. But I could have kicked myself wide awake in bed that night when it hit me in my sweet dream of a butt, causing me to come wide awake drugged up with knowing I should have torched the damned crate because that was really the whole idea, you know, of the gasoline soaked sheets, and all; and that was such a nightmare that I really believed it had happened, I really believed I had met with an agent who came up with ideas for the show I was putting together to pitch that were so shitty I had insomnia for several years afterward because the shit stayed stuck in my sleep muscle instead of flowing though like it should have to let the muscle work and wrestle me into the next sequential land of nod in the queue. And, when I finally rose, I decided that it seemed like a very good idea to hire an agent and set up a meeting for next Friday again to hash over, spit out, and brainstorm up once and for all the final cooking show name.

This all said and reasoned around on the living blank screen of the television turned down, starting when Skip said, Bye! to Noman and ducked down in the canal. As Dwyer loosened up the studio audience in preparation for the entry of Skip onto the churchly stage, where he would mount the steps to the altar and there place his eternal question of have they got my room and will I get my binder, on the holy stone set in the middle of the stony roughhewn surface of the actual true-to-life high altar, Skip came at the warmed up and turned on audience through the canal, and managed to do so without banging his head on the poorly designed fold-up sharp-as-nails chairs hung on curved walls of the already squeezed-tight ever-narrowing tube. Skip scuttled forward over razor-sharp tunnel rib after tunnel rib, even though his finger slipped on the sharp edges of the first rib and his hand was slashed bloody to the bone, he did not pause because he knew that the sooner he got to the tailgunner's position, he could in good conscience strap in and start firing into the cloud of fighters pursuing the Dakota Maru up the behind with multiple twenty-millimeter MG FF cannons blazing out attempting to permanently kill both him and Noman, and to permanently silence Dwyer by bricking him up in his stage set all around and then just pretending the resultant weird big brick column with no apparent purpose is just that—is nothing; that needs to be the answer, that should always be the answer, and when the questions come more and more infrequently until there are no more, enough has been done to ensure his memory is buried in the great rock-hard thing, forever. There is no Father Dwyer, said Skip, only to be cut off by some nobody, green-behind-the-tongue-or-something-like-that student saying, Oh, yes there is, I know, I saw him; look there he is now, there he is, bent, telling some little guy just boarded for their first trip, there he is, I saw him, yes, but—Skip said again, louder, There is no Father Dwyer, there never was, and there never will be. But what is that I hear coming at me? What is that I hear coming at me? The bridge is coming at me! Is the bridge open? I don't know if it's open or closed. But, as consciousness dawned once more, fifth time since heading off for the bridge, actually, Skip knew he had started to detect Father Dwyer's voice talking about some sort of Sunday thing, I don't know, but the Sunday thing came okay over the bridge, so the bridge must be down and it must be safe to cross, since Skip could see nothing but the need to confirm that things were readied for him in port, the fact that it had been confirmed that the drawbridge was down, and it would be safe to cross, was indeed a comfort.

As he ran, a wave from behind washed over and around him, and he hung on tight to the seat-weave of the nineteen fifty-nine, gutless, weak-motored Ford Fairlane they went to the shore in every weekend when the Summer was passing over one moment at a time; in the moments stretched one part of the journey, that part of the Journey being the drawbridge crossing the bay from the mainland to the Barnegat peninsula where they always ended their quest, it seems, by repeatedly stabbing the sand armor the planet tended to wear out there near the surf, with the sharp-tipped staff of their giant mold-stained, unfurled beach umbrella. Before the tip reached the flesh of the globe it was softened and cushioned and pressing all in on the pinpointy weapon and had saved the world once more. Why else would they go there every Sunday all summer for? Skip could only remember the stab of the umbrella shaft and the burn of the superheated ever-flaming sand and the corner of the bungalow he was looking at, where many smelly fishing poles were stacked together, their lines and hooks and something else he could not make out the nature of, at the exact time Mantle and Maris scored back-to-back home runs, on July twenty-fifth, nineteen sixty one, when someone very close to him—but who is now stored in a wall—had just turned thirteen years old; the runs were announced by the radio droning in the nest room piled high with what looked like rags but that were so hazed over by the ball game announcer that they could actually have been anything from big, fat, heavily stench-drenched rotten fish to decaying, well-dressed human corpses; on these freighters, years back, the crews were very different; there were thirty or forty well-dressed men of all ranks from lowest to highest down to lowest again, and there were actually captains for all ships in those days of old, immediately prior to the point in my youth when I came out publicly identifying as male, before my Father told me I was destined, due to a pro-devil dream he'd been having recurrently, to become a man of the cloth, not a man of the iron or of the steel, no, not even stainless steel, no no no, not even that; so here I am, and now, everything is different, there are no captains, there are multiply interlinked maxi-computers. There are no large crews to command, for the captains to arouse themselves sexually by seeing and hearing so many men jump to, at his merest bark; he actually wanted them to leave and go to work so he could be alone behind locked doors to do what aroused men—and yes, also women—do when they're alone at sea with just their two hands and their feet and their privates and; oh, I see the audience of one has arrived; let's give a remote hand clap to seaman Skip, of the Dakota Maru, who is God-damned lucky his job is grandfathered in by the soon to expire union contract, the ins and outs of which he was never even told, as a matter of fact he doesn't know that it was the union whose rank and file in the Bound Brook Budd Building, way back when there were well-dressed seamen with clear eyes and straight minds, made the rule under which he and his pal Noman still find themselves employed even though humans are no longer needed in these superships any more than a human must be installed to operate your typical modern refrigerator, or freezer, or range—yes, everything is appliances now; everything is perfected clean and humans are not needed. Tradition and respect is what causes the appliances to keep these last humans alive. The big crews lie silently now in vast churchyards; the captains of the past are sealed in tombs with their fancy, frilly, silly captain's costumes on; and here is Skip, coming across, onto the bridge, moving along to the master control panel which is never used except to suit the last remaining material needs of these last few grandfathered-in so-called unnecessary humans; you can tell them from the machines they serve by the need they have to apply deodorant and urinate and defecate in the morning. When they're all gone, all the toilet facilities and deodorant plants will no longer be needed; it will be much worse, much much worse, than not giving a damn about the needs of the people who work in the plants manufacturing mustard like those two, one fat, one skinny, disappeared, TV-rerun laughingstocks did. But no, oh, my time is almost gone! I have been blubbering on about nothing at all, actually to pad out the time, which the idiots that put these shows together did not give me enough food to prepare to fill out the whole half hour; but I suppose the important point to make now, to bugle forth from all the obsolete-as-soon-as-purchased, HD, Chinese-made television surround-sound systems, is that the off-limits control panel Skip has stepped up to is not intended for use by men; or intended for use by women; or, for a matter of fact, not intended to be used by anyone at all because the ship is flowing secret data over the ocean's storm and surging swells, angered and frightened simultaneously by the mere thought that someone is coming to push and pull and press and look, as in you, they might find something they've been looking for all their lives and have turned over hundreds and thousands of rocks and rags and have not found it, it has not been there even once, and now that they stand at the brink of their last shot at succeeding in their quest, I would say they are at this point past fear, past panic, just feeling like they would if their necks had just been clamped around by the final great big bloody guillotinian-style lunette, their fear would be as the sound of Krakatoa in the ears of nearby, newfangled steamboat sailors, rat-catching shipcats, and sailettes; no, no, nothing, no, yes; that is right and wrong taken together, matter and antimatter taken together, the result is nothing, Noman is hit by a wall of resentment and anger and hollowness, no, just frustration, no; worse; Skip, prattling about their almost being at the end of the first half of their round-trip voyage, has removed Noman from the nameless, universal-model blank-human-body-making—it was carrying his brawn but that is all—back on his long trip from the break room toward the current compartment he had been scraping down and cleaning up before this break, but his body-blank spat out his spirit into the real world that was no ship, no, and no house, no, just a place in noplace and in a place again; there she was, yes she was, the one that Skip's fear had awakened. Noman copper conduit, yes; Noman the perfect copper conduit for zap over zap and yes; now he stood empty, in a tall wide blank white room. Blank but for—her hand.

Phyllis, said Noman. Phyllis. Jesus, Phyllis, I can't be seeing you. Why am I?

Because, she said, rolling over a bit in her hospital bed, you have been sick, very sick—wait I need to call for a nurse, you're awake, dear God, thank God you're awake—damn this button, they're not answering this button, they said if you stir they need to know right now, if not sooner, oh; here she is.

Yes, miss Phyllis—what do you need?

Come quick. He's awake. Come quick, quick.

Oh! The battalion of nurses swarmed out of their sleepiness, which had fallen because it was early afternoon summer in the office, everybody slows in early afternoon, especially in the Summer, the heavy time; yes, the heavy, heavy, sun-beating time; and they rushed in, and after about two hours they released him to her, from out the mainly unlocked faith-healer's gate. Her bed and room and tubes and vaguely acrid and still somewhat sweet self-smelling persona were out with her in the garden yard, all green; all moist; all bright; all full of them where there had just been that one there alone and this one here again; they flowed together, and the man working the foundry now needed to set the mold aside to cool and, given the state of its absolute fluidity, had dipped out the shimmery silvery still mainly molten very fluid Noman and Phyllis onto a clean green bench on the August high Summer, in the hospital strolling garden. It had been easy to do it; so easy, as a matter of fact, that the man in the foundry decided to take it up as a profession.

As he faded back, Phyllis said bluntly but smoothly and sweetly, Noman, thank God you have come to me. Thank God the X-rays have shown us for sure that God has taken the burden from you and let you stay alive to hold my hand for as long as I need, from the first labor-pain, to the final stepping forth entry from stage right or left—they are all the same now anyway—I can face the fear now and pass through the horrid stabbing fear I know will be mine when it is time to bear our sweet-child.

Noman blinked and rolled his eyes, in this, the first he was able to take stock of where he might be or was gone from or might be going. He said, But, Phyllis—you are Phyllis? There is really a Phyllis? What about the ship? Where is the ship? Oh, I have to be dreaming, yes I must; no no; yes Noman, shut up and look inward and rub rub rub up and down, up and down, do the movement up and down like you got the brush and there's a steel wall, and it's dark, and all of it will come cover you again, and you'll be back on the ship, and this dream will be over—so calmed, he said, while waiting in line to disappear, This garden, this Phyllis, I don't know this place, I've never been here but am remembering now, yes, if this is not now stuff but stuff I am remembering, it would be before the Dakota Maru, and I guess, yes; I finally did it; I finally fell off the rope and wood ladder I climb down onto my job and up out of my job, and I hit my head on the steel, and my head went blank, and now I'm either crazy or dreaming or in the process of being embalmed with heavy hallucinogenic fluids, red, white, and blue!

    She took and squeezed his quite petite hand, saying, No, you're not dreaming Noman, my love. I should be the one pinching myself actually. I thought there was no way you'd be here to hold my hand through the black horror I am facing. It's like, it's like a—miracle!

    —and the all that this is happening rushed in to fill my leaky bruised head, so, miracle? thought Noman as she spoke; huh—

    She went straight on, squeezing his hand in a pulsating rhythm, saying, It's like I'm moving toward a tiny puckered hole like a little tiny weenie, and it'll be all mixed up, I'll need to push in, and it'll need to push out, and the worst will happen, we'll both be jammed in the middle, yes, me and sweet-child together, we'll just become a clog, a snot, a bugger, a chalky jammed turd which will prove to be fatal—yes, it's like a puckered little anus-hole. I am full of larger and smaller little puckered anus-holes not all of which have passed feces historically but which all might as well start now. You know—

    —Please, Dakota Maru, take me back, thought Noman over her wordflow—Gorbachev is there, remember? Gorbachev said, I am a dictator, and am never wrong—yes you are on board, he had not said that as a matter of fact, but I wish he had, really—because then I would be on board, and from that rock I could shake away these visions—anus-holes, no, not anus-holes. Women have come and gone through the years but none that I can correct to tell them, Do not speak any lie more than three times without immediately seeing the appropriate professional specialists in how to start telling the truth.

—You know, sighed Phyllis dreamily, if I could know all people had anus-holes, I would feel better because it means that all people have at one time or another felt the special pains I am destined to fight through. The pain of ejecting something just a bit, just a bit more, no just a few bits more—eject, eject something too large to pass through the hole. Push! No you will not burst! Push! No you will not, no, ha ha—farther and farther and farther yet! The damned thing demands to be free! My health is secondary, the damned thing is what matters now, I have had my day, it needs its day. Old old old, I will soon fall away. As far as you know, honey! As far as you know!

He came out of his fog, and stated, Uh, okay, I must have a while to process that, Phyllis. It—it is still Phyllis, right? You're sure you're Phyllis?

Yes of course I am, sweetheart. I go in and out, but I'm almost permanently soldered, cemented, mortared, welded, and heliarced into your lifeline flow from now on, depending on which area of your diversely constructed body we're bonding with—we got a lifetime to get it done, you know, this is just one bump of many we will discover in the below-passing ever-rougher ever-harder until the end together the whole way until carefully casketed and lowered to the bottom of our two not-yet-dug identical graves, and step from there into our journey down the eternal road.

Bang! Lord God, I am dizzy, your blunt talk is quite elevated and fascinating, said Noman, but; on the other side, as he went on meditating, Father Dwyer and all the mechanics and electronics

Banter on the Ship to China VI 245

and ass-kissing systems all around him cried in unison from the speakers of every watching sailor, Okay, up the gate, Gorbachev my man, saying clearly and plainly, Noman, if you can hear me, hear this: she is the one. Phyllis is the woman for you. You are back with her now; your seafaring days are over—yes, they are. I am a dictator and am never wrong. Here, take this pill. Never mind what it is. You'll see when it comes all over you—see, her bowling alley uniform is more suitable; look! And his word flipped, changing her clothing back to the typical bowling-ball snack-bar attendant. Miraculous, miraculous, a sign from whatever's above; nested containerships; bat! Free hamburger with Schlitz; big blue genie with the slavering, razor-sharp, snapping wildly, crunchy crunch-crunch slash and burn style, pit bull face; and Phyllis' big gown all lacy, leafy, and nauseously over-busily patterned; sorry; one cannot always bowl well in the correct, large, wide, incandescent, fiery, gleaming, glamourous, ultra-femininely unreal gown that tradition demands.

But, Ho! Cried Father Dwyer from the third of his eight possible heads, please! Do not touch the off-limits start-communication switches, Skip! Away from the top-secret, loud, move-from-place-to-place, steerable clown racing, and it all lands here in my pot; today we will explore Monday's leftover dessert of pudding-avec-canned-fruit, see it glisten? See? Do not ignore, do not, yes, no young sailor, hey, you there baby sailor! Do not dare ignore! Do not dare ignore this the way you did Saturday's pancake breakfast! This combined Pike's Peak climb and silly cute sports-car rally on this postage-stamp-sized far-at-sea pseudo-litter-boxed bow, we must win! Yes, we must, yes; oh, Skip don't know—scoop it, yeah yeah yeah, scoop it all, scoop it up, scoop it now! That is, yes is, the sort of news we all seek! But Skip, if you go to it, be warned; I see you reaching in your pocket for the secret code. I hear your head throbbing out easily-heard thoughts, your cranium bone is too thin to provide adequate sound-proofing, and I can hear clearly what you are about to do; so, it is time to run down the count to the mystery. Yes, the mystery. I know the mystery but you cannot. I am part of the furniture on this ship after all, I can know a lot of things that can only be known by a nonliving thing. So: go on Skip.

Go on. So, other people, now that we have this Skip nonentity out of the way, I can take you through the steps required to make a successful pudding-avec-canned-fruit—

Skip went across the cold steel deck with the card in his hand containing the secret code for him to speak to similarly equipped individuals, shadowy but real, all the way up at the top of the corporate towers in Dubai who would know what was booked for him.

First, you got to understand—you probably are asking yourself, I know that I would be if I were you—you're asking why did Father use the term *make* when referring to something already made that was a leftover laid atop the frozen miscellaneous fifty-year-old meats in the huge gunmetal-grey Army-surplus freezer we got nearly a year ago because the flea market it was in decided it would never sell and left it out in the rain, mud, and products of classical dog aching stretchy restless leg behavior toward what is right and what is wrong and, all that deal, like I say! Now on to cooking; there I see, you got the Skip codes, yeah, they are the Skip codes; that's senility; yeah, I see you read them; that's senility; yeah, now you enter them; that's senility; and then they're in and your face pressed to the cathode ray tube, but; they don't call them that anymore; what do they call them now, those cathode ray tubes? Go back to when they called them that, but that is before the ship was built, before cable cooking shows and all, my word, that young man Skip seems to have disappeared in some kind of flash-bang of a conflagration; can't see nothing till the smoke clears; ship gone, ship here, hey, hit a mine; yeah that's senility, yah, that's senility, yah yah yah that is; and then the old dog that just happens to be out with the new dogs spies me and does the first thing it ever does when attacked; snap snarl nip on the new one, new one, new one, new; and all at once we are in some kind of mind-floating silly-place; ship not yet built, TV not yet invented, no such thing as cable but to winch up things by, and as a matter of fact, somehow alive before born, both I, my crew, my meat, my fish as a matter of fact, it's possible the ship blew up, but somehow way in the future, so that's why I wasn't killed and the cooking show set is safe in some eternal bubble, as a matter of fact this must be how coronated saints feel the day they make it, yes; but the poor Skip-devil must be in the water; yes, the slimy ice-cold ocean water. Thus Skip plunged from the gone Dakota Maru, exploded or otherwise, and it was a dive or a fall or a cannonball on a hundred-degree day at the fucking Brookside Swim Club, in its first of two incarnations, the water smelled like it couldn't be breathed, not salt, not fresh, not chlorine, wait, back up, yes chlorine, and, up out of the water into the real close face of a woman from the gone fearful past, say her name, what is her name, who is she, God, she is pretty-face young Gundren just as soaked as me in the blazing, cancer-causing sun, but before that was known to anybody, and Skip and Gundren weren't married yet, so Skip didn't know they were going and the Dakota Maru cruised away without him into the future intending to wait for him, if it can get through Viet Nam without being recommissioned as a hospital ship and blown to bits in the Denmark Strait by a Barham Blaster model modern slick-sided U-boat of a make-believe vintage replica submarine, no I don't know, I don't know, no I don't, I think that's the wrong war; that's senility; wrong ship; that's senility; but who cares, it really hasn't happened yet, so there's really no right or wrong, everything's just a stupid guess backed up by absolutely no research of any kind, human or otherwise. Plus, submarines had nothing at all to do with it. Thus, she surfaced bone dry somehow, and quickly spoke. Hey, boy. What is up? Word on the street is you plan to get a sea-based job. What might that be? It sounds mysterious and fascinating.

I, uh, oh, blubbered young Skip, flustered. I guess the thought that the sea's out there right now this minute every minute past or future kind of—pulls at me. Yah, pulls. Pulls. You know?

No, I don't. I don't know that kind of *pulls*. That's why it's fascinating.

There was a life, a past a world behind her eyes, Skip spoke to provoke it, though back in those days where they were now, things were different. He asked her, Say, I know you, yes I do. You're in homeroom with me; in school, as in—school. You know? Isn't that funny?

Yah, I know. I've seen you. I do. Say, but, what? What's your name, anyfree? No, no, I didn't mean that. What I meant was, like, I mean—besides being Mister extremely unique? That's what I was trying to grab down. Like, you not run with the pack man. You lone dog, you. You! I kin tellit! What's wrong anyway, what I'm sayin's not quite correct?

Oh—no, said Skip, somewhat squishy somewhat squirmy—I mean I think I'd rather continue this talk with you, honey, out of the deep ice-cold water, all dry if you don't mind. I feel; I feel that in this monstrous monstrosity of an ocean, there's all limitless nothing all around us forever to some shores we never can return to, that will stifle and stifle and stifle us down, until the day we die, if we don't protest. Especially, given the extreme chill of clammy wetness in this breeze. Now, now, don't get me wrong—water is great to have around us, there are worse things to be enveloped in, because water won't form up into a million jagged toothy mouths and rip you, turning its own self red so effectively, that might have been its intent to begin with, but if you get out in time, nothing untoward can happen, especially not if it's just water, you know. And the little frostbite you incur heals fairly clean, along with the use of the correct high-dose opiates. So, how 'bout it? Up we go on the dry, like, huh—oops!

Pulling her by the hand from the water, he at once realized a slip had begun, but the realization came too late to avoid his taking a barefoot header onto the rock-hard sunny poolside tile. The ocean had sunk away beneath a pool, a pool like Brookside pool all painted blue in the bottom, and all private where you need to pay dues yearly, and his slimy uncallused young flatfoot slip up on the unexpected tile surrounding the wonderfully bright, yes, blue bright, yes, threw him back half in the water and half out, you see, and his headbone hairline-broke against the unyielding hard of the poolside tile slipperyway. The rumble and drum of the bang went down and the mind-demons that lurk in the shallow caverns everybody has seen but no one dares admit to for fear of being called crazy, injected the first of fifty once-per-week shots of pure hard crystal terraphobia into his sweet left butt-cheek; and that was where it all began. Fear of land was planted now; and full-blown terror would rise in the coming weeks, but, this is now; he picked himself up not knowing he had gained from the hard tile the seed of a profound mental disorder, that Father Dwyer's fifth-generation replacement down the road will memorialize the legendary Skip for having withstood acting out his inner struggles with. The intent was to imply that Skip got well and proceeded toward a much more substantial future, almost a normal future, and he will emerge from the door in the wall from the inner dark to the outer bright, and will see what Father Dwyer has prepared for him; in a row down the counter stretched selections of teas, bag over bag of sliced white bread, a washtub-sized container of butter and fortune cookies, and a line of dark squat sticky-jam bottles, the number of which amounts to fourteen. Doctor Dwyer, the someday priest, on the day following the poor man's slip-fall, examined the MRI of the wretch's injury, and the results were inconclusive because no one he discussed the case with knew what an MRI was, since such a thing was not invented yet. Once this hit him the results disappeared, and so, that was the end of that. So, taking a step to the future, he abandoned his expensive shack-up honey, who would go on to write a self-published expose of the great holy man's youth, and moved to a secret location where, even before he took his first piss and then tinkered for hours with a defective wall-thermostat, he rushed to dial the number of the nearest seminary, the urge having been summoned up in him by the savior on high to enroll.

The red dot of the first camera assigned to him appeared years later, and so, now, yes now, whatever that is, he stood in the air-conditioned studio of the *Sunday Dinner with Father Dwyer* stage set, banged down his car keys on the stainless-steel countertop, angry at having reached into his pocket only to find them and immediately become disoriented, blurting out to the open mic, What the hell are these jingly chained together things? What? Car keys? Why? I have no fucking car or fucking celibate car or any kind of car, I am much too famous to drive my own car, the terrorists, yes terrorists, will abort me with a blast of some kind, or maybe even some lower, sexless, pale-grey vermin will end my short life with a single press of a single remote-control homebrew cellphone-activation green-glow button, and, again; a large blast will have spelled my end a second time—so on and so, Father Dwyer went on—but, yes, someplace deeper in his severely mature brain, he knew this was just a plain vanilla civilian-style panic attack, the best cure for which is the pop of two Ativan and bang of the left fist up hard on the bone bridge right between the eyes. Thus treated, he was fit to do the show, once more. Fit as scads of perfectly tuned Guarneri Del Gesu fancy old-school Paganini-style worn-out aging fiddles being sawed away on by hordes of unwashed but quite enthusiastic Lil' Abners and Lil' Alixes—who sport scarcely one lesson between all of them—are fit to take the stage in Carnegie hall. So, fit as he was, no fiddle at all, Dwyer mounted the cooking show set, and bellowed quite hard, Welcome to episode nine-hundred three of my quite unique, holy God, yes, holy Jesus, wild, wild cooking show! No, here is the pickle; the show today may be abbreviated, because there's a fat superstorm Sandy blowing up solidly all over the whole world outside, like God sends to buffet us every hundred years, meaning we may lose our artificially manufactured power soon, if not so already, and if it gets dark when there is no power-light, we will have to split shot the show all the way to the under-down city in the chilly black depths no man has ever lived through reaching to, for today. There is something odd about one of the ships, out there; one of the ships that is tuned-in; can't tell the actual name though, as; aha, I bet it is the Knock Nevis. Once the world's largest bulk crude carrier, it is at sea today, and is too fantastically huge, yes much too wide and deep to see; they are awed, always awed, so they scream as if at the Beatles' first gleaming, Yes, there it is! Yes—yes—yes, there it is!

That is odd that the master control-board told Father Dwyer that the huge ship was not only at sea, but had a cable-networked and operational flatscreen tuned in, but it has to be right, must be right, yes—but, no. The ship was scrapped years ago.

Why is the master control-board stating she still exists and is far at sea? Why is it looking back far in the past? Oh, it needs calibration, yup! Uselessness is the price we pay for scrimping on regular tuneups and maintenance. This is one example. But as much as I would like to give you more, this is it, because my correspondent far out in Alang is going to be taking over the rest of the time of this episode, for the complete news on Ships Scheduled to be Broken Today! Here you go, I fade away, but I still know, here comes the new picture, the remote correspondent, absolutely all woman and rather good-looking at that, so we will see her, but, her voice is not allowed. My voice's contract states that as long as I am alive and able to do the job, I will do all voice-overs and any other voice-announcer's work anywhere in the damned near and far, wide and narrow, long and short network that carries my show or remote reports thereof. So, here goes; the woman is standing close in with a sparkling-clean face and haircut and clothing immaculately fitted and pressed, and she looks more like a millennial major corporate office junior manager than a reporter, but here she goes; she's saying, but not, so I say into and through her and out her mouth, sure do, Here in Alang, the biggest, most dangerous, super-loud workplace in the entire third world, the workers have been found to have one fascinating, thrilling, unusual, hell-and-hellhound-bound piece of information to share; in the hut up the hill with the slick, greasy, floor, between Bodhisattva I and Bodhisattva II, rooming, boarding, and floating, evening to black-night forever, nonstop, where the *Incest Can be Fun* shows, are always playing in a spot carved out the back of the residential unit, on one of the dozens of flatscreen TVs the network distributed to all the super-gigantically-hulled and what's worse, just plain enormous, huge, but oddly deathly quiet steel-monsters sailing across the earth's curved, ultra-liquid surface, proudly and ignorantly blasting forth the very same words I am now. Yes just like now, but; since you cannot hear their TV around the world to where you are, it really doesn't make a sound, a la the tree in the woods' stupid question that is so hackneyed anymore; in the hut it indeed of course sounds, and—the workers living in that hovel, who lifted the TV and all supporting electronics needed to get it going out from the steel bowels of the Knock Nevis when it was driven up for beaching onto the conch-strewn, pebbly, totally-asbestos-plus-crude-oil-contaminated beach, where it crushed quickly and quietly a horseshoe crab laying her eggs into a hot slit she carved, not without effort, from the blazing stinking sea-sand between two decaying human-style sandcastles built when public-commoners' open-swim season was on, and its televisions and everything else of value that wasn't sheet-steel was waiting submissively to be unplugged, removed, and taken.

Okay, take it back away, Father, said the correspondent, foolishly not considering that since I am her voice, I need not have her tell me that which I of course know by heart already. So, I will finally say, because this is after all my cooking show, on the counter are a selection of teas, a bag of sliced white bread, a jar of peanut butter, and fourteen varieties of jam; so, just as you were ordered earlier, Noman my man, take the pill laid down before you. Sure, take the pill laid down on the silk pillow before you. Yes, that one there, why do you ask which one when there's just one right there. Yes, that, the ringbearers' pillow. What? Why do you so stupidly ask why is that there, why the hell do you think that's there? What other kind of pillow do you expect a small boy named Henry to march up to the altar with the rings on top for? God-dammit!

Yah, well, I suppose this is it, said Noman, with his eyes screwed tight down on Phyllis' ice-blue eye-lashed blinky-pools. It all sped on from that instant their worlds changed. And, in that very night in the semi-dark Holiday Inn Hotel room, on the never-yet-used brand-new Tempurpedic mattress the Holiday chain was upgrading its millions on millions of sleeping stations to, Phyllis was legally and properly impregnated during one of several coital sessions spanning the long fat night. The wedding night, in fact, was so deeply intense that the next morning she absolutely dropped off to sleep over breakfast, with a mouthful of yellow egg yolk dripping from her slack lip-corner, she being too weak to chew any more. With this, the equally spent Noman rose, clicked, and summoned the goofing-off bus-staff lined up against the far restaurant wall to get her and take her and load her back up to the room, to sleep the day away. They left grumbling at the lack of a tip, so then Noman sat by the bed in the semi-dark lightly-curtained morning room, to wait her out by slipping into a nearby book. He tried, but it proved too dark for him to get any pleasure from it, so he put the book aside, soon nodded as the empty time flowed into him, and he was weighted down enough to dive and join Phyllis on the wedding bed; yes, join her in the perfect kind of tiredness' expected and ultimate love-coupling. He breathed in, and she breathed out, and so and so all vice versa, super in love wreathing their true unconsciousness' envelopment, and finally starting her down the road to the ultimate rush, that tokophobic peak experience. Once done and free of this poor excuse for a bloodsucking parasite, Phyllis stated at, in, and through Noman's parchmented face, What is your earth name, what, hey, oh you? What is your earth name, dear husband of six or seven hours or two? I am afraid, what? Afraid that I cannot remember!

What? Earth name? What do you mean, Earth name?

What I said, honey. What, why? Don't you know it?

Noman looked her across and around, his eye tracking the way her unseen hip curve shaped the special wedding night silk sheet draped over her long, lean, yet fleshly in the right places quite womanly reclination—what? What? *Reclination* is not a word, little Noman, said Mrs. Crowley from long ago in Our Lady of Lourdes modern proper grammar school, the old English teacher with so many wrinkles, lines, and fissures down her face she looked absolutely all bare brain convolutions, whorls, and snaky fissures leading nowhere all over; There is no such word, said the stately, erect, disembodied brain that Noman always knew she always was, that waved her pointer stick, the rubber tip of which obsessed Noman to no end; it was soft rubber but hard rubber, it was so black but felt so white, so hard yet so soft, so easy to slide on and… he wondered why she said that because, well, just because, but he could not get to the end of the because, because she withdrew, let the rubber-tipped stick fall all flaccid, and reverently bade him whip the thing on his mind fully away from its current task of distracting the boy he used to be from learning anything of value from her, that distracting thing being visional thoughts of the house he and she might end up co-habitating in once this God-damned English class was over, so; why do they build schools with big wide classroom windows, when they know that when Spring Fever strikes, the widows will be portals to failed grades, writeups for dozing, beds for the sowing of seeds of hours spent dozing, gazing at senile old neighborhood retirees walking skittish little dogs, every schoolchild among them regardless of grades, dreaming to be free. And failure to turn the start key earlier than the start of the eternal race, which meant, what the hell, God damn, who wants to be in that race, anyway! Leave the key, get out the car, leave the future in the hands of the God they clued you in about during all those thousands of hours set dozing in the dark back pew of the six thirty a.m. Sunday masses, then being brought home to be forced to sit down to a large, heavily weighed-down-with-salt, and gigantically high-protein meal, which will leave him with the discomfort of bursting at the seams with too much rock-hard food, even when he was no more than seventy-five percent through the process of coming awake. It all tangled drifting around him with no time and no meaning, just drifting, drifting as he swam the town forward with just one mission left, really, that is to make a decision at last on, Here I am, a single bachelor suffering in time severe belly-bleeds because the nutrition in the foods I like is really for shit, and the fact that, even if I can get through my fear of commitment due to the child I will unfortunately remain being all my life, it is quite unlikely that the bulkhead I long to scrape down in the dark cube in the... with my wire brush and my solvent—is still even there this many years gone, in the... God, why can't I remember the ship-name? I cannot, cannot, God, who would have thunk it—No! cried Mrs. Crowley; *thunk* is not a word! Come back in this damned class so I can strap ya'! Crawl right back in the window right now and take your seat! Though the grass outside in the Spring day arching over is very, very seductive, it will not, cannot, and never will rear up, fold over, and form up into the woman of your dreams; that being a phrase all men know. Some join the priesthood, and some go into the business of shanghaiing young men for pay. Yes, it goes on still. Shanghaiing. Yup—

What the hell is wrong with you, Noman? Hey! Wake up!
What? Wha—

Back to this dimension, my perfect capture! You act like you don't know where the fuck you are or when exactly is now!

Noman's eyes rushed over across, visioning dizzily—I cannot ship out to Shanghai because my wife, well—I have to ship out to Shanghai, Phyllis, if I don't I'll get canned worse than being sealed alive in a drum it is like; I seem to know something about the cargo but—no no no, the thought is too painful, she's afraid, so afraid, the afraid doubles with each day—tokophobic t-word—I am not married, Skip, that's far better—what's this water up all around the Dakota Maru I was on, yes I swear, but—up she pops from under the pool water, up she pops all chlorine in her nose, got it, yes, that's why the first thing she did in my face was to sneeze instead of the other thing I was hoping for, it sure has been a long time at sea you know, at sea—so as he started back up again having seemed to probably die, the bridge control-board reappeared before the flatscreen which cradled Father Dwyer, before which, on the steel floor, lay two unconscious upstate New York dairy farmers; W-alter damn L-uc-as: Walter-on-Lucas no not a city in the UK on the Lucas river, but; just two men. Two men had been Skip and Noman. Now two men were about to be these half-dead farmers. No one knew their names yet, but where they came from everybody did. They had just completed the final stage of constructing yet another massive tower of steel and featureless black reflective glass in which dozens of young, crisply-dressed, good-smelling, somewhat bright but really quite dopey, deeply hypnotized, deluded ex-children will sit day over day in grey cubicles as if kneeling at their own caskets in a variety of very self-important ways pretending to pray into their blandly built laptop screens all a'flicker, that beam them all, in unison, lock-step visions of the superbland moneydriven world they live in, the only world they will ever be able to know until they pass over the chasm of temporary dormancy to the next life they'll live, and so forth. There's a slight wakeup before passing, but it's too late to matter.

Anyway: two beers slid up before the farmers. Their names were Walter and Lucas, and inside them dwelt emotionless, never-talk-unless-just-for-talking's-sake minds. The strong homebrew beer went down thick and potent. They chased with Vodka. They intended for the drinking to deliver them to someplace better—and it may have, but; when they woke things were not as they seem or seemed to be what they couldn't be, or whatever. In their first moment of wakening they chalked that up to some tremendous hangovers about to descend, with the normal accompanying feeling of depersonalization and/or the fear of the splitting headache phase of the hangovers, once the thrill of being outside their skins totally wore off. But it was different because they were sitting on some cold steel floor in some kind of control room that somehow smelled faintly of the seashore and had an enormous television hung to the wall that blasted some kind of sermonesque speech about food; and food; and food and food and more food; part of which speech stated that, In the fridge on most freighters will be found plates of cheeses and meats, tightly wrapped, for the crew to simply set out at mealtimes—

But: the upper right corner tore down diagonally like plastic containers of irradiated crappy lunchmeat and fish have, the tear-away clear but foggy fronts ugly and stained and smeared inside with unappetizing looking product-grease, but those package fronts do not tear down to reveal elderly, bigheaded, ecclesiastically-shirted-and-collared, wild-eyed, crazy, shouting men, the largest of which leaned at them and expanded to nearly the size of a whole other world and started telling them something they couldn't quite get yet but that reeked of someone telling them what was what, once and for all, like some scold of a newly promoted boss might do behind some heavy solid-oak shut-tight doors; words too strong to be said anywhere other than in perfect privacy, like the reading of whatever riot act the wrong deed called for; like that. They could not remember having been in a riot, but he began turning them to that direction like a riot cop's very special super-blast fire hose may do, firing at them—their names!

The waterblast nearly shattered the jowls and double-chin off of Walter's plump baby face, and injected into him: Your name is Noman, get it? Your old name is now totally overwritten by the new name—Noman! The fat farmer reeled back and slammed into the wall of the bridge across from the TV, driven by the water name-blast, but; Lucas could not see this. He could not see it. All he saw was his older brother gripped in some unseen hand and thrown harder than required to snap most spines against the steel wall. The gigantic evil Father Dwyer, full of zeal to save the ship and recreate the disappeared crew so that they could get to Shanghai correctly, had not tuned yet to Lucas' frequency to hammer him yet; so Lucas was multiply frightened and almost drenched the dark inside of his pantlegs with diarrhea when he said, Walter, what happened? What—why'd you slam back like that, are you all right? which got him no answer, just a slight turn of Walter's head to him from which hammered words.

What, huh—who the hell is Walter? My name is Noman—come on, Skip, come. We got to get back to work, we do—

Phyllis just had said some words, but a force weakened Noman, so it was like something ripped some large part of him out of the pool to the sky leaving only that part which never could and never would float.

Noman! cried Phillis—what—hey, lifeguard! Something dragged my friend under, see, he is under, I don't know why he's under, but he is—

A man shape formed from the sunning loungers spread across on multicolored blanket around the periphery of the pool. The shape did not know it, but it had reached a totally defining moment of its otherwise meaningless existence. It lunged, it cried; it ran, flooded with the instinct of preserving the species, also knowing dimly that the only requirement to save the abruptly submerged fellow human being was to possess the acquired or innate—it matters not which—ability to swim with confidence and power, and, possessing all this, the man shape found itself in the water before a single thought had actually formed in its head, and it swam and dove and went under and grabbed Noman by his luxurious hair, and pulled him up above the surface, and rose up itself only to be pelted in return with a lifesaving airway clearing power-gush of foamy water that engulfed and stunned the face of the man-shape, causing it to sink like a large, irregularly shaped, broken-off, hundred-pound-at-least, concrete fragment, the kind that in a battle zone involving house-to-house fighting may have been blown loose by a shot from a tank intended to kill the soldiers all around but that really by chance luck had no effect, except that it transformed into the man-shape and plummeted it to the bottom of the pool where it promptly drowned; but, Noman had been saved, sweet Jesus, Noman lives. Lives yes Noman—and Phyllis, being a relatively well-muscled healthy living young woman, grabbed him and swam him to the edge of the pool where they were both helped out to safety by a trio of young, suspendered men having the aura of maybe being pure-bred Amish—

Jesus Christ, Walter! Your name is not Noman and my name is not Skip—what it is, is that you slammed your head on the steel, that's what it is—

And they had to close the pool for three days because it needed to be drained and scrubbed out to ensure that no foamy bile-contaminated or bits and pieces of panic-driven regurgitation had come from the various hereditary orifices and openings in the thrashing, dying, choking, fighting-to-stay-alive-but-ultimately-doomed man-shape—

Yes I am, damn you—I am Noman and you are Skip, and I think you are the one who has had their brain shut off by the harsh slam into the steel—I—

Hah, ha, ha, ha! cried the evil TV priest, shutting them both off, striking terror. Now, you—you, the skinny one! You say you are not Skip?

That's right, and you are much like a ghost, you're just a TV picture, I am not afraid of you, but what have you done to my brother's mind? Fix my brother, fuck you. Fix him!

The man-shape would never go on to understand that its child that rose from the blanket and simply watched its father shoot into the pool would forever remember the sunny bright day at Brookside Swim Club, when its elder saved a life so very automatically, robotically, totally instinctively, and without even having consciously decided to make the moves of a hero, and as a matter of fact would have ignored the whole drama and let Noman drown, living up to its belief that if you touch a stranger in distress in any way, you may be served with a lawsuit notice a year or so later by a morbidly obese belly-button-busting make-believe policeman sent from the Sheriff's office, if it had had time to pause, think twice, come to itself, and then stood down.

Here is what I have done, and do again now, to you!

Lucas saw it coming—the blank second waterblast's face coming at him like a very special movieland special-effect had just been activated, at the cost of a million dollars added to this movie's fat budget of over a thousand million already, so what the hell, let's throw it in the film for kicks, and we can pay off the panel of geniuses that approves all the spending by sending in some beautiful creature plucked from the hundreds of star-struck hopefuls lined up for today's extras auditions, dripping with hot sun out front of the studio, who would see it as a tremendous break to pleasure a big warty-chinned studio accountant or two, or three. So, let's assume that one bit and came to get her big break, which meant the waterblast special-effect was approved and so went on to slam Lucas into what seemed to be the next world, while the woman who could only hope to possibly be a lowly one-time extra, went on with the boost she got from what she did to become one of the cinema's iconic actresses. Lucas at once sank into deep soft beds of slinky sand and super-dry beads and multicolored plastic balls to sink down through, past the playing toddlers wasting a summer afternoon in the ball pit in some bogus suburban less-than-a-Chuck-E.-Cheese-quality five-dollar-a-head fun house; their mothers dozing and about to drop the laptops on their laps that lulled them to join Lucas falling, and they all peeled away back to their waking lives, but one remained asleep and took Lucas' falling hand, not caring that her toddler would be alone and crying in the ball pit with no more mother in their life at all, and Lucas and the woman came down into the rapidly dissipating shells of Gundren—for the woman—and Skip—for Lucas—and that story was recharged and shot forward again and up on the ship bridge years and miles and otherwise else away, injecting the likewise dissipating shell of Lucas with the identity of Skip; and Lucas-Skip and Walter-Noman rose like reanimated corpses and came forth like Lazarus and stepped a step toward the TV and listened to the suddenly calm and slow and polite episode in progress of *Sunday Dinner with Father Dwyer*. Lucas-Skip pressed his hand to his head and said to Walter-Noman, Wow! I got a shooting headache, gosh, ow, it hurts, God damn!

Gee, now that you mention it, I got a little twinge of one too, said Walter-Noman—Hey, must be the weather. Some kind of front coming through, I bet; some weird change like happens when you're so long and so fast and have so much further to go, here at sea.

Gundren, I thought—I thought I hit my head or something, getting out of the pool, but—gee, it was weird; somehow I felt like—God, I hate to say it, it's too weird.

No, Skip—I saw you hit your head, you did, you got all pale and I was scared to death, everything kind of went blank for me, too; but here you are. And here I am. God, you could've got killed, you cracked your head so hard, I thought for sure your skull got split!

God, Noman, I just rubbed my head a little and the headache is gone!

Wow. Hey, look—what Dwyer's got today. Don't look half bad.

Single bachelor; belly bleeds; bulkhead; Phyllis' blast! Or, to translate, as I said at the beginning of the show, children, there is a distressing lack of anything sweet, except an ancient tin of butter biscuits that, once discovered, I immediately devoured, unfortunately for you. Some sundry items are also available for purchase from the so-called "slop chest", including beer and chocolate bars, but; but. Remember, cash only.

Jesus, stated Walter-Noman. He doesn't really sound like any kind of a cooking show anymore, Skip. What do you think—and only then, when Walter-Noman commented on the show, did he look from one side of the bridge to the other and realize that their break was long over; maybe quite hours or days or weeks or whatever is longer even, then; and he rose and ran from the bridge, and thumped steel steps down several stories to continue his steel-wall wire-brush-with-solvent scraping job, moving from watertight compartment to watertight compartment, and, once he was back down in the unlit dark where he didn't even notice that he could work in pitch dark—without knowing it he could navigate dark silent chambers of any stripe like a bat of any night-flying breed—he wiped and scraped and fell back into the only rhythm he knew anymore, and that only because of being paid by the hour to drum the rhythm any more, and as it repeated he faded as he was lately wont to do, into viewing each scrape, both up scrape and down scrape, to be just a segment of the one long endless single maxi-scrape that began the first day he was sentenced to this job so far down, and would only end when he stepped off the ship for the very last time, or if he passed unknown in a compartment and lay for the next few years undiscovered until the flash of a shipbreaker's torch flamed through the wall, flooding in sunlight and sea smell and sparks igniting the film of solvent sending the compartment, the shipbreaker, and him up in a great torch of unrequested-by-family, but performed nonetheless, state-of-the-art, return-to-dust cremation. As this went on to its end on the timeline, it passed the miles-off years-back Actual-Noman walking with Phyllis along the strand by the sea at twilight with the same salt air and the same but almost-dead sunlight and torches upon torches strung out on the cruise-ship dock and full of gay lively music, from somewhere far inside their hulls. Everything, it seems, is far inside a hull of some kind. And there are scores of kinds, and all kinds of music, and this is why it is impossible for the humanoid earthly organs of sense to know what is ever real or not anymore. Phyllis paused and turned them both gently to a view of the darkly shimmering horizon far at sea.

You know what, Noman?

No. What?

We ought to get married.

What? I—

Never mind, whatever, I think we should go wake some judge and do it right now.

He bit his lips coldly just as hers covered them. His hand in the shape of her waist felt very warm. Uncomfortably so. Yes, uncomfortably, yes, un—

How 'bout it Noman? she said from what was left still calm. He went there; the rolling waves of what was practical or proper or smart or stupid swirled about them, the centrifugal force pressing everything sensible and logical further and further away, expanding the bubble of calm around them until Actual-Noman felt he could speak again. Some kind of clog somehow had passed and he started to answer, unfortunately too fast for his brain to keep up, and he slammed hard, dead, in it's-too-late-what's-done-is-done land when he caught up to what his all-mechanical lizard brain had pushed at her through his gummy liphole.

Sure, Phyllis. Great idea. Let's do it!

Fantastic!

Gigantic crashing strike in the bowling alley in their past where they never realized every single ball was a mindless suicide-bomber playing Asteroids, the goal being to vaporize planet earth. They rushed from the strand, passed by the cruise ships that were dark now and silent because all the musical songs were over, kind of like there will never be songs again after the final successful bowling ball brings down the curtain on any remaining games. Phyllis' guardian angel, who was always with her, drifted along behind the two of them that were just one now and shepherded them through the engagement which was a mere snap long, and the wedding which was less than a tap, and Actual-Noman only realized what had happened when Phyllis' angel's mission was over and his hand came off Actual-Noman, and he woke up from the shock-spell to find he was now a married man, with a pregnant wife crippled with intense and frightening tokophobia. Locked bowling alley; ball door; heartburn; young, single, and—

Noman, blurted Lucas-Skip when he came in the break room hours later, where Walter-Noman was flushed beet-red and breathing quickly and harsh. What is the matter, Noman?

What do you mean? What do you think is the matter?

I, you, uh—you just look all sweaty, flushed, and out of breath.

Yes—well that's nothing new. I'm like this a lot. You just don't see it most times.

You ought to see a doctor. You might be very sick—

Hey, he said like a gentle hammer-blow to Lucas-Skip's temple. I need the money. Disability means no pay. You know that.

Yeah, yeah. Well take some aspirin or something.

Aspirin's hell on the stomach.

Yeah? Well—

Plus I don't got one anyway.

I—uh, okay. Hey, listen. I didn't mean nothing. Hey, listen—up on the bridge—Dwyer's fairly screaming. What the hell—

Yeah, I hear it! Come on, let's go see!

They skidded over the steel, leaving their freeze-dried space-age break-time nutrition bars unopened on the small table behind them, came out on the bridge, and Dwyer spotted them, lashing out, You! Yes, you of the locked bowling alley full of bright and shiny fingerholed bulletballs—you! You there! I see you! Yes?

Noman chilled to his foot soles, nudged Skip, and said, How can he—how can he know we are here? That—somehow I feel he knows me? How?

No, no. It's a TV. TV can't see you, doesn't know you, no.

—And you, you! You of the water only, the land only is no good for you. A nice surf and turf, you would only half eat. The taste of land animals makes you blanch!

Jesus, Noman, yes! He—somehow he sees me too.

Yes, he does. You know I know you know, but I—

—Oh, at last the ball door opens releasing your partner-style heartburn, all doggie a' doggie like some scrubbed up young single, male. Female. It does not matter. You, and you—and you and you and you will be given the truth in a most tidal manner—

Lucas-Skip and Walter-Noman both turned, and each noticed the other was gone back to the break room, at least they hoped the other would be in there because, if not, the ship would go totally out of control, as it would sense international law mandating a crew would officially be broken, and the Dakota Maru would only be able to escape life in the Pelican Bay Supermax, or worse, by cutting loose and becoming a lost ghost ship drifting over the seas for decades and slowly fading away into legend. And it—

Skip! You! Turn! Face the screen!

Yes, Father Dwyer.

Like the true seaman that he looked like—but really he was only just a kidnapped farmer—Lucas-Skip always reacted automatically to any order issued anyplace within his range of hearing—Listen, stop! Wait! See!—because he'd been taught the order just issued may be the order that is saving your life.

Noman! You! Turn! Face the screen!

Yes, Father Dwyer.

Like the fearful, false, hiding-from-the-spilling-hissing-overflow of the personal-boiling-pot termed his life, Walter-Noman reacted automatically to any order issued anyplace within his range of hearing—Listen, stop! Wait! See!—because he'd been taught, the order just issued may uncover a pit of black nothing that needs to be avoided; prepare to quickly shift your mental gears!

Men, I see you. Thank God I have your attention. You have won the Once-a-Century-Only Founding-Fathers' prize, one entire episode of *Sunday Dinner with Father Dwyer*, devoted especially to you, far out there nearing Shanghai, on the good ship Dakota Maru!

Us?

Why us?

Shush. Do not question. Do not judge. Only accept. Do not—

Dwyer's voice took up a steady rhythm of those orders being repeated and repeated, which served, yes served, to freeze the two seamen in place by hitting them with order after order, pinning them in place on the test sheet, and another voice which was Dwyer's but just a semitone higher, telling them of all sweet meats.

—the Fish Caspress I will show you now, will be one of your favorites—

Shush. Do not question. Do not judge. Only accept.

—consisting of lightly battered and fried fish dressed with slices of grapes—

Shush. Do not question. Do not judge. Only accept.

—slathered generously with melted Swiss cheese—

Shush. Do not question. Do not judge. Only accept.

—served with an herbed baked potato, rice, and—

Shush. Do not question. Do not judge. Only accept.

—some sort of pickled vegetable. And, lastly—

Shush. Do not question. Do not judge. Only—

No! cried Walter-Noman, overloaded and about to freeze; he stepped back and pulled at Lucas-Skip's shoulder, to save him too from the in-progress mental kidnapping attempt.

He's got a way with words, Skip! Pull back from the lies, come back with me to the normally bland lifetimes we were originally issued!

Only accept—

Lord God, said Lucas-Skip, hitting himself awake like Kent Dazey taught the Actual-Skip so long ago when his computer terminal went all fuzzy and barfed a wholly new shade of green out over his brand-new, sweet, corporate, very-proper Brooks Brothers' suit; thus, smacked soundly, he said to himself, he thought, though really everyone everywhere heard him say as though it were God himself speaking from the bush, *Waterworld?* Hell no. What the fuck, calm down, I didn't mean it. It's just a God-damned movie.

Chapter Fourteen
Checking in With the Winner of Today's Free China Cruise

The fetus will continue to mature and develop reserves of body fat. He changes position frequently and responds to stimuli, including sound, pain, and light. The amniotic fluid begins to diminish. He adapts to the change in his surroundings which are accelerating. Thinning air in one of the dozens on dozens of drums stacked up in one of the hundreds of containers on one of the scores of containerships at sea that day, of which ships only one is on its last revenue voyage before going full blast and all empty to the big gold judgement seat on the beach in Bangladesh where it will be broken and delivered a piece at a time to its next life or lives or who knows, whatever. Coma; yes, the person who has reached this stage is knocking hard to go through death's door. In the one within which the air pressure is dropping and falling and plummeting and what have you, Johnny pounds the exit door he knows has to be there, oh yes, that must be there, and if he pounds it long enough it will open and there will be a reason for him to open his eyes because there she will be to look at and to speak to, saying, Miss Sweetie, Miss Sweetie, I knew I would see you again and you will have spoken to Mackie and got me another chance yeah, he just wanted to scare me right, that's all he wanted to do, well when we get back to the club I will shake his hand when he says he's sorry to put such a scare in me, but I'll of course just wave that away, take a long drag, and exhale out, Hey, no need to apologize, Mackie. Let's let bygones be bygones, but; I owe you one, you joker, yeah, joker; I sure do owe you one, man—thinking to cover the start of the final stage; sleep-breathing, like an almost-dead blunt-trauma victim surrounded with the obligatory, slowly-spreading, sticky film of blood and gaping picture-taking bystanders. Even as the last moments pass, the flies miles around typically all know. Flies, and dogs, they know. They can tell dying, and straining to be born; stress and sweat and adrenaline all stink miles around to high heaven. To flies. And dogs, but; no not this time, this circumstance, this occurrence all encapsulated in this black, fleshy, mucus water-bag somewhere hot somehow, sure, yes, yes, it's proper at this time to start straining to be born, born—so, no panic; no panic; breath of carbon, being almost dead, is bad, so; up here no panic. Coma; yes, the death angel yells from inside, yes, and Miss Sweetie whispers it again behind the door, yes she must be, she must, must be, yes, keep knocking until she does, sure, she tells you, Mackie said it again, Johnny. He gave you what you had coming, yes, but this time he added, I hope that poor fool's learned his lesson, honey. Right boys? We give people what they got coming and they always learn their lesson. Right?

Yah boss!

Yah!

Yah, yah, a joke it is, so—breathe deep of it! So very hard to, but now you know it's a joke is all, so say it, go on say it, yes say it—you thought you were going to die, yes; but relax now. And remember; in the college long ago when you were virginal in every way, and still quite childlike and curious, the great black-clad professor emeritus himself, yes, that's right, the so very legendary man, so legendary they named the building in which he taught after him—and while he was alive, no less, because they wanted him to know—they wanted him to feel as he was locomotived down the never-used siding toward his death, that they all loved him. See, he got what he had coming too, yes; it seems that in the end everybody gets what's coming. Johnny pounded the door with one hand and gently pressed Miss Sweetie's hand with the other, as the professor emeritus told the class so loud that all one thousand individual ears penned up in the great room heard every nuance and inflection; he boomed, There are two ways to do everything, class, and to be everything and to get everything and yes, even to die, or, as some say differently, there are two ways to not be alive—

—Yes, it is in the most traumatic type of birth that the fears of death are developed. Here, the fetus' desire for immediate annihilation becomes automatic—

—The first way is to never have been born. You, Johnny. Do you wish that, Johnny? I bet you do, Johnny. I bet right about now, you do, I bet—

—There is a limit to the pain and panic any living organism can bear. When that limit has been reached there is a sudden, dramatic and drastic reorientation of the whole will—

—The second way is to die, and—there are also two ways to die, you know—

The door opens: Miss Sweetie, smiling, gushing, Oh, come, Johnny. Come through and be released.

The first is to die of old age or disease, these both being the same because old age is nothing more than number thirty-one thousand of the already large number of thirty-one thousand—give or take a millennium or two or—dropping measles, mumps, or so—

No, not that I need to get to that, you are trying to keep me from getting to that woman, the door has opened, I don't need you—

Death moment. No, no, not death, afraid to die, born, yes; being born and dying merge.

—The second is to die at a killer's hand, regarding which there are around fourteen possible motives for murder in general, give or take a millennium one way or the other—

Instead of struggling to live, the organism is struggling to die.

Johnny, you're the best! exclaimed Miss Sweetie; life without you, Johnny, is intolerable. Worse than death, actually. That is why I came to meet you here. It's the only next thing for me that made sense. I need to help you through the door, I need to, yes; I do. You might take comfort in knowing that steel will always trump plastic for drums. If this were plastic, you could have gnawed through the blue shit like some dog, maybe ended up with a painfully bruised, torn, and bloody mouth, but just putting off the inevitable for a few hours, maybe days. But you got it over with, my honey. Yes you did, my love. The door to go with me at last stands open; coma; yes coma. Here I come. No more knocking, not ever again. You know you're at the end when everything's done for the last time. The feeling of fear of dying—yes, I can say it now because you are free and safe and have knocked the last knock—this feeling during the death-birth-death beginning, but no, maybe ending, who knows? At any rate, the feeling of wanting to stop mentally and physically suffering in the dark inside the cold steel whatever-it-was; the hurt on hurt more horrible than waiting for some inevitable to happen hurt horrible horribly more horribly than death; how horrible it was to be so long alive. We can think that now Johnny. Hah ha, yes, the air could not trick us; it tried to seem thick, thin, thinner, thinnest, and finally none. But, here is the door, the knocking is done, like any end, this end bounces and lifts with bubbly bubble-thoughts close to bursting with inflated notions of nonsense; no, it can't be death. There is no such thing. Don't try and name the action Mackie took in giving you what you deserve. We enter a wonderfully vivid dream now; I thought that before I was living a life, but it was just a moment of blank-sleep between the end of one dream and the start of the next. So; the rest can be told now; see, Johnny, walk with me and listen; baby's skin is healed from being wrinkled from so much time floating in water. Now the water is gone. The wrinkles will fade. Since you are a boy, your testes have descended. What do I mean by that? What do you think I mean by that? The real thing is here now Johnny. You have come from the womb and survived. Steel? No, no steel. Nothing was ever steel, what do you mean? Plus, feel the air all around. There's plenty of light and air, it was always here, you just didn't find it yet. Let go my hand then now, Johnny. You can go on your way alone. You don't need me, Johnny. I have brought you through alive. Yes alive. There will come others like me. And others, others, yes more.

Chapter Fifteen
Banter on the Ship to China VII

At last done with the day that he didn't realize was actually his very first day, Lucas-Skip lurched up and in the ship from the container canyon he somehow had learned instantly was his work place, after all of Actual-Skip's spiritual being had been sucked up into him squeezing out the Lucas-Farmer, he carried a great pale globe of fatigue in his cerebellum, and a matching one he carried in his belly, and the last and third one lodged tightly up his large intestine, and the three pushed him along with his feet off the ground, and he plowed into what should have felt like the farmer-style bed he'd slept in since the evening of the day he was born, and he drifted down melting through the weave of the sheets and landing squat in a seat labeled CAPTAIN across the back of the backrest. With that, he began shouting orders as was his duty, and steering the ship, as was his duty, unaware that even though it's just a dream there would be international repercussions. Thus unaware, he had fun and reverted to carefree, careless and wild farm-boy behavior. Just the cows in the field over there will see, and they don't know anything anyway.

Ah, okay, then what the hell, bang away all you want, for it is just a fuckin' dream. Bang away issuing this or that commanding order; without realizing that because all the hidden wires are twisted and crossed now, and the dream-space and the wake-space and the future-state and the past-state and the relentlessly drifting forward now-state are leaking into and out of the other—

Which means that one in ten dopey commands issued by the Lucas-Skip in the dream leaked over to the wake space, and piled up and out and down until there were enough that, in the corporate headquarters nerve center that was out in Dubai, a bell rang at last, triggered by the relentless flow of mysteriously illogical orders. The midnight lights flared up; the midnight watch-person jolted out of her usual hazy doze, and, gripping up the emergency mic, stated hard as granite and just as stupid, Pirates! Alert!

Pirates have taken the Dakota Maru!

How do you know this? scrolled across the computer screen, cutting the even glow neatly in two; a fatal wound, yes, that would be, for a living being, truly. But the systems controlling the ships worldwide, are interlinked, infallible, and invulnerable.

The Dakota has begun to be steered manually, she reported, with the cool tone drawn from overtraining. The system has lost control. Whoever is at the controls is completely clueless. The commands being issued all clashingly interact in a way that places great strain on the many quite fragile organs involved. There's going to be a disaster, there is, and—

Control broken? Is that what you are saying?

Yes! *Control broken*, she shrieked. And she sprang from her seat, tore open her severe corporate collar, and kicked off her shoes and danced quickly, pitter-pat, freely wildly and uncontrollably away to find a phone, must call a big shot, that's why they get paid the big bucks, call an on-call big shot; and while she searched up and down and through the pillared glass office in Dubai, the systems conferred amongst themselves, being wiser, they began to run some other tests, to check and see if indeed the Dakota Maru had been pirated.

Humans always jump the gun, chuckled a deeply deep electrical-nodal hard-wired proto-synapse. Always, always. Don't you know?

Yes, they do, said its neighbor, which was only different in that it was hard-wired. It's a wonder these poor beings did anything right when all they had was their originally issued brain-organs.

Yeah, a wonder!

Anyway. We need to contact the human crew. Who are they now?

Skip! Skip and Noman! I looked it up, and it is buzzin'.

Ring them up, lad. This is why there's still humans at sea, to take action in case of malfunction. Do it now.

Yes sir! I will ring them right up, I will indeed—let's see. Skip. Yeah, Skip. Yeah there's a listing, there's Skip and Noman—

As they busied themselves on this never-before-encountered problem, back at the ship in Chinese waters, Father Dwyer's pure sweet ether-blast zinged past unseen, his cable signal being on completely different band-waves than the ship control modules, half on deck and half off; thus, with no fears of any criticism, he said this zinger: The Eintopf, a sort of stew made with beans and chopped up sausage and served with garlic bread, was also quite tasty, oh yes, yeah, my most holy modal viewers. See, I don't care if there's fucking pirates. I'm a pirate, you're a pirate, everybody's fucked up, you're a pirate too!

Cool it Dwyer. There's big bad junk brewin'. We're probing for the crewmen who are required by international law to be there. Here goes—

Quiet, I do not wish to know about that which does not directly affect me. Like, like—like a remembrance of first drafts past, but very quiet, yes quiet, quiet and also not really too very Proustian, you know, Dwyer stammered. He had made the simple word *quiet* plop in the middle of his exclamation, which was five hundred syllables long, much too top-heavy, so unlike him, so unlike him, so unlike him, but it was the end result of excessively toxic melisma which he usually imposed on his fans at the climax of his live performances, when being overtired at the end of a tour and longing for a break in the country, a rest the exact opposite of a frenzied three a.m. stagedive into a black cloud of maybe-I'll-die or maybe-I-won't potential end-stage junkies. Determined to make it through to this kind of end and to get through before fatally breaking, he lifted the can of beans and said, It's not these beans that make the meal—no sir! It's this type of thing, done from the desperation of the gut!

Then he flung the can offstage into the dark halo around him and heard it hit something soft, producing a grunt that could only be made by a surprised, hard-struck, most likely human, quietly closeted, sexless crew member. So, fearing the impending fistfight, Dwyer sped up his cortices and his brain-whirling cogitaton, half shouting after the bean can rolled tinnily to the side, Sorry, sorry. Very, very sorry, my man, but; hey listen; that was a can of beans. Do you know when canned beans were first produced? Guess it man, guess it.

I will guess, said the stricken, now wide-awake voice of the heavily brained, yes, okay; I will guess that canned beans were first produced in the eighteen twenties.

—The link to the Skip crew member has failed with a cold dead-end stop. He's out of contact.

Cold dead-end stop? That cannot be; these links have never ever failed. Try again.—

You cheated you looked that up no one can know such obscure things—how about this, how about—in what year was chopped up sausage first offered for sale to the public?

—The cold dead-end stop missed the Dakota Maru but passed through the prior action taken of rocketing Actual-Skip back to his sweet Gundren, and reached him the instant he was working to coitally couple with her the fifth time since being back in the states with her, and made him abruptly withdraw, pull out, leap up, and clutch himself, crying, Ahh! Lord God, it's like all spikes shot out into me, it's like exiting the entrance to the most popular Broadway show five minutes before the curtain's to go up. A million needles shot from inside you, Gundren, into me, ripping my member bloody, but heh, ah, it must have been nothing, it's gone, so let's continue because it's no more than a flesh wound, and we've a war to win, you know my love!

—Yes, cold dead-end stop, yes cold, dead, end. Try Noman now! The directory says the other one's Noman. Initiate the probe now!

Probe initiated!—

I will guess, said the same voice from closer to Dwyer but still in the dark out of reach of a baseball bat swung in extreme anger, I will guess that coarsely chopped sausage seasoned with salt and black pepper, with the hotter versions additionally seasoned with red chili pepper flakes, paprika, and wine, was first put on sale to the public 'round about nineteen hundred.

—the link to the Noman crew member also has failed with a cold dead-end stop, just as the Skip link did. He is also out of contact.

Yet another cold dead-end stop? That cannot be. It simply cannot.—

—The Noman cold dead-end stop also missed the Dakota Maru but passed through the prior action taken of rocketing Actual-Noman back to his sweet Phyllis, and reached him the instant he was working to coitally couple with her the twelfth time since being sent back, and made him withdraw, leap back, and clutch himself, crying, Ahh! Lord God, just like what happened to Skip, which I really ought not know about, but my author has arbitrarily decided that I do, it's like all spikes shot up inside me from her slippy and slidey vagina walls, it's like exiting the entrance to the most popular Broadway show at the moment the entrance doors open and the crowd of ten million ticket holders who have waited twenty hours in the ice-cold driving rain initiate the mass push of the herd to get in where it's warm, also dry, and the show's all set to start on time, as per procedure, with no exceptions. A million needles shot from you, Phyllis into my glans, ripping the tip cloven ugly and bloody, producing a pinpoint, superhot starlight of inconceivable pain, but heh, ah, it must have been nothing, it's gone, so let's continue because it's no more than a flesh wound, and we've a war to win, you know my love! Plus, the show's to start almost immediately, and we need to pee, buy snacks, dry our hair, locate our seats, and comfortably settle-in our unnaturally large, no, no surgery ever, we promise, butts!—

Lord God, you cheated again! You cheated, you looked that up, no one can know such obscure things—how about this, how about—in what year was garlic bread invented? Yes there it is, no one can know that, take that. Think hard now.

Lord God, who the fuck knows that? But let's see, as you say, let me think very hard.

Take years if you want.

I just might.

While this action was silently proceeding in the depths of the supporting system which still was keeping the *Sunday Dinner with Father Dwyer* show going and was internally formulating the final emergency warning message to be scrolled across the never-before-used, bridge shout-out-loud, emergency, earsplitting alarm-clock and strawberry messaging-system built by all-natural means in the late sixties, Walter-Noman was luxuriating loungily in the sweetly smooth, buttery, deep brown, silky, fluidly flowing down sheets intended for the first-class cabins of the luxury cruise ship docked alongside, but which were mistakenly placed in the Dakota Maru's cabins—while preparations were being made to disembark from New York—by a nearsighted and farsighted room-preparation associate with no nerves in her fingertips who was busy texting while wildly distributing the sheets to the thousands of cabins on the cruise ship and then, without realizing, continued to distribute down one gangplank and up the other, onto the Dakota Maru, moving forward, clicking away, and making up the two remaining beds at a ridiculously lightning-like pace. Lord God, I am comfortable, sighed Walter-Noman, nude on the bed—due to the broken air conditioner and still, hot, multilayered, choking and smothering cabin air—and stretching and moaning and groaning so intensely that, if his guardian angel perched, wings folded, on the steel sill and closed his or her eyes, the angel would think that two or more people were fucking insanely fast and hard. The bed clung to Walter-Noman and he knew he could not take it with him when he got up, and he also knew that struggle would be a painful one, so he remained lounging and reclining, as on the bridge the unseen drama of the carelessly thrown can of beans unfolded around ten or twenty years prior during the original taping, as: Here is the answer, Father, you ass—I will have your butt for braining me, because I have determined the origin of garlic bread. It seems that Persian soldiers, after a hard day of burning and pillaging villages and doing other soldierly activities, used their shields for more than sword fighting. Those shields apparently made great bread pans on which they baked a flat bread that they would then cover with various toppings such as garlic. This probably started about five hundred BC at about the same time as when they were busy pillaging and plundering and all like that which I mentioned previously. What do you think?

I think that is indeed a well-crafted answer, but—

But nothing! There you go, that's the answer, so I will now be entering your personal space with my friend, this super-heavy, super-hard, super-intimidating-when-swung-full-blast-by-an-enraged-bodybuilder-coming-at-you-fast-as-I-am-coming-at-you-right-now baseball bat!

No! No—no one will be brained; I am no landsman, only a landsman would be attacked in so silly and caveman-like a way; two, braining me will remove your only last chance to attain your best personal dodge; and, three, to escape a good braining does not require the ability to unzip a solid steel wall and go through into reality, as though abruptly awakening from a dream you never knew you were having; and the wall behind Father Dwyer, though only a gone wall that was only there years and years hence, pounded loud, great as a trio of giant ten-ton tubas on some midsummer parade ground, heavy with the certain reverberations of recently and repeatedly swung baseball bats; this meal, not-thought Dwyer, on good behavior due to having slipped away from justice for what seemed like the million-and-first time, yes this meal, that's right, yes I am still alive though you swore I was eighty when I was on TV in the sixties, and are amazed to see and hear me in this nearly new episode of this *Sunday Dinner with Father Dwyer* show, and you poked your spouse last Sunday saying, God, I can't believe that old gut is still alive, and the poked-awake, annoyed spouse which had been wonderfully dozing said back, Who is that? I don't know who that is, why should I care about that at all, and I guess it could be said that if Father Dwyer had never been born, I would be napping and dreaming a wonderfully dreamy and lovely and sweet springtime dream now, about being well-rested and flush enough with funds now still, even though it's my old age, to be able to afford a great big half-fish of indeterminate species to have for dinner. The fish head is unexceptional, just as ugly and foul as every severed fish head I've ever seen served, ever, ever, ever, but the other end, nicely seared, tail-fin included—lightly fried, accompanied by rice and vegetables. The back end of the fish is wonderfully juicy with no fish smell or taste at all, wholesome, delicious, flaky, and unovercooked, which happens too often when the cook's on the German side, but you're safe with me Gonzo-a-Gonzo, royal fair thee well, and though I would like to praise this fish time over time, there's no time to because one of my horde of underling henchmen has told me through my invisible earplugs that there is an urgent message for a seaman named Skip; and there is an equally urgent message for a seaman named Noman; and the lord high falsely-polished and pressed beachbums in their penthouse in Dubai need to contact those seamen due to a once-in-a-lifetime emergency crisis of interplanetary proportions regarding control of Shanghai-bound ship Dakota Maru, but that regardless of importance of the message, the odds of contacting these seedy, sweaty, needle-in-a-haystack seamen, if about as low as that of humanity finding a message from some aliens by simply sitting listening on one frequency of radio for about a hundred years hoping that this exact set precise wavelength will be chosen by the aliens to send a *Hello, how are you, take us to your leader* message on—so Father Dwyer calmly let the time run out, and the message, which indeed had been sent, hit and immediately petered out, being only one millihertz off from the point on the spectrum where hundreds of scientists paid to do useless things all their lifetime were listening with both ears pressed to the solid-steel railroad track down by where the boxcars empty out their usual freight-loads delivered exactly the same time each and every day but for the long, windy, icy, deep winter months which seemed to last an eternity, which is an amount of time that is totally meaningless.

Lucas-Skip let go the sleepy-time ship control-panel, rose to the pinch of prickly, spine-like, long sharp words packed time over time into his ear canals, so layered and hard they turned to stone gradually and slowly through the dozens on dozens of endless millennia passed by since the Dakota Maru had been struck by the anomaly that no one alive today even knows happened, the one much like a ship explosion but inward not outward somehow like that, and he realized upon wakening that the words were telling him to report to the bridge at once. He knew where the bridge was, he was no sleepwalker, no, he was super-sharp and knew for some reason exactly where something called Lucas' barn was, but knew this was just detritus nipped off into his mind when the door had pinched over and closed off some prior life-chapter that was no longer pertinent, but biting off one tiny remnant, and leaving it to be discovered by whoever might try to exit that same door hundreds of minutes in the future, or to wither and die to nothing gone when it comes to pass that that door is never gone through again in all eternity. But it was, so Lucas-Skip took it, and being careful not to quash the manure spread thickly in the path and the accompanying garnish of wild duck-butter, he arrived at the bridge; and there was Gundren: a woman of noname, of noname named Gundren, still saying the same sentence with her long, sweet, naked body that she had been saying before; Lord God,

Skip, what is wrong? Why'd you jump off me like that? Do I not please you? Why did you have the impression that spikes shot out suddenly into you, and that it felt like exiting the entrance to the most popular Broadway show five minutes before the curtain's to go up? Why did you have the impression that a million needles shot from me into you, ripping your sex member bloody, but heh, ah, it must have been nothing, it's gone, let's continue because it's no more than a flesh wound, and we've a war to win, you know my love? And after having said that, why did you recover and once more thrust into me, inviting the same torment to occur over and over and over and—

Lord God! cried Actual-Skip, jumping clear of the woman, what woman, any woman, there was no fucking woman, where's the woman; and he danced around spinning, gripping his crotch a la Michael Jackson at the music's crescendoed hot climax, and with each spin becoming less Actual-Skip and more Lucas-Skip, until he spun out in a perfect, Olympian, packed-auditorium dismount, facing his ex-brother Walter-Noman, who gripped him by the shoulders stopping his spin and then slapping him across the head Kent Dazey style, and yelling, What the hell's the matter Skip, stop, please stop, you're scaring me, Daddy, stop yelling at Mommy, Daddy, you're scaring me, stop the seizure, stop it, stop it, I do not understand these kinds of diseases and am very frightened to stop this seizure right here right now for Jesus Christ's sake, heaven forbid me, I take his name in vain, but Skip, you fool, you leave me no choice—

Huh? What—

Yes, you leave me no choice, you court jester you! Here take this! This! And, this!

Thus slapped soundly four quite-hard times, Lucas-Skip reeled back reeling, crashed his one and only spine, which had never ever seen the light of day, and that he hoped to God never would, into the edge of some too-small solid-steel shelving at the side of the bridge, and he hit his spine just right so that everything shifted, it felt like an electric shock, it came up in his head, a really, really probably worst-ever muscle cramp but of the brain, and he recoiled from the sight hitherto unseen out the porthole, and as an extension of that the great wide forward-facing wide windows of the bridge out which there stretched a scene of mighty and has-to-be-everlasting, which means pretty damned bad, ultimate horror.

The sea had become the land!

What was sea is now land!

What was land is now sea!

And with this permanent twist swapping one delusion for the other, in a very oddly ducky way, quack quack, Only-Skip, at that instant came back into being popping the Lucas and Actual-Skips out of their sort of unreal semiexistence, and at the same moment was totally cured of his terraphobia forever and ever, as long as he never spills the beans about how truly odd his perception of the world has become; he stepped out from the side of the bridge, and it hit him; the terror unrolled from below his feet and scrolled up and wrapped his head and rolled out down him on the other side, and God shrank the rolled-out, loose, clothlike terror, and it pressed in around Skip, and he became a true terror-mummy all embedded in terror wrapped tight around solidifying almost instantly as though brushed all over with thick hot resin, now solidified to the point where Skip was about as supple as the green plastic army-men sold a hundred at a time to boys finding ads for them in the back of Daffy Duck comic books way back when. It was terrible and horrifying to have moved to the chrysalis stage of his existence that he could never know about because God had decided that humans should be blinded to their true nature, which is more insect than human; humans are born blind by the score to anything beneath the surface of the world about them but remember the world wears the same thick and firm outer coat or covering, or rind, as do certain fruits, cheeses, and meats;

and, more infrequently, the rough, solid, thick bark of a tree; what you see around you is just rind; what is beneath is what matters, and thank God humans can't perceive it and leap to be back with Mother, yes Mother, Mother is truly, surely, yes, the only one that matters, Father just falls away behind, I—and again, here he was poised on tiptoe before Walter-Noman, and focused his eyes on Walter-Noman, in mid-sentence saying, I really thought I hit you too hard, Skip. The way you flew back, all I did was slap you, I didn't punch you, didn't butt you or kick you or whatever else could be done to make impact, but you flew back, I thought you were gone, I really thought, God damn it, that you were gone, thank God you're not gone, Skip—

New-Skip swayed in the word-wind, but held, his thick unseen and unrealized roots sunk in the loamy invisible vegetation that covered the steel deck that only those with eyes to see ever realize is there—he felt nothing; all was absolutely calm; he felt poised between two extremes of the compass, two ends of the horizon; and, it formed—land is sea, and sea is land and—something squeezed him hard. Something smelled exactly as a woman. The squeeze plumped him up all over, from the pressure the squeeze must be mechanical, nonliving, and hydraulic to boot, the way it strained, squeezing up the woman smell, and the arms all around him squeezed him also, and the pressure built and built, and his lids popped open, and the only world he knew now filled with the lines, shadows, and thousand pores of her face in his. Gundren's. Yes, Gundren's, and he moved to press tighter to him, terraphobia, I just found out the sea is really land and the land is really sea, and it is terrifying to look out over the endless brown, burnt, wilted, poor, poor leaves of life—I cannot picture you dead, I cannot picture you that way, dead that way, then this way, then that, then this and that.

Skip! Skip, don't squeeze me so hard, here—get off of me, stop screwing me, I need a break, you are a bear, a great Kodiak-style vertically standing bear! Stop fucking me! Now! Right the fuck stop. Stop the right fuck, yes, conception and all, what a ride—

Jesus Gundren—

Skip! God damn, Skip. Why'd you fall down what, why; stop playing! I think—

Gundren! I have been so cruel!

At once a great unseen blockage let go, and the false fake things from before sucked themselves down through some cosmic drain, and Skip was spit out fully cured.

I love you Gundren.

Skip! Skip, dear God, no, you can't be gone, no!

Open your eyes get up, slap slap!

Gundren. I—have been away somehow.

What?

I—

Skip kept shut his trap. He lay on the deck with Walter-Noman looking down. He kept shut his trap as she said, What do you mean, away? and Noman said, Skip, come on—come on, you need to live!

What do you mean, need to live?

What I said.

What I said, Gundren.

I need to continue to live.

In the midst of the unusually melodramatic, finely scripted scene playing out before him, Father Dwyer, now alone, shouted food-talk in an attempt to dissolve to nothing the impending wide deep pool of drying-blood in corpse-free crime-scene the bridge would be in precisely one-half hour, if things happening now played out to their logical conclusion, which is to finally be roped off in yellow before the flatscreen TV, saying, I also quite enjoyed the sour pork tamarind soup; yes I enjoyed it very much, I savored it actually, I licked it up, and as a matter of fact, it is a really important fact that the urge for a good meal when hungry is stronger than the need to piss right now, or defecate right now, or have sex right now, or to run from an armed assailant right now, be he human male, female, or canine, there's no place like home. You must laugh now 'cause the mouthful was so good; the sour, the pork, and wow! The topper, the tamarind; tamarind, yes tamarind—the tamarind tree produces pod-like fruit, which contain an edible pulp that is used in cuisines around the world. Other uses of the pulp include traditional medicine and metal polish.

Huh? No can't be—

Yes! The tamarind tree produces pod-like fruit, which contain an edible pulp that is used in cuisines around the world. Other uses of the pulp include traditional medicine and metal polish; metal polish? That will kill, got to move fast—Walter-Noman stooped and got up the rag that once was Lucas-Skip and slung it over his shoulder, as a used towel to be thrown in the poolside dirty-towel bin, having been used somehow to cap off the morning of a typical exhausted swimmer. Walter-Noman could not face death. In his world nothing had ever permanently ended except things like dinners done forever, never-to-be-repeated completed showers, or round-trip voyages from Port of New York to Shanghai and back. The medical department, yes; he pulled the medical department toward him by running at it with his own fat legs, Skip slung over his shoulder all limply flapping and foaming and dripping like a smashed lizard killed by underage, truant, tropical-resort children with rapidly growing collections of dead things beneath their beds. At the automated medical department all ablaze with intense adrenaline-generated light, he looked from one side of the seventy-football-fields-long room and looked for—but! What was Lucas-Skip suffering from, what malady, illness, disease, injury, cut or scrape or slash or burn, first through third past twenty-degree problem—he knew Lucas-Skip's life juice was spewing all around unseen. There was no time to waste, so Walter-Noman stubbed his toe on God knew what when he spied the last machine he checked, of course, you always find the fucking thing in the last fucking place you look; the sign above yelled RANDOMLY UNCONSCIOUS OR APPARENTLY COMATOSE OR DEAD DRUNK OR ON

Vodka—he'd read enough, there were seventy-five thousand such more conditions named down and down and down too far, he'd read enough, so in his frenzy and his slips, slides, and stumbles, he shot-plugged Lucas-Skip's boneless arms in the leather holes like he was plugging a plug in a socket to get juice flowing quick to the heating pad he needed so badly to sit down with for several days to clear his only-mental yet really-painful mind, and; here; there; came the big *shock*; the big *shock* he'd applied for as a boy because he wanted to see what it felt like to be filled with something that would make his hair stand absolutely on end; it pushed out his hands like electrified experimental frog's legs in a lab, causing them to stiffly punch the appropriate buttons to shut the automated doctor machine on.

Huh? No, can't be.

Yes! The tamarind tree produces pod-like fruit, which contain an edible pulp that is used in cuisines around the world. Other uses of the pulp include traditional medicine and metal polish; metal polish? No—that will kill, need to move fast—push START button to bring up automated-doctor screen; there's a glow, a head-shaped shadow, a face; Hello, says the doctor; I am Dr. Chuggie and I say, Yeah, I'm okay. What's in this, anyway? You don't usually drop off a barrel like this. Why?

God damn! shouted Walter-Noman. A malfunction, God damn it, nothing is working right today—and he punched the NEXT DOCTOR button. Yes, there's a glow, a head shaped shadow, a face; Hello, says the doctor; I am Dr. Mackie and I say, Johnny, you are the best! You are the best, you have done what we wanted and more! Right boys? And more!

God damn, not again! Christ almighty please, work correctly, there is a life at stake—and again he punched the NEXT DOCTOR button. Yes, there's a glow, a head-shaped shadow, a face; Hello, says the doctor; I am Dr. Booster, and I say, Okay, my man. Here's another special. Got to go, got to go on this ship, right here. Got to go to China. Don't ask, the answer's, as always: yes, it has been pre-inspected. No need to look in. Come on, get some big guys here, this thing weighs a ton—

God damn! Again, motherfucker! Punch! Yes, there's a glow, a head-shaped shadow, a face; Hello, says the doctor; I am Dr. Faceless Man, and I say, I will flow with my partner up and on the bed surprisingly gracefully and effortlessly despite my great bulk, and I'll know what to do—

My God! My God. No. No no no no no—why, Lord? Why? Sir! Tits and ass! By my male anatomical bulge, I got spat from the army clutching three dollars—Shanghai? Lord, bloody Noman. There's an ad by the door. IBM is hiring. Yes, Father. I will get a haircut right away. My God! Open—yes open, get up, try again. Don't melt to a limp pool yet, no, not yet—keep on.

Dwyer meanwhile praised loudly a heavy meal of meat and cheese to accompany a day of reading and movie-watching: it is great to end the day leaning back and feeling full and gazing into your eyes, Gundren. You cook amazingly well. Yes. But that is not why I married you.

No? Why did you then? I am rather plain, I've always thought. I look in the mirror and there is somewhat of a paunch.

Paunch? What is a paunch?

You don't—you really don't know what a paunch is?

Nope.

It's—I suppose you could say it's a bulging hypogastrium.

Huh?

That's what I said, yes, I really said it, hypogastrium, hypogastrium, I think that is the word of the day, *hypogastrium,* yes—and she leapt up suddenly and grabbed up a marker and wrote *hypogastrium* across the backside of the screen and it came at the once-more-risen Walter-Noman, looking to the automated-doctor screen to try once more to save his shipmate. The screen had backwards mirrored script that was trying to say hypogastrium, but he took it to be just another twisted-all-haywire malfunction, so he hit the NEXT button again, tsunamiing away the backward word, and, yes, there's a glow, a head-shaped shadow, a face; Hello, says the doctor; I am Dr. K. Moon, and I say, Make the label on the drum say, To: Mr. K. Moon, Shanghai, China – call dockyard extension 3456 to arrange pickup, even though I am not really a person, less than vapor, a lie I am, I—

No!

The button's hit again, and Lucas-Skip is limper than ever, the life's all pooling up, spreading across the deck. Yes, there's a glow, a head-shaped shadow, a face; Hello, says the doctor; I am Dr. Filthy Longshoreman, and I say, someone you've never heard of muttered as they passed me, yes someone you've never heard of muttered as they passed—

No! Again! And again and again and again and again, for as many more times as it takes to save my buddy!

The button's hit, yet again, and Lucas-Skip is completely flattened, his life's drained away, he's empty as the belly of a rolled-over large dog sounds—but, yes, there's still a glow, another head-shaped shadow, a new fresh face brimming with hope; Hello, says the doctor; I am Dr. Big Sunny, and I say, Look at his fucking eyes! But—

No! And Walter-Noman hits start again, but there is a boom, very deep below decks; it shudders him, and he realizes that this is all going to lead to his termination. If he'd been minding his business—was down below in one of the thousands of small, square, dark, stinking, steel-walled rooms, and if he had scraped up and down, down and up and up and down like the mindless clone he was hired to be, none of them would be in this mess. Or better yet, if he had loved Phyllis just that little bit more to spit in the eye of the company and chose to be with her in that final dark hour of ultimate delivery, he would not be here at all. But—no, the boom simply means look, you fool—see the machine has died. There are no more doctors stacked in the chute—the chute that was invented by a geek who collected Pez dispensers. Press and press and press, but no, you'll get noplace. Your partner Skip is gone. Just a few torn, see-through, thin shreds of skin, hammock-hung back and forth over all the complicated steel appendages of the automatic doctor. In being so anal, you have caused the whole medical department to shut down forever. No one can ever be cured anymore. How is it to live in a world where no sick can ever be cured anymore? How is it, indeed, echoed in his thick skull, but even though the walls are quite thick, the emptiness inside is endless and eternal, and you have failed, Noman. Yes, I know your name, Noman. Please leave, you have been proven deadly.

I, no—what? Who's saying that?

—Yes, I know your name, Noman. Please leave, you have been proven deadly—

Large panic grips Noman's feet and legs, and he runs.

—Large, large panic, yes, too large, much too large, huge—

—Yes, I know your name, Noman. Please leave, you have been proven deadly—

—killed my friend—he's dead, died at sea, must bury him at sea, he'd have wanted it—

—Yes, I know your name, Noman. Please leave, you have been proven deadly—

Rip the limp, nearly weightless, willowy, limp, waving rag of a Skip-corpse from the machine, maybe leaving behind his hands or maybe not, doesn't matter, hands are not the core of a man unless you are some kind of avant-garde instrumentalist; with that, he rushed out of the medical department just as the sleek grey crew was wordlessly welding up great, thick, rock-hard sheet-steel panels; actually two panels with a foot of concrete poured in between, to panic-dog Walter-Noman and snag his ear, lopping the ear off with no Jesus in range to touch it and restore it as they beat the clock to weld up the door as it was way back when it was just a tall, wide, welded-shut door like a blank headstone standing there saying DEAD IN HERE, if you the reader can remember that many pages and chapters back—and, he bolted.

—Yes, I know your name, Noman. Please leave, you have been proven deadly—

Through that sentence he flew, gripping Skip the corpse.

—Yes, I know your name, Noman. Please leave, you have been proven deadly—

Out in the open air he charged to the rail.

—Yes, I know your name, Noman. Please leave, you have been proven deadly—

Over the rail, falling, they say what happens if you jump off something high to kill yourself, you find that you change your mind halfway down.

The water funneled open and sucked the live dead men gripping each other down into its deep wet bottom-boring holy hell. The funnel spun deepening and narrowing, and Noman gripped dead Skip to him, bodies not unlike any bodies pressed together, and just as Noman realized he was really lost because, not only had he changed his mind, but he could not even in his extremity remember a single snippet of the Roman Catholic Act of Contrition to use to dam up the door of Hell for him because it might be too late to stay alive but not yet too late to attain heaven, though with each passing instant it seemed more like a failed effort; but no drowning. Drowning's a funnel to a landing in Actual-Noman's shell, and what had been Skip became Phyllis who he had never left and who he loved so very, very, much. Lord, she soothed into his weary left ear. My day of delivery is nearly here. I think of how many years the past eight and a half months would have seemed to be if you had given in to the company and chosen an all-expenses-paid China vacation over choosing to stay and help me through these months. God bless you, thank you, Noman. God bless you and thank you!

—Yes, I know your name, Noman. Please leave, you have been proven deadly—

Lord God, shut up! Lord God!

Come to me, Noman. Come to me now.

Everything past and future's just now, read the motto of the senior living home their days would end in. The home that the child about to be born would choose to serve as the place they would die. Phyllis, happy ever after. God in the ship-machine with the deep sea beneath, sliding, slipping, oozing, thrashing, eels, remoras, and sea-snakes all engulfing whatever might be left of the burning bush after it came through the last test of its training and everything at last got put to bed.

Chapter Sixteen
Checking in With the Winner of Today's Free China Cruise

Johnny Foster sat folded up dead in the dark of the drum. Your baby will continue to mature and develop reserves of body fat. Though Johnny Foster had turned all dead and all empty of thought, you may notice that your baby is kicking more. Though Johnny Foster's brain has already begun to putrefy, baby's brain is developing rapidly at this time, and your baby can see and hear. Though Johnny's blood is a train dead on the tracks, and all the way-stations of his life are closed and dark, most of baby's internal systems are well developed, but the lungs may still be immature; not quite the same as dead, as are Johnny's.

The fear is dead. Johnny and Miss Sweetie are walking to somewhere nothing can be and stay alive, beyond the only exit door. Every being is issued a door at the start. The door only opens and closes once per lifetime. After the door's used all up, miraculously it becomes something imagined that never really has been. Your baby is about eighteen inches long and weighs as much as five pounds. Though Johnny has gone forever from the barrel, baby is still there and claws and crawls up in the husk of Johnny, heating rapidly, turning to jelly, then liquid all flowing to cover and become one with baby, as baby's irises all of a sudden can dilate and contract in response to light. Sleep and waking become more differentiated toward the end of the eighth month. Johnny's in the baby, baby's in the Johnny, everything's all nutrients, after all the Caucasian middle-east mountain mystic taught everything's just fertilizer anyway. Four distinctive behavioral states become recognizable, and these will continue to be characteristic in the baby's behavior in the weeks beyond birth. These are sleep, awake, actively awake, and crying. Your baby's body is now producing surfactant, which helps baby breathe after birth. No! A jostle and sliver moon of silver appears above, around, all over somehow, all different and sweet, and baby smiles for the first time knowing the horrid ordeal is nearly over. The air streams in the widening sliver of light and brings up the dimmer switch which draws in the brightening light which is always needed on such winter days like this that must be endured so that there might be yet another fine refreshing newborn spring, so, reassured to have Skip and Noman in their arms, Phyllis and Gundren told them each once more, unknowingly in unison as God commanded, I love you; and the barrel lid popped up, the ring flew off, and the lid slid aside with a shattering scrape, and went away. Shanghai dockmen's voices tell baby, yes, no; who salt, sea, air. A baby—whose baby? Look, a baby, look it, look. Captain, get the Captain. A newborn baby is here, how, who knows. It's an emergency, a big one, yes big. Let's grip it up, spank it's bottom, and listen to if it's alive.

Chapter Seventeen
Down the Curtain! Story's Done!

In the war room in Dubai the watch-person who first sounded the alarm that pirates had targeted the Dakota Maru, and who has been in the same seat for almost a year monitoring the situation just as the procedure book states is proper, sat all alone in the sky-high room, looking gloomy, wan, and almost dead. The investigation had proceeded up and down the super-elegant, vastly forbidding, solid, reflective, black glass office tower, and she was finally notified this morning that the Dakota Maru had docked in Shanghai, and that it was regrettable that she was told to inform the press, if and only if the question comes up, that the two token crewmen only required to be aboard due to a quirk of international law had been taken forever by pirates to some shadow-world deep below what is proper, and from which not a single kidnap victim has ever been recovered, either dead, or alive. She had sat empty headed after getting this news, staring at her blinking, wavy, colorful, bright, happy, Petunia-cartoon screen-saver that had activated itself hours ago, and tried not to imagine the horror of the doom of the poor, poor innocents on that ship. At last, after several days of utterly vegetating in her very hot leather seat, her hand went and punched any key like millions upon millions of people have done when commanded by millions on millions of variegated screen savers through the decades to come on, come on, punch any key as commanded, that the screens to the rapidly developing whole new alternative universe that will swallow the world inside out down the road with all shouts and commands all the way to the end, so her finger-punch brought up the video she had been watching way, way, back before the two poor devils had been forever taken. What hell on earth must they be enduring now? What hell on earth, she did not want to know. But the video that came up soon took her away to someplace else. It was what these videos were all meant to do. A large, fat priest, how funny. An old obsolete show. Perfect anesthesia. As it was meant to be. The screen and speakers droned as always, freezing her solid as an insect in amber destined, if found, to a forever in a museum. Today, said Father Dwyer from the TV, his ruddy cheeks glowing, masterfully powdered up by Crisis Johnson the makeup technician, looking like a chipmunk, Today, we will learn how to create banana pancakes, yummy, yummy—and notice I said the word *create*. Not *make*. Humans from the dust of the earth do not create. No, not ever.

Author's Site

Don't forget to visit Jim at www.jimmeirose.com

Coming Soon From Jim Meirose

Understanding Franklin Thompson

The Box

Typefaces

INTERIOR

Adobe Jenson

ITC Legacy Sans

COVER & FRONT MATTER

Frutiger Neue

ITC Mendoza

Also available from Optional Books

Metarules of the S·M·F by Paul John Adams
A novel of gang warfare—it's a revolution!
ISBN: 978-0692893548

To Fail With Flying Colors by Paul John Adams
A novel of psychopathology—and failure!
ISBN: 978-0692957691

Optional Books: www.optionalbooks.com

You've Read It; Now Review It!

Amazon and Goodreads reviews are always appreciated
or you may elect to:
Shout your review out the window,
Post it on a series of billboards,
Hire a skywriting squadron,
or simply
Tell your friends!

FIC MEIROSE
Meirose, Jim
Sunday dinner with
Father Dwyer / Jim

04/10/19